THE UNHALLOWED HORSEMAN

Based on characters from
The Legend of Sleepy Hollow
By Washington Irving

by
Jude S. Walko

Blue Falcon Productions LLC
101 Washington Ave., Ste. B-148
Grand Haven, MI 49417
USA

This book is a work of fiction. Any references to historical events, real people, or real places are used fictitiously. Other names, characters, places and events are product of the author's imagination, and any resemblance to actual events or places or persons, living or dead, is entirely coincidental.

For information about special discounts for bulk purchases contact the publisher at theunhallowedhorseman@gmail.com

Content Warning: adult and derogatory language, gore, substance abuse (drugs and alcohol), uncomfortable sexual situations (one is non-consensual assault), death, child abuse, mention of pedophilic tendencies, mention of suicide

Manufactured in the United States of America

10 9 8 7 6 5 4 3 2 1

Library of Congress Cataloging-in-Publication Data is available.

ISBN 978-0-5783-0357-4
ISBN 978-0-5783-0356-7 (pbk)
ISBN 978-0-5789-7692-1 (ebook)

"Leave Her, Johnny" (Sea Shanty)

aka "Leave Her Bullies", "Time For Us To Leave Her", "Leave Her"

Public Domain derivatives.

To Washington Irving, who inspired me to pick up a book,
and
Anthony R. Muskas, Sr., my "Pop Pop," who inspired me to
pick up a pen.

ACKNOWLEDGEMENTS

If I truly had to thank everyone who helped exorcise this demon from my brain-housing unit into something consumable by the rest of the world, the list would be encyclopedic. There are simply too many. But I'll try to mention some of them here.

My financial backers. During an international pandemic, money is hard for everyone to come by, and these people still managed to encourage the arts: Ann Stein, Ashley Meg Eng, Barbara Woltag, Bart Plaster, Bobbie Sobel, Christopher DeBenedetto, Dan Campbell, Daniel Suhart, David Reyes, Donald Cantwell, Dylan Kellogg, Edward Chiodo, Erin Krajewski, George Parker, Heather Lehigh, Hilary Lee Capellari, Jake Bowen, James Harrington, James "Marty" Swearengin, Jeff Lamb, Jeremy Briggs, Jerry Chappell, Xavier Calvera (Songwriter X & The Skeleton Band), John Lueken (RIP Joey & Go Dawgs!), Jonathan Kruk, Jose Ramos, Katherine "Katie" Lueken, Kristi Frankenheimer, Margaret Merlino Frye & John, Mary Diedrich & Lana Winters, Mike Barroga, Mouncey Ferguson, Ricky Lloyd, Roger Bojarski, Sebastian Muñoz, Stephen Statler, Susan Dziama, Taryn Conant, and William Barger.

The artists who helped contribute. Rezki Akbar, who did the amazing cover art. Andy "Doctor" Bernet, who did the highly stylized graphic on page one, of which I also have a tattoo. Jake Bowen, who did all the illustrated concept art. Photographer Dave Oscuro of Certain Dark Things Photography for his Hitchcockian black and white photo of me in the About The Author section. My daughter, Preeya Marie "Fah" Walko, for her rad photograph of me on the back cover, and the amazing red and black hair dye job that helped me shed fifteen years off my look. Boontawee "Thor" Taweepasas, who helped with the graphic design and is my ride or die Production Designer of choice.

To the editorial team, without whom my lack of inner monologue and overuse of commas and exclamation marks would be abundantly clear. Editor Elizabeth A. White was a godsend. Believe it or not, there were 10,000 more words to the original manuscript, but in her wisdom she persuaded me to "kill my darlings" to help the flow of the story. That's something every creator always finds hard to do, but is the most necessary part of the process. I assure you if the story is ever choked up, or there is an obscure pop or historical reference, that is solely my ego to blame. Any grammatical errors are definitely me adding things after she completed her work. She's an ace and deserves tremendous recognition. Rasel Khondokar helped prep the novel for digital and physical distribution. And a shout-out to all the beta readers, particularly Michael Amman for his extremely well thought out insight.

I have also been lucky to have a tremendous group of established authors who were willing to give me advice along the way. Ask me about filmmaking and I'll give you a confident answer from decades of experience. Ask me about book publishing and I'll look at you like a deer in headlights on a Texas freeway in the dead of night. Alyson Noël of Evermore fame and her agent Elizabeth Bewley over at Sterling Lord Literistic gave indispensable moral support. Fellow Thailand expat Christopher G. Moore of the Vincent Calvino series and Wounded Tongue author Garrett Dennert both gave their invaluable time and sage advice. Fellow scribe A.E. Rought, author of Broken, has always been a sounding board and shares in the excitement and disappointment of being a novelist. I highly recommend you check out their work. They are all extremely talented, but better yet, wonderful human beings.

To my muses… Of course Washington Irving for creating the greatest and most endearing antihero even known. You, sir, like the Horseman, are a Legend, and I look forward to our parties with the dead someday near the Old Dutch Church at Sleepy Hollow

Cemetery. My literary influences are vast, but if I had to single out a few it'd be Charles Dickens, Edgar Allan Poe, Roald Dahl and Stephen King. I have visited all of their former homes across the world. In the cinema world there are so many, but the highest pinnacle for me is Tim Burton. I simply admire all of his artistic endeavors. Alongside him are the usual suspects of Danny Elfman, Pee-wee Herman and "Weird Al" Yankovic. I am blessed to call Richard and Anastasia Elfman, Derek Frey and the Chiodo Brothers not only colleagues, but friends. I am honored to be in their wolf pack. I also want to thank Lia Marie Johnson, who was originally attached to be in the film version. I can say unequivocally without her there would be no Lorraine "Rayna" Constance. And too, Jeremy Briggs, the original face of Vincent.

I want to give a special recognition to the people of the real life Sleepy Hollow, formerly Tarrytown, New York. Their visitors bureau, cemetery and Old Dutch Church, Police and Fire departments, curators and historians, and all the businesses and inhabitants honor Washington Irving each and every day and put up with infernal tourists, like me. I hope I have in some small way contributed to your endeavor to memorialize all things Irving, and if anything in my novel is historically inaccurate or offensive, I sincerely apologize. I can assure readers the abusers, corruption and sex offenders in my novel are the most fictional thing about it. Sleepy Hollow is the most beautiful, diversified and friendly place on the planet. Please visit if you have a chance, and tell them I sent you. To the sleepy little village on the Tappan Zee, you are the true Legends!

Similarly, I'd like to thank the Irving Heritage Society in Irving, Texas, a town purportedly named after Washington Irving himself.

Master storyteller Jonathan Kruk, who was kind enough to write the foreword, deserves his own recognition. The man has spent a lifetime carrying on the oral traditions of storytelling. Not only is he a noted historian and Washington Irving and Sleepy

Hollow expert, he primarily uses his powers of emoting to encourage children to engage in history, reading and specifically the magic of storytelling. Having him involved in a horror project with very adult themes is about as far away from his brand as one could imagine, but he eventually agreed to break his Golden Rule, as he saw the value in spreading a variation of Irving's tale to future generations of Young Adults, dark fantasy fans and horror aficionados. Jonathan, you sir, are a true gentleman, and I sincerely thank you for coming over to the "dark side," albeit briefly. I've long been an admirer of your work and writings, and consider you amongst the utmost living authorities on Washington Irving, Sleepy Hollow and all things Hudson Valley. Thank you.

Finally, my close friends and family. Without you I am nothing. My PALS: Set Dec Johnny, J Ags, Doc Pete, PalookaMA and MunsterVision; I'd die for any and all of you. My bros in the trenches, fellow Blue Falcon Actual, Dan Campbell, Andrew Reyes, Cort "Fish" Johannes Maclean and Boontawee. My support group, Gary, Julie, Erin, Connor, Garryowen, Jennifer and the Sullivan Clan. To the Steins: Chris "Scrappy," Ann "Barnacle," Prudence and Nate, Jake & Thunder (Jake 2.0); I could never repay you for your generosity, friendship and love. To my family in Georgia, who despite being pretty conservative Christians, still welcome my version of the Horseman into their homes; I love y'all. (RIP Flyboy Pappy Bob and Julie Baby Zultar). And to the loves of my life, Preeya "Fah," Orion "Monkey Dog," and my rock and partner in life, Pranom "Tilac" Thumcha-Walko…without them, I would be a shell of a man with no real purpose or motivation in life. I am grateful for their love and continued support.

And to you, the reader! Thank you for helping the Legend live on, one gallop at a time. MIND YOUR HEADS!

With Much Love & Respect
Jude S. Walko Khon Kaen, Thailand – Halloween 2021

CONTENTS

Foreword 1

Prologue 3

Chapter 1 5

Chapter 2 9

Chapter 3 16

Chapter 4 24

Chapter 5 30

Chapter 6 40

Chapter 7 49

Chapter 8 59

Chapter 9 65

Chapter 10 69

Chapter 11 74

Chapter 12 80

Chapter 13 85

Chapter 14 90

Chapter 15 96

Chapter 16 108

Chapter 17 112

Chapter 18 123

Chapter 19 135

Chapter 20 147

Chapter 21 153

Chapter 22 162

Chapter 23 172

Chapter 24 182

Chapter 25 191

Chapter 26 196

Chapter 27 204

Chapter 28 208

Chapter 29 214

Chapter 30 220

Chapter 31 228

Chapter 32 233

Chapter 33 241

Chapter 34 250

Chapter 35 255

Chapter 36 261

Chapter 37 266

Chapter 38 271

Chapter 39 276

Chapter 40 282

Chapter 41 288

Chapter 42 292

Chapter 43 296

Chapter 44 302

Chapter 45 307

Chapter 46 311

Author's Note 316

About The Author 321

Foreword

The *Unhallowed Horseman* reimagines the horror of the "galloping goblin" unleashed in "The Legend of Sleepy Hollow." Jude Walko embraces the mysterious intrigue at the conclusion of Washington Irving's classic to create this novel. This a book of horror... bold, ambiguous, and diabolically compelling.

Twenty-five years ago, when Historic Hudson Valley hired me to perform "The Legend," I felt any change to Irving's tale would be sacrilege. Best to stick scrupulously to the original when retelling it to audiences in Sleepy Hollow. Delving into the tale, however, I discovered Irving adapted his classic from myriad sources. He took hold of local lore, Dutch-American customs, German Märchen, Robert Burns's "Tam o'Shanter," and personal experiences to stitch together, like Frankenstein's monster, the tale of the Headless Horseman. Author Jude Walko follows Washington Irving's imaginative lead.

Many of my longtime fans and Irving purists will recognize Walko's novel as out of the realm of my usual family-friendly fare. Indeed! I believe as a storyteller there exists room literally for all types of expression in this ancient art. The beauty of stories, of all art, is in the infinite interpretations. "The Legend Of Sleepy Hollow" has inspired countless retellings, reimaginings, and reincarnations.

This rendition is certainly not for the faint of heart. It is part "Legend," part *Nightmare On Elm Street*. Here, parents in a town harbor a shameful secret. There's a 'demon' bent on exacting revenge on the younger generation for 'sins of the fathers,' and a protagonist driven mad in relentless pursuit of the monster. In the tradition of a Stephen King novel, the town itself is a character in the story. It has an energy of its own, affecting all those who reside there.

And, as many of you who have visited Sleepy Hollow know, the real environs have a palpable mystical, magical quality. There, one gets the feeling of something supernatural sensed yet unseen. The same is true in *The Unhallowed Horseman*. Horror fans will enjoy this detailed novel with its twists, turns, and clever references. Sleepy Hollow fans, read it like I did, with an open mind; it will open your eyes. You will be thrilled.

A modern interpretation of the iconic story. If Washington Irving lived in these times, he may well have written a novel like *The Unhallowed Horseman*. Presuming to speak for the man himself, I believe he would approve from the grave this dark, intriguing contemporary rendition of his beloved American classic!

— Jonathan Kruk
Sleepy Hollow, New York
October 2021

Jonathan Kruk is the master storyteller known for solo performances of "The Legend of Sleepy Hollow" for Historic Hudson Valley. His unabridged recording of "The Legend" garnered a Parent Choice and a National Publishers award. His book *Legends and Lore of Sleepy Hollow and the Hudson Valley* reveals the origins of the Headless Horseman. Mr. Kruk has been featured on *CBS Sunday Morning, The Today Show*, The Travel Channel, appeared in the *New York Times*, and has performed before countless school children.

Prologue

The lines in the jack-o'-lanterns were carved with surgical precision, but not by your average surgeon. More like one with the tenacity and skill of decades of practice, but who was entranced within his own mind, listening to the beat of a distant rhythm while staring doe-eyed at the task at hand.

This feeling, when the entity in question actually felt like a passenger on the flea-ridden back of the planet as it hurled through space, seemingly circling an invisible drain of gravitational waves, was inevitable and came often. Yet, how was it one could feel so claustrophobic, like the walls and ceilings were sinking in, when the vastness of space was endless?

So, too, was Sleepy Hollow.

Like a spike in a soundwave making its mark through the oceans of time and space, not understanding, itself, if it was approaching or leaving. Indeed, we have come to love Sleepy Hollow and its Revolutionary War nostalgia and tales of All Hallows' Eve. But that's the here and now; what I speak of is something bigger. That undeniable, yet indescribable and indiscernible Thing, with a capital T. The essence, nay the very Spirit, that inhabits Sleepy Hollow. We've tried to put a name on it. Washington Irving came closest to describing its overwhelming Power and induced Fear with his embodiment of that Hessian equestrian.

It is in that world that we mark as a starting point. For we cannot yet begin to understand the vastness of our universe without first starting with our very own star and the surrounding galaxy. Let it be said, though, that this Thing that is Sleepy Hollow is perhaps vaster than the universe itself. It transcends time and space as we know it because it exists in the very core of our being, in the very stardust we are composed of and the neurons that fire deep within the synapses of our brains.

Words, words, words. They can't begin to amply warn us of the impending doom. Yet, however futile our attempts, we must try. For survival as a race, it is what we are programed to do. But long after we are gone—deceased, extinct— this Thing will continue to thrive.

Chapter 1

We open our tale at the beginning of the third millennium of so-called written history, at the turn of the 21st century. But let us not trick ourselves into thinking of it as modern. Instead, let us treat ourselves to the rustic and rural village burrowed in the leftover wash of the haunting Catskills of upstate New York.

Subdued grays, browns and subtle bleak color palettes paint the countryside as brambles creep over crumbling brick and faded granite. Dark cast iron wraps its way around Dutch and Victorian edifices like the metal kudzu of some lost gothic civilization. Occasionally, a splotch of autumnal orange or a splash of red, bloodred to be exact, entertains this otherwise stark environment. This is our sleepy little hollow.

Nestled just east of Pennsylvania's land of the squonks, wedged between Mother Leeds's Jersey Devil and the Eastern seaboard of the continental United States, sleeps a quaint little town. Perhaps originally named Tarrytown because restless New Yorkers had preferred to rest here. They tarried, if you will, for a while amongst the lapping shores of the Tappan Zee, often after a long, arduous journey from the confines of the crowded Big Apple. Once known as New Amsterdam, before the Duke of York took a proverbial piss on the Dutch colonists there, NYC's overflow generally settled in its more pastoral upcountry and upriver cousin. Like the pregnant swell of the mighty Hudson itself, the region would soon bustle with teaming life. That is, before being terrorized by a nagging fear of speaking out loud a name that may cause him to appear over one's shoulder, like Bloody Mary, Beetlejuice, Candyman, or even Voldemort—The Headless Horseman.

But just as all good things must come to an end, so too all bad things eventually somewhat placate themselves into inactivity and mediocrity.

And so it is in the aptly named Sleepy Hollow. So much so, not only have the local village folk begun to go about their daily lives again after the Horseman's Reign of Terror, but in fact, they have embraced it. In a strange twist of human adaptability, people have adopted him as their preferred mascot, much like medieval castles may have logos of feared dragons or how the French countryside is dotted with pubs bearing the mugs of broom-riding witches and goblins who were once feared to the point of persecution. It is said that all things eventually become the thing they hate the most, and so Tarrytown now irrevocably identifies with its own nemesis. They have become inseparable, if not indistinguishable, from each other. So much so, the town currently bears the name of the very tale of horror that once plagued it, but now defines it.

In a confusing Ouroboros-like fashion, the tale has now doubled back on the town in which it was first conceived to re-identify itself—the head eating its own tail. Life is cyclical, one might say.

But I posit the Thing of which I first spoke was always here and will continue to be long after we are gone. This particular Thing lends itself to the darker side of the spectrum of Being, but every Yin needs a Yang, and vice versa. That is to say, in this sleepy little hollow one can only really rest with one eye open.

Life presents itself as tranquil, sometimes mundane, even normal at times. But it is anything but. Despite the pleasantries one feels while drinking morning tea on the banks of the Pocantico or watching black squirrels do tightrope aerobatics across moss-laden oaks, therein always lies a sinking feeling of impending doom. A feeling that at any moment the hand of God in the form of a meteorite or tsunami may decide to pull the plug, just for fun, and end it all. But perhaps it's not the hand of God at all, but rather the cold steel of a blood-stained battle axe in the gnarled hand of a horseback mounted apparition. We can lose ourselves in pumpkin spice or gingerbread, season dependent, but like a manic episode, that feeling only lasts so long.

But like people living in stilt houses on the crumbling edge of the San Andreas fault or high atop an eroding shoreline's ledge, let us go on pretending nothing bad will ever happen to us.

Indeed, the sleepy hollow has adopted dread as its mascot. Every firetruck, police car and ambulance bears his likeness. Halloween is not an annual occasion like the viewing of Capra's *It's A Wonderful Life*, but rather a constant way of life, almost to the point of absurdity. In a town full of mostly immigrants, not very many tourists, and that is relatively off the beaten path, one wonders where this obsession with all things Horseman and Halloween, the least of which are jack-o'-lanterns and hayrides, stems from. Orange signs with his silhouette dot the city streets, and the local high school students are collectively known as the Horseman. Even the cemetery now bears the legend's name.

Armchair psychologists will tell you this is a leftover coping mechanism from the terrible events that once plagued this otherwise peaceful village. After all, even serial killers are mailed scented panties and marriage proposals behind the boundaries of solitary confinement. And so, villains become heroes, terrorists become mascots, and the very people who once burned purported sorcerers at the stake now go about their daily lives embracing the very Pagan rituals they once feared.

And here this story begins.

The mindset of the people's denial of past transgressions remains the status quo. The youth here don't know their own history, nor the origins of the town's fable. And most, dare I say all but one, with their noses buried in electronic devices pondering objects of their desire, both material and corporal, never will, until the next such catastrophic event occurs. For as every scientist knows, it is not a question of if, but when, the next cataclysmic event will happen.

Enter Vincent.

Chapter 2

Vincent Douglass' unruly mane of auburn hair hadn't been combed a day in his life. This small detail is telling. It shows that the few adults in his life, mainly his mother, never gave him the care a child deserves. It also illustrates he had neither the desire nor the attention span to do it himself.

In fact, Vincent had no attention span at all. He had been diagnosed at an early age with severe ADHD, and his many psychiatrists over the years had alluded to early onset paranoid schizophrenia, as well as him perhaps being bipolar, but no one knew for sure. He certainly couldn't afford proper medical treatment, and it had been easier to pretend these things had never existed. Until, that is, the more and more common occurrence of the symptoms rearing their ugly heads.

This, however, was a convenient excuse for his mom, Marisa, to blame his actions, or at times lack thereof, on a vast array of mental diagnoses and a litany of prescriptions rather than her extremely poor parenting skills. In fact, she never wanted kids to begin with, and she simply was not wired to be a doting mother. Unlike most girls born with maternal instincts, that particular gene skipped Marisa. She enjoyed the freedom of one-night stands, the constant imbibing of drugs and alcohol and, most of all, not having anyone to answer to—societal expectations be damned. These were the reasons she'd dropped out of school, ran away from home, and currently spent government checks on tattoos rather than childcare. At thirty-seven, she still did not have a GED, a steady job, or a driver's license. As far as stipulations for sleeping with a man, she didn't have many. Perhaps the only one enforced was that he needed to have wheels, and he more than likely would get ass not gas from her. Her revolving-door policy of men made her feel oddly liberated. All this free, and often unprotected sex, would eventually lead to impregnation, which for about six months of the total necessary incubation time needed, seemed like a sign from Jesus to get her life back on the right track. Fortunately for Vincent, or unfortunately if you ask him directly, that was just enough time as required by law to keep him alive.

And here's where her two worlds collided.

Her current boyfriend, Jack, was only four years Vincent's senior and had gone to the same school, the only public school in town. His legend preceded him, as he had been the sole man among boys in the entire school who had somehow convinced the otherwise Puritanical drum major to let him finger-bang her on the bus to band camp. Carried away in years of pent up sexual frustration, said drum major allowed her first orgasm to be witnessed by a third of the junior class, a fair share of sophomores, and a particularly perverted and predatory snaggletoothed bus driver in his mid-fifties. Jack instantly became the fodder of high school legend. However, unlike the town's famed Horseman, no roads would be named after him, and he certainly wouldn't be appearing on any police car logos anytime soon.

Vincent, Marisa's only son, was used to an endless cocktail of the entire spectrum of "dex drugs" taken for his various ailments. Previously, as an impressionable young child, he actually methodically took them and followed the directions to the letter. Now in his teens, he barely paid any attention. He would often stare at his own foggy reflection in the bathroom mirror, confused, and mindlessly dump a handful of prescription drugs into his hand. These drugs, often expired or even obsolete, were extracted from the faded and cracked orange translucent bottles in his expansive collection. The sink was filled with Walgreens receipts and discarded pill bottles, yet he never took the time to move them from under the flow of copper-stained water. All he knew was that the drugs kept coming. And as long as he took them, he was fulfilling his minimal duty, just like his mother did hers, for battling his mental degeneration. In some twisted way, the government was directly paying Big Pharma, using his body as a vessel and his disease as an excuse. But like most, he refused to give two shits. Like a mob boss weighing a stack of hundreds by feel rather than actually counting them, Vincent would often pop just the right amount of pills into his hand. Somehow, each day he remained functioning.

At least until now, that is.

Vincent was definitely not knowledgeable enough to be labeled a geek, and certainly not smart enough to be a nerd. What he was, though, was an armchair horror aficionado. Posters of 60s and 70s horror classics plastered his walls in an uncalculated homage to those who were at their peak long before he was born. Among the most notable, Hammer films starring Christopher Lee, the original *Exorcist* and *Amityville Horror*, and a rather obscure James Brolin vehicle and cheesefest known simply as *The Car*, complete with George Barris signature in its lower quadrant. A bevy of second-hand McFarlane toys from various franchises also dotted the landscape amidst a smattering of pizza boxes, laundry and the occasional crusty cum sock. It was the den of a typical teenage boy, except for the exorbitant number of discarded prescription pill bottles scattered throughout like uncut stones.

It was Saturday, and Vincent had fallen asleep in his previous day's attire of dirty jeans, Chucky T All-Stars and a faded flannel over a stained Vincent Price T-shirt. The faux-wood paneled alarm clock on his nightstand refused to do its job. Either that or Vincent in his current lucid dream state was having absolutely none of the idea of bringing his astral-projected self back to consciousness. Instead, he clutched a comic entitled *Zero's Journey* while he slept, along with a crumpled $20 bill. The comic was open to an ad for the latest statuette of the Headless Horseman—a hand-painted, limited edition, resin Chiodo Brothers original, which was purported as being quite the steal at the reasonable price of just $69.99. It was this imagery that would dance around Vincent's brain as he slept and it reared itself into his REM-induced dreams. It was currently the object he most desired, although that would change in the very near future. The one thing that would afford him said artifact was his slightly more than minimum wage job, which coincidently, he currently had mindlessly overslept for.

Sweat crept across his brow and upper lip as he found himself standing mere paces away from the Horseman, in the exact spot where Ichabod once stood just a blip over two hundred years prior. The two stood motionless just across the creaky planks of the rotting covered bridge. The steady, rhythmic breaths of the Horseman's Hellsteed filled Vincent's ears and drowned out the rushing water down below, giving Vincent the feeling as if he was floating in air and neither ground below nor air above had any finite boundaries, bearing, or even orientation. Vincent tried to focus on the fire-burnt glare of the horse's fully dilated, piercing red eyes, if only to avoid looking up above the shoulders of its rider at a countenance that was no longer there. As he could feel his muscles begin to tighten and spasm, he slowly tilted his head up, uncontrollably so, and his line of sight began to crest the powerful, wide shoulders of the statuesque Hessian. Vincent's eyes racked into focus on the severed stump of the protruding vertebrae column and chunks of bloodied flesh garbed in thick, aged, black leather. He tried in vain to suck in air to relinquish a scream; nothing would come.

Instead, the Horseman raised his weapon of choice, a Revolutionary War battle axe, and its bloodstained and tarnished metal glinted with the sheen of alabaster moonlight. With ax raised, counterbalancing himself as the horse reared on its haunches, the Horseman rose to unparalleled and indeed unhuman height above Vincent's head. The rider dexterously lobbed a flaming jack-o'-

lantern illuminated with a devilish visage into the air and, catching it with the same hand in one fluid motion, launched it full force at Vincent. Vincent dodged to his right, diving headlong off the bridge into the unseen murky black waters below, but not before feeling the sharp pain of the projectile hitting with bone-shattering speed across his shin.

"Hey, dipshit, you're late for work. Again," Jack said, accompanied by a man-sized kick to the exact spot the Horseman had aimed for.

As Vincent's eyes slowly came into focus, he was relieved that it was indeed just a nightmare. His next thought was that this man-child Jack was merely chopped liver when compared to the devilish foe he had just came face-to-face with. His contempt for Jack paralleled his fear of the Horseman.

"Hey, jamoke, you deaf? I said you're late," Jack said a second time.

Just as the thought of a witty retort begin to formulate in Vincent's foggy head, the realization of his real-life problems harshly dawned on him.

"Oh shit! I'm late." Vincent leaned past Jack's glare to hurl choice words toward his mother, presumably somewhere else in the house. "Mom, why didn't you wake me? I'm gonna lose my job over this."

"Yeah, good luck with that, loser," said Jack as he took the last swig of Jack Daniel's Tennessee Honey. He tilted the fifth upward, then threw the drained bottle into a pile of laundry next to Vincent's bed.

"Whatever. Get out of my way." Vincent pushed forcibly past Jack while shooting him a go to hell look, but then took the moment to return and savor one last insult to Jack's face. In a whisper, he snapped, "Don't worry, flavor of the week, she doesn't keep boy toys around very long."

Jack tried to push Vincent back, but in his current inebriated state, his hand-eye coordination was way off. Instead, like the Neanderthal that he was, he spat in Vincent's general direction, missing his mark.

"Fine. Next time I won't even bother wakin' your goat-smellin' ass up," Jack snarled as he stumbled out of sight.

The bathroom looked like something out of a horror film, notwithstanding the one from Hitchcock's *Psycho*, which was decidedly cleaner even after the iconic scene. The web-wrapped, mangled corpses of crunchy flies dotted the windowsill like aging fighter jets on an abandoned air base strip. Every tile within sight was covered with calcium deposits and other questionable stains. A multitude of half-used toothpaste tubes, dirty towels and the ever-present myriad of pill bottles littered the space. The stench from the stains in and surrounding the porcelain god matched the grimy spatter of their colorful ambiance.

"Don't forget your pills," came Marisa's strained voice from an adjacent part of the house. To her mind, this was the extent of her maternal duties for the day fulfilled.

"I know, Ma! Jesus," answered Vincent. "All of a sudden you're an expert now?"

He reached into the medicine cabinet above the sink in a sleepy stupor, as he had mechanically done so many times before. Not bothering to read labels or check expiration dates, he downed a concoction that, by the touch, felt right to him. Grabbing a plastic cup full of stale water and backwash, he downed the cocktail, before nearly gagging at the taste of his own spit. After the first two previously worn shirts draped over the back of the commode failed the smell test, he decided on a third and quickly changed. A quick spray from a rusting Aqua Net can substituted for his misplaced deodorant.

He gathered his composure and cleared his throat; it was once again time to face the outside world. In order to do that, he would at least have to appear functioning and ignore the voices embedded inside his head. He also would need to avoid the images of the Horseman from his dream, which seemed to becoming all the more familiar and befell even his waking thoughts as each day passed.

Chapter 3

Clear across town, which sounds a lot further than it actually is, the highest ranking police officer for miles, Sheriff Eustice Van Wart, defying the war on stereotypes, settled down with a box of warm Dutch crullers and Oly Koeks fresh from the oven of Von Landshort's bakery, his one early-morning stop on the way in. Looming and quite overbearing, he stood somewhere between the lofty realms of six and a half and seven feet, one's imagination adding on several inches simply by the preceding of his reputation alone. Although the sheriff's utility belt was a little too tight and his cuffs a little too short, giving him a somewhat comical appearance of a ripening knockwurst trying to split its own webbing, no one dare laugh, or even smirk, in the presence of this literally and figuratively larger-than-life presence of a man.

After heroic Bufords, Sheriffs Pusser and T. Justice before him, Eustice would have preferred to have been thus aptly named, but they were slightly after his time. Instead, he was christened Albert; Albert Eustice Van Wart, a name he had despised all his life. He was only addressed as Big Al once, by his high school wrestling coach, who received such an infamous stink eye—even though the occasion was winning the Regional Championship, and one worthy of celebration and camaraderie—that it was never uttered by anyone, coach included, ever again. It was well known throughout the area that if you happened to be a perpetrator of crime, misdemeanor or otherwise, and you called the sheriff Al or any derivation thereof, whether it was inadvertent or not, you very well might find yourself on the wrong side of some back-country police brutality. No sir. He was to be addressed simply as Sheriff, sir, the sheriff, or the preferred Sheriff Eustice. Anything else was completely unacceptable. Sheriff Eustice gladly embraced his stature and at times the largesse for charity against would-be offenders which his manly reputation afforded him. That is if, and only if, the mood emerged.

That is not to say the sheriff was a stranger to criticism or heckling by the youth within his sphere of influence. Just never, ever to his face. In fact, the donut-eating, stuffed sausage, bellowing face of authority in the town was quite often met with the ruddy faces of prepubescent boys holding back a snigger or joke, saved only by the deliverance into safety afforded them by a chiding mother's swift backhand upside their head.

The rumor mill labeled him as a direct descendant of Brom Bones himself, although this was unprovable and contentious to say the least. The fact Sheriff Eustice was related to the Van Wart family, however, was not. The family tree was as gnarled, curved and moss-ridden as many of the century-old oaks that bedecked the Colonial cemetery on the hill due to its many violations against the sanctity of marriage, subsequent bastard children, and inaccurate recordkeeping due to either incompetency or bribery. However, no tree in the area, family or otherwise, was without blemish or ill repute at one point or other. The arcane language—a mixture of Dutch and English of the period with the occasional Native colloquialism thrown in to keep the hounds of history off—within the village's archaic record books kept in the cemetery's cloistered vaults illustrated that a gentleman known simply as W. Van Wart had been most active and noteworthy amongst General Washington's finest in the several skirmishes of the area. It was this undeniable fact of ancestry that gave Eustice not only an air of pride, but an actual birthright as cock-of-the-walk and rightful arbiter of justice amongst the inhabitants of Sleepy Hollow. And if ever there was a man reincarnated in the likes of Mr. Bones himself to fight off, or even mock, the dangerous Hessian as Brom had done before him, it was Sheriff Eustice. Although these days, the smooth worn leather seats of a powerful automobile were much preferred over the often uncomfortable and teetering orientation of horseback.

The town coffers could not afford much in the way of luxury. With little to no crime, save the ever-present vandalism and petty theft, there was really no need for such amenities for law enforcement. So the sheriff spent the department's little funds quite wisely. His steed of choice was an inherited 1978 Plymouth Volare Super Coupe. A 360 cubic inch engine monster of a beast, with a 4-barreled, 5.9 liter V8 providing over 250 additional horses, rather than the single one his forefathers had strode upon. Add the louvers, matte black trim, racing stripes and custom sheriff's logos, and this was one badass piece of machinery rivaling any other rider in town, headless or otherwise. It was, however, ironic that the rearing Horseman logo on the cruiser read "Our Service is Legendary," as it was anything but. Though as often is the case, more times than not in small towns looks were everything. The car, mirrored shades, and the sheriff's handlebar mustache meant he was a force not to be trifled with, and he definitely looked every inch of a badass while doing it. At least he did in his eyes, the only ones to him that actually mattered.

The town's three-cell jail and bullpen style police office was something right out of Mayberry and, like times of recent past, was usually reserved for the sleeping off of inebriation rather than the frigid hearts of hardened criminals. The jail-cum-office was so small, in fact, the village's lone deputy, Deputy Constance, gave a spare key to his daughter, Lorraine, so she'd have a safe haven to study in after school hours. Neither the sheriff nor the townspeople had any objection to this. In fact, the keys to the cells only had two copies, one on the oversized key ring on the sheriff's utility belt, and another set in his desk drawer. Deputy Constance simply had no need for another set.

The last time the town had seen real crime was a few decades earlier amidst a killing spree during the Triduum of the Hallows surrounding All Hallows' Eve. Like the "Call of Cthulhu" itself, those exact dates coincided with unparalleled events of destruction and abnormalities across the entire spectrum of the space-time construct. The town's elders were anxious to cover up the blemish that tarnished their otherwise wholesome reputation, lest it drive away the steady flow of tourist dollars around that time of year, so were conveniently quick to forget it ever happened at all. They proceeded to remove any evidence of said unfortunate events faster than one might change the distinct windows of the infamous Amityville house, and it hadn't been spoke of since. In would only take one generation, unlike their unfortunate cousins in Salem, to erase the unsavory happenings from the historical blotter.

Eustice was not around in those days, as he was rushed off to a Big Apple police academy for proper training in hallowed halls amongst the ranks of New York's finest upon the first sign of distress among the community. It is of note that his predecessor, whom he would eventually replace, no longer walks among the town's living.

"Eustice, eyes on the ball." This was Deputy Constance's typical greeting of his superior every morning. He loved his baseball metaphors, and was perhaps the sole inhabitant of planet Earth who could call the sheriff nearly anything—but still not Al.

Constance was a mostly by-the-letter guy. Being a single parent with a hormonal teenage daughter was even more challenging for him than his stint overseas as a combat-hardened Marine. At least there he was in the company of only men, all of whom he could relate to. Expressing his emotions was never his strong suit, and growing up in a household steeped in toxic masculinity didn't help matters much either. But since his wife's untimely death sometime back, he vowed to give all he had to raising his daughter, Lorraine. Though hed rather be engaging in crossfire than having his toenails painted glitter pink and would rather talk about anything other than his daughter's monthly menstruating episodes, he endured all, and then some, for her sake.

He liked to think of himself as a reasonable guy as opposed to a traditionally stringent patriarch of a man. He had a passion for God, country, Corps, refurbished muscles cars, craft beers and Fellini films. He was an everyman's man—likeable, relatable—but one who could easily slip into the figure of authority in a heartbeat when duty called. He used this same mixture of real-world experience and empathy as tools in raising his daughter.

Like with all teens her age, her perception of self-importance and adolescent erudition were quickly outpacing the archaic knowledge and parenting skills of her father. But when the times it really mattered arrived, they put their head-butting differences aside and assumed their respective roles in the long-honored tradition of the filial-parental relationship. Like the time he threatened to borrow the Super Coupe squad car and race down to her elementary school to take her sixth-grade boyfriend away in cuffs because he reneged on being her date to the Sadie Hawkins dance only days before the event. Or the time he played the Headless Hessian at the annual Dutch Down-Home Days Parade, but allowed her to ride with him in the saddle to keep her from crying, even though it broke the fourth wall for observers and fans of the genre. In those instances, he solidified his place as not only father, but friend.

"Hey, Constance," came the lazy retort from the sheriff, who had his boots up on his desk and his nose buried in the morning edition of the *Daily Voice*.

"So, what's crackin?"

"Kraken?" puzzled Eustice as he slowly lowered the paper to just underneath the bridge of his nose in order that Constance could properly see the look of consternation on his face. He looked like a librarian shushing someone in the rare book section.

"Yeah, you know, like happening," said Constance, followed by an awkward silence.

Finally, Eustice broke his gaze. "Then why not just say happening?"

"My daughter…the kids at school… Never mind. What's happening today, Sheriff? Any official business I need to know about?"

"Well, Kimberly Ann called. She said you left your casserole dish at the potluck last Sunday. Claims she'll bring it by next weekend, unless you need it sooner, and she wants your pigs in the blanket recipe."

"First of all, that's my Grandma Babinski's recipe, and no one's getting it. And furthermore, I meant police business."

Eustice straightened his glasses and sat upright. "Oh, you mean like cat in the tree type stuff?" he said.

"Yeah. Cat in the tree type stuff," Constance agreed.

"Well, the only thing of note is that old Van Ripper thinks some saddles and tack might be missing down at his farm. The phone rang three times before I could even get to it at six. But to tell the truth, between his forgetfulness and wild goose chases, I honestly don't even feel like investigating."

"I'll take that one. It's on my way to the high school anyway. I'm taking Lorraine her flute at lunch. Band practice after singing lessons. She forgot it again."

"How sweet," Eustice said as he unconsciously and involuntarily rolled his eyes. "Other than that, not a whole lot. That is, unless you want to file a missing persons for that casserole dish." The glint in his eye and the upturned corner of his mouth was about the max emotion the sheriff ever offered in their partnership.

Constance smirked a crooked smile. That same crooked smile got him laid in the band room when he was just a junior, after innocently stalking the only girl, Tina, in the drumline. He knew from her adroit ability to play the quads at lightning speed that she was very good with her hands, and would never forget the universal smell of stored instruments from the experience. That same smile caught him much shit from his COs during boot camp, and was the same exact one that eventually would give him a daughter. It was his trademark, and it was adorable. Irresistible even. Even his daughter knew it was hard to stay mad at him when he flashed it alongside his baby blues. It was the most powerful weapon in his arsenal, even more so than his Glock 19 sidearm.

"Alright, well I'll do a couple of rounders in the neighborhoods," said Eustice. "Probably head down Riverside past the manor and check out the cemetery. Been a couple a vandals tagging some stuff. Nothing serious, just pumpkins and skeletons and the like. The usual shit this time of the year."

"Okay, great. So, you want to meet up around one or so, after lunch?" asked Constance.

"Yeah, but keep the walkie on, just in case," instructed Eustice.

"Copy you, Sheriff. Oh, can I at least put a half a tank on the card?"

Silence.

"Come on, you know there are federal mileage laws and stuff. I'm using my own vehicle for work."

After a brief moment of reflection, Eustice responded. "Alright, but I want you to start keeping a log. And runs to the school to deliver flutes don't count." His eyes rolled back, ending any moment they'd had, as he drew breath for the impending eruption of nostalgia. "You know, this used to be a volunteer position, back before—"

"Whoa, whoa, whoa. Let me stop you right there. You're seriously going to be that guy?" He blinked. "Never mind. I know the answer to that. Thanks, Chief." Constance said with a smile in his voice as he headed out the door. It was an honorary title he called Eustice pertaining more to his stature, than his actual job title.

Eustice would have crushed any other mere mortal for such jabs. Instead, he mumbled something about a company card as he wheeled around in his chair and pirouetted his large frame into a standing position. He was surprisingly graceful for a man of his stature. He picked up one last cruller, but halfway to his mouth thought better of it. He replaced the pastry and proceeded to the key rack on the wall and grabbed the ones with the pewter Headless Horseman keyring. Still, after all these years, nothing quite had the enchanting power over the sheriff's sensibilities as did the Super Coupe's guttural purr and harnessed horsepower. She would be forever by his side, the Gunpowder to his Crane, the Rocinante to his Quixote. Besides, Constance already made the perfect Sancho Panza.

And just like that, the Village of Sleepy Hollow was deemed safe once again, as the fine representatives of its upstanding, law-abiding citizens went forth to restore order to chaos, ensure their safety, and keep trees cat-less... until that fateful day when they once again weren't.

Chapter 4

Vincent stumbled out the door, nearly spraining his ankle on the awkwardly constructed half-step of splintered wood that inexplicably separated his front porch from the questionably solid earth beneath it. He couldn't help but notice how everything old in the town seemed to have been built for pint-sized humans. Being gaunt and taller than average himself, he had hit his head on many a door frame in the old Dutch Colonial homes around town, and steps always seemed to alternate between full-sized, half-sized and random-sized. Vincent's house, a one-story, three-bedroom stone and mortar, was ramshackle to say the least. Between Jack's discarded booze bottles, the ankle-deep grass, and the tears in the porch screens, it looked more like something out of *Deliverance* than the Victorians and Colonials that mostly dotted the village.

Marisa, on one of her half-high walks home, had bought him a pink, girl's 5-speed. It only cost $20 at the yard sale, and was customized with rainbow tassels, a pink straw basket, and glitter infused banana seat. His friends liked to remind him of its sissy bar and sloped frame, to which he always responded, "Better than a nut crusher." Clearly it had belonged to some Amazonian preteen girl refusing to transition into adolescence. Not so clearly, at least apparently to his mom, Vincent was not a girl, pre-pubescent or otherwise. In her mind, however, this was a very motherly purchase and spending the money on Vincent rather than a pack of menthols and a whippet was above and beyond. Vincent, not wanting to offend her and actually happy to have the freedom of some kind of wheels, had reluctantly accepted the bike. What he hadn't realized was the amount of bullying and mocking the bike would bring to his already troubled life. Right now, girlie or not, the bike would get him to work much faster than he could walk.

Vincent fumbled through the first few gears as rust fell from the bike's chain like powdered cinnamon. He finally gained up enough speed to cruise through the mostly empty streets and inhaled a much needed gasp of air, filling his lungs to capacity. The thoroughfare leading toward town was long and wide. Several centuries ago, someone had had the foresight to line the street with oak trees, which now formed a dense canopy over the entire road. It shaped a beautiful natural infinity tunnel as far as the eye could see and would have made Norman Rockwell proud. Vincent soaked it in and daydreamed as he cruised past the wooden giants. Some might view the gentle sylvan giants as protectors, but in his mind, Vincent always had felt they were more ominously foreboding.

It was late fall and the leaves had just began to show their colors. In fact, the deciduous trees in the area were famous amongst New Englanders and many, tourists and city folk alike, traveled on the weekends to bask in the glory of color tours, soaking in the bright oranges, reds and yellows of the decaying plant life as the chlorophyll died inside. It struck Vincent as odd how there could be such beauty in death. As a fan of horror slashers and gore-fests, such picturesque scenery was not his idea of transitioning from living to dying.

All Hallows' Eve was just around the corner, and this town took its Halloween seriously. As such, every yard, front porch, and even the municipal building were decorated with jack-o'-lanterns, ghosts, ghouls and of course the ever-present mascot, the Unhallowed Horseman of Hallowed Grounds. Several incarnations of him seemed to peek out around every corner. They ranged from handmade effigies fashioned from hemp rope and corn maze, to antique renditions peering from third-story crow's nest, and even the unsightly full-on animatronic the village treasurer had convinced the people at a town hall one year was a good investment in the village's perceived reputation as the birthplace of Irving's demonic antihero.

As Vincent pushed the bike to its bare-bones limits, he rounded each corner of town, his mind easily picking out the Horseman from the myriad of other decorations. Almost as if his soul sensed where they would be before his eyes actually registered them. There seemed to be more than usual this year. Vincent thought perhaps he might even have imagined a few, but the 5-speed was cruising too fast for a second look, and he was still noticeably tardy for work.

Vincent's brain once again drifted to the limited edition Chiodo Brothers figurine. If he could just manage to beat Mr. Price, the owner of the mom-and-pop video store where Vincent worked, he could save his job and within a couple of weeks would have saved up enough to get it. Unbeknownst to all but one town cuckold, there was a good chance he could do it, as Mr. Price was known by nearly the whole village to visit Mrs. Guerrero on several mornings a week. This, of course, happened once he was informed by her that her husband had safely arrived two townships over for his position there as a record keeper and municipal attorney. Luckily for Vincent, that town was in the midst of an audit by the State and this was once such morning, even on a Saturday. Vincent smiled to himself, picturing the frumpy, balding Price with the vivacious and curvy Doris Guerrero.

Opposites attract, he thought with a smirk.

Vincent cruised past the one and only high school, where he and every child of age attended. The prominent marquee read: GO HORSEMEN! BEAT THE FALCONS! DUTCH DOWN-HOME DAYS October 31st! Halloween costumes welcomed. Then no school til MONDAY!" The Blue Falcons from Hanover Township, Pennsylvania, would make the three-hour sojourn once a year and were considered the Horsemen's most illustrious football rivals.

Vincent rounded a corner full speed, just in time to receive a taunt from two of the high school's most renowned bullies. They were a dynamic duo known as Mack & Saunders, and were often accompanied by a third boy. Mack had inherited a Napoleon complex pickup truck from his now deceased older brother, who had been killed in action overseas by friendly fire. Needless to say, his parents gave up on the little parenting skills they had at the point, resulting in Mack and his group of undesirable miscreant friends to spend more time drinking and avoiding truancy officers than actually studying. Most adults in the town, however, felt sorry for the family, so unfortunately gave the boy and his friends an otherwise undeserved pass.

Mack slammed the brakes on the lift-kit fitted, tan-and-creme-colored Chevy pickup, bringing it to a screeching halt. Saunders and Robert Greenfield, the other occupant, affectionally known as 'Billy Bob' amongst his friends, were so taken by surprise they spilt half the contents of their beers on the console and chrome skull gear shifter.

"Asshole! I should make you lick that up," blasted Mack. "My cousin brought that Ichabod from New Holland, you dicks."

In a throwback to 80s villains, whom Mack idolized, he wore flannels with ripped sleeves showing off his muscular physique, but leaving him one mullet short of a caricature.

"Do you see what I see?" Mack revved the engine, pulling within earshot of an unsuspecting Vincent, still lost in thought over Mrs. Guerrero's hip-hugging red dresses.

"Hey, Dougl-*ass* Nice bike, faggot."

The boys laughed as Vincent looked over his shoulder in disgust at them, trying to think of a witty retort.

All he could muster up on the spot was a heartily shouted, "Up yours, asshole!"

Suddenly, Vincent's world literally and figuratively came to a stop. Unluckily for Vincent, at that very moment the front tire of the five-speed crumbled like a Coors Light can at a redneck mud bogging.

"What was that? You trying to be funny?" came a deep belt of a growl.

Mack and the other boys discretely lowered their beer bottles and slowly turned the truck onto West Elizabeth Street.

Vincent dusted himself off, realizing he had dented the sheriff's Volare, hitting the Horseman logo on the driver side dead center like a bullseye. Everyone in town knew it was the sheriff's most prized possession. Besides Deputy Constance's waxing duties, only the Fire Department volunteers were allowed to touch it, and even then, only for repairs. It was going to take more than a plunger to get that dent out, however.

A pair of policeman's boots slowly revealed the pot-bellied Sheriff Eustice as he alighted the vehicle. It raised a good three inches on its chassis as he stepped out. With a pompous air, he lowered his mirrored shades, not at all offering to help Vincent to his feet.

"I was talking to those…" Vincent trailed off as he realized the other kids had left the scene and that excuses would most likely be futile at this point. He was right in his assumption.

Eustice lowered his aviators down the bridge of his nose to the tip, starring daggers. Only a pissed librarian or Dana Carvey's Church Lady could do it better. Eustice took out a ratty notepad and a Holiday Inn Scranton pen and began to write a ticket.

"You can't be serious," pleaded Vincent. "Please, I can't afford that."

"Save it, son." The towering lawman sized up the boy like a choice cut at the butchers. "Douglass boy, right? Knew your mom." The peace officer chuckled to himself. "Better watch where you're goin'. Boy could get himself killed." He ripped the ticket from his pad. Heartless. "That'll buff out, but it's gonna cost ya."

Vincent shouldered the full weight of the bike, the tire now nearly a perfect square, and limped his way in the direction of the video shop, crestfallen. Eustice mad-dogged the boy until he was nearly out of sight. He got a kick out of it, and besides, the cemetery and its occupants weren't going anywhere.

Chapter 5

Mr. Price's video shop, unoriginally but aptly named For The Right Price, certainly was no Blockbuster, mostly due to its appearance and lack of organization. But for Vincent and his best friends Allister and Aaron, it was gainful employment. Price had started the shop after abruptly leaving the Carolina Wrecking Company in 1978 over a dispute with his then boss about being caught leering with a pint-sized boner at her bikini-clad high school daughter through a hole in her adjoining wooden fence. The only thing bigger than his penchant for young girls was his obsession with the, at the time, newly released format known as VHS. Price's father had still been receiving a pension from retiring as a POG in the 'Chair' Force's accounting department and gifted his son his life savings of twenty-five thousand dollars. This was just enough for Price to leave town, avoid scandal, and settle in with his cousins in upstate New York. In addition to the money, Price was able to sell off some of his valuable comic book collection and use that as seed money to start up the shop.

Over the years, and with the eventual invention of Al Gore's internet, Price was able to amass a vast collection of VHS tapes, and eventually DVDs, ranging from studio titles to Serbian gore horror, bootlegs and even Japanese Hirsute porn. Those beauties were of course kept in a locked room behind a faded pink curtain in the Adults Only section, reserved for the discerning eyes of middle-aged perverts and the occasional out-of-town teen with a fake ID that no one cared to bother verifying. Needless to say, he had something for everyone, and although the shop didn't make a lot of money, it kept the kids off the streets and allowed Price a nice distraction from his past life and penchant for underaged girls.

The shop had one faded yellow computer monitor and one boxy TV mounted above the rows of new and obscure titles, so that anything shown on them could be displayed to customers as they browsed. Price had gotten that idea after reading a biography of Quentin Tarantino, and it had since become a long-honored tradition of movie rental shops. Unfortunately, only one of them worked, and it happened to be the shittier of the two. It was on this that the boys were scrubbing through a VHS copy of *Donner Pass* that had been recorded off of cable with a jury-rigged VCR setup. The image blipped up and down before finally centering itself on the screen.

"Watch this shit," said Aaron as he fumbled over a remote that looked like it hadn't been swabbed with sanitizer since the 1980s. Its carcinogenic plastic had yellowed from decades of UV light. On the screen, a hammer nailed a villain to a wall through his eye socket. The boys belly laughed.

"Classic! Now back up to the Crypt Keeper guy." Allister unsuccessfully tried to wrestle the remote from Aaron's hand.

"No. No! Titties in the hot tub."

Aaron rewound the tape back with surgical precision to an underwater scene where a half-naked woman is choked out and slain in a hot tub by an unseen assailant. Bars of garbled static striated the screen into pixelated snow, indicating this part of the VHS had been watched on numerous occasions. The boys celebrated the pair of ample appendages as if it was the first ones they'd ever seen. Behind them, just past the mountains of clutter in the display window, a tired Vincent was just out of view as he dropped the 5-speed down in disgust.

"Never gets old," Allister said. The remote jammed on a still shot of the blood-covered boobs. "Damn! It's stuck again."

"That's what she said." Aaron playfully socked Allister in the shoulder, causing him to drop the remote onto the ground. They fumbled bent over to get it, then rose up to see a sweating Vincent towering over them.

Vincent gestured to the monitor. "Classy. I don't know what else I'd expect from you guys."

"Oh hey, V.D. Didn't see you come in," quipped Aaron.

Vincent shot him a look. Although V.D. were his initials, that joke was getting old.

"What, you never seen tit-tays before?" said Aaron.

Vincent ignored the playful duo, as he was in no mood for joking after hauling his incapacitated bicycle for nearly a mile. He went to the cash register and began busying himself with a pile of receipts and jumbled paperwork next to it. In Price's shop, everything was handwritten and manually accounted for. In fact, no one would be shocked if they found out he used an abacus for his accounting.

Vincent noticed several unopened boxes stacked on the floor behind the counter. "Damn it, you guys, you didn't even stock the new releases? Mr. Price is going to be pissed."

"Says the guy who shows up nearly two hours late." Allister did have a point.

Aaron put down the remote and walked over to Vincent. The freeze frame, seemingly with a mind of its own, had moved forward a couple of frames. Now, a single areola encompassed the entire screen, like the tip of a Zeppelin submerged in watermelon juice. "Well, lucky for you, Mr. Bedhead, he hasn't shown up yet."

"Yeah, we all know he's partaking of some hot tamales for breakfast," said Aaron with a laugh.

"Luckily for us, he's a marathon runner not a sprinter," quipped Aaron.

That got a good laugh out of Allister and Aaron both. Even Vincent couldn't help but crack a smile.

"You guys are idiots." Vincent chuckled under his breath as he searched for a box cutter.

He pulled a sweat-matted magazine out of his back pocket. It was worn and damp, the tattered pages showing white in spots. He had forgotten it was there, what with being late and his literal run-in with the police. He peeled back the pages to reveal the advert for the Chiodo Brothers figurine. "Did you guys see this?"

"Of course," and "Hell yeah," were the rapid-fire responses he received in unison from his friends.

Vincent got lost in his own daydream as he continued. "Over 150 years of Legend, started right here in this very town. Our forefathers must have seen him. You know, sometimes late at night, when everything is still and quiet, I think I actually hear him. The Headless Horse—"

"Man of Unhallowed Grounds," the boys chirped in unison. "Yeah, we know, man. We hear this same shit from you every year," retorted Aaron.

"You guys are so immature," was all Vincent could muster in his defense.

"We're immature? We're not the ones jerking off to a plastic doll of some imaginary phantom." Again, Allister had a point, albeit a crude one.

At that moment, Vincent's eyes fixated on something behind his friends. The other boys turned around and saw standing there —— the most beautiful, purest, innocent girl in their one-horse town. Lorraine "Rayna" Constance was also the most popular girl at school. Not because she was cool, but because she was angelic. If one could take all that was sweet about a bubble gum princess, wrap it in a porcelain doll with sandy blonde hair and ice-blue eyes, and breathe into it cotton candy flavored breath, you might come close to her. She was in a word, perfection. Unfortunately for the boys at the school, her father was the very overprotective Deputy Constance.

All three boys just stared at her.

"Sorry to interrupt," she said softly. "I wanted to hand these back in person, to avoid late charges."

"How long have you been… Sorry about that jerking off thing. It's a figure of speech," rationalized Aaron.

Him bringing it up only made it worse. Lorraine's cheeks blushed as she averted her eyes.

"We really need to put a bell on that door," Allister said. He then suddenly looked up at the massive titty filling the screen. "Oh shit!" This, of course, only drew everyone's attention to it. All three boys slowly turned a crimson red. If Lorraine hadn't seen it before, she certainly stared it down now.

Vincent rushed over and yanked the cord from the monitor out of its socket so hard that it nearly fell from its bird's-eye perch. As first impressions go, this was a zinger.

Lorraine handed the videos to Vincent with a smile that could cut through even the cruelest villain's heart. She was the Nikita to his Elton John. "I actually love the Horseman Legend. To think it all happened right here, perhaps in the very spot we're standing now."

Aaron and Allister stared at each other in disbelief.

"How long was she there?" inquired Allister under his breath.

Aaron shrugged.

It was final and indisputable—Vincent was officially smitten. "Uh, yeah. I mean exactly. I really want to research the backstory of it all," he managed to get out. He couldn't have felt more awkward if his pants were down.

"Vincent, right? You're in my history class with Mr. Crane. I'm Lorraine. My friends call me Rayna." She extended her hand.

Vincent was beside himself.

Aaron had a shit-eating grin across his face. "Yeah, he knows who you are. Everybody does."

This warranted him a swift and cautionary shin kick from Allister. "Shut up, asshole."

Vincent reached his cold, sweaty palm forward. She remembered him? His hormones made his heart beat right out of his chest. The thought of physical contact with a girl, much less this girl, was almost too much to bear. He remained doe–eyed and speechless.

"Hey, maybe you and I could research it together sometime. It's super intriguing. I better be going, though. My maw maw's waiting for me at home."

"M…Mm…Maw Maw?" Vincent stuttered.

"My grandma." Lorraine retrieved her hand and flashed a smile so brilliant Vincent felt as if Thanos himself had just neutralized him. "Bye." She waved on her way out. Vincent barely managed to lift his hand up and reciprocate the gesture.

A moment of silence hung in the air as the boys soaked it all in.

"What in the hell just happened?" Aaron said, breaking the stillness.

"Her dad's a deputy you know," Allister said. "Probably not a good idea with your track record."

"Our boy's getting' laid!" Aaron ran over to Vincent, mussing his hair.

Vincent gently pushed him away, flipped him the bird, then playfully sent one Allister's way as well. "Dude, she just said she also liked the history. Nobody said anything about fucking anyone."

"Our boy's getting' laid," Aaron repeated.

"She did say maybe you two should study sometime. I mean, it's kind of implied," reasoned Allister.

"Dude, do you hear yourself right now? That's nothing to do with getting laid." Vincent deflected his embarrassment by feigning anger.

"No one's getting laid around here, especially you three nitwits," Mr. Price said as he burst through the door and rained on their parade. His combover hair was dangling, shirt half-tucked in. Clearly, he was a man out of sorts.

"We really need to put a bell on that door," Allister said again with just the right comic pensiveness.

"No one getting laid but him," whispered Aaron to Allister. They laughed.

"What was that, Klimchak?" Price gave him a side-eye so sharp it nearly cut him.

"She's my cousin, you know," said Allister softly to Aaron.

"Wait, what?" replied Aaron.

Price watched the exchange play out like a cat eyeing its mostly dead prey. The boys, caught up in their conversation, remained oblivious to his glares.

"Yeah, like three times removed or some shit."

"You guys are like the same age, dumbass."

"Whatever. Then like forth cousin or whatever. I don't know. And it's Dumás," answered Allister with a curtsy and some flair.

"Dude, your cousin is fucking hot." Aaron mimicked an air banjo and twanged out "Dueling Banjos."

"Shut up, dick."

The boys looked up to see Price staring at them over his bifocals on the bridge of his nose.

"Are you through now?" he asked.

The boys fumbled over themselves, knocking over a few titles as they went to busy themselves.

Vincent had been avoiding Price and the other conversation, and had made himself busy by dusting the countertop. The whole time, he uncontrollably smiled to himself. Finally something had gone right for him. He pulled the magazine on the countertop closer to him. His aptness for daydreaming and ADHD again took control of his here-and-now and he fantasized about the figurine, but also about Lorraine. He pumped his fist in quiet victory.

"Are you all a bunch of retards? And you're late again, Douglass," said Price.

"My mom says that's not a nice word. And no I wasn't. I've been here all morning."

"Your mom? I got a word for her too. It rhymes with door, which is where I'm about to send you."

Allister and Aaron registered the burn from Price.

"And don't bullshit me, you little prick. I just ran into Sheriff Eustice and he told me all about *your* little run-in. Calling him names, damaging police property. You're lucky he didn't take you in."

It was difficult to argue with Price when he had been caught red-handed, and Vincent was in no position to talk back. He needed this job because he needed that figurine.

Allister tried to interject and defend his friend. "I'm sure he didn't really—"

"Am I talking to you? You stay out of this, mister." Price wagged his finger obnoxiously. "You're lucky I don't fire all you losers. And what's with this?" Price picked up a handful of the new releases, among them *The Incantation* with former Superman Dean Cain's face plastered across the cover. He flung them at Aaron and Allister. "Get on it!"

"Hey, I wanted to see that," thought Allister out loud. "I bet he banged Eva Longoria."

"You mean Teri *Snatch*-er?" Aaron couldn't ignore the lob pass. They sniggered.

"Faster than a speeding bullet," said Aaron. They literally could do this all day, and would have if it hadn't been for Price's interruption.

"You know, I can't for the life of me possibly fathom what it is you imbeciles did all morning. And don't play all innocent over there, Douglass. I know you haven't accomplished shit today."

The boys exchange a 'busted' look, then Aaron's mouth wrote a check his ass couldn't cash.

"I'm sure nothing as fun as you," he said with a smirk.

Price waited for a beat, one that clearly registered across his face. *That's the second innuendo today. Did these kids know something about his affair? Doubtful, they're idiots.* He started a slow rant, like a locomotive building up steam until it blows a gasket running full bore. "I want all these releases stocked by tonight and everything inventoried and alphabetized. I don't care how long it takes."

"But, Mr. Price, please," said Vincent. "It's Saturday night and they're running *The Legend of*—

"Don't push it, Douglass. You're on thin ice. Very thin." Price began to walk toward his tiny office in the back, before spinning 180 degrees on his heel like Michael Jackson in a Pepsi commercial. He ripped the magazine out from under Vincent's nose. "And I'll take that, thank you very much." He took the rolled up magazine and waved it front of Vincent's nose as if chastising a puppy that just crapped the carpet. "Get your head of the clouds with this shit, kid."

He sauntered off, the smell of bad cologne and sex still lingering behind him.

"No overtime," Price yelled as a parting shot before he slammed the door to his office shut. An Arnold *T2* cutout blew down with the force it made. Outside, the boys could still hear Price's muffled condemnation of misspent youth. They clearly weren't getting out of this one. Dejected, they begin to mill about and take in the daunting task ahead of them.

"This is bullshit, man," Aaron said as he threw a VHS tape down. "VHS, seriously? Who outputs new releases on this shit? Haven't they heard of YouTube?"

"Retro, bro. Vintage. You pay more for shittier quality because it's the hipster thing to do," Allister retorted. "Plus, we still use ours."

Vincent looked up from his stack. "Poor but proud."

The boys again shared a round of smiles in spite of themselves.

Vincent's eyes wandered again through the old, outdated and obscure titles on the display racks. "I mean some of this shit is pretty cool. Got to give him that," he mumbled under his breath. Between Lorraine and the pageantry of classic horror creature features before him, his head was spinning. So much so, he'd forgotten all about his disabled bike, the sheriff's ticket, and the fact the demons in his head were preparing for a masquerade ball the likes of which he had yet to ever experience.

Chapter 6

The low-hanging moon was beginning to rise over the claw-shaped and gnarled branches of the crippled forest on the no-man's-land side of town as night began to slowly encapsulate the village. In just a few days, it would a full bloodred harvest moon, but until then, it managed to dip in and out of blankets of heavy fog. Much like the lighthouses that dotted the Eastern seaboard, it too served as an ominous warning to all, seamen and civies alike. The universe was always putting signs out there, if you were willing to see them.

Rayna was saying her goodnights to her eighty-something grandmother, affectionately known as Maw Maw Williams to the community. She had just had her nightly warm milk and rat poison medicine, which she took for high blood pressure. Rayna and her father had moved her three houses down from them, as the flights of stairs in her old former Victorian were one accident away from a hip replacement, or worse. In her middle-aged years, Maw Maw had been quite the socialite and proved to be the very toast of the town. She never could quite give up that independence and, despite her various infirmities, was in no way ready to give up her freedom. It wasn't all one-sided though. She was still able to care for Rayna's younger cousin, Bobbie, who had been orphaned in a freak accident, for various short periods of time. Not to mention, her cooking was still magical. The family loved her, and she them, although periodic bouts of dementia were starting to set in, and that was a hard metaphoric pill for anyone to swallow.

Back in his office, Price looked through the photocopies of the boys' school files, which Principal James Carter, no relation to the former President, had shared with him. It may seem counterintuitive that a borderline former sex offender would be offered access to children's sensitive information, but Price truly had tried to reform himself since his early days in Tarrytown. In Carter's defense, he was unaware of Price's indiscretion, as it had never been made public record. As much as Price shit-talked the kids, he wanted to make amends by helping them succeed. As such, he purposefully and privately campaigned to the school and the PTA's retinue of parents to start after school programs and work-study ones, like the one Vincent, Aaron and Allister partook of in his own shop. In a small way, he was giving back to the community. He did have the foresight, however, to never be alone with young teenaged women, so as to avoid any improprieties that may creep back into the recesses of his brain.

Aaron had been an Army brat. His father had deserted his mom after a stay in Germany when she fell prey to a Jody Grinder back Stateside. The kid was heartbroken, but Captain Klimchak couldn't take the heartache and his own COs calling his wife a Susie Rottencrotch. It was too much for him to bear, so he simply didn't come home and Aaron became collateral damage.

Allister, on the other hand, was anyone's guess. He came from a picture-perfect home, surrounded by love, wealth and encouragement. But for some reason, he always acted out. From a very young age, he would get into fights with other children and steal things. Luckily, he wasn't quite up to squirrel-mutilating psychosis or the type of paranoia surrounding Damien Echols' childhood yet, so his idiosyncrasies were mostly forgiven. He did, however, continue to be a handful, although his mischievous side usually materialized itself as playful pranks and horniness these days.

Vincent was no different. As a child with a clinical disease and an absentee mother most of his life, he had no real role models to look up to, hence his obsession with imaginary creatures, scream queens and horror icons. The doctors never really cared for him either. Everyone in his life seemed to take the easy way out. Syphoning off insurance money and a plethora of prescriptions, Vincent's personal welfare seemed to be the last thing on anyone's mind, including his mother's. Price, ironically of all people, ended up being more of a caretaker to him than most, despite the fact he was indiscreetly fucking a married woman twenty years his junior. Not all heroes wear capes.

Price had spent the day trying to translate quarterly statements from his Japan titles and testing his skill as an amateur ham radio operator. He only qualified for the technical license, and after exhausting the limits of his skillset, he finally decided to call it a day. Call him nerdy, unattractive or even perverted, but the libido department was one in which he was far from lacking. He would spend the rest of the evening at home with a couple of bukkake selections from his Adults Only selection and still be plenty reloaded for Mrs. Guerrero come morning. He pushed aside a stack of jacket-less DVD burners of Dolph Lundgren movies off his desk and got up to leave.

The boys, now deep in their due-deserved misery, had had plenty of time to think of the errors of their ways and were sitting around a couple of pizza boxes doing the last of the inventory when Price exited his office.

"Alright, fellas, finish that up. I'm heading out," said Price. "Vincent, be sure to lock up, and I swear to God none of you better leave before this is all done. You can drop the keys in my mailbox on your way home."

"We're almost done, Mr. Price," said Vincent.

The boys had the piss drained out of them and were too tired to talk back or protest. Even Aaron was focusing on the task at hand, along with the others' robotic pushes to finish.

"Thanks, kids, see you next Saturday. Have a good Down-Home Days and a great week." Price closed the door and took a good fifteen minutes warming up his beige '82 Chevy Chevette before it gained the willpower to accelerate out of park. He waved goodbye and the boys let out a collective sigh.

"Oh thank God! Finally. Let's go." Allister stood up to leave, his legs cramping from sitting Indian-style so long.

"Am I the only one thinking he was weirdly nice?" Aaron asked.

The others shrugged.

"Wait. There's a good half hour more of work left. Plus, let's wait at least fifteen to see if Price comes back for something he forgot," said Vincent.

"Like what, his Fleshlight?" Aaron could never resist a jab.

"I mean, *Hollow* doesn't come on 'til after the cartoon, so it probably just started, so we got a beat," reasoned Allister.

"Alright, but fifteen minutes only," Aaron reluctantly said as he sat back down.

A half hour had quickly passed before any of the boys bothered to check the time. Finally noticing the hour, Aaron sprang to his feet. "The Horseman! Let's go, dudes."

Outside the shop, it was mostly black save for the moonlight and the sign, which with its burnt-out P now read FOR THE RIGHT ★RICE, something the boys thought was hilarious so they hadn't bothered to tell their boss about yet. They also thought it strange how he felt the need to pay to advertise the closed shop all night, but instructed them to conserve water with their flushes and would only allow fans, not AC, in the summer months. It wasn't like he'd be gaining any new customers in a town so small anyway. Price was a weird dude indeed.

Vincent searched though the pockets of his hoodie for the keys, but they simply weren't there. His two fingers poked right through a quarter-sized hole in the single front pocket. As he did so, a pill bottle clattered to the ground, but remained unnoticed by him. He continued to obsess over the missing keys, checking his jeans pockets as well. "Damn it, I can't find the fucking keys!"

Allister picked up the errant pill bottle and read the label, a look of shock immediately registering across his face. Whatever it said prompted a look from Aaron as well when he was shown it.

"Here, dude, you dropped this." Allister flicked the bottle back to Vincent.

Vincent caught the bottle, looking somewhat embarrassed. "Oh, thanks, man. Hey, you guys go ahead. I'll catch up later."

"Are you sure you're alright, man?" Aaron was sincere for once.

"Yeah, man, totally. Laters."

"Alright cool. We're gonna try and catch the last half of *Sleepy Hollow*. It's a tradition at this point." Aaron gave Allister a playful nut tap and they jogged off into the darkness.

Back inside the shop, it was extremely dark. Cardboard cutouts of James Dean and Pee-Wee Herman cast eerie shadows over the displays. It didn't help that titles like *The Creature From the Black Lagoon, Re-Animator,* and *Child's Play* starred back at Vincent from the prominently placed horror section. Vincent stumbled around in the dark looking for the light switch and nearly toppled an entire rack of 80s action films. The multiple Schwarzeneggers seemed to mock him, until he eventually found it. He flipped the switch, and with a ZAP, a shower of sparks flew. "Piece a shit," Vincent said as he felt his way around like a blind man looking for Price's office door with the moonlight outside as the only source of light.

The desk and file cabinet barely fit in Price's tiny office. It was chock-full of at least three decades worth of clutter, probably more. Outside, branches and autumnal leaves scratched the surface of near ceiling high windows like the claws of invalids who had been trapped in padded cells. The wind started to kick up vehemently.

Vincent carefully moved around the desk. The keys could be anywhere. Then some luck; a sudden glint of metal. *Voilà!* The keys. As Vincent reached for them, outside the window something big, dark and mysterious fluttered by. It was way too quick and impossible to make out, but nonetheless frightening. *It seemed almost… airborne? Couldn't be.* Beads of cold sweat began to appear on his forehead.

A buxom Queen Doris of the Sixth Dimension starred down at Vincent from a signed *Forbidden Zone* poster. It was unnerving under the circumstances, and caused him to loosen his grip on the keys. The *clank* of the key ring hitting the floor made Vincent jump back, clearly out of sorts and scared of his own shadow. He was now sweating profusely. He slumped against the wall, breathing heavily, as his hand searched out the keys.

Seated on the floor, he fumbled in his pocket for his medication. Thank God for Allister. Vincent searched the desk with his hands, like a blind man reading braille, trying to find a bottle of water, or anything, to swallow the horse pill. Again, something large and dark winged by outside. Its silhouette dwarfed the windows high above Vincent's seated position and seemed to hover a beat before fleeting off. *Is it there, or did I just imagine it?* Hard to tell, as the wind had really kicked up now.

Vincent squinted and again looked around for some water. Nothing but a half inch of coffee in a dirty Shin-chan cup; God knows how old. He pulled it to his mouth, grimaced, and ultimately rejected the putrid smell. He decided instead to put the horse pill on his tongue. With a look of determination, he dry-swallowed the pill with an audible gulp. After a few seconds, he composed himself, grabbed the keys and mustered up the courage to bolt for the exit.

Back outside, Vincent locked up and went for his bike. *Damn!* He had completely forgotten about the incident this morning. His front tire was more trapezoid-shaped than circle. He grabbed the bike by the handle bars and began the longish walk home. The thud of the flattened bike wheel made a disconcerting sound as he walked.

On he went down the beautiful but eerily silent streets of Victorian homes. Dutch names like Beekmen and Depeyster seemed to mock him from bright orange street signs emblazoned with tiny little headless riders. Blackened chestnut trees with claw-like branches formed canopies on either side. The dying leaves of fall and occasional gusts of wind seemed other-worldly. Vincent couldn't help but feel like he was being watched by someone, or some Thing.

As he limped the bicycle down the street, demons of his own imagination seemed to get the better of him. Not a sign of life anywhere, other than eerily lit jack-o'-lanterns with grimacing faces, and the occasional reflection of the flicker of a late-night TV screen. Each home seemed to be looking at him, but oddly not a soul was stirring in sight. Bloody mannequins and masked effigies lined the upper windows. People had gone the extra mile. Stuffed Jasons, Freddies, Michael Myers, and of course the Horseman himself, peeked from behind trees and under brambles or basement lattice work. Their victims were strewn out or draped off of parapets, as if dying. Only the occasional Jack Skellington gave him a fleeting sense of comfort.

Then, in the distance, almost echoing on reverb, the distinct sound of a horse's hooves hitting the pavement. Vincent stopped and looked back. Nothing. He continued, but quickened his pace. He wiped his brow, deep paranoia again setting in. He reached in his pocket for the pill bottle. It was there, but empty. *How many pills had he taken at the shop?* He couldn't remember. Something scurried across a lawn. *A cat? A squirrel? Was it even there? Okay, Vincent, get a hold of yourself. This is all in your head.*

Having reassured himself, he continued. Then he heard the sound again. This time not so far away. It was the distinct whiny of a thoroughbred. Vincent turned toward the unfathomable noise, and got nothing but an unnatural gust of wind for his troubles.

Now panicked, he ditched the bike and began a full-out sprint. As he ran, he heard the clear, terrifying sound of a horse's hooves at gallop speed not too far behind him. He covered his ears, hoping this would drown them out. It didn't. He kept running, too afraid to look back.

Finally, completely out of breath and unable to run any longer, he stopped in his tracks and panted heavily. Then, close enough to feel its breath on his neck, the snort of a larger-than-life horse gave him chills. The hairs on the back of Vincent's neck stood at attention as he slowly turned. Not wanting to believe what he had heard, and sure that this would be his final act in life, Vincent accepted his fate and began to timidly open his eyes, knowing the Horseman would be there.

"Vincent!" shouted his mother. "What the hell is wrong with you?"

Instead of a ghostly apparition on a demonic Hellsteed, Vincent instead saw the one person who haunted even his waking dreams—his mother; tagging alongside, her boy toy, Jack. The two were clearly readied for a night on the town. Marisa wore a miniskirt so short it made her son blanch at the thought of potentially seeing his own mother's kidneys. Bra was optional, heavy makeup was not. Jack, on the other hand, looked like he could either go line dancing or milking cows; the difference was indiscernible.

"Vince, answer me. Are you okay? You look pale," she said.

Vincent snapped out of it, not sure if he'd actually pissed himself or not, and managed a response. "Yeah, Mom, I'm fine." He wasn't.

Marisa matted his hair like a grandma would to a child at their First Holy Communion. "That's good. I was worried sick about you. There's cold pizza on the table. We're going out. Don't wait up for us," she said, then turned her affections toward Jack, as if her underage son wasn't even present. The not-much-older man already seemed like he was half lit and reciprocated her lustful intentions.

As the two walked toward a decade-old F-250 dually pickup, Jack turned around to wink at Vincent and grabbed Marisa's ass so hard it fully exposed the cheek and left behind a red handprint. He then used his full hand like palming a basketball to hoist her into the truck. "Oh, stop it," she playfully protested as she climbed onto the lifted sideboard.

Vincent grabbed his temples as if to defy the torrents of raw emotion now descending down upon him, as he was often prone to do in situations like these. This had long been one of his nervous ticks when life became too overwhelming. A roller coaster of emotions had wrought hell on him. From disillusionment, to being scared for his life, and now anger in just a matter of minutes. This would be enough to fatigue anyone, much less someone in his frail emotional state.

Vincent kicked the screen door open and grabbed a piece of cold pizza off the coffee table before switching on the TV. He couldn't even taste it over the rage on his palette. Tonight sucked, but he found solace in the fact that perhaps his favorite movie would allow him some much needed escape. It took the TV as long to warm up as the Spruce Goose had to take flight. Finally, after a horizontal flash of light the picture realized itself. Instead of his favorite antihero, the end credits of Tim Burton's *Sleepy Hollow* crawled up his screen. Not even Danny Elfman's score could soothe the savage beast inside.

Disappointment—the perfect end to a perfectly disastrous night. He would instead end it as it seemed he always did, in a pill-induced rage, lulled to sleep by cacophonous death metal.

Chapter 7

The New Dutch Reformed Church was not quite as antique as the Old Dutch Church of Sleepy Hollow, but it had a lot in common with it. Both were built on bookends of the 17th century, both were adjacent to the trickling section of the Pocantico River, both were nestled somewhere between Phillip's Manor and Sunnyside, and both had similar architecture. It was rumored that General George Washington himself had once sought repose at the oldest of the two churches after barely missing a fierce interrogation by a Redcoat Commander that would have surely ended in him hanging for treason.

Powder keg colored balustrades, bone-white retaining walls, gambrel roofs and wrought iron weathervanes were among the similarities. The newer church of the two also boasted four giant stained glass windows which had been retrofitted by Louis Comfort Tiffany himself, and his colleagues at the Pacific American Decorative Company.

Just about the time the village had finally embraced its Washington Irving heritage, the designers decided all things horse-related were fair game. This timed out perfectly with the resurgence of the fire and brimstone era in the area. Each panel depicted one of the Four Horseman of the Apocalypse from the Book of Revelation descending upon the earth for the final judgment and destruction of the world. They were, of course, each mounted on horseback riding plumes of the four classic elements: earth, wind, fire and water. Although these New Yorkers didn't have quite the reputation as their Salem compatriots, the crushing stones and hanging trees of this town were much more fierce. The pariahs they were intended for would have to survive public ridicule and scorn as social outcasts instead of simply dying off. Whether tis nobler in the mind to suffer the slings and arrows of outrageous fortune or actually die by the sword was still up for debate.

Nevertheless, every Sunday in this town might as well have been Easter Sunday and today was no exception. The congregation politely seated themselves in the wooden pews of New Dutch Reformed Church facing the intricately carved wooden pulpit wearing their Sunday-best pastels, heirloom jewelry and quaffed hair. They greeted each other with pleasantries and smiles, even to the faces of their own private Judases and worst enemies. There were plenty of stones to be thrown around this town, though that would never happen in this glass house or under the heedful eye of one Reverend Graham James Todd. The town collectively joked never to trust a man with two first names, much less three, but of course not to the good ol' reverend's face. Like the Reverend Ritzema before him, he warned of speaking to foreigners outside the trusted circle, especially those suspected of witchcraft or its modern day equivalent, atheism.

The sun reached high noon up above the steeple and it split its rays though each of the Horseman in the grandiose windows behind the pulpit, simultaneously giving them each a celestial glow while also striking the fear of God into their onlookers. Although many were uncomfortable, no one stirred. The reverend was bathed in the yellow, pink and blue hues of the stained glass behind him, and in this particular instance, it didn't take much to imagine him as the actual Voice of God.

"And the number of the army of the horsemen were two hundred thousand; And I saw the horses and those who sat upon them, having breastplates of brimstone and jacinth and fire!", and so the reverend droned on.

Mr. Price stole an awkward and uncomfortable glance toward Mrs. Guerrero, whose was seated across the aisle in a dress most of the Puritanical members would have deemed a bit too short and a bit too racy. In their eyes, there was no need to brand her with a scarlet letter, as her own choice of attire seemed to take on that task welcomingly. That's not to say, however, every human under the holy roof didn't try to sneak a peek of her ample cleavage, save maybe Rev. Todd. The attractive Latina housewife was seated next to her staunch, older and three-piece clad husband. He remained oblivious as always, but the eagle-eyed reverend, on the other hand, caught everything. He studied his flock religiously and didn't need confession booths to understand their transgressions. He turned his attention to Price and continued.

"And out of the horses' mouths issued fire and smoke and brimstone. By these three was the third part of mankind killed, by the fire, smoke, and brimstone, which issued out of their mouths."

The rays of sun singled Rayna out as if the heavens themselves had placed her in the pew. Even God, Himself, couldn't deny her innocence, and the heavens seemed to be revealing as much right there in front of the entire congregation. She listened attentively, surrounded by her loving, all-American family, including her grandmother, Maw Maw Williams, her younger cousin, Bobbie, and the ever-by-her-side father, in his full dress deputy sheriff's uniform.

Todd often kept the doors of the church open during his sermons, in hopes of fulfilling his personal fantasy of converting some errant passersby. A disheveled Vincent, still dressed in yesterday's clothes and sporting bedhead, snuck in said ajar doors and sat in the very last row, trying to go unnoticed. The derisive reverend, however, closed the dog-eared Bible roughly on the podium and gave Vincent a condescending look as he addressed the congregation.

Following the reverend's gaze, a few church members, Lorraine included, turned and noticed Vincent. She and Vincent briefly locked eyes, and although shocked to see him there, she managed half a smile.

"And so is the wrath of condemnation on those who don't repent and atone for their sins." He briefly paused to single out Vincent with his eyes. "This concludes our service. Let us pray."

As the congregation stood, Vincent made a stealthy motion to Rayna to meet him outside, then darted out the door. It was so fast and fleeting that even Reverend Todd didn't notice, nor did Deputy Constance. Rayna and Maw Maw did, but this was a perfect instance where the 'girl code' won out over pitchforks and torches.

Several minutes later, outside, the reverend shook hands with his flock. Mr. Price took special care to avoid eye contact with nearly everyone, but especially Mrs. Guerrero and her surprisingly handsome and rugged husband. Deputy Constance and his family passed through the vestibule and exited through the double recessed doors and out through the Gothic archway. Out here, the reverend seemed to drop his austere facade in favor of a much more congenial one. "Morning, Maw Maw Williams," the man of God said as he stooped lower to meet her eye to eye. The elderly woman just nodded with a crooked smile.

Rayna took this small distraction as an opportunity to cross the quiet two-laned road that separated the church from its centuries-old cemetery. Vincent was already there, visibly brooding and shuffling his feet nervously, when she finally saw him.

"Rayna, you coming to the social hall? Pancake breakfast," her father shouted, not caring if he embarrassed her. She didn't answer. "Lorraine, answer me."

"Yeah, Dad, just give me a minute."

The look on her father's face showed his disapproval. The reverend and the deputy now saw that her attention was on Vincent. Constance pushed his sidearm tighter into his holster —a subconscious move by an overprotective father. "Okay, but make it quick. I'll save you a plate." He turned to the reverend just as Price had come to greet them both.

Vincent had noticed the gesture and took the opportunity to sit on the closest piece of horizontal granite near him, hoping to brace himself for the wave of emotions he was feeling.

Constance locked his eyes on his daughter like a tracking beam as she walked toward Vincent. Reverend Todd and Price also gave a disapproving glare. "I don't trust that kid. Some boy from school," said Constance absentmindedly.

Price butted in, like he always had when he was trying to fit in to the boys club. "That's Vincent Douglass. He's about as harmless as they come, Constance. Works at my store on weekends. Come to think of it he still has my keys."

Constance let go of the grip on his sidearm with an audible sigh.

Unlike its eternally resting counterpart in Sleepy Hollow, the cemetery was much more grandiose, though equally as ancient. In fact, it had been said on several occasions that only Bonaventure Cemetery in Savannah could even come close to rivaling it. But Little Gracie be damned, if its one-upmanship wouldn't allow for it to be adorned with larger-than-life saints, cherubs and every angel and demon known to man. Some were draped in granite cloaks and praying vestments, others seemed to mourn their occupants, while still others warned of the finiteness of life. The moss-ridden gardens and spectral displays were beautiful, but extremely daunting at the same time. The weathered statues, tombstones and mausoleums from ages past surrounded by black cast iron fencing created quite the menacing menagerie. The older parts of the cemetery weren't even all that well maintained. Anyone who ever set foot in the town and died, and a couple who hadn't, were buried either here or next to the Rockefellers. It was the kind of place most people wouldn't feel comfortable in alone even in broad daylight.

Vincent had inadvertently sat on a tombstone lost in thought. From the corner of his eye, there seemed to be a dark figure slightly out of focus at the edge of a large structure. He turned to look, but no one was there. Whatever it was seemed ominous, foreboding. Unlike the sandstones, granites and lime that most of the cemetery's statues had, this apparition stood out from what the other tombstones and mausoleums were made of.

Rayna alighted out of nowhere, almost, it seemed, as if gliding above the ground. It was practically sinful to have such a young girl so full of life bounce into a place so filled with death, but the sun seemed to light Rayna's pathway as she made her way over to Vincent. She was simply beaming. Her blue and beige floral sundress radiated in the patches of light, making her stand out like a blooming lotus in a briar patch.

"Hey," she said cheerfully.

Vincent finally snapped out of it. He knew he had seen something, but Rayna's ebullience was too much to ignore. "Oh, hey. Do you mind if we talk somewhere a little private?"

Rayna giggled in spite of herself. "More private than this? I don't think you have to worry about anyone eavesdropping."

Vincent made a gesture to Rayna's father, who still eyed them from across the street. She threw her father a "Seriously, Dad?" look and he reluctantly sauntered off.

"Don't mind him. He gets a little overprotective sometimes. Single Parent Syndrome. You know," she said mockingly to a singsong beat, "Daddy's little princess."

"So, about that talk," implored Vincent. He seemed distressed.

"Yeah, sure. Of course. But could we, um, do it over there?" She motioned to a concrete memorial bench. Immediately noticing his error, Vincent jumped to his feet, made an awkward, apologetic gesture to the tombstone he had been sitting on, and followed her over.

"So, what's up?" began Rayna. "What in the *heck* are you doing here?" She was intrigued that Vincent was actually opening up to her and had gone out of his way to meet her in public.

Vincent was a bit taken aback by her bluntness, but hadn't come all this way and put his heart on his sleeve just to clam up now. "My friends would just make fun of me. And my mom…"

"It's okay," she said. "Just tell me."

Vincent felt the frog in his throat swell as he began. He couldn't believe he was about to say this out loud to the cutest girl in school, whom he had only just met. "Last night I…" He could barely get the words out. "I thought I heard something. I can't explain it. But I never felt anything like that before."

"Like what?" The suspense was killing her.

Vincent's rational side started to emerge. He felt belittled and stupid again. Of course it was all in his head. "It's stupid. You wouldn't believe me."

"Try me," she implored.

"A horse." His face contorted in embarrassment as the words left his mouth.

Rayna burst out laughing in spite of herself, not realizing how sensitive a subject this was for Vincent. "I'm sorry, a what?" She giggled again. "A horse? There are definitely plenty of horses around here."

Vincent looked defeated. His shoulders slumped. She didn't get it, or him, in the least bit. Then he found his resolve. He would make her understand.

"No! This was different. Like it was chasing me. Like it was him, the Horseman. I was walking home alone when I heard these pounding hooves and whinnying and snorting, and felt its God-awful breath on my neck."

Vincent's eyes glazed over as he relived the moment. As he told Rayna the story, he experienced the feeling all over again, how it had made him feel threatened.

The whole time, Lorraine watched him. Her first reaction was to feel sorry for him. As he went on, she concluded this could perhaps be a much bigger issue. Still, though, she wasn't frightened.

She was drawn to Vincent, and one strange episode was not going to deter her. At least he wasn't a child molester or an axe murderer, despite what the kids at school joked.

"Are you okay? You know, maybe it was just a reaction to some bad medication. And all this Halloween stuff everywhere can't help either," she reasoned.

There was an awkward moment of silence between them. Lorraine nervously fumbled with the gold, heart-shaped locket around her neck. You could tell by the tarnish that it was more than a few years old.

"You know about my medication?" he asked.

She shot him an 'as if' look. "Yeah, Vince, everyone does. Kids at school talk, you know."

Vincent looked a bit shocked and possibly a little offended. The thought of being the center of gossip at school, particularly amongst the popular crowd, left a bitter taste in his mouth. "You guys talk about me?"

It was the worst thing she could have possibly said. Although she was a genuine and caring individual, her teenage mind hadn't quite taught her the art of diplomacy just yet. To her credit, she realized her faux pas immediately.

"No, not like that. Just in passing." She was making it worse. "I'm sorry. This was not a very good start was it?"

"A good start to what?"

She smiled at his naïveté. They sat there for a moment, soaking each other in, the tip of the iceberg slowly starting to melt.

Suddenly feeling shy, Vincent wanted to change the subject. "Nice locket."

"Oh, thanks. My mom gave it to me. See." Rayna opened the heart-shaped pendant, which had a picture of her mother and a photograph of her as a much younger child. By looks of the pictures, they were obviously very connected and happy when together.

"She's beautiful," Vincent said. "And so are you."

Rayna looked up and her tearful eyes met his. "Was. She's gone now." Her eyes darted around her surroundings, an untimely reminder of her mother's passing.

"I meant you look just like her." he said, trying to backpedal.

She scanned the empathy deep within his eyes, then leaned in for an innocent peck on Vincent's cheek. Maybe now he would understand what the "not so good start" was to.

"Lorraine H. Constance, are you coming? It's getting cold," belted Constance as he stepped on the edge of the lawn. Chances were he had probably seen the innocent gesture.

Rayna blushed so hard the red of her cheeks clashed sharply with the baby blues of her summer dress. She bolted upright. "Okay, Dad, coming!" She turned to Vincent. "Look, I really have to go. I'm sorry I laughed at you, I didn't mean to. Can we talk about this at school tomorrow?" She stood fully up to leave, not really intending to wait around for an answer.

"Yeah, I guess. I guess so," came Vincent's sullen reply.

Rayna started to walk away but suddenly thought better of it. She abruptly turned and bent down toward Vincent, whispering close to his face. "And by the way, it's really sweet you came all the way out here to talk to me about this. If my dad wasn't standing right over there, I'd give you a better kiss."

Their eyes meet for an intimate beat and Vincent felt the surge of adrenaline and hormones come to life below him. As bad as his world was right now, she seemed to make it brighter, and this new revelation was beyond anything he could have hoped for. The Horseman was momentarily forgotten.

Constance was not pleased with even this minor show of affection. Vincent briefly met eyes with the deputy, but quickly skirted any further direct eye contact. He stared down at his scuffed shoes as he sauntered deeper into the cemetery.

As Lorraine and her father walked away, the dark figure appeared again in Vincent's peripheral vision, then once again suddenly vanished, never quite coming into focus. Vincent, more confused now than ever, walked toward where he thought he had seen the figure.

In the place where he thought it had stood, he found a large, weather-beaten gothic memorial from the late 1700s. The tombstone was protected by a larger-than-life granite knight statue. It stood at attention holding the hilt of its sword firmly in both hands. Black moss had begun to creep over the massive guardian, filling all the porous holes of the stone's granite like a deathly cancer. The sword it held was firmly planted on the base of the marker, which had only a single word upon it in bold, period-style font—ACKER.

Chapter 8

As the cool of the approaching evening turned the brisk afternoon a little more chilly, Vincent found himself standing on the wooden inlayed porch of his school psychiatrist. He didn't come here often, as he got his share of Dr. Paulding at school. It was juvenile court ordered that Vincent check in with the good doc three times a week, so the weekend often felt like a much needed respite from his pedantic drilling.

But something felt different this time, and if there was one thing Vincent knew, it was that Dr. Paulding would at least take the time to pretend to listen to his woes. He shuffled his shoes on the fading and paint chipped wood flooring of the porch. He imagined how many decades of feet it must have taken to wear away the wood beneath him. The porch and house were raised up off the ground, and broken pieces of once–fancy whitewashed lattice work partially blocked the crawlspace under the house. At any moment, Vincent half expected Stephen King's Cujo to run out and take half of his foot off. *Man that dog could slobber,* thought Vincent.

The porch was filled with brightly colored corn husks, an autumnal wreath and some hand drawn, anamorphic black cats wearing orange pinstriped suites and playing jazz instruments. To Vincent, they almost appeared as racist caricatures in black face. But if there was one house in town that could get away with such questionable decorations, it was this one. Dr. Paulding was a member of one of the few African–American households that had made their home here long before slaves had ever been emancipated; no one would question his choice of decor.

Vincent shuffled his Converse a few more times and then sheepishly knocked on the door. After a few beats, the middle-aged psychiatrist swung the screen door open wide with a look of surprise. He was hiding something behind his back.

"Oh, Vincent, it's just you," said Paulding in a smooth, deep voice not unlike Darth Vader's.

Vincent didn't know how to take this. *Was the doctor expecting someone else? What was behind his back? Was he preparing to defend his home from an intruder? What was wrong with being just himself?*

In fact, what Paulding was hiding behind his back was a half-finished scotch and soda on the rocks. Being Sunday, he wasn't expecting any company, nor patients, and certainly not the often elusive Vincent.

"Give me a minute," Paulding said as he ducked behind the door and polished off the other half of the drink. He set it down on the end table near his door, which normally was used to hold a bowl of keys and an African-themed Poole pottery piece his aunt in Amsterdam had gifted him. He poked his head back out, wiping the wetness of the whiskey off his lips with the back of his sleeve.

"You said anytime I needed to talk, right?" implored Vincent.

"Sure, son, of course. Come on in." He motioned Vincent in.

He hadn't fooled anyone, as Vincent could smell the pungent tinge of alcohol on the doctor's breath. But that was fine. It was after hours, in his own home, and Vincent had ambushed him after all.

Vincent took a seat on a royal green couch covered in plastic. It made awkward fart noises as his butt scooched across the protective cover. The decorations in Paulding's home seemed a bit depressing to Vincent. There were a lot of browns and dark greens, and the furniture seemed like something a person much older than the doctor would have around. There were framed pictures of heroic African-American figures adorning the walls, along with sonnets, landscapes and quotes from Martin Luther King, Jr. It felt more like a museum than a home. All in all, though not to Vincent's taste, it was tidy and organized. Something he was not at all used to in his own household.

"What's on your mind, Vincent?" the doctor asked.

Vincent fidgeted in his seat. A row of Dogon ceremonial masks stared down from the walls. They seemed to be asking Vincent if the cat, in fact, had got his tongue. He shifted again, his jean pocket sticking to the plastic cover.

"Oh, come on now." The doctor's voice was as smooth as the sixteen-year-old scotch on the back of his tongue. "You're the one who came over here on a Sunday afternoon. This couldn't have waited 'til tomorrow? If you're not going to say anything, I'll pour my next drink." The doctor chuckled to himself.

Vince remained motionless. The ticking of an old grandfather clock seemed to come into sharp focus in his ears. The Dutch longcase had made is way over as precious cargo on a schooner bedecked with an equally as intricate, hand-carved St. Nicholas effigy guiding its bow back in the late 1600s. Vincent hadn't even noticed it before, but now it seemed to be taunting him. The seconds seemed like eternity.

Finally, the imaginary ball of molasses on Vincent's tongue dissolved and he managed to speak. "It's just that I feel like such an outcast. What do you call it? A social piranha?"

This was too much for the doctor to bear. He let out a super-sized belly laugh before catching himself. Vincent's brow furrowed. This was the second time today he had worn his heart on his sleeve and had been laughed at.

"I'm sorry, Vince. I didn't mean to laugh." He paused. "It's pariah. A social piranha's a good one though. Plenty of those around here." His laugh tapered off.

Vincent neither smirked nor stirred. Why was it that after everyone laughed at him, they immediately felt the urge to apologize? *If you're going to make fun of me, at least be man enough to own it.*

Dr. Paulding leaned in and engaged Vincent with full eye contact. "Vince, listen. You wanna talk about social pariahs? My family comes from a long lineage of slavery, and people here won't let me forget that. I grew up in this town that's over 75% white. If anyone knows about being a pariah, it's me. So let's talk. This's probably the one thing I can actually relate to you on."

That got Vincent's attention, and after a moment of quiet reflection, he lifted his eyes to meet Paulding's. He could see the inherited centuries of anguish and pain in the older man's eyes, and new that his plight was an earnest one. Then he again turned his thoughts inward to himself. "But at least they don't look at you like you're crazy," he said.

It was a strange flex, but the doctor understood that Vincent needed this moment to be about him. "No, they don't. But they look at me like I'm going to hit them, or steal something, or take their women. And the messed up part? My family has been here longer than most of theirs."

"So how do you deal with it? I'd really like to know."

The doctor sat with his hands on his knees, elbows jutting outward. Then, with a hefty sigh, he leaned back. "Look, Vince, you're only responsible for your own actions. In the end, all you have is between you and your God, whatever that means to you personally. No one else matters. I guess what I'm trying to say is forget about what other people think, or what you think they think. In the grand scheme of things, none of that matters."

Vincent sighed audibly. "I guess so. It's just sometimes I start to believe them. Like maybe I am going crazy." Vincent looked imploringly at the doctor. They both knew where this conversation was going, and once again subconsciously assumed their respective roles in the relationship.

"We don't talk nonsense like that in this house. It's a chemical imbalance. You know this, and you have to keep reminding yourself of it," Paulding said as he grabbed a large bottle of medication from a newly opened box that held samples. He pulled out a white plastic bottle labeled Neuropreen and tossed it to Vincent. "Here. These won't hurt either."

Vincent caught the bottle and pretended to be interested in the label, but they both knew he couldn't care less about what it actually said.

"Reps dropped these samples by just this week. Was going to suggest them anyway. But use only as directed, alright?"

"Okay."

"Promise me, Vincent," said Paulding. Both knew the implications of overprescribing, especially to a minor.

"I promise," said Vincent with the same scoff of a petulant teenager promising to take out the trash or do his homework. Then he caught himself and restated, "I promise. Honest."

That did the trick. Paulding rose from his felt chair and walked toward the door. Vincent knew the conversation was over and pulled himself off the couch. "Thanks, Doc. See ya tomorrow."

Paulding gave a playful eye roll and shuffled Vincent out the door, anxious to return to his own bottle of self-medication. He, too, had his addictions to feed. "Bye, Vince," he managed as he shut the door.

As Vince practically skipped home and the good doctor nestled back into his comfort zone, neither gave a single thought about the pawns they had just played the part of.

Big Pharma lobbied the politicians. The politicians, in turn, gave them tax breaks. They also supported prescription medication programs for young adults, like Vincent, throughout schools to allegedly help treat their infirmities. The politicians, of course, received kickbacks from the lobbyists, and the schools received much needed additional funding. The doctors would receive free dinners, fifty yard line tickets, exclusive club memberships, and often under the table payments from Big Pharma. Bribes, all in the name of helping the children.

The drugs were highly habit forming and proved to be the easiest part of the equation. All Vincent wanted was his fix, and Neuropreen was it. And with government funding, insurance policy payouts and pricey co-pays, doctors like Paulding were all too happy to oblige. Neuropreen, of course, being a portmanteau of pristine and neurological. It was no coincidence it was spelled and rhymed with teen, the impressionable and vulnerable demographic it was intentionally aimed at. Big Pharma, like Enron's inside jokes about rolling blackouts before them, got a good laugh at everyone else's expense.

It was a win-win situation for all, unless you counted the headache-inducing, often hallucination causing carcinogens Vincent and others like him pumped through their bloodstream. Not to mention, the toxic neurological cocktails made it hard for these kids to function.

But just as Paulding had assured Vincent, "In the grand scheme of things, none of that matters."

Chapter 9

Vincent popped a Neuropreen, and the tingle at the base of his skull welcomed it like an old friend. The pill had a slight minty taste going down, unlike its chemically flavored predecessors. How nice of them. At this point, they might as well just call it candy and name it Radical Raspberry. The marketing tactics aimed at young adults were old hat. Vincent's buddies could have their vape sticks and flavored chaw, but to him nothing beat the kick of Pez-like amphetamines.

The sunset seemed to dance in especially exuberant colors. The rainbows of yellows and pinks turning to devilishly brilliant Halloween oranges, bewitching purples, and fiery reds before Vincent's very eyes. The smiling jack-o'-lanterns and dancing skeletons along the street seemed to be singing in unison to the cheerful chorus Vincent imagined in his head. It was such a magical moment, he felt even the Horseman himself couldn't have ruined it. He was terribly wrong.

Vincent walked through the door to his house sideways. The high had been kicking in pretty good for a minute now, so he wanted to avoid solid obstacles, like a door frame, at all costs.

"Mom, you home? I'm starving," he bellowed down the hall.

Marisa had been a teen when she became pregnant with Vincent. What that meant to his friends was that she was the perfect MILF candidate. The sad part is, knowing she was a bad mother, she often sought attention from young men who were just a few years Vincent's senior. She had been sexually abused at a young age by her father's brother and often equated sexual acts, incestuous or otherwise, with love. Those wires had been permanently crossed and fused together in her youth, and now she repeated the cycle with men nearly young enough to be Vincent's barely older brother.

Jack was no exception. Marisa had met him at a career day at Vincent's high school, where students and recent graduates could mingle with prospective employers in the hopes of finding gainful employment. This, in turn, helped the students afford to pay for their necessities, but more importantly, their addictions. Vape sticks, White Claws and Swisher Sweets weren't free after all, and despite what the next mumble (c)rapper told you, being an influencer wasn't really that lucrative. Unless you were a dummy thicc teenage girl willing to get butt-naked of course, then the collaborating partners would slide into your DMs by the dozen.

Jack didn't walk away from the fair with a job that day, but he did end up with the best and sloppiest blow job of his young life. Marisa had gone down on him right there in the faculty parking lot, where she had double parked, and also forgotten all about the reason she had even been there—picking up Vincent.

Now in the throes of passion, Jack fucked her like one of the high school cheerleaders he had helped taking turns on under the bleachers during a prep rally. Literally balls deep, with her legs high up in the air and her bedroom door ajar, Marisa didn't care who heard her moans, even if it was Vincent. Just as Vincent walked by the open door to see his mom getting plowed by Jack, Jack turned and saw Vincent in the doorway, mouth wide open. Jack pushed her panties off his face and chortled like Bane as he used the full force of his body to swing Marisa up reverse cowboy, making sure to give Vincent a good glimpse of her pussy and tits. This was a game he enjoyed playing with Vince. A literal *fuck* you.

"Fuck me, you animal," she said, unintentionally making eye contact with her son at the door. For a brief moment, she seemed mortified, but Jack's relentless pounding beneath her was too much for her to bear. She gushed forth an onslaught of an orgasm, barely having the wherewithal to throw a stiletto at Vincent though the doorway. "Fuck!" She came loudly. "Get out of here, Vince."

The high heel barely missed his eye, and the pungent smell of sex it wafted toward him was everywhere. With the *THWAP* of the shoe hitting the doorframe, Vincent snapped out of his initial shock. "Jesus Christ, Mom! Are you fucking serious?" The dancing pachyderms in his mind were quickly being replaced by flaming skulls and iron clad demons.

Vincent punched a hole in the corridor wall, leaving plaster of Paris and trickles of blood in his wake. He stomped off into his bedroom and slammed the door so hard one of its hingers turned askew. He jumped on the bed, nearly breaking the frame, and began to pull out small clumps of hair. He screamed as loud as he could and cried snot and tears into his already soiled pillow. This was not the first time this had happened, but that didn't make it hurt any less.

Suddenly, Vince remembered the bottle from Dr. Paulding. "Use only as directed, my fucking ass." Vincent's dark side began to take over. He popped two of the minty Neuropreen back-to-back, not even bothering to look for a liquid chaser. He fumbled on his nightstand, knocking over a *Killer Klowns* figurine. As it hit the ground, its ear to ear demonic smile chipped off its visage and fell onto the floor. It seemed to be staring up at him, maybe even blinking. Rows of its sharpened dagger-like teeth mocking his loser status. This only infuriated him more. He shuffled through the drawer, and mountain of a mess, until he finally found a battered Walkman he had received from one of his previous psychiatrists. Ironically, that was the one guy who actually had seemed to care, and he had been beheaded in a freak jet-skiing accident. *Good looking out, Universe!* The Horseman parallel wasn't lost on Vincent.

After digging through his collection of The Cure and a stack of goth metal tapes, Vincent finally found what he was looking for. Some scream metal nursery rhymes that were so loud, vulgar, and obnoxious they probably could have summoned Beelzebub himself. Just what the doctor ordered. "Mary's Little Slaughtered Lamb."

Now dazed, he picked up a graphic novel of the *The Legend of Sleepy Hollow* impeccably drawn by Gris Grimly. He flipped through it, but it was way too tame for his foul mood. He picked up another, *The Unhallowed Horseman,* much more imbrued and gory. This was more like it. Each page depicted another gruesome scene that played out in time with the rants of the scream metal bombarding his eardrums. He envisioned the faces of Jack and Marisa in place of each and every victim on the page. A cartoon Horseman wielded an axe and a whip, making short work of unsuspecting victims.

Marisa screamed, 'Fuck me, you animal," on repeat in Vincent's mind. The cartoon version of her was now shoving her supple breasts into Vincent's face. "Fuck me, Vince," the animated woman begged. A waterfall of blood began to flow from her succulent nipples. Reality and fantasy were blurring in Vincent's mind. "I said fuck me, Vince." A sharpened axe slit across her chest, flaying her breast meat, sheering it right off her sternum. She died in a horrific heap of blood and copulation. In his mind's eye, she was begging to be fucked, begging to be killed.

He slammed the graphic novel closed. His brain was full. The music pumped hatred. His dick was hard and his mind was numb. *Fuck that bitch!* he thought as he drifted out into unconsciousness.

Chapter 10

Not far from Wiley's Swamp, on the border of Sleepy Hollow and Tarrytown, a group of Redcoats hastily jumped over brambles and briars. There were four of them. Three were Caucasian, with prominent European noses and brows. The fourth was of African descent. They scurried about, tripping over muck, fallen trees and withered vines. It was clear by their haste they had been compelled to achieve the task at hand as efficiently and quickly as possible, no matter the cost.

"There. Just past that row of hedges." The black man pointed.

It was clear something heavy and bulky had been camouflaged under shrubbery and a stack of disjoined kindling. It had long since decayed from the verdant stage in which the disguise was set. Now, the makeshift hide was brown and earthen and the outline of a cannon became clearer as they approached.

"Here, help me with these," whispered the tallest, strapping one. He clearly acted as the leader amongst them. He removed a small axe from its leather sheath and began chopping away at the more sinewy of branches as the others cleared away the mound of detritus.

A robust man among them tried to pick up the hitch that was designed to pull the cannon. He only managed to lift it centimeters off the ground before the weight crushed back down on his hands. "Yahhhh! Help me!" he screamed in pain.

The others rushed to dislodge his trapped digits.

"It's too heavy. There's not enough of us to move it," said one.

The most logical among them pondered for a moment. "Okay. It's on a slope. Everyone to the uphill side and push. The weight should shift it. Once it's pointing in the general direction of the path, we just need to time it right and it should take him out." It was far from a perfect plan, but it was all they had. The men lined up on the uphill side.

"Wait," said the black man. He got down on his knees and began burrowing underneath the cannon's loop. "That will slick out the ground and loosen it. Should make it slide easier. Gravity will do the rest."

"Three. Two. One," instructed the leader. The men heaved but the cannon barely budged. "Again!"

This time as the men pushed, the cannon edged at least half a foot. The men could feel their hearts nearly beating out of their chests and their spines buckling under the pressure. It didn't matter; the birth of a nation was at stake. It took them five tries, but in the end, they were successful. Once the cannon reached its tipping point, it slid decisively into place, just as the smartest had predicted. The cannon stopped perfectly aimed at the path in the woods that was just wide enough for a skilled equestrian to navigate. It was almost as if it had been predestined.

The robust man noticed a tear on his coat where one of the buttons had caught on a thorn while they had maneuvered the artillery into place. A sizable piece of fabric had torn with it, exposing a pair of burnt-mustard breeches underneath. "God save the Queen, indeed," he scoffed.

"In God we trust," said the logical one.

"George can take his tax and get fucked," said the slave.

The fourth remained sullen and quiet.

They were not British Redcoats at all, but rather American Revolutionaries impersonating them. The men gathered around and uncovered a box of ammunition, some flint, oil, and a wheelless caisson that had been left with the cannon specifically for times like this one. They hastily readied the cannon and snapped a dry branch that would serve as a torch. Now all that was left was to lie in wait for their would-be prey.

Although no one amongst them had noticed, the date was October 31, 1776. The Dutch men present knew of Sint-Maarten, but it wouldn't come to be known as Halloween in these parts until over 150 years later.

Above them, a full bloodred harvest moon pierced through the blanket of low-lying clouds that carpeted the battlefield. Over the marshes, a lone wolf howled an ominous warning. Ghostly shrieks seemed to permeate the air. Suddenly, in the not-too-far distance, the steady rhythm of a horse galloping at full speed grew closer. The four edged lower in the muck, ignoring the dampness that now filled their boots. Only one of them had a musket, and although he nervously aimed it, it was doubtful any of them had the marksmanship to pick a rider off of horseback at full stride.

"If we miss, there's a good chance it's all over for us. He has the plans, the secrets… everything. If he makes it to those British frigates offshore on the Tappan Zee, all is lost. West Point fallen," said the tall man. His eyes were wide and full of blue moonlight.

The Tappan Zee had long been where two opposing forces collided. Just like wind and mist, water and fire, now was no exception. When the stakes were high, the heroics were unparalleled. And now more than none other, the will and resolve of the men of the American Revolution was tested. There was no need to think of the alternative; failing simply was not an option. This very moment was tantamount to the colonists' will to survive and gain an important step toward independence and freedom from the cruel talon of the ever-domineering Crown.

Almost out of nowhere, a black stallion seemingly twenty hands high leaped airborne over a massive fallen tulip tree Nature seemed to have deliberately set in its path. The horse and rider stopped and stood flush at the sight of the torch and the cannon aimed squarely at them.

The rider, equally as daunting as his steed, wore the black and brown leathery frocks of the American Militia, a tricorn hat atop his head, and had his long black hair braided in a ponytail fashionable among Revolutionaries at the time. A harrowing battle axe and a long whip were his only defense against the four men and their massive weapon.

"What party are you from?" queried the quiet one.

Upon seeing the Redcoats lying in wait for him, the Hessian's mind quickly calculated his odds for survival. "Wait!" he exclaimed. "I'm one of you."

But his German accent, the filth of a former prisoner, and the decidedly Alemannic cut of his teeth proved to them otherwise. They immediately lit the fuse.

"Hi-Yah!" screamed the Hessian, giving the horse such a jolt with his spur that a steady stream of blood immediately flowed from its meaty haunch. The horse reared back, took two unfathomable strides and once again leaped into the air just as the massive iron ball erupted from the gun's muzzle. The force of the projectile was so fierce that it took with it the words of the manufacturer, which were embossed on the gun, and flung them at the rider in a fury of molten metal.

The four men ducked simultaneously, some taking shrapnel from the weapon. Once they had mustered the courage to again look up, there before them was the Horseman, sans head. A jutting vertebrae and still-smoking stump smoldered where the man's head once was. The horse died from fright on the spot, and it, with Rider, fell in a massive heap to the ground. An ungodly cry escaped into the night air, along with what was left of their crushed and cursed souls.

Not far along the coastline, the sloop-of-war *HMS Vulture* had been waiting for the Hessian's arrival in the very spot south of Croton's Point where *The Phoenix* and *The Rose* had been embroiled in battle less than three months prior. The abnormally loud report had served as the only signal its crew needed to realize their plan had been foiled. The *Vulture* made her way down the coast to Dobbs Ferry. The victory had indeed been won, but the war was far from over.

Chapter 11

The eraser hit the cracking green slate of the chalkboard with a resounding _thud_. A cloud of white chalk dust permeated the air like the remnants of cannon fire. The words REVOLUTIONARY WAR were spelled out in the elegant cursive writing of Sleepy Hollow High School's history teacher, Mr. Crane.

Mr. Crane's first name wasn't Ichabod, it was Peter. It was, however, believed that one of his great-great ancestors was the inspiration for Washington Irving's character; Not the War of 1812 veteran colonel, but rather the renowned Kinderhook pedagogue Jesse Merwin. Much like the lanky schoolmaster of Irving's yarn, Mr. Crane could have been a spitting image of what most people pictured in their mind's eye when they read the haunting tale of the choirmaster with a penchant for pastries. Like Ichabod, Peter was thin, tall and had a very pronounced nose, second only to that of Stuyvesant's prodigiously pronounced proboscis trumpeter Anthony Van Corlaer. Luckily for _this_ Crane, unruly students, and not larger-than-life moss bunkers, were all he need worry about at present. And like Ichabod, he, too, loved pursuing the single mothers of the PTA. What's more, again like Ichabod, he was known for his harmonizing at the church choral practices. Furthermore, a legion of tapeworms couldn't have blessed the man with more of an appetite, and no matter what he did—carb loading, protein shakes, and cholesterol fats by the gallon—he never seemed to gain an inch around his waist. It seemed his appetite for food, as well as for members of the opposite sex, simply couldn't be satiated.

But unlike others in the town, Crane was respectful of his peers, especially members of the opposite sex. He had control over his compulsions and urges, and unlike some, actually conferred with his inner monologue before speaking out loud. Beautiful blossoming girls could not convince him for higher grades with the batting of eyelashes, nor prominent bosoms. He took his job as village and school historian quite seriously, and he expected those students going through the hallowed halls of such a historical town to at least respect the culture of all things then and now, if not to actually retain it. In short, he had his flaws but, at his core, was a gentleman.

Between the Revolutionary War, General George Washington's sojourns through the village and surrounding areas, Washington Irving's collection of literary masterpieces, and the long history of Dutch colonization, there was plenty of rich history and cultural significance for Crane to keep busy with and certainly more than enough to fill the burgeoning minds under his care.

Today, Crane's lecture spoke of the historical significance of one of the area's lessor known personages. "William Acker, the illegitimate child of a famed Dutch tax collector, was born into the Van Tassel family out of holy wedlock, which back then had serious consequences." He belted the words out loud enough for those in the back row not paying much attention to hear.

In the front row, attentive and studious as always, Rayna took a flurry of notes. As she had mentioned to Vincent in Mr. Price's video shop, the history of the area intrigued her, and it was a subject she quite excelled at. Her favorite area was the many ghost stores, the Headless Horseman notwithstanding. She especially liked the tales of the White Lady of Raven Rock, or Widow Rock, stories that seemed so prevalent amongst *Dark Shadows* plotlines.

Mack & Saunders threw spitballs at each other, while Billy Bob Greenfield tried to edge his cellphone, which was recording, under the seat of Marlene Munpan, a pretty Asian girl in front of him who loved wearing tartan skirts and bobby socks. If he could pull off a decent upskirt, he'd have bragging rights for at least a week and the chance of his video going viral. And doing this while class was in session with the pedantic Crane was a virtual trifecta.

Somewhere in the middle of the classroom, a few desks in front of the boys but a few behind Rayna's, was an empty seat. This was Vincent's, and as of yet on the frosty autumnal Monday morn, he was nowhere to be seen. Of course, after his weekend and drug-induced slumber, Vince being late for class was not a surprise, nor much out of the ordinary.

As the classmates' brains churned through the lesson, Mr. Crane droned on.

"Then, in the American Revolutionary War, it is believed that Acker, although then an outcast from the Van Tassels, was an important part of local history."

Most of the kids looked bored with the exception of a few sycophants taking notes, just like Rayna was.

As the lecture continued, a frazzled and unkempt Vincent came stumbling through the door. His stained shirt untucked, bedhead unchecked, he fumbled for his pill bottle, but was hampered by his backpack sliding down his shoulder and a handful of dog-eared schoolbooks.

Mack & Saunders made a quick plan to trip Vincent. Just as he looked up and caught Rayna's flirtatious smile, Mack kicked the heel of one of his sneakers like a well-timed PIT maneuver and caused him to misstep. Neuropreens and dignity went flying airborne, like Pez candy from a busted piñata. Most kids chuckled. Some, like Rayna, were taken aback. Vince tripped face-first, using Marlene's midriff to break his fall. That she smelled nice was all that registered in his dulled brain. As she pushed him back, he heard Billy Bob's smartphone's screen crack into tiny slivers under his shifted weight. Finally, some instant karma had been served. Viral video thwarted, Marlene's reputation intact.

"Hey, you're gonna pay for that, asshole," barked Greenfield.

Mr. Crane stopped mid-sentence, but didn't even bother to turn around. "Mack, Saunders and Greenfield, principal's office. Now. Leave the phone. And, Mr. Douglass, next time you disrupt my class with tardiness, it will be detention, understood?"

The three bullies packed up their things. "Whatever," Saunders said with a sneer.

"And don't talk back, Mr. Saunders."

The boys left, but not before shooting a look to Vincent, who quickly scooped up what pills he could and tried to slink into his chair. He managed an almost undetectable wave to Rayna. Marlene suddenly seemed interested. He was practically facedown in her crotch, after all. Bad boys always seemed to have a *je ne sais quoi* about them.

As Crane continued his lecture, Vincent began doodling frightening sketches on a tattered notepad. Demonic faces, a reared Horseman, the name ACKER from the tombstone, the chalkboard in front of him, and an axe.

Rayna exchanged a few playful glances with Vincent, but he was deep within the recesses of his mind and barely noticed her advances.

"Acker did his part in the war and defended our town against the British invasion. However, because of his illegitimately and unofficial military registry, you won't find his name on plaques. Your ancestors, however, and all of you owe him a debt of gratitude. He risked treason for the sake of a fledgling America."

Crane noticed Vincent scribbling and walked up to his notepad to take a cursory view. He quickly confiscated it and walked back to the front of the classroom. He threw the pad on his desk, just close enough to where Lorraine's front row seat gave her a full view. The contorted faces of demons, the Horseman and the jumbled and sinister tones of Vincent's art didn't sit well with her, but she chose to ignore it.

Crane looked up at the clock ticking away monotonously on the sterile wall. Like the trained professional educator he was, he began to wrap up his lecture. "In summation, what's the moral of the story?" He paused, waiting for the volunteered answer that never came. "Okay, we'll pretend that was rhetorical. The moral of the story is history may forget you, but those close to you never should."

Just then, the class bell rang out with impeccable timing, and the students began to chaotically gather their books and belongings. Crane called Vincent over to his desk. Lorraine slowed her pace just enough to eavesdrop on the teacher and student huddled over the desk speaking in hushed tones.

"Vince, you alright? I really want to help you here, but you're making this extremely difficult."

Vincent shuffled his feet for a moment, feeling more than vulnerable. "I'm sorry, Mr. Crane. It's just I haven't been sleeping well, and my mom's boyfriend…sss…"

Crane knew all about Vincent's mom's reputation in the school, especially among the boys of the senior class. The point was taken. It was an unfortunate situation, to say the least, and one he had sympathy for. To Crane, Marisa was off limits even in his seemingly never-ending quests for sexy mothers amongst the unturned stones of students' single-mother households.

"Vince, as much as I feel for you, and I do, you can't just come skulking in at second period and expect there to be no repercussions. This is the last time I can protect you."

Both of them avoided eye contact. Vincent again shuffled his feet. His go-to move. His eyes darted toward his notebook, which remained splayed out across Crane's desk for all to see. Rayna pretended to check her phone as she stood in the doorway leading to the corridor, purposely just in earshot of their conversation.

"And save this talent for art class," stated Crane as he handed back the notebook.

"Yes, sir," said Vince meekly. "Can I go now?"

"Of course. But you missed the lesson. I want you to read up on William Acker and his part in the Revolutionary War before our next session. Understood?." Crane was serious, which caused Vince to be.

"I will." Vincent took his things and slung his backpack over his shoulder. He noticed Rayna leaving the classroom and quickened his pace in hopes of meeting up with her.

Chapter 12

In the few moments since Rayna had left the classroom, she had already been surrounded by a group of her popular friends in front of a bank of candy apple red lockers. They included Marlene and two adorably gorgeous girls, Anita and Samantha, who went by Sammy. Anita was filled with enough charisma for two girls, a true friend, and a pleasure to be around. As such, she couldn't get laid to save her life. Sammy was a textbook tomboy, and although not choosing pronouns and gender fluidity just yet, it was clear to everyone but herself that she would soon experiment on any of the girl group who would be willing. The group popped bubble gum and laughed as Vincent scurried around the corner. The site of the herd was a bit daunting to him, as he would have much preferred to speak with Rayna alone. She noticed his awkwardness and subconsciously bit her lower lip. She thought it was cute.

"Guys, can you give me a minute?" she said to the gaggle of girls.

Marlene remembered the tingling sensation she had got in her panties when Vincent had tripped and inadvertently practically muff-dived her. "Oh sure, girlfriend, but save some for me," Marlene teased.

Rayna stepped away and approached Vincent. Unbeknownst to him, the fact he was considered cute by one of the group made him desirable to all of them, even Sammy. That's how things worked amongst hormonal teen girls.

"Hey," she said as she slid up to his side.

"Hey yourself." It came out sounding ruder than Vincent meant it to be.

"Can I ask you something?" Rayna asked, not really expecting an answer. The two walked side by side, starting to look almost like a couple. The answer, as expected, never came. "What's going on with you? I'm starting to worry a bit"

"Like you care," he scoffed. Ouch. He was two for two, batting a thousand. His nerves were making him appear conceited and aloof.

Rayna stopped in her tracks, visibly offended.

"I'm sorry. I didn't mean that, Rayna. It's been a rough couple of days at home." His apology was heartfelt and sincere.

She took notice, and it worked. It didn't take much to win her over, as she had made up her mind in the cemetery that she was smitten.

"I just meant you being late, always looking like you just woke up. And what the hell were those drawings?"

Vincent didn't respond. It was going south fast. After a few awkward beats of silence, Vincent had an epiphany and yelled to drive his point home. "I'm a jerk, okay, Ray-Ray?" He smiled at her. "A jerk."

All the other kids and a few faculty members took notice. Rayna held her own for a moment with her best poker face before breaking character and the two burst out into laughter.

"Ray-Ray?" She laughed. "What the hell?"

He flashed another handsome smile. His impromptu planned had worked. The ice had finally been broken.

The hallway had been adorned with Halloween and Horseman themed decorations and streamers. The traditional orange, black, yellow and purple were mixed in with a few standouts. Several posters hung from the walls announcing the Dutch Down-Home Days Ball. It was traditionally the big dance just before the holiday, and the town's one festival that it completely embraced. It was a big deal to the kids, bigger than any prom or homecoming festivity.

The festival had its roots in the old barn-raising celebrations that were popular among the Colonial Dutch settlers back in the day, and had evolved over the years to include Pagan holidays like Samhain and All Hallows' Eve. Throw in some of Irving's legendary Horseman for spice and you had yourself a recipe that nearly everyone in the region could get behind. It included period costumes, hayrides, corn mazes and all sorts of seasonal foods and pageantry. It was primarily a celebration of mischief, spookiness, and trickery, in keeping with the season.

As both teens avoided direct eye contact for a few moments, Rayna noticed one of the posters and finally mustered up the courage to ask Vincent the question burning inside of her. "So do you—"

"Were you serious—" Vincent interrupted unintentionally. His teenage awkwardness knew no bounds.

She laughed again as he blushed. If this got any cuter, a unicorn would have to be sacrificed on an altar of cotton candy somewhere. Ever the picture of perfection, Rayna gestured for him to go first.

He began again. "Were you serious about wanting to find out more about this Horseman stuff?"

Her eyes lit up. They were like two geeks talking about Christopher Nolan movies. Finally, something they could both be insightful about while avoiding conversation that might still be considered a bit too personal. "Of course I was."

"So what are you doing after school?" Vince stared at the ground, not ready for the rejection he was sure would come next.

"Nothing. My dad takes my little cousin and Maw Maw Williams to Little League, and they usually go for pizza afterward at the Mellow Hollow."

"Maw Maw Williams?"

"It's a nickname. It's what we call my grandma. Remember we talked about it at the video store?"

He didn't.

"Anyway, it's fine. I already told them I wanted to skip this time."

"Ruh roh," Vincent said, doing his best Scooby Doo. He was warming up to her, and although his mind might have been a garbled concoction of chemicals and dark thoughts, his humor was always on point.

His charisma struck gold again and Rayna busted up laughing. If there was a way to warm the cockles of the most popular girl in school's heart, humor was definitely it.

"Perfect. You want to meet up at the Township Library this evening after school lets out?" he said, this time with renewed confidence.

"Great, it's a date," she said matter-of-factly, then kissed him on the cheek.

Vincent turned fifty shades of red and saw Marlene and Rayna's gal pals smile their seals of approval. Did that really just happen in front of half the school? He felt like everyone was watching him, but actually could not have cared less. This was the first time in a long time he didn't need a pill to achieve a sublime high. Boy had things changed for him.

Vincent finally got his head out of the clouds, if only for a moment. "Yeah, I guess it's a date." He began to shuffle away, still lost in dreamy thoughts.

Rayna was imbued with a feeling of power. There is nothing a young woman enjoyed more than knowing how her seductiveness could create control over the object of her desire. This was a relatively new feeling for Rayna, and much needed break from the submissive relationship she usually had experienced with her father. She smiled sideways as she observed Vincent, who was clearly lost in his own thoughts.

Then, after a moment of revelation, Vincent turned to her. "Wait. What was it you wanted to say to me?"

Rayna looked at a hot-pink poster for the ball. This was too easy. Rather than risk a possible rejection though, she opted out. This was not the time to use her feminine guile to outwit such an enamored opponent. The shoe was on the other proverbial foot, but she would save that for later. "It's okay. It can wait. See ya," she sang as she waved her goodbye delicately.

Vincent nearly walked straight into the bank of lockers ahead before looking up at the poster Rayna had been staring at. Any other boy would have figured out the proposition on Rayna's mind. Instead, Vincent's gaze became fixated on one thing inscribed on its iridescent surface. Although glitter-bedecked and riding in a sea of sparkly rainbows and fluorescent pink, looking back at him from the Dutch Down-Home Days Ball poster was an axe-wielding and very sinister-looking Headless Horseman.

Chapter 13

The bright day's October sun started to dull, blending the sharp yellows and oranges of morning into the monotonous blues and grays of an overcast evening. In the distance, the faint crackle of thunder and flashes of lightning highlighted the translucent clouds.

As Rayna sat in psychology class, the pitter-patter of rain started to blanket the window. It was a welcome distraction from Mr. Washington's lecture. Even the ever-studious Rayna was beginning to get bored. All day she had thought about studying with Vincent. Not only was the Horseman her favorite subject, but the thought of spending some quality time with a boy would be a nice change of pace. And what better place to flirt on a rainy autumn evening than in a centuries-old library full of books, with the added risk of getting caught. Plus, with Halloween and Dutch Down-Home Days just around the corner, the unmistakable feeling of mischievous and otherworldly spirits was in the air.

Friedrich Washington had an interesting past. His son, Eddie, had been abducted and murdered near Seneca Lake, New York, back when Washington was a young single father. There was a lot of media frenzy over the incident, and for quite a prolonged period of time, Washington himself was the primary suspect. This had caused him to lose his teaching credentials and his dignity, not very long after his wife had left him. He'd been on the brink of suicide. Then came a serendipitous meeting with John Walsh of *America's Most Wanted* fame, in of all places the cake line at a Catholic wedding reception. The two became fast friends. Each had a very similar story of tragedy and pain. After several years of counseling, and several breaks in the case, including DNA evidence, Washington was eventually cleared of all wrongdoing. He and Walsh remained lifelong friends.

It turned out the killer was a teenage boy, who was the spawn of a severely incapacitated mental patient at the Willard Asylum for the Chronic Insane. The patient had been repeatedly raped by a particularly savage group of orderlies, and the boy who killed Washington's son was the tangible result of the ungodly tryst. Some patients considered too drastic for treatment were literally left to their own accord in the subbasement of the institution, where staff turned a blind eye and they eventually formed an unruly commune beneath the bowels of the aging building. They were essentially left to fend for themselves, like animals. The boy was sent there to hide the staff's transgressions.

As the boy grew, he had no mental disability or handicap to speak of, other than being raised by elders who were clinically insane. Killing toddlers and younger children born into their pack out of animalistic sex had been the norm in the secret society of reprobates underneath the asylum, which often led to cannibalism of the weakest to satiate the others' hungers and sexual appetites. So when Washington's young son had strayed into an adjacent field during a family picnic on the lake one summer, getting lost as the sun went down, it was not a stretch that he would fall prey to the cult like subbasement-dwelling inhabitants of Willard's outcast community. Eventually everything came to light when the asylum was fully investigated after a particularly brutal rape above ground and was eventually shut down. Most of the inhabitants in its very bowels went undiscovered as by now they had learned to become quite stealthy, but the teenage killer was among the patients discovered.

Washington never did get his son's remains back, but in a surreal twist of fate, he legally adopted the very teen who, unbeknownst to him, had killed his own son and named him

Freddie Washington, Junior. In a rare act of mercy, Washington taught the boy about the expectations and norms of society and raised him, and in fact loved him, as his own. Washington then furthered his own education with a Masters in Child Psychology, defending his thesis on the behavioral patterns of the abandoned. Once the State of New York felt he was fully cleared under the law, his credentials were reinstated, and he was assigned to none other than Sleepy Hollow High School. Of course, by looking at him, he was just another humdrum middle-aged man on a mission straight out of the lore of Carlmont High School, trying to save one underprivileged kid at a time. However, many of the older generation of townsfolk remembered the extensive media coverage of Washington's son's murder, and a few of them, with sharpened pitch forks, still believed he was guilty. At least he was in their personal court of public opinion.

Rayna just wished he would stop talking.

The standard black numbers on plain white face dollar store clock clicked away at a snail's pace. It almost seemed to Rayna as if the timepiece's seconds were actually going in reverse. The desks in this classroom had yet to be refurbished. They were the classic tiny all wooden kind, and had at least a decade of graffiti on the tops and backs. There was equally as much discarded chewing gum on the bottoms of the furniture, which seemed too small for human utilization, even that of adolescents. Rayna pulled out some Peanuts' Great Pumpkin pencils from her Lisa Frank backpack. It was a CVS find, whose receipt would be longer than its perceived trendiness. She was all about the retro stuff and could think of no better time than the moment to entertain herself with it. She began scribbling a classic Stussy S on the back of the desk in front of her. This was pretty out of character for her, but since she would actually have some alone time with a boy this evening, without even telling her dad, she was feeling a bit rebellious.

"And that concludes the section on early onset dementia. For tomorrow, I want you all to read section 8 on peripheral hallucinations."

Rayna smiled to herself. *A psychology book with a section 8? Let me guess, it must be on page 5150!* This time a laugh snuck out from the side of her mouth, causing Mr. Washington to turn around dead in his tracks.

"Something amusing, Ms. Constance?" he asked over the top of his bifocals.

"I… I…" she stuttered. The period bell rattled its signal and there was a flurry of activity as a bevy of students, including Rayna, packed their things.

"Ah, classic. Saved by the bell," stated Mr. Washington. This time, it was he who laughed from the side of his mouth. "Don't forget midterm first reports due after the Halloween break," he shouted over the din of the students.

Rayna was happy to make a quick getaway and was excited to see Vince.

Outside in the corridor, the same group of girls were gathered in a defensive huddle. But this time there was a fifth wheel with them, Patti. Anita and Marlene coddled her as smeared mascara ran down her cheeks. Patti, like Anita and Rayna, was a genuinely good girl. She was smart and good-looking. The dreaded double threat to teenage boys. As such, most of them lacked the confidence to date her for very long, at least once it was their turn to reciprocate second base or better. This wasn't the first time the young women had had to console her.

"I can't believe that bastard broke up with me," Patti sobbed.

"It'll be okay," comforted Marlene.

"Just let me at that son of a bitch," ranted Sammy. "I'm gonna send that tiny-ass dick pic to the whole school!"

Marlene shot Sammy a look. "Now's not the time to stoop to his level."

"The fuck it's not," spat Sammy, delivering an Oscar-worthy eye roll.

The girls looked up to see Rayna fast approaching. As their undeclared figurehead, the girls shot beckoning stares at her, eyes begging for leadership in the looming teenage crisis.

This was the last thing Rayna needed. She checked her watch, but realized this was much more pressing on the pals Richter scale of teenage drama. With slight reluctance, she put her arm around Patti's shoulder as they all walked and talked.

"It'll be okay. Come on, tell me all about it," sympathized Rayna. Ironically, getting dumped by a boy was something Rayna could not actually empathize with, at least at this point in her short life.

"I can't believe he did it right before Down-Home Days, too." Patti sobbed so intensely that snot and spittle flew from her. In an unprecedented move of solidarity, Marlene took off her school girl outfit tie and used it to wipe Patti's face.

The pals stopped at a vending machine, where they loaded up on Funyuns, Skittles and soft drinks. Rayna readied a playlist and Anita double-checked that she was carrying her glam bag full of nail polishes and lip balms. The group headed to the band room, where Rayna knew they actually wouldn't find any band nerds; they'd be too busy at the Band Boosters' annual "haunted car wash" which would leave the room all to the girls to commiserate about Patti's painful loss. Being the popular girl and a first chair flutist, Rayna's peers had given her a pass from cleaning coaches.

Thunder rattled the windows in the corridor as the girls walked along. Rayna was so occupied with Patti, she soon lost all track of time. There was a foreboding feeling in the electrified air outside the school's sheltered walls. Like the doleful lamentation of John André before them, one could almost imagine the shrieks of ghosts and unknown phantoms riding the splashes of symphonic thunder, which resonated an announcement of the oncoming dead of night.

Chapter 14

It was a gargantuan, two-storied gothic structure filled with books from the beginning of the town's history as a settlement. The cornerstone of the library was dated March 20, 1820, but many of the books and artifacts therein were much older. Complete with spiral staircases, oakwood carved paneling and late 18th century decor, the combination library and museum was a virtual cathedral to the historical and literary attributes of the town's past. Many Dutch artifacts and antiquities had made their way across the Atlantic from the Old Country and ended up here in the private collections of the aristocratic elite of New Amsterdam and Forts Nassau and Orange.

Like everything in Tarrytown, there was a legend surrounding the building. Folklore said the library's centerpiece, a mostly wooden spiral staircase with no newel for support, was commissioned by Dutch settlers from a group of wood-dwelling Benedictine monks. The settlers had built themselves into a literal corner and lacked the skillset to continue construction as envisioned. It was said the group of monks, wearing matching alabaster-colored robes, came looking, from hence no one knew, for food and alms amongst the townsfolk. They agreed to continue the construction and only requested to be fed and that prayers would offered up to St. Joseph in lieu of payment. Although no visible nails or solid structure was used to support the staircase, it had lasted the test of time. After the mysterious disappearance of the monks without a trace or even a name, the locals insisted they were angels and that their work of unfathomable carpentry was a heaven-sent miracle. In fact, if ever the library would be destroyed, the villagers were convinced this "stairway to heaven" would remain standing. The Picea Spruce trees used in the staircase's creation were not indigenous to the area, but not one person had witnessed the wood being shipped or carried in. To this day it remained a mystery.

The walls of the ancient edifice were adorned with old oil paintings, mostly of vicious battles and the ravages of war. Tarnished sabers, flags, war implements and various American Revolutionary War and historic memorabilia were displayed in every nook and cranny It was the kind of place Edgar Allan Poe might have imagined an underground stairwell full of corpses, or H.P. Lovecraft an entombed portal to lost civilizations of reptilians or albino simians.   The library was a page right out of a fairytale, enough so that it sparked one's imagination just being there.

Mr. Martin, the geriatric librarian, sat at a giant, old oak desk on the solid marble of the first floor. The immense desk was so expansive and sturdy, one could imagine scores of Egyptian slaves might have had to set it in place. Yellowed papers, dusty manuscripts and an outdated manual typewriter adorned his desk alongside fountain pens, quills, rubber stamps and comic books. A looming grandfather clock swayed its pendulum behind the aging man. It was hard to tell what was older, the librarian or the contents of the library. An Emeralite banker's lamp gave the old man's features a gaunt effect, making him look even more cadaverous. The only thing making him appear slightly younger was his yellow-tinted aviator specs.

Vincent entered wearing his backpack and holding a vending machine coffee. The kind you don't really want to look inside the bottom of the cup at for fear of remnants of its actual ingredients. Vincent just stood there, waiting, not quite sure what do next.

Mr. Martin looked up over his worn copy of Poe's "The Raven" and pulled down his amber 70s-style specs to address the youth.

"Looking for something, kid?"

"Someone." Vincent paused. "I'm looking for a girl."

The librarian belly laughed so hard he nearly spit out his dentures. "Ain't we all kid! Ha ha ha! Ain't we all." His horse laughs were the kind of wheeze that made it sound like he had smoked two packs of cigarettes a day since he was twelve. Vincent instinctively looked for an inhaler. "Sorry to disappoint you. Nobody here but me." He went back to reading with total disregard for a further line of questioning.

The grandfather clock behind him struck six o'clock. Mr. Martin never bothered to look up, but Vincent absentmindedly honed in on the chime, which seemed ominous and forbidding. Just then, a large thunder clap crescendoed so hard it sounded like it was right on top of them. Vincent's heart skipped a beat, and he nearly spilled his drink.

Vincent could see through the high, arching, cathedral-like windows that it had already gotten unseasonably dark outside. Not only was daylight saving time robbing them of sunlight, but the oncoming storm had squeezed the pulse out of any tendrils of sunset that were still trying to survive. The wind howled against the glass of the upper stories, its gusts giving them the appearance of breathing.

Mr. Martin noticed the boy still standing there. "Anything else, son?"

"Mind if I take a look around?" Vincent asked.

"What are you special, kid? It's a library, you don't need to ask to take a look around." He lowered his book to really take in the agitated adolescent's face. Vincent stood there, silent. "Look, leave your student ID. You want to check out anything, bring it to me and I'll get you sorted." He licked his thumb to turn the page of the book. The man's thick New York accent reminded Vince of one he had heard say "Excelsior" in plenty a cameo. It distracted Vincent, which didn't take much is his heightened state of alertness.

He gave the librarian his ID card, then turned to walk around, soaking in the immenseness of the structure and its contents. There were easily a hundred thousand books on the seemingly never-ending shelves. The place might as well have been the Smithsonian as far as Vincent was concerned. The vastness of the space was overwhelming. The number of sliding ladders that stretched into the rafters alone seemed daunting. Vincent realized this was probably too much for him and returned to the old man who seemed as still as a waxen corpse. He was in the exact position Vincent had left him, holding the book. His shallow breathing was imperceptible to the naked eye.

"Can you tell me where your local history books would be?" Vincent managed.

With the tinted specs catching the already subdued lighting of the library's archaic chandeliers, it was hard to tell if the man's eyes were looking at Vincent, or if they were even open at all. Suddenly, he sprang back to life.

"Never used a library before?" asked Martin.

"Sorry, don't get out much." This was a classic foot shuffling moment if Vincent had ever had one.

"Get to know your friend Dewey Decimal. But in the meantime, here's a clue." Martin softened his tone. "Reference section's upstairs. In the very back." He went back to reading the pigmented passerine's quotations.

"Thanks," said Vincent. His lowered anxiety finally allowed him to catch his breath again. He got to the base of the famed spiral staircase before the elderly guardian called out to him.

"And don't go spillin' anything on my books neither," said the librarian, not waiting for a response.

Vincent noticed a trash can at the bottom of the stairs and dutifully disposed of his mostly drained coffee cup before attempted to ascend the timbered masterpiece. On the second floor of the classic establishment, Vincent was again in pure awe. There was so much to soak in. Why had he never visited this place before? It made him feel small and minuscule, but not insignificant. In fact, it had the opposite effect. All the history here made Vincent feel like he was part of something. Just like his ancestors before him, he now walked the same hallowed halls surrounded by collections of their former belongings, some of which had even been used in the pangs of battle. The combination of clutter, muted lighting, and musky smell of old books was womblike and wrapped Vincent in its collective arms. He felt encased in a loving embrace of bygone sagas. It felt good, comforting.

As he walked deeper into the shelves, however, the mood of the decoration started to get considerably darker. Along one wall, a Revolutionary Colonial belt axe tomahawk was mounted and framed, crisscrossed with an aging riding whip. It was hard to tell, but they might have even been stained with the crimson hues of spilt blood. The red velvet backings and pewter fixtures started to blend together before Vincent's eyes. The sensory overload was perhaps triggering an episode. Either way, he wasn't afraid. He felt strangely at home in a place he had never even laid eyes on before. Painted eyes of Colonial Americans and embattled Revolutionaries seemed to stare holes through Vincent from their tarnished canvases. Countless unknown generals as well as traitors followed his every movement with their gaze.

It was obvious by the sounds from outside that the storm was kicking up. This broke Vincent's train of thought, and now slightly creeped out, he made his way to the reference section. In the farthest and most deeply buried area of an oddly conceived wooden alcove, which was lit only by a few flickering, aged yellow lights. He found the local history section, and his hand traced along the splintered spines of a multitude of aging books. Titles such as *The Colonial American War, American Revolutionary War, Wolfert's Roost: A History, Tribulations of Tarrytown, Washington Irving: A Biography,* and many more. A thick, rust-colored dust enveloped the oldest of the texts.

He knew not his own quest, when suddenly his hand stopped, almost by itself, on a particularly antiquated tome. Vincent instinctively pulled it from the shelf. *William Acker: Revolutionary War Hero, Social Pariah.* He stared in disbelief. *What were the chances?* he thought. He cradled it, along with a stack of books from the section, and headed toward a vast mahogany table. Vincent's mind raced imagining what tales of yore lay in store for him.

The vaulted ceilings of the lengthy and otherwise uninhabited room embraced him like an ancient and colossal sarcophagus.

Chapter 15

In the music recital and dance classroom, Rayna was braiding Patti's hair with multi-colored Halloween-themed ribbons. Marlene was strumming a beat-up guitar in front of a bank of mirrors, while the other girls sang along to an acoustic version of Lia Marie Johnson's "Moment Like You." Patti's tears had dried, and her smeared mascara made her look like a disgruntled Harley Quinn. She had chosen to leave it that way as a badge of breakup honor, as she was unwilling to let a boy defeat her pride. The girls seemed lost in a sugar-induced jamboree. Empty Faygo cans and candy corn wrappers were everywhere.

Anita was painting alternating black and white stripes on Patti's long fingernails when she happened to look up at the clock, which read quarter past six. "Shit, look at the time. I got to book or my dad'll kill me." She stood up and started packing up her things.

As the trio of singing girls stopped, the wind whistled outside. The disfigured fingers of tree branches gesticulated on the window panes. The janitor hadn't even bothered to check the band room. It was always kept spotless anyway, and the girls hadn't really noticed the time, nor the torrential storm that had been brewing outside.

"Damn, it's pouring. We'll get soaked," said Marlene. "This is gonna ruin my dress."

"You guys can ride with me," said Sammy.

"I thought your license was suspended," said Anita.

"It is," came the rebuttal. They all shared a laugh.

"Come on. We'll just follow the overhangs around the side of the building and then bolt for the parking lot," said Sammy.

"Lessssgetit," said Marlene in her best ATL twang. Anita gave her a well-deserved eye roll.

Rayna's brow furrowed. "I'll catch up with you guys tomorrow."

"What? Why?" asked Patti.

"Oh, we get it," said Marlene, lewdly thrusting the index finger of her right hand into a circle made by her left.

Anita started to twerk her ass and immediately Sammy play-mounted her and enthusiastically dryhumped her ample curves. The other girls joined in. "Vincent! Oh, Vincent," they cried in playful, feigned orgasms.

Even Rayna was laughing now. Their antics were too much. "Shut up, you guys. It's not like that."

The girls stopped in unison as if part of a trained choreography piece. The "oh really" looks they shot her were almost palpable.

"Not yet, anyway," she finished.

"You get it, girl!" teased Marlene, as the other girls chimed in with similar jabs.

The girls gathered their things, said their goodbyes amongst kisses on the cheeks and fist bumps, turned out the lights, and left. Rayna headed out in the opposite direction, down a long, dark corridor. The janitor had already turned out the lights for the evening in the rest of that wing, and Rayna would've been lying to herself if she didn't admit she wasn't at least a little bit scared. Outside, the thunder and lightning raged on. She wasn't looking forward to her rain-drenched sprint to the library.

As she neared the single-paned door at the end of the hallway, flashes of light strobed against the shiny red surfaces of the bank of lockers. It was almost as if the hallway was extending the closer she got to it, like some twisted Kubrick shot in *The Shining*. She finally got to the door, took a huge inhale of air, and readied herself to depress the metal bar that would open the door. Then, just as she did, a flash of light backlit a hulking figure's full form through the crisscrossed wire pattern embedded in the glass. Its silhouette seemed to fill the entire glass panel.

Rayna reeled back when the door pulled open from the outside, but a strong veiny hand seized her by the forearm. The mysterious figure pulled her out into the rain-soaked night amidst a powerful clap of thunder.

★★★★

Vincent was immersed in the books spread out before him. This was the most reading he had done since the Reaves' and Neil Gaiman's *InterWorld* trilogy had been released. At least three of the books were open to long historical descriptions of the American Revolutionary War. His nose was buried deep in a fourth The sketches of men gored with bayonets, who'd had limbs amputated outside of field cabins, or were disemboweled as cannon fodder were beginning to make Vincent get lost in unpleasant fantastical thoughts. He popped a Neuropreen to settle his nerves.

Vincent read a paragraph in a book easily ten times his age. The grimacing faces of the violent battle on the adjacent page seemed to stare back at him. He could have sworn they were mouthing warnings to him and melting like some war-torn Dali painting. He greedily popped another adult-coping, candy-coated pharmaceutical and gulped a half-empty water bottle from his bag.

He picked up an errant pencil someone had left on the desk and began circling the names listed out before him. *Even the pencils here look old as hell.* First, he outlined ACKER in the text, then he paused, tapping on the name VAN TASSEL. These were the names Mr. Crane had been lecturing about, but this never registered to Vincent, at least consciously. He might as well not have been present that day, as his mind certainly wasn't. He read from the cracked pages and ancient typeset.

William Acker, illegitimate bastard, was all but written off by his Van Tassel birthright. However, the true colors of his near-royal lineage and pedigree would shine through in one of the bloodiest confrontations of the American Revolutionary War.

Further down the page, he again circled names.

Williams, Van Wart and the slave Paulding lay in wait.

His ADHD kicked in hard. He grabbed his temples and had to stop reading. He almost decided to take a third pill, but even he had the common sense to know this would be too much. He waited for the pleasant trickle of the medicine to start to work and numb the base of his skull.

As Vincent got lost in the shadows and intricate details of the gothic architecture, the book seemed to settle on its spine by itself, causing the page to turn, almost supernaturally. What the book then revealed, next to a thinning and yellowed piece of tracing paper, was a beautifully inked wood etching depiction of the Unhallowed Horseman rearing up on his charcoal-black Hellsteed. This version had flames leaving its nostrils like a medieval dragon.

Vincent was taken aback by the image. A thunder clap outside jolted him out of his seat, and he started to get an uneasy feeling. His mind took an aggressive turn. *Where the fuck was Rayna?*

Vincent slammed the book closed, not wanting to be reminded of the Horseman right now, or Rayna, more particularly. *She promised to meet him here to discuss the Legend. That was over two hours ago! He knew she would stand him up. Even an idiot could have told him their relationship was too good to be true.* His mind, almost in third-person, told him not to let some girl get to him. He pulled over another archaic book with a foldout map, that like the others, dated back to the American Revolutionary War. He blew a cloud of dust from its pages, which caused him to sneeze hard, jarring the nape of his neck. He placed his fingers on a portion of the map that read Van Tassel Manor. "Van Tassel... The name from History class he said to himself under his breath. So it had registered after all.

Vincent looked to see if anyone was around. He wondered if the old man downstairs had managed to stay awake, or was even alive at this point. *That guy probably has the blood pressure of a hibernating bear*, Vincent's inner voice whispered. A quick mood swing and Vincent violently ripped the map from the book, as well as the page with the circled names from the other. He quickly stuffed them into his pocket.

Suddenly, as if out of nowhere, an ominous black figure appeared to be drifting along the floor, visible only through the limited spacing between the shelves of aging books. Scared out of his mind, Vincent knew there was no way the old man could walk that fast.

"Hello? Is someone there? Rayna, is that you?"

An agitated Vincent rose to his feet. Thunder beckoned, lightning taunted, then the failing lights threw him into pitch darkness.

★★★★

Rayna was dragged out the door and around the corner of the building. Although it wasn't a Headless Hessian waiting to kill her, her assailant was revealed to be Mack, who had equally sinister intentions.

"Calm down, Rayna. I was just playing," he gaslit her. A flash of lightning highlighted the stretched skin over his high cheekbones. His ear to ear grimace gave away that there was more malice in his intent than he was letting on.

"Let go of me, asshole," she barked as she broke free of his grip and started a hasty retreat. Unfortunately, Saunders and Greenfield revealed themselves from the shadows, blocking her path.

"Where you going, beautiful?" leered Saunders.

Rayna wouldn't have been any more creeped out if Charles Manson, himself, had accosted her. Mack leaned into her. She could smell alcohol on his breath.

"I never noticed how full your lips were before now." He was close enough to kiss her. Thunder crackled above his soaking wet body. He didn't seem to care.

She pirouetted away, appalled by his stench and lascivious demeanor. As she spun out from under Mack, Greenfield adroitly scooped her up in his muscular arms.

"Whoa, whoa, whoa, you little hussy. What's your hurry?" He gripped her arms tight, filling her with apprehension. She wanted to lash out, but she wasn't about to let them know just how scared she actually was.

"What do you guys want? I'm running late. Move out of my way." She tried to break his grasp but he was much too strong for her.

"What, you got a date or something?" sneered Mack.

"I want a date," piped up Saunders like the suck-up toady he was.

"Yeah, me too," said Mack a lot less playfully as he leaned over and licked Rayna's cheek.

"Gross!" She pushed him away hard, nearly gagging with revulsion. The boys laughed insidiously, except for Mack, whose ego wasn't good with bruising. "I said let go! You're hurting me!"

"Or what, princess? Your scrawny little boyfriend's gonna come save you?" He leaned in for a sloppy kiss, this time forcing his tongue into her unwilling mouth and grabbing a handful of breast. "Don't act like you don't like it, either, bitch."

She kneed him as hard as she could right in the balls. He doubled over in pain, nearly falling to the ground. His groin hurt so bad he thought for sure he would cough up blood. One knee on the ground was now holding the rest of the weight of his entire body. "Motherfucker! Hold that bitch, you fucking idiots," he said as he slowly rose to his feet, a menacing and determined look on his face. The other boys did as they were instructed and pinned

Rayna to the rain-slicked bricks of the side of the building. Her books and belongings feel into a puddle on the ground.

Inside her backpack, her cell phone hummed to life with several messages from her father indicating that he and her cousin were back home and expected her return very soon.

★★★★

In the library, Vincent was wrestling with a few demons of his own.

On the floor below him, the old librarian mumbled something incoherently to himself. He fumbled for some matches in his antiquated desk drawer and lit a vintage kerosene lantern. Its orange glow on his emaciated features gave him an almost maniacal and haggard appearance. The lantern only lit a few feet in front of him, so he placed it near his face so that he could continue to read his poems. "Stay put up there, boy. Lights'll come back on soon enough. Genny will kick on any minute," he yelled up to Vincent, not really caring if he heard him or not.

The old man's voice was so shallow, upstairs Vincent didn't hear him over the din of his own thoughts. True to the librarian's word, a generator somewhere in the far recesses of the building tried to spur to life. However, like most things there, it was dilapidated and in much need of care. The result was an endless sputtering sound and flicking of lights. Between that and the storm surging outside, it created a chaotic and agitating atmosphere.

Vincent was sure, however, that he'd seen something. He followed the inky apparition through shelves of antediluvian books and artifacts. Like a stealthy cat, he tracked glimpses of the figure through small holes of confined space between tenuous, overladen shelving hoping he was imagining it, but letting his curiosity get the best of him.

As he moved through the multitude of bookshelves, there were simply too many of them obstructing his view. He couldn't seem to get a clear line of sight to whatever had been gliding along so fast. The intermittent flashes of lights made it even harder to see, and he was finding it hard to focus and was losing all frame of reference. Regardless, it was obvious it was a larger-than-life humanoid figure of some sort. Whatever it was, it seemed to be dressed in dark clothes and was moving swiftly.

Just as the shelves came to an apparent end and it seemed the figure would be revealed… there was nothing. It was inexplicable.

Vincent stopped dead in his tracks, shocked. There had definitely been someone, or something, there. He began to frantically look everywhere. *This is not happening. There was definitely someone there this time.* As he neared the wall by the stairs, the frame Vincent had seen holding the belt axe tomahawk was illuminated by another rapid flash of lightning.

The death instruments were now clearly missing.

★★★★

Rayna's blouse was ripped open and the boys pulled down her bra, exposing one of her breasts. They took turns groping her and forcibly necking and kissing her. She managed to bite Greenfield on the cheek, and she tasted the warm iron of his blood on her taste buds.

"Son of a bitch! She bit me!"

This caused the boys to pause, but only for a moment.

"Stop it! This is assault! My dad's a cop! You don't want to do this!"

Her words seemed to have had an effect on them, and the boys stopped. Then Mack leaned in so close to her ear she could feel his breath tickling the tiny hairs inside her cochlea. "If you tell a single Goddamned soul about any of this, I *will* fucking kill you," he said as he brandished a switchblade and opened it mere centimeters from her face. "And just to make sure," he continued as he traced the sharp blade over her exposed pink nipple and up over the curve of the breast, "I'm taking this as insurance."

Rayna whimpered and tears flooded from her eyes as he cut the gold-braided band of her locket and caught it with his free hand as it fell from her pulsating neck. Rayna flinched, and it was all she could do to try and stifle her uncontrollable sobs. This was more than even her utmost defiance could handle. There was a visible mark on her neck where Mack had leveraged the blade against her sternum to create enough pressure to break the chain. Any harder and it would've surely bled.

"Please don't take that," she pleaded through stilted breaths. "I won't tell anyone. I promise. We can all just forget this ever happened." The locket was one of the few things of her mom's she still had, and without it, Rayna would feel emotionally lost.

"Insurance," he said with a Hannibal Lecter-like smile, the yellow of his teeth matching the glint in his eye. He closed the blade and blew her a repugnant kiss.

★★★★

Mr. Martin had drifted off to sleep in the soothing mood lighting of the kerosene lamp. It, combined with the rain outside, had lulled him into a catnap. He was too old to be afraid of things that go bump in the night, though tonight maybe he should have been.

As he awoke and tried to focus his eyes, the silhouette of the Horseman cast itself over the flicker of the lamp's light. The old librarian languidly looked up. What he saw sent him into a deep state of shock. The shadow of the belt axe loomed over Martin, who now clutched his chest with one hand and Vincent's ID in the other. The book he had been reading fell to the ground with a thud, its spine opened to an illustration of the Raven high atop a book shelf, with the extremely apropos caption, "Nevermore."

From upstairs on the second floor, the shadow of the Horseman was visible as it descended upon the librarian.

Martin fell backward and plunged through the gold-embossed glass of the grandfather clock, dead, a wide-eyed, hellish grimace of pain plastered across his face. The sound of the breaking glass shattered any semblance of normalcy in the otherwise serene surroundings. The clock's pendulum swung methodically for a moment over his no-longer-beating heart, then the weight of the clock settled and the pendulum smacked in time against the librarian's lifeless countenance.

Outside, the dissonance of the storm, like the breath inside him, suddenly came to an abrupt end.

★★★★

Rayna and the boys remained in a standoff. She was resolved to never let them get the upper hand again, even if it meant risking her life. Suddenly, the headlights of Sheriff Eustice's patrol car swung around, illuminating the group. The boys acted as if nothing had happened, while Rayna, partially obscured behind the three boys, instinctively tucked in her breast and straightened her bra and shirt.

From the sheriff's point of view from within the squad car, everything seemed calm, if a bit odd for the kids to be outside in the storm. The mountain of a man alighted from the patrol car.

"What are you kids up to over here? It's late, you should be at home. This storm's been wreaking havoc everywhere."

"Yessir," mumbled Mack.

That was an unlikely affirmation coming from him, and made the sheriff suspicious. He turned his attention to Rayna "Lorraine, You okay? They weren't bothering you, were they?"

Rayna wanted to tell, but was too embarrassed. Plus, she doubted the sheriff would take her side. That was just part of being a woman—always to blame, even when the victim. Mack gave her a sideways glance and flashed her the locket in the palm of his hand, hidden from the sheriff's view. She thought better of it.

"I'm okay. We were just rehearsing," she lied.

"In the rain?" The sheriff didn't exactly believe it, but he wasn't the world's best detective. Besides, he had other things on his mind. "Alright, look. I want you kids to go home. The late-night custodian called in a death at the Township Library. Lorraine, have you seen your dad? He's not answering his cell."

Panicked, Rayna suddenly remembered Vincent, whom she was supposed to meet at the library. "A death, but how?" *Could the body be Vincent, or worse yet, her father?* She forgot all about the lecherous boys; they seemed insignificant in light of this news.

"Old man Martin. Probably heart attack. Your dad?" inquired Eustice for a second time. Patience wasn't his best virtue.

Rayna involuntarily let out a huge sigh of relief. The others seemed curious, but were just glad she didn't bring up the altercation. "He should be getting home soon. He's never out too late." She, in fact, had no idea where he was, as she hadn't checked her phone in hours.

"Come on, I'll take you home," offered the sheriff. "Cell service has been shit with the storm. I'm sure he's worried about you."

Rayna gladly went into the protecting arms of the massive law enforcement officer. She shot a look back at her attackers.

"Hey, Rayna," said Mack. "You must have dropped this." He held up the broken locket.

Rayna looked at the boys, then the sheriff, and like a skittish cat on a tightrope, decided to approach Mack.

He handed her the necklace, but as her hand reached for it, he pulled her in just close enough to be out of earshot of Eustice. "I'm gonna go ahead and give this back, but this is far from over. You cross me, and next time I'll be stealing a lot more than kisses." Their eyes locked. She knew his threat was serious.

She made her way back over to the police cruiser.

The sheriff had a fleeting feeling that something wasn't adding up, but had learned long ago that lazy law enforcing was much easier than digging for clues and asking questions. "You boys take care," he said as he purposefully pivoted the mounted spotlight on the vehicle into their collective eyes, momentarily blinding them. "I'll be keeping an eye on you."

He lit up the red and blue lights of the car, which strobed splinters of color and shadows across the shiny wet surfaces and uneven lines of the school building. The torque of the big boy under the hood engaged the fat radial tires as they slung mud and water in Mack and Saunders's direction. It was the sheriff's version of a warning shot.

The boys exchanged worried looks, hoping the threats to Rayna were enough to keep her mouth shut on the longish ride home, and more importantly, to her dad, who wasn't quite the pushover Eustice had been.

The Volare glided through the darkness with lights ablaze, the steady hum of its engine constant. It looked like a cat prowling the depths of the dark unknown, casting colored lights everywhere as it searched for prey.

A man was dead, and somewhere, a Horseman remained to be found.

Chapter 16

The next morning, the sun rose over the sleepy little hamlet as an orange glow draped the skies. Birds chirped. Squirrels sorted out bad nuts from hollowed-out tree trunks. A stillness was in the air.

At Vincent's house, Mrs. Douglass, wearing just a bathrobe and with a severe case of bedhead, tried to compose herself. She hadn't been expecting company, but a determined Sheriff Eustice had forced himself inside and now took up three quarters of her sofa. The large law enforcement officer was always imposing, but even more so in Marisa's compact home. He looked like a bull mastiff sitting on a pin cushion. Under any other circumstance it might have appeared comical, but the look on his face was serious. She brought him a cup of coffee and some store-bought Halloween cookies. They had a layer of icing on them thick enough to induce a diabetic coma. It was clear the minimum wage worker who had painted faces on the jack-o'-lanterns wasn't an art major. The gourd-themed pastries looked like they were either orgasming or constipated.

Jack was passed out on a La-Z-Boy, a myriad of discarded beer cans strewn about his feet. He was shirtless and snoring loudly. The only thing more immature than the young man was his collection of large-breasted manga tattoos. Marisa didn't mind, and in fact had even paid for one of them.

She noticed a bong on the floor and discreetly pushed it behind the recliner, as the "devil's lettuce" was still illegal in their county. It spilled, and a puddle of swampy bong water started to spread on the already hideously stained shag rug. Marisa bent over to right the blown glass, and as she did, her robe sash fell, exposing her bra and her barely contained abundant bosom. She caught the sheriff stealing a glance and quickly adjusted the wardrobe malfunction.

"Sorry, Sheriff. It's just that I wasn't expecting company." She was hoping whatever it was Eustice was so eager to speak with her about would be over soon. She pulled a brush from her bathrobe pocket, and as she did, a fiery red G-string fell to the floor. Marisa stood there, mouth agape, mortified.

The sheriff didn't hesitate a beat before picking up the undergarment in his hands like a piece of material evidence. He held it close to his nose, giving it a deep, longing, almost loving look. Marisa couldn't bear to watch. *It was no wonder*, she mused, *people referred to cops like him as pigs.*

"That's okay, Risa, you and I never hid much from each other."

She preferred not to be reminded of their past. The truth was, however, that several years ago when she was pulled over for a DWI Eustice had convinced her that a blowjob could make it all go away. Drunk and broke, she reasoned that sucking one more dick for the night wasn't that bad in the grand scheme of things. Jail time, court fees and bail money were certainly less easy to swallow. She failed to realize, as she always did, that there might be long-term repercussions to her actions. This very moment, and ones like it, was a prime example of the lifetime of harassment she had come to expect from the officer. All thanks to her blind-eyed policy toward responsibility.

Eustice gave her a crooked smile as he slurped his coffee, the sound of it every bit as lecherous as Marisa's memories of that fateful night. "This won't take much time. Just wondering if I could talk to you about Vince real quick." He watched her face for reactions. After recalling her indiscretion with him, she wasn't worried about him taking his time. The thought made her smile. The sheriff thought this an odd reaction as he tried to read her thoughts.

Marisa wrongly believed she knew what this was about. "Is this about that bike incident? I'll pay for that, of course"

Eustice had barely remembered. That, too, was nothing a quick fellatio couldn't settle. Having passed the first test with blissful ignorance, Eustice decided to fire a rapid series of statements at her in hopes of gaining a reaction. "No. It's probably nothing, but his student ID was found at the library last night near a body, and he wasn't at school this morning. Is he here?"

"That's odd. Vince doesn't seem like the library type," she said, foot inserted into mouth.

Eustice nearly spit out his coffee. Wasn't she at all curious about whose body it was? "Is he around? I'd like to talk to him."

"No, I don't think he came home last night." Either the caffeine hadn't kicked in yet, or she wasn't the sharpest tool in the shed. She was batting a thousand and now Eustice started to take notice. That was two solid strikes against the boy.

"Is Vincent—" she started.

Eustice held up a sausage finger, stopping her mid-sentence. "Give me a minute, will ya." He keyed his shoulder mic. "Constance, copy?"

"Copy," quickly came Deputy Constance's muffled voice over the squawk box. He sounded like he had fallen in a well.

"He's not here. Check the school one last time before we put out an APB," Eustice ordered.

The hamster in Marisa's brain finally kicked its wheel into overdrive. A look of realization dawned across her face as she stood up to address him. "Eustice, is Vince in trouble? Did he do something wrong? And what body?" The revelations were flooding in torrents now, and she started to panic like only a mother could.

Eustice stood up to lock her gaze, suddenly all business. "No, ma'am. Just need to ask him some questions. See if he saw anything." He had put his arms on her shoulders to drive the point home. He noticed her robe now fully open and gave her shoulders a shrug as he pushed his weight off her. This was a trick he had learned from a police academy RA, and it came in handy when interrogating female suspects, or victims, whatever the case may be. The movement caused the meat of her breasts to bounce noticeably. She felt the jolt, and although too distraught to say anything, immediately knew what he was doing. Her gaze rose up to find his shit-eating grin. His breath smelled like coffee and corn syrup. Even living with two less than hygienic young men caused less of a gag-reflex than he seemed to trigger from her.

After an awkward beat, he finally stepped back and put his hat on to leave. "Oh, and Marisa? Wouldn't mind stoppin' in for some more treats again sometime soon."

The jab made her extremely uncomfortable. She could deal with lecherous assholes, but having one who was supposed to be the town's safety net made it particularly repulsive. Offended, she covered herself and pulled the robe tight, then closed the door on the Sheriff without answering him. The standoff was over for now. She needed a shower.

Chapter 17

On Tuesdays, Peter Crane taught home economics all day. This time of year, and especially this Tuesday, the halls, offices and classrooms of Sleepy Hollow's high school were filled with the sumptuous smells of autumnal baking.

Crane had the brilliant idea of starting the cooking class early in the morning, and rather than rotating the dishes for each class, he would simply let the new students pick up where the last class left off. This ingenious plan had had several positive outcomes as a result. For one, it allowed him to cook and bake large quantities of items with no particular limitation on time as long as it fit into the school day. On occasions like this, however, he was more than happy to stay late if it meant squeezing out a few more batches or baker's dozens of seasonal treats. Also, since the Down-Home Days festival was just days away, it allowed him to utilize school resources to create a litany of foodstuffs for the annual bake sale. The bake sale was a favorite among the townsfolk, and it provided much needed funding for many of the school's extracurricular activities. Not only did it teach the kids much needed cooking skills, but it also propagated the continuance of long honored holiday and cultural traditions.

There were the obvious Dutch favorites like apple tarts, pepper cakes, Christmas sweet breads, almond cookies, butter cakes, ollie bollens, Bankets and spiced nuts. But the area had also been heavily influenced by the Polish as well. As it was, Crane had his eye on the particularly curvaceous Emily Jiompkowksi, a temporary teacher from Scranton. He had invited her down for the day to assist in the class, and she had surprisingly accepted. The real reason he invited her, however, was because the first time they had met at a regional schools conference he had accidentally caught a glimpse down her very loose and braless blouse. Under any circumstance, when God blessed you with a serendipitous nipple, it was not to be taken lightly. Crane had been smitten with her ever since, and she and her errant areola were on heavy rotation in his prolific spank bank. Along with her ample breasts and winning smile, Emily was bringing with her an arsenal of culinary skills with a specialty in Polish cuisine. The fact she was half the distance between his age and school seniors also mean he was robbing the proverbial cradle.

Crane had prepped the classes to churn out potato pancakes, pierogis—the cabbage, pork and tomato finger foods known as "pigs in the blanket"—and classic nut and coconut rolls. Both Peter and Emily had really wanted to include poppyseed rolls in this year's lineup, but were worried the delicious pastry might trigger a positive opiate test on an unsuspecting faculty or staff member, or worse yet, a student. They opted against it, but Emily had promised to teach Crane how to make them in a private in-home lesson. The thought of her giving him personal instruction in his home sent his mind reeling. *Was he going to have to take a restroom break in order to be able to focus today?* he wondered as his powerful hormones raced inside him. No, he could do this. For now, he would have to manage to subtly flirt and woo her without offending her, all while completing the task at hand of instructing over 500 students how to bake as much product as possible without burning the school down. As a fairly good-looking man, he had convinced himself that the difference between being creepy and flirtatious was directly correlated to how handsome the man saying it was. In his mind, he was ready.

The scent of pumpkin pies, nutmeg, cinnamon, chocolate and various sweetbreads wafted through the building. It was hard for one not to be in a good mood while inhaling the aromas. It seemed that everything was leading up to the joyous celebration of the sacred holiday of All Hallows' Eve and its local cultural significance. However, just down the hall from the Home-Ec classroom was Dr. Paulding's musty office. Despite the school's strict no-smoking policy, Paulding had negotiated the occasional cigar in his contract with Principal Carter. The school couldn't have reasonably afforded Paulding's salary, but the ace up his sleeve, which he hadn't divulged to them, was that he thought working with youth was his way of giving back to the very community that had given him so much. In fact, he thought it would be an easy retirement and wasn't worried that much about salary. He certainly didn't tell them that, but used this knowledge to leverage what benefits he could. Cigar breaks, front lot parking and leaving early on Fridays were among his better benefits.

The sign on his door read *Dr. Conrad Paulding, Faculty Psychiatrist & Youth Counselor*. Rayna shifted in the high-backed leather chair as she waited impatiently for the physician. The smell of pumpkin spice mixed with the dank cherry tobacco odor that had infiltrated Paulding's furnishings, created a pungent and sweet fragrance. On this particular morning, it made Rayna's stomach churn. She was nervous too. She needed to get the incident off her chest and certainly couldn't tell her father. If she had, he would have mounted a shotgun lynchmob and hung Mack & Saunders from the highest gallows or tree, as was the case with the dandy Major John André near the DeWint House back in the golden days. And that's if they were lucky.

She shifted again nervously, tucking her face inside the collar of her sweater to avoid the smell. As she stared down inside the homemade tunnel, she saw that the red mark from Mack's blade was still there. An uncontrollable sensation of guilt and sadness suddenly washed over her, followed by a flush of anger. A second wave of depression followed and she finally succumbed to it.

"Lorraine, is that you?" came the doctor's voice. "Please come take a seat in my office." He made his way past her, inviting her in.

Rayna popped her head out of her sweater like Punxsutawney Phil from his burrow on Ground Hog's Day, more embarrassed than shy. She took a deep breath, gained her composure, and followed the doctor into the adjoining room.

Paulding sat, surrounded by a mountain of medical and psychology books. There were several students' dossiers on his desk, and a collage of medical certificates, degrees and credentials adorned the walls. It all seemed very official, but for some reason made Rayna squirm.

"Everything I tell you here is secret right?" she asked. "Because I really need to tell you something."

"Yes, dear. Doctor-patient privilege protects you. Besides, that's what I'm here for," He grinned wide. It was more disconcerting to Rayna than comforting.

"Promise me you won't repeat any of this to my dad," she said.

"Lorraine, are you in some kind of danger? Did something happen to you?"

Rayna averted her eyes, staring down at her blue and gray Converse shoes. She swallowed hard and then began, " I was… I was almost…" She couldn't get the word out. She had spent all night fluctuating between being catatonic and crying into a lukewarm bath miserably stewing in her own menstrual blood. She hadn't wanted to admit it to herself, much less anyone else, that she had been victimized. There was a long pause as she finally brought herself to continue. "I was… bullied." It was a safe, albeit not partially accurate, compromise.

"By whom? You can tell me." Paulding began to automatically switch into an authoritative tone. "Ms. Constance, I can assure you I'm trained for these types of situations." He was going to need a better bedside manner if he planned to win over a vulnerable, victimized teenage girl who was also headstrong, like Rayna.

A flow of tears burst forth from Rayna's eyes. She could no longer hold back the tears, nor the emotion. It all started to come out. The words were at first stifled, then flowed in rapid succession. "I just felt so hopeless. No one has ever laid hands on me before. I've never not been in control of a situation like that." She sucked in air through her mouth as snot clogged her nose.

Paulding stood up and handed her a pinch of tissues. As she reached for them, he noticed a handprint shaped bruise on her wrist. "Who did that to you? Was there an altercation? Lorraine, you must tell me. Did someone hurt you?"

Rayna quickly covered up the bruise with her sleeve. She didn't want him to ask about her attackers. *Couldn't he just prescribe me something and let me leave, like he does everyone else?*

BOOM! The door nearly flew off its hinges as Vincent stormed in. It bounced off the wall and swung back toward closed, but remained slightly ajar to anyone within earshot in the corridor outside. The hall was full for a class change, and it hadn't taken much to alert others, as Vincent's voice quickly reached a feverish pitch.

"What's in these things, Conrad?" shouted Vincent. He subconsciously wasn't going to give the doctor the sanctity of his title, even if it had taken him a decade of school, two residencies and several fledgling practices to earn it. He held up the Neuropreen bottle in his hand like an armed hand grenade.

Paulding's first instinct was to stand up. "What's gotten into you, son? Can't you see I'm with someone?"

"Sit the fuck down! I said what the HELL is in these things." He wasn't going to ask a third time.

Paulding eased back in his chair, a look of apprehension plastered across his face, and tried to reason with the unruly teen. "Now, Vincent, calm down. I already told you that your severe ADHD requires—"

"That's bullshit and you know it!" This round of medical jargon and textbook reasoning was not going to appease Vincent. Surely, even Paulding could see that.

Paulding was at a literal loss for words. He blinked feverishly at Rayna, as if to ask, *What should I do?* Vincent followed his gaze, and it was the first time Vincent even noticed her seated there. He heard the sound of his own panting, like having an out of body experience, as he soaked in the sight of Rayna in the chair. *What the fuck was she doing here?*

"And you? Where were you last night?" The words picked up right where his mind had trailed off. Sometimes it was hard to tell where one ended and one began, the line between reality and the metaphysical was constantly diminishing. "Answer me!" raged the other Vincent, the one he didn't have full control over, especially in moments like these.

Rayna had already felt extremely vulnerable talking about the incident to Paulding, and now this line of questioning came out of the blue. To make matters worse, she wasn't used to being yelled at. Her teenage mind and hormonal fluctuations were not yet equipped for this kind of onslaught. Since her mother had passed, her father tended to be more sympathetic, albeit stern with her. He had tried to take yelling off the menu, as it never seemed to accomplish the desired effect he had intended. The emotional barrage proved too much for her to bear. Her defiance started to win over timidity. "Don't yell at me like that. I didn't do anything wrong," she managed to stutter between tears.

Paulding had seen enough, and knew he needed to take control of the situation. He again started to edge forward in his chair. "Vincent, you need to leave now." He took an aggressive tone. "This is completely unacceptable."

Vincent squared up to the doctor like Kimbo Slice in a street fight. "You sit down, right now! And as for this…" He brandished the bottle in Paulding's face. "I will never put this shit in my body again. They'll have your license for this."

Vincent flung the bottle of pills at Paulding, taking aim at his face and squarely hitting his mark. He could now add assault to the police's list of charges. As it landed on target, the already loosened cap had popped off and pills flew everywhere. The humiliating blow had the desired effect, but somehow the frightened doctor managed to keep his calm. He managed to pull out his cell phone and, under his desk out of Vincent's view, began typing an SOS.

Vincent approached Rayna like a prowling velociraptor. She silently cried, trying to avoid his gaze. This was the exact feeling she had felt just before Mack had licked the side of her face last night. It was an unconformable violation of personal space, even from someone she had previously kissed.

"I waited for you," he said softly, and unnervingly. Jack Nicholson couldn't have delivered the line better as Jack Torrance.

Rayna's sobs morphed into weighty breaths. It was clear to everyone in the room, except Vincent, a panic attack would soon ensue. Suddenly, Vincent noticed the bruise on her wrist. He turned it awkwardly toward him to get a better view, the arm bending unnaturally in its socket. Paulding was attentive to the manhandling as Rayna let out an audible wince.

"Who did this to you?" Vincent demanded.

An underclassmen peeked past the doorframe to check out where the shouting was coming from. Vincent shot him a glare from his position hunched over Rayna that was so fierce the boy immediately wheeled around to bolt. The excited teen ran smack-dab into a group of seniors standing by a nearby water fountain, prompting them to further investigate.

"Vincent, why are you acting like this?" Rayna managed to ask.

Vincent got in her face. He was sweating, and his pupils were dilated beyond recognition. For the first time, she was afraid of him. "Don't make me ask you again," came his cold response.

Paulding fumbled through a typo-laden text under his desk. He sent it to Principal Carter, as he was the first person listed on his most recent call log. It was simply a matter of convenience in an ever-increasingly dire situation.

Vnce Dglss in my office. OUT OF CONTROK! Cll cops!!

Since Columbine, there were protocols for these kinds of messages amongst faculty, even in a school this small.

Vincent was still hovering over Rayna. At this point, she was more scared for herself than the fear of any retribution from Mack. Besides, maybe subconsciously pitting her maniacal would-be boyfriend against the lecherous reprobates was some sort of vigilante justice. Either way, she was unaware why she confessed to him. Her voice was so muted only Vincent, not Paulding, could hear her. "Mack. Mack & Saunders and that other kid. Maybe more, I can't remember all of them." It was a half-truth that only Rayna knew and had already blocked out, but nonetheless, the main culprits had been outed. It felt good to her just to let the words go and get it off her chest.

There were about four boys now gathered outside of the office in the hallway.

"Son of a bitch," screamed Vincent, now more agitated than ever. "I will fucking kill them." He stood up straight, meeting eyes with the group of gawking boys. They scattered like roaches when the lights come on, even the ones who were bigger than him. Any sane person knew not to mess with anyone with a darkened-pupil, sharklike dead look in their eye, no matter their size. Like Paulding, many had witnessed Vincent's rage and threats before. Should the need ever arise for character witnesses, this wasn't going to end well for him.

"What the fuck you looking at?" Vincent barked a spittle-laden tirade at a senior twice his size who was the slowest to make a path. Vincent muscled past him with a gut check and bolted out the exit.

Back in the office, Paulding let out a sigh of relief and tried to compose himself. He picked up the pills, one by one, along with tiny fragments of his dignity. Rayna sank deeper into the chair, weeping, and tried unsuccessfully to stifle her whimpers. Her body convulsed with each emotional wave.

★★★★

Vincent was seething. He pulled his hair at the temples, trying to get a hold of his rage, wondering where it all went wrong. Some strands actually came out. He'd started to come down out of the cloud of his aggression, when Deputy Constance drove by in the Volare squad car, lights and siren blaring. Eustice had let Constance use it to inquire about the librarian's last known contacts, and he'd be damned if he would pay federal mileage for an entire morning of driving. Luckily for Paulding, Constance had just circled back to the scene of the death when he got the call from Principal Carter. It wasn't lost on him that the boy in question was the same one who had talked to his daughter, alone, in the cemetery just a few short days before. Constance felt a surge of adrenaline spike his veins as his inner monologue pondered his daughter being in the line of danger. He unknowingly was inches away from practically running over Vincent, whom he barely missed as he was lost in the bombardment of thoughts within his head.

Like a scene straight out of *Maximum Overdrive*, Vince ducked behind a row of parked cars just in time to avoid the deputy's line of view and the protruding, toothy grin of the Volare's cow-catching front bumper and grill. As he stooped down and caught his breath, he blinked rapidly at the reflection staring back at him from the shiny chrome bumper of a late 70s Chevy Vega. Vincent didn't recognize the deranged monster staring back at him. He had to look away. The bumper sticker of the car behind him, now at eye level, read, *Stay in drugs. Eat your school. Don't do veggies.* The irony was lost on Vincent in his altered state. If he hadn't thrown the bottle of pills at Paulding, he would have been popping one this very moment. *What the fuck were you thinking, man?* came the belligerent voice in his head.

When the coast was clear, Vincent ran off toward the nearby tree line of some adjacent woods. His mind was reeling, and his head was pounding like the very hooves of the demonic Hellsteed.

★★★★

Rayna absentmindedly sipped water from a glass she held with two hands, like a timid squirrel would a stranger's peanuts. She hadn't quite registered yet what had happened, and her eyes were still red and puffy from crying. Paulding gave her a nondescript pill; his answer for everything.

Deputy Constance burst through the door, his hand on the butt of his holstered but unstrapped gun. He did a quick sweep of the small office, accidentally knocking over a small globe that had teetered unbalanced atop a filing cabinet. The sound it made hitting the floor gave Rayna a jolt. She startled upright in the chair, spilling some water on her shirt.

"Where is he? Where is that son of a bitch?" Constance demanded. He finally noticed his daughter, and her obviously upset state of mind and knelt next to her. "Rayna, are you okay, baby?" he asked. Crouched at her level, he noticed the bruise on her wrist and bolted upright once again, his anger reigniting in an instant. "Did that little prick do this to you?"

Paulding just sat there, nodding in affirmation. He thought Vincent fully capable of anything after his outburst. Furthermore, he wasn't happy about being humiliated. Sending Constance on a manhunt for his daughter's suitor seemed like a nice dish of revenge, her personal feelings for either of them be damned. "That boy made death threats," stated Paulding, making himself the clear victim in the room.

At this, Rayna's intelligence immediately kicked in. She knew exactly where this was going and wanted no part of it, regardless of how pissed, or even scared, she'd been of Vincent at the moment.

"No, Daddy. No," she implored, but she could tell by the look that registered across her father's face he would be having none of it.

"Don't you dare protect him. I forbid you to see that kid ever again. We'll talk about this later."

As if more insult couldn't add any more injury to the occurrences of the last few hours, there it was. She had been expecting it, and like a Parisian train scheduled by a Swiss clock, the other shoe had just fallen precisely on time. There was no way she was going to win this argument right now, and honestly, she was too drained to even try.

Constance hurried out, spitting police jargon into his shoulder mic, not even waiting for her response.

Rayna crumpled in her chair, quietly sobbing into her hands. The salt water of her tears mixed with the tap water from her glass forming microscopic tempests of emotion. Why did she feel like she and Vincent had both been victims in this situation, and why was it always the adults who either refused, or proved unable, to help them? Her mind began to stop reeling as the active ingredient in the pill began to dissolve away her concerns.

Finding herself slowly disarmed, she was a newfound Alice going down her very first rabbit hole, and the scariest part was, she didn't exactly hate it.

Chapter 18

Vincent didn't even notice the splinters from the withered and broken tree stump that were biting his ass like some sort of sadistic ants at the concession stand of a diabetics' convention. Gnarled branches and decrepit moss reached up to his sneakers like the hands of so many decomposing corpses, each finger reaching for a second chance at life but ultimately snapping under the weight of Vincent's feet as he tapped them in time to the rhythm section pounding inside his skull.

Vincent, too, felt like he had snapped. Despite what people said behind his back, losing control was actually his least favorite thing to do. He had hoped he would have more intimate times with Rayna before introducing her to one of his episodes. *Too late for that now.* He doubted he could ever regain her trust. His head continued to pound as anxiety settled in for the long haul. *What the hell was he doing out in the middle of the woods at this hour anyway?* The realizations were beginning to dawn on him again. Oh, that's right: his mom was fucking someone young enough to be his brother; the cops were probably forming a manhunt for him; and he had insulted and injured the one person he thought he could relate too. *Way to go, asshole.*

The cognitive side of his brain told the rest of him what he had been thinking subconsciously all along. He reached into his pocket for the tattered map he had ripped out of the old book in the library and unfolded it for a better view. Normally, he would have had a hard time holding on to things like this, but considering he hadn't changed his clothes in a few days, it was no wonder the filthy denim still held the booty. The seat of his pants was black from the countless filthy surfaces he had rested his ass on. It wasn't coincidence he had been taunted for shitting his pants on more than one occasion. *The map, Vincent. The map!* Jesus Christ, he could not get out of his own mind sometimes.

He tried to focus on the tarnished paper. Upon closer inspection, the outdated markings became clearer to him. Its details showed the towns of Tarrytown, New York, Sleepy Hollow, Wolferts Roost, Spook Rock, the Van Tassel House, the Hudson River, Delaware Indian grounds, and a covered bridge. They were surrounded by a style of calligraphy so intricate and embellished it was doubtful anyone other than a seasoned cartographer could have read it. Vincent studied the map and gathered his wits about him. *Wait a second.* The fog of his mind started to dissipate. He checked in the watch pocket of his tattered jeans and found two pills covered in lint and questionable substances. They were so old, their outer coatings had actually started to congeal into a brown liquid. *Perfect. These are the good kind that give you the best rides.* He would save these for when he really needed them, but not quite yet. Hopefully they would last him through the night, until he could get back home to his ample supply of medication. Perhaps in the morning things would have cooled down and everyone would realize he actually meant no harm.

Fucking Mack & Saunders, the belligerent voice came back. But he didn't have time for that now. *I'll deal with them later.*

Vincent got up, dusted himself off and looked at the map one last time before putting it back in his pocket. He didn't know where his hike would take him, but he knew it would last him well into the evening. No matter, as he certainly couldn't return home or go back into town just yet. He sucked in a deep breath of air and tossed trepidation aside.

Growing up, this part of the woods had been one of legends. It was the kind of place parents told their kids to avoid at all costs, along with legends like Krampus, La Llorona, or in his case, the

Unhallowed Horseman and the Great Witch Hulda. Part of him knew those fairy tales were meant to get kids home by supper time or keep them from being alone in the woods, where more sinister adults could take advantage of them without prying eyes, but this was also the kind of place the West Memphis Three types would go to spray-paint abandoned cars, huff whippets, or get their first hand job. All those things were scary in their own right, but Vincent's mind was obsessed. The Legend of the Horseman seemed to be the only thing that could help him stay preoccupied and away from the torture of emotions that only seemed to be getting progressively worse the older he got.

Vincent could barely make out any of the cursive on the map, but he knew from local folklore and the rudimentary illustrations on the map that somewhere out here was the Van Tassel Manor. Maybe if he was lucky, he could do some cool urban exploring, or perhaps even find some clues. *What if a bum fight with some squatting derelict was in order? That would be great.* Beating the fuck out of a homeless guy would be a refreshing way for him to get out his frustrations with the authorities, his mother and his own damn self. He nearly salivated at the thought as his fist balled up and clenched his fingers so tight the nails bit into the flesh of his palm. It would definitely be time to take his happy pills soon.

He stomped on with exactly zero fucks to give. The sweat in his socks made uncomfortable squishes as he trudged through mud, trampled briars and scattered subterranean wildlife. The sun had already crested and was on the downswing. He bent down near a stream, which one could only imagine was a tributary of the great Pocantico. He imagined himself an Algonquin warrior on the hunt for some cryptological beast unseen by mortal eyes. He scooped a palm of murky water, swallowing filaments of moss, dirt, and God only knows what kind of natural detritus. Either way, it was natural, and that's all that mattered. *It certainly couldn't be worse than any of the shit Paulding had pumped into his system*, he thought as he swallowed more robust gulps. Water and mud had splashed down his shirt. He would look like a raving lunatic to anyone who might have come across him out here in the woods, but as he looked at his reflection, all he saw for once was a kid. A kid free of pollution. No amphetamines, chemicals or magical medications tainting his thought.

"No," Vincent actually said out loud, before thinking, *I won't let them feed me that shit anymore.* He was like a coffee drinker at an AA meeting, in constant contradiction to what he felt he needed and what he wanted. He knew he was kidding himself, but it felt good to be assertive.

He took one last gulp from the stream. As a heavy metallic taste hit his tongue, his entrails slithered around inside him like Medusa's tangled hair. *Maybe that wasn't such a good idea.* As he held his abdomen and continued on determinedly toward the direction the map had indicated the manor would be, the sun dropped a few more finger lengths from the sky.

★★★★

Marisa sat drinking coffee on the couch. Hopeless. Braless. One of Jack's open shirts barely covering her nipples. She didn't care. Jack sat next to her, drinking a fifth of bourbon; his go to.

"You think he's alright?" she asked. A furrowed look spread across her face showing small indentations of wrinkles in an otherwise unblemished countenance.

Jack poured a hearty portion of bourbon into her coffee. She didn't protest. Her breasts were freely exposed, and Jack noticed the sculpted upward curve of her ample tits that ended in a seemingly airbrushed and flawless dark-brown nipple. It was perfection. He nearly salivated. He could give two fucks about her son, and he couldn't resist her.

"I'm sure he's fine. The cops will find him.

He forced the cup close to her lips. It had faux-granite paint on the outside, with a cat in a Santa hat smirking back. The way her thick bottom lip latched on to the mug made him tingle. He was horny as hell. *God she sucked a mean dick, ask anyone.*

"Here, this will make you feel better," he bullshitted, hoping his empathy might get him laid.

The slurping sound she made was too much. His dick was getting hard. *What an asshole*, he thought, even about himself. But who cared? In this house, hedonism was king. *Wasn't his kid anyway.* Besides, she had offered to fuck him first, back in the day. He had been an innocent bystander at their first encounter as far as he was concerned. He didn't ask to be put in this situation with raging hard-ons all the time. He put the bottle down and started greedily kissing the nape of her neck, grabbing a full handful of the meaty flesh of her breast. It filled his entire palm. He squeezed harder. He was throbbing now and could no longer hold back.

"Damn it, Jack. My son is missing," she said, pushing him away and nearly spilling her coffee. She may as well have slapped him in the dick. But anyone who knew Jack knew he wouldn't let this minor hiccup stop him. It was his assholishness that had attracted her to him in the first place, after all.

"Oh, now all of a sudden you're mother of the year? Better call Oprah."

She shot him a quick look of disdain, but then realized he was absolutely right. She hit the coffee-bourbon mixture hard. She couldn't act mad that well, so she spread her legs and let him ravish her. Maybe it would take some of the sting out. After all, in this house hedonism *was* king, and she knew it. Worrying about Vincent would have to wait. She reminded herself that she was a terrible mother. Herself agreed.

She fucked him robotically.

★★★★

As the sun began to set, a cool chill began to ever so slightly snake its way through the spindled groupings of severed saplings. Overturned roots and felled logs created a tapestry of decaying cadavers. Vincent clumsily navigated them until he stumbled upon an old wagon path that was partially overgrown. It led to a covered bridge near the Hanging Tree, which had long been the landmark demarcation of the end of town's civilization and the beginning of where the lower-class peasantry resided. From here on out it was no-man's-land and private, mostly abandoned, property. Shotgun shell casings and bullet holes marred the few remaining rust-covered signs warning of trespassing. A solitary county line sign was so overgrown and ramshackle that the rust made it practically illegible. Neither logical townsfolk, and certainly not maintenance personnel, had visited these parts in quite some time.

Vincent continued on until he came across a handprinted sign on an old wooden plank. All that was left on it was an arrow pointing to where he now stood, with the only legible word, ASS, right in its center. *That's rich.* Rather than take it as a personal affront, he continued in the direction it pointed, knowing full well it had most likely once been emblazoned with the words Van Tassel Manor. He was close now. He could feel it in his Brom bones, as the locals were fond of saying.

The sun unsuccessfully tried to hang on to the last vestiges of light in the sky, slowly losing the tug of war as gravity spun the earth into the darkness of night. The day died away, a faint orange glow all that was left of its very existence. Vincent didn't feel so well, but felt a calm come over him. This was probably the way those subject to bloodletting felt when drained of the battling phantoms of their boiling hemoglobin. He carried on.

Now inside the covered bridge, Vincent was a nervous wreck and visibly frightened. He stepped across the wood planks with great trepidation. As he did, the unmistakable sound of a horse's hooves on hardwood planks matched his every move. They echoed off the wooden walls in eerie fashion and cascaded down the sides like a mist over an enchanted waterfall. As Vincent picked up his pace, the hooves kept time. *Was this some sort of sick joke?* Maybe Mack or one of his cronies had followed him here. Just as he left the bridge, a horse whinnied from its soul—or lack thereof, as the case may be—and belted out a godforsaken war cry. Terrified, Vincent took off running down the wagon trail much deeper into the ominous forest. His mind was racing. It seemed like the eyes of ghouls, goblins or other apparitions peered out from behind every tree. Vines looked like serpents, and the terrifying sound of nocturnal wildlife clamored in the treetops above. A jet-black cloud of bats screeched through the treetops. Vincent ran, then paused, as his eyes darted around for any other signs of life. Suddenly, all was still save the continuous sound of an approaching gallop.

Panicking and running once again, ominous shadows, mistaken shapes, and the sound of the pursuing Horseman drew him deeper into the woods. He could have sworn he heard a disembodied, hellish chortle.

Vincent took pause near a field. Years of sedentary video game streaming and comic book reading meant he could no longer carry on at this pace without first catching his breath. He couldn't understand why, but something definitely put him ill-at-ease here. An enormous oak tree loomed like a foreboding scarecrow, almost purposefully anthropomorphic. There was an eerie silence here that seemed unworldly. Even the horse's hooves had stopped their pursuit. A slight wind blew and Vincent shivered, then quickly moved on. He had noticed clay mounds of earth and grayish-white slate river stones stacked in deliberate piles. These were known as "pumpkin patches" amongst the locals. The wind howled above him, the air uncannily and unseasonably warm as it circled his torso. He didn't know it, but he was standing in a long since abandoned Indian burial ground.

Like much of the Native American heritage and civilization in these parts, the Colonials had chosen not to recognize its cultural significance. It was left far from the pubic's eyes, overgrown, and in a continued state of disarray; long forgotten. The spirits hadn't forgotten though, and now there was a stranger in their land. No one was an intruder until they had proven otherwise. That didn't mean they were welcomed, however, especially given the history of the region.

Vincent sensed a large, ominous figure just out of view at his five o'clock. The snort of a colossal Charger was expelled and he could see what seemed to be its enormous head bobbing on the reigns behind him, literally chomping at the bit. He was too scared to turn and face his fears head on, so he did what anyone would do—he bolted. In his mind, the Hellsteed reared and made chase. He couldn't be absolutely sure, but he wasn't going to stop and ask it for directions either. The pursuit was on, and Vincent was getting weaker. His options were quickly running out.

★★★★

Rayna wore her comfy Doraemon sweats for sleeping. Marlene had turned her on to Asian stuff that her other girlfriends always talked about in chats. Among them were the robotic earless cat with his magical pouch, BTS, and Korean ASMR eating videos. Rayna hadn't yet worked herself up to the brutality of *Battle Royale* or *High School of the Dead*, but she could handle Sanrio and Studio Ghibli just fine. Her eyes were still slightly red as she listened to K-pop tunes and surfed the web. She sipped a large hot chocolate and warm milk concoction with a dollop of marshmallow puff, trying to forget about the day's previous events. It wasn't working so well.

She turned up the volume and tried to zone out so she could forget about Vincent's outburst and ever having to see Mack's wannabe gang again. Right now, she was safe and far from all the men who seemed to cause trouble in her life. Funny how it was always men.

★★★★

Vincent passed a decrepit barn. Old and worn, splintered wood and antiquated hardware adorned its rustic edifice. Antique riding gear, equestrian tools, boots, picks, shovels and various agricultural implements that looked more like weapons than farming tools leaned against the crimson-red planks of the old building. Although worn, it appeared the items may have been recently put to use. In the near distance, Vincent saw what he could only assume was the Van Tassel Manor. There was, after all, nothing else reportedly even out here.

Tired and out of breath, Vincent arrived outside the mid-sized Dutch manor perched high atop of a grassy knoll, surrounded by overgrown moss-laden trees. It was clear by the architecture and spaciousness that in its day this would have been home to quite the affluent family. The house was definitely of rustic origins, with a large, sweeping porch meant to be more utilitarian than elaborate. Now weathered, it still gave the impression that in its heyday the place was one of majestic glory. Two large parapets formed the base of a third one, giving it an almost steeple-like appearance. The broad paned windows, when combined with the elongated and sagging porch, gave the house the demeanor of a grinning face, much like its *Monster House* and *Amityville Horror* counterparts. Only the owner ever knew if the grin was intended to be malicious or congenial. The house was dutifully bound together by a tall, cobblestone chimney and dovetail framing. A light dusting of ash flit from its rafters almost like a powdery fine snow.

The pitch-blackness of rural night had now fully set in, and the only light source emanated from a flickering oil lantern burning inside. Vincent thought he could still faintly hear the plodding of horse steps in the distance behind him. He pounded his head, shook it off, and decided to investigate once he determined here might be a place to seek refuge, if only for a moment. At least he could theoretically find a place to hide from the equestrian apparition that had been following him.

Above the slightly ajar door of the house was a weathered sign that cryptically read *Rust in Lust*. The sign was older than any known creature still living. It made no sense to his young mind. Vincent lightly rapped on the door. "Hello? Anybody home?" He spoke softly, filled with apprehension.

Now inside the home, it appeared larger than it had on the outside. *How was that even possible?*

As Vincent walked through the aging Colonial home, the floorboards creaked. The furniture was outdated and unkempt. Warm hues of orange and yellow flowed through his occipital orbs, not from lighting, but from the blood rushing through his skull. The place appeared not to be lived in for quite some time. Vincent's eyes tried to focus and make the dulled edges of surfaces into noticeable objects in his mind. Brown waves of blurry color subdued the perceived orange hues as waves of blood washed inside the torrents of his temples. He didn't know when the last time he had taken any medication was, but he knew it had been a while. Perhaps the longest in a very long time. He soldiered on, determined to try and ride out the withdrawals his body was experiencing.

Vincent took in everything slowly, following the path toward the flickering light. Ghastly figures peered down from wall paintings. All the high-backed furniture and antediluvian fixtures seemed foreign to him. Tim Burton, himself, couldn't have painted a more elaborate or daunting setting; only Rick Heinrichs maybe could have. Vincent reached a doubled-paneled door. He slowly pushed it open to reveal a vast, open parlor.

As he peered around the corner of the door, he saw what appeared to be an ethereal crone covered by a mountain of Tartan blankets rocking in a wicker chair. The sallow-faced woman looked, improbably, every bit as old as the house. Certainly, at least a century had passed under her gaze. She rocked back and forth with purpose, not startled in the least bit. Vincent thought he heard a music box chiming out a ghostly melody. It appeared to be coming from one of the rooms at the top of the expansive, colonnaded staircase. He crept forward.

A voice with the timber of an injured falcon ripped Vincent back to reality. "Come in, son," said the wrinkled and emaciated woman who sat facing a massive ivory and stone fireplace. She wore a shawl around her head and was surrounded by the distinct smell of drying herbs. The two carved ivory lions' heads of the mantle flanked her profile. Small flames flickered in the firebox spitting tiny embers onto the hearth at her feet. The flickering light silhouetted her ghostly appearance.

Vincent came closer, cautiously slow, so he could get a good look at the woman. Now that he could see her, she was aged so much it is almost incomprehensible that she still breathed life. The blue-green veins under her skin created an unnerving patchwork of spider's webs. Her eyes were red and sunken.

"Hi, ma'am. I'm sorry to disturb you. It's just that—"

She motioned him to sit, silencing him with a single wave of her feeble hand. You could almost see the bones through her translucent skin.

"What is it you seek?" she croaked.

Vincent pulled the crumpled map from his soiled pocket. I was looking at this and thought maybe I could find..." He thought better of it and changed course. Do you know the Van Tassels?

The woman nodded as a toothless grin split her face like a demented jack-o'-lantern. The mere mention of the name lit a fire in the dusty cobwebs of her soul. A boney digit pointed to a huge painting of a woman standing beside a man bedecked in an

American Revolutionary War uniform. Then the hand made a flitting gesture worthy of one half its age.

Vincent shifted in his seat and wondered how ridiculous he might come off to the geriatric spinster. Look, this is going to sound crazy, but I was wondering if I could ask you about the—"

"Unhallowed Horseman?"

Vincent was stunned into silence, mouth agape.

After what seemed to be an eternal pause, the woman continued. On All Hallows' Eve over two centuries ago, a Hessian spy for the British stole floor plans to some key military installations. If his ploy had been successful, we would still be paying taxes to the King.

"All Hallows' Eve? Vince barely got the words out.

"Halloween, All Saints Day, Dia de Los Muertos—same rituals across many cultures and countries. The one night a year the living and the dead can coexist on earth." She smiled to herself, suppressing a cackle.

Vincent felt the sharp pang of the words deep within in his bones.

Chapter 19

Less than eight miles west of where General William Heath was engaged in the battle of White Plains, Acker meet up with Van Wart, Williams and the slave Paulding. He informed them about the spy and setting up the ambush, and explained that some imperative clandestine papers were hidden in the Hessian's boot. If the skilled equestrian were able to reach the British blockade offshore before they got to him, it would be the end of the Revolution and they would all be hanged as traitors to the Crown. So much for Independence. They had one shot to get this right.

Acker had just got out prison and was a target himself. He had always been in trouble with the law because he didn't fit within its Puritanical codes of conduct. But this time the very fate of the burgeoning colony was on his shoulders. It was a chance for him to redeem himself in the eyes of his soon to be countrymen.

In a small prison, especially during Revolutionary War times, anyone could be your cellmate. There was little room as it was, especially with transgressions of treason increasingly daily. As a result, the inebriated town drunk or fornicating adulterer might end up sharing a cell with an actual traitor.

So was the case of Acker. Although the Hessian who bunked with him on the cold slab of the concrete floor didn't speak to him outright, he did have a bad habit of talking in his sleep. Being of German and Dutch descent, Acker had learned both languages and one Mahicanituck dialect by the time he was twenty, allowing him to understand the Hessian's nighttime ramblings. The single night he and the Hessian had spent sharing the same filthy and confined space proved to be just enough to give Acker all the info he needed to try and subvert the traitorous plot.

Acker had learned that the Hessian had stollen many of the plans of the Revolutionaries, including blueprints, shipping details, a codified language and plans to attack the British Naval fleet the following night. The Hessian was scheduled for the gallows, without trial. He had plans of his own, however, and was determined to deliver the information he had acquired to the British. He had committed most of the plans and blueprints to memory, but carried a small folded paper of them, which he had hidden inside his boot. During the few minutes of physical exercise he was allotted, he planned to execute the escape he had successfully cased out the previous night. The colonialists were revolutionary, but they weren't barbaric, so they took him out for his nightly stroll as was customary with all prisoners.

Spotting several grazing horses in the field near the town's public gallows where he was to be hanged, the Hessian used his superior agility to scale the wall and mount a nearby horse before his guard could get off a single musket shot. The guard had been warned to preload a cartridge, but in his laziness decided not to. It would be his downfall, as it took the skilled equestrian less than fifteen seconds to sprint to a nearby stallion, mount it mid run, and begin his adept race toward the shoreline.

Acker had been released that morning and would stand trial later for a multitude of sins, including abetting witchcraft practitioners, infidelity, adultery, sex out of wedlock, and many others. But for now those could wait, as in the midst of an uprising cases like the Hessian's proved to be more pressing.

Acker had spent the morning rounding up the vestments, red coats and weaponry that had been salvaged off British corpses after battle. Most people didn't want the attached juju of evil spirits that was believed to follow such objects around, much less the literal stink of death with which they were permanently imbued. Acker, already a social outcast who spent most of his time down on his luck, had no such reluctance. He knew the items held some value, even if were mere farthings to the pound. Little did he know how valuable they would prove to be that evening. He had gathered the items, cleaned them best he could, and was taking them to the village marketplace to see what he could buy or trade for them.

Upon his arrival, mere seconds after the Hessian's escape (in fact, had he turned around he would have witnessed the act firsthand), he was accosted by the young guard, who confessed his faux pas. "The German, he's gone. Escaped!"

Acker went pale as all the blood rushed from his face. Acker, who had forgotten about his cellmate's nocturnal outburst, thought the German had been in the good hands of the local authorities with a one way ticket to the gallows. Although himself previously scheduled to be hanged via mob, justice, or a combination of the two, Acker immediately came to the realization of what he had to do next. As a third generation child of the area, Acker knew what the Horseman did not. There were several shortcuts to the roads that led to the British Navy offshore, and if he was betting man, not only could he reach them faster than the Hessian, but he knew exactly which way the wanted man would try to proceed.

He slapped on one of the red coats mid gait, gathered the items and got quick word out for Williams and any of the militia men in the immediate vicinity to meet him. The ones in the know would understand exactly the spot in question, where they had hidden a cannon for safekeeping for exactly unpredictable times like these. It had been eruditely positioned ahead of time in the direct path of the British frigates favorite anchoring spot just offshore. It seemed tonight fate may actually be on their side.

At the site, the men hurried to uncover the camouflaged cannon and get it ready to aim. They would not have the five men it normally took to fire the massive armament, as they were fewer and even lessor trained. However, they did have some luck on their side that night, which was absolutely necessary to pull this off. First, since the cannon hadn't been fired in a while there would be no need to clean the muzzle of any residual gunpowder. There would be no glowing embers. They did give it a quick swab with the dry sponge, though, just to get out any moisture that might have built up over the course of countless dawns. Also, since this wasn't an official military maneuver, they could skip protocol. There was no sergeant to inspect or give orders.

Van Wart, a former military man, had served as a number five and a number two gunner in a cannon regiment. In fact, he was missing one of his thumbs from an incident as a young soldier when he was swabbing out the barrel only to be met with some residual gunpowder. His regiment and he had developed the open hand policy ever since that particular incident. Regardless, he knew the necessary steps, but time wasn't on their side. The Hessian may come bolting around the bend at any moment. Fortunately, the men had pre-prepped the round and shell specifically in case a need like this should arise.

Williams had a necklace with a brass friction primer that he had always wore around his neck. He figured that the small item may get lost or stolen by some curious rodent if left out in the wild. Better not to chance it. His spark of foresight proved most beneficial. The men carefully seated the round, softly at first, and then with a firm tap from the ramrod. The sound it made as it snapped into place confirmed it was perfectly flush deep within the muzzle. Now, they would hope and pray and wait.

Acker had learned enough from his hunting uncle and infantry buddies to properly load a flintlock musket. There was only one, and there was no doubt he had not the proper marksmanship to pick a man off a galloping horse at full speed. However, he reasoned it couldn't hurt matters, and any extra help was better than nothing. He leveled the firelock across his chest and pushed the pin forward. Next, he removed the paper cartridge from the pocket of his woolen red coat. It was actually quite warm, albeit bulky. He chewed off the end of the wrapper, getting a metallic taste of gunpowder for his troubles. His tongue was black with the substance, but now was no time for particulars. His hands shook as he nervously poured a pinch of powder on the pin, before upending the other end and placing it down the barrel. A cloud of black dust spilled outside the muzzle. *Would it be enough to set off the gun? How dangerous was this, anyway?* He used the metal rod to ram the cartridge down the musket's barrel and then hastily threw it aside. There would be no time to get off a second shot, and he only had the one cartridge anyway. He had no desire to find the hole to reseat the rod, so in his nervousness discarded it.

He hunkered down, took aim at the imaginary rider…and waited.

★★★★

Vincent's eyes slowly came into focus. He had no idea how long he had been drifting along in his mind. The skeletal-like jaws of the mysterious Lady Van Tassel were still moving. She continued her tale, and he was mesmerized.

"On that night, Acker became a hero. What happened next was legendary, but also a curse. It happened on the Triduum of the Hallows. A night just like this one so many, many moons ago."

★★★★

The black Hellsteed let out a hellacious whiny that seemed not of this world. It leaped the distance of three outstretched men in a single bound and came to a sudden stop in front of those who lay in wait.

The Horseman, with a black, braided ponytail, earth-tone civilian clothes, belt axe and bull whip, loomed silently aback his black steed. He had stolen a tricorn hat, a distinctly American cloak, and boots from a farmhouse to hodgepodge together a quick disguise. He stood there a mere thirty yards away looking very much like an American footman. They could practically feel his breathing permeate the air. Like a demonic vision, he towered before them as they trembled, having vowed allegiance to Teufel in exchange for a successful escape. Then, in a thick Germanic accent, he got out the little English he knew. "Friend, not foe."

Acker and the others looked at each other, astonished. This was rather anticlimactic compared to what they had built up in their minds. "What party are you from?", they questioned, but needed not to waste time for an answer. Then at the same time, Paulding and Acker looked down at their red coats. "He thinks we're British." In all the nervous excitement, they had forgotten about their disguises, with which they had unwittingly fooled him. Acker raised the musket to fire, but the Horseman had already received the message loud and clear.

"Hiya!" He spurred the animal hard, nearly cracking its rib. It leaped with abnormal ability, instinctively aiming its trajectory over their heads.

Van Wart leaned with the full weight of his body, causing the back end of the cannon to dip. It was in God's hands now. He pulled the lanyard and shielded his face and ears. Acker pulled the trigger on the fully cocked musket. Rifle and cannon rang out in unison in a plume of fire and billowing gray smoke. The earth shook beneath them, as if it was physically opening up to receive its prodigal son. In the distance, a waiting ship's captain read it as an inauspicious sign.

It turned out the shot had been perfectly timed as he passed above them; they had fired the cannon with deadly accuracy.

Gravity pulled the dead weight of the horse and rider back to earth. His body was sheared off above the shoulder blades. A jutting vertebrae and brown muck appeared where his head and neck had once been. The blood had immediately cauterized upon impact.

The body of the Hessian stared at them as if in disbelief, though it had no eyes with which to see. They incredulously starred back.

★★★★

"They ended up shooting the Hessian spy's head clear off his shoulders with a perfectly aimed cannon ball."

The lady's voice grounded Vincent back into his earthly surroundings. He came to, once again frightfully aware of his current situation. He tried unsuccessfully to shake off the grogginess. "The Headless Horseman," he simply stated.

"It was believed no corpse, even of enemies, should be left uninterred. To this day, no one knows where they buried the body," Van Tassel said ominously, although she knew the Ancients believed it to be tied to the Grand Hokohonkgus chestnut tree.

★★★★

The newfound American Independence heroes stood in the same Indian burial ground where Vincent had stopped. A full blood moon illuminated the field. The clay mounds were pristine and well preserved. They dotted the ground in nearly concentric patches. The slave Paulding had taken the initiative and was digging a hole where one of the previous burial sites had been. The men had reasoned that since the Natives were no longer a threat, and locals were too skittish to come here, it would be the perfect place to dispose of the body. The mutilated head of the former Hessian was wrapped in the purplish-brown horseman's cloak the Hessian had tucked around his waist and thrown into the crude hole.

★★★★

Vincent was half awake, as if in a dream state. He could feel his body in the chair across from Lady Van Tassel, but was picturing her words as if he were actually there in the field with the men. He was having some sort of surreal out of body experience as he surfed the waves of time and perhaps dimensions.

The woman droned on. "Out of pure hate for his traitorous act, they buried what was left of the head in an old forgotten Wecquaesgeek burial ground."

Vincent heard the woman's words as he envisioned the burial in his mind's eye.

The disfigured head looked up as scoop after scoop of shoveled dirt filled every crack and crevice of its mutilated disembodiment. It was a sight the men would never forget.

"Hoping the spirit's mind could never again be reunited with its body, they planned to bury the corpse separately. They prayed that even in the afterlife the two could never be united. It was as pure an act of revenge as ever there was. Turned out, neither the Indians nor the patriots wanted anything to do with his corpse, so that wasn't a problem."

★★★★

Ringlets of fog began encircling the men. A distant howling could be heard, sounding neither human nor quite animal. Something snapped a branch nearby.

"Did you see that?" Acker was still holding the musket for show in case they got in a dire situation, but everyone knew he had already spent the only cartridge. He instinctively raised it across his chest.

Then another snap, followed by more. There were seemingly surrounded. The men started to panic.

"Retreat! Let's get the hell out of here," screamed Van Wart above the ever-increasing din.

"What about the body?" asked Williams.

"Leave it!" someone yelled. It was now too chaotic to tell who.

The men made a hasty retreat, only God himself knowing what would have happened had they stayed. They fled as fast as they could, as behind them swirls of ominous fog circled the freshly decapitated corpse. The body lay exposed, the head rocking to and fro in the makeshift grave, the menacing grimace still plastered across its face, as if to taunt them.

★★★★

"Thus, he was posthumously nicknamed The Unhallowed Horseman from thenceforth," said Van Tassel, so low Vincent could barely hear her.

She and the room came into full focus now. The dream state had ended, and there was no denying this was a starkly cold and bitterly harsh reality. Vincent had no need to pinch himself. All his senses had returned. He looked around the unfamiliar surroundings, slowly feeling the full weight of the impending doom of his current situation like an anvil on his chest."

"Do you believe it?" asked Vincent.

"Believe it? I know it. Seen him many times in my lifetime, son. You see, every couple of decades or so, just like this year, the full moon falls on All Hallows' Eve, the first day of the Triduum of Hallows. Also the exact anniversary of the Horseman's death. It's said that on this day he seeks revenge on the descendants of those men."

Thoughts of the Horseman who had chased him, this old lady who looked like a living cadaver, the cops, his outburst, Rayna… everything came rushing in upon Vincent in a tsunami of emotions.

"That includes me… " the diaphanous creature continued,— …and that includes you!"

"Me? What do I have to do with any of this?" Vincent's eyes were as wide as saucers, even without the influence of fresh drugs in his system. He looked more like a caricature of himself than a sane or mortal boy.

"Like most of the natives of this town, we are related to those four men responsible for the killing. Acker was a bastard, but still blood related. Like him, you were too," the woman chided. She was having fun taunting him now, like a spider with a paralyzed fly. Her face seemed to distort from the refractions of the shadows cast by the dim firelight, almost as if she had many countenances. Not all of them were feminine, most ill-intentioned.

Vincent pushed himself straight up in his seat. It wasn't until that point that he felt the dampness of the sweat sticking his clothes to his body. The density of the air and the moisture in his clothes made him feel trapped. He fumbled his fingers around in his pocket searching for the pills. *Where the fuck were they?* Had he said that out loud or was it in his mind? He thought he heard the woman laugh. *Is she mocking me? Is any of this even real?*

Vincent tried to calm his breathing. He had gotten himself into this situation, and he could get himself out of it. The left side of his brain looked for clues. His mind was reeling with scenarios as it chewed on the woman's last soliloquy. He decided to address her head-on, no more time for games.

"That's impossible! My dad—"

"Is it? Ever ask her his real name?" Lady Van Tassel interrupted.

"What are you saying?" Vincent was asking himself as much as he was her. His brain went in to overdrive calculating scenarios, dates, relationships, possibilities. It was too much.

His fumbling fingers finally found one of the pills. He immediately dry swallowed it, the capsule biting the back of his throat on the way down.

Lady Van Tassel began to snicker at the boy, then drove the point home. "The sheriff, the teachers at your school... Hell, even the black folk in this town are descendants from the slaves entrusted to defend Tarrytown from the British that fateful night. Understand, boy?"

Just then, a horse could be heard as clear as day outside.

"Oh my God, it's him. It's him!" Vincent bolted upright so fast he nearly toppled his chair, and the woman along with it. She swiveled her torso, locking in on his every move.

"Of course it's him. You made it easy for him." She sneered, seemingly having not a care in the world. Her voice rose with each utterance.

"We've got to do something." Vincent picked up the iron poker from the fireplace. Its tip glowed a yellow-orange, as it had rested in the slowly burning fire the entire time. He raced to the window and threw back the curtains. In his heart, he was hoping he wouldn't see anything. A large, dark silhouette skirted by just out of view. He felt it as much as saw it. It was like a horrible, unescapable nightmare. Vincent knew wholeheartedly that it was the Horseman, and that It was coming for them both.

"There's nothing you can do." She began her hideous cackle again, even louder now. Her smile was so wide that it pulled the skin over her cheekbones in a fiendish, contemptuous sneer.

"Shut up, you freak! He's going to hear us," Vincent yelled, ignoring the reverberation of his own voice.

She laughed harder still.

Heavy footsteps could be heard mounting the porch stairs just outside the main door. Whomever, or whatever, it was, was big and mere moments away.

"God damn you, bitch!", Vincent blurted out in an irrepressible rage.

"He already has, son. He already has," croaked the woman, who seemed strangely at peace with herself.

With that, the belt axe from the library came hurtling toward the woman. It caught her right between the eyes, firmly imbedding itself from the bridge of her spindly nose all the way up to the tip top of her forehead. A putrid spray of grayish blood painted the off-white walls in an homage worthy of Jackson Pollack himself. Axe now firmly implanted in her skull, she continued to laugh, out of reflex more than anything, before slumping over, dead.

Vincent heard what sounded like the melancholic tones of a church organ. The eerie music was drifting a funeral dirge down the stairs and through the halls. He didn't understand why he hadn't heard it before.

It was at that moment, Vincent saw Him.

Chapter 20

Now, for the first time, Vincent got a good look at the Horseman. He was seven foot tall if he was an inch. He wore the earth-toned clothes of an American civilian during the American Revolution, just as Vincent had imagined them when the woman had told the tale. His clothes were torn, tattered, dirty and weathered. His period riding boots shuffled slowly across the floor as the heavy belt axe he drug behind him etched into the wooden floorboards. The old whip was wrangled in a circle and attached to his waist.

Vincent fell to his knees and scurried backward in a crab-walk, shocked at the ungodly sight before his eyes. He was still holding the red-hot poker in his hand, but didn't even flinch as it briefly rested on his shin, searing the flesh.

As Vincent's eyes slowly moved up, they revealed to him that the Horseman indeed had no head. Instead, a gruesome stump of a vertebrae jutted out of charred flesh. It was hard to tell if the burnt flesh smell was coming from the Horseman or Vincent. His senses swirled. His nose was attacked with the stench of decomposing flesh, singed hair and the fresh iron smell of death. Vincent soaked in the sight before him, unable to turn away. Like Alex DeLarge in some sick and twisted visualization experiment, the images rushed upon him in a torrent of stimulation. The history, the legend, the folklore. The pop culture, comics, movies and literature. Here it was, standing before him.

Vincent didn't have time to rationalize how his eyes were trying to fuck his brain. The Horseman took a step forward and swung at Vincent, who ducked back just in the nick of time. His adrenaline had kicked in, fight or flight time. He was no match for the superhuman, apparently undead entity. If his love of horror films had taught him anything, it was that villains like these were unable to be killed and never stayed "dead" for very long. Flight it was, but first he would have to defend himself just enough to get by the titanic being. His odds seem insurmountable, but he had to try.

Vincent countered with a swing from the fireplace poker, but a swing and miss made him smash the kerosene lamp, sending shards of glass and ignited kerosene oil onto the Horseman's arm and up his sleeve. As it did, the Horseman instinctively swung the burning arm, setting a nearby curtain ablaze. It draped all the way down to the floor and provided just the right kindling to ignite the rest of the wall. The creature flailed its arms about wildly, and the centuries-old artifacts and tattered furnishings proved to provide the perfect fuel for the combustible tinderbox. The room quickly was ablaze.

With this distraction, Vincent seized the opportunity to make a run for it and darted from the house.

★★★★

Vincent stumbled through the detritus of the barnyard. He hadn't realized how many obstacles would prove to hinder his progress once the time to make his escape had come. The now story-high flames threw flashes of light across the implements in the field. Tools, old tractors tires, wagon wheels, yokes and even an oxcart were among the many things scattered about. Behind him, Vincent could see the interior lighting up, fully engulfed in flames. Inside, the dark shadow of the Horseman battled to escape. The chimney collapsed in on itself, hurtling a thunderclap of dust toward Vincent. The walls drooped in on themselves in a deluge of flame. The manor couldn't support its own weight much longer.

Vincent tripped roughly, skinning an inch of flesh clear off his kneecap. A rust-eaten scythe had proven a most worthy adversary in the dark. He screamed out in pain, as he ripped the chunk of flesh the rest of the way off. Blood and a creamy white fluid drained from the kneecap. The pain was searing, and who knew what combination of germs, bacteria and evil voodoo accompanied the gash. Not even a tetanus shot would've helped at this point. Vincent limped closer to the barn, the only shelter nearby. Smoke billowed out from the burning manor house, choking his lungs and stifling his breathing. Embers fell from the sky, burning out like tiny meteorites on his scalp and clothes. It was a virtual hellscape. He ran to the broad side of the barn to take cover from the firestorm and gather his thoughts, but his mind was equally as engulfed as the structure behind him.

The Horseman continued to bash through the flaming debris inside. It tore down walls with the unprecedented strength in its bare hands and crashed through ignited obstacles with ease. Its progress was hindered, but not completely impeded.

Finally at the barn, Vincent was going into shock. He stumbled backward into the barn wall. All he could do was sit on the ground, his back to the structure, and watch in horror as the house disappeared into the envelopment of flames. He tried to scream but nothing came out. If it did, no one heard it, including himself.

Inside the barn, an unmanageable Beast let out deep, guttural bellows. The animal reared back and kicked at the aging walls of the barn, which were barely holding it upright as it was. As dust and debris filled the air, the wood began to splinter. Vincent tried to get up, but felt paralyzed from within, his fear once again having physiological effects on the outer mechanics of his body. The yet unseen animal used every ounce of its predatory brute force to try and escape its confinement.

Vincent got a sinking feeling in his gut. He instinctively put his hands over his head and crouched into a fetal position, like a middle schooler in a tornado drill. He clenched his teeth down onto his good knee, biting hard as he tried to suppress the pain, anguish and fear that had overcome him. He screamed as he tasted his own blood. Above his head, the rearing Hellsteed crashed forward through the wall, which disintegrated into matchsticks. It leaped over Vincent's head so closely he could smell the manure on its hooves. An ungodly wave of hot air washed over Vincent as the Beast barely cleared him and was immediately splintered off by the bite of the cold night air.

The animal turned and recognized Vincent as the enemy. It looked every bit as supernatural as its rider. Its eyes burned a fiery red. Smoke forced its way through its nostrils. It looked more like a medieval dragon to Vincent than some barnyard livestock. The braided black of its mane matched the Rider's and seemed darker than the night itself—a complete absence of color. The expanse of its gargantuan muscles glistened in the reflection of the flames. They were grotesque in size and did not seem possible, and certainly not natural. Vincent could not even in his wildest imagination have created as hellish, yet simultaneously awe and fear inspiring, an animal as this one. Stricken with fear, he was too petrified to meet its gaze. Something told him that a diabolical behemoth such as this one had many more powers than what the sight of it alone would deceive one into believing. Like Medusa before it, even in his altered and excited state Vincent knew better than to make eye contact with the brute. Luckily, the monstrosity of a Hellsteed had a sense of loyalty to his Rider. It speed full force into the melee that used to be the manor and sought out its Master.

Vincent took the opportunity to dart away as best he could on a smashed knee. Sometimes limping, sometimes dragging his appendage, he no longer had any desire to know the intricacies of the legends surrounding the Unhallowed Horseman.

★★★★

Inside the house, the Horseman put his boot on Lady Van Tassel's head to acquire the leverage needed to dislodge the axe from her skull. He wasn't leaving without his prized possession. Her skull made a popping sound as the war implement dislodged. If he'd had had any eyes, he would have enjoyed watching the rest of her flesh melt off the bone and her eyes drain through their socket holes. The skull again popped with the spark of a flame, like a yule log at Christmas, before it split itself in two along the laceration. The grin remained permanently plastered across the hag's unsightly visage.

The Horseman exited, his clothes still flaming, seemingly impervious to flame or mortal restrictions. With axe in hand, the apparition mounted his black Hellsteed and rallied into hot pursuit of the wounded Vincent. Behind him, everything of this world remained ablaze. The house, now completely engulfed, collapsed in an inward implosion of fire. The flames licked the night sky, and like the Horseman, destroyed everything in their path.

Vincent ran in a complete panic. He had gotten a head start and put a reasonable distance between him and his pursuer, but sounds of the Horseman were soon not too far behind him.

★★★★

As he entered the covered bridge, Vincent mistakenly took the time to catch his breath. All those Yahoos and late night Mr. Nick's pizzas had finally caught up to him. He reflexively looked back, just in time to see the Horseman arrive. For some reason, it wouldn't cross the bridge. The horse breached the night air nervously as the Rider reared it back. In one fluid motion that only a skilled equestrian could perform, it simultaneously hurled the axe at Vincent while commanding the animal's reigns with its other hand. The axe barely missed his head, sinking deeply into the wood plank of the bridge's wall just inches from his face. So close, in fact, Vincent saw the panic in his eyes within its reflection. He tried to extricate the death instrument, but after he finally realized this was futile, he had no choice but to run.

The culmination of his worst fears was now chasing him down like the scared, broken and fragile child he was.

Chapter 21

Deputy Constance parked the Volare cruiser in his driveway. He looked up and noticed the glow of the bedroom light in Rayna's upstairs room. He wasn't looking forward to making amends with her, but as a dutiful father was up for the task. He walked inside, plotting the reconciliation in his head.

Constance had unintentionally let the house remain retro. After his wife's death, he'd had neither the time, money, nor inclination to do any remodeling. Raising his kid was a full-time job, on top of his duties as a peace officer. As a result, the rooms looked like the early 1980s, but with all the newest technologies from the current decade. Baby-shit green tiles adorned the countertops and backsplash. Wood paneling made the living room look like a Moose lodge, and there was clutter everywhere. The only thing missing was mustard-colored shag rugs. It wasn't messy, per se, just slightly untidy, and extremely lived in. Children's things—clothes, toys, books and documents—were everywhere. More than enough, in fact, for two households. Most of Maw Maw's belongings were here, as were those of his deceased wife. The family loved it though. If there was one thing that was not arguable, it was that it felt very much like a home their home. Even strangers felt welcome and an immediate sense of comfort upon visiting their humble abode.

Now in full *Mr. Mom* mode, Constance saw little Bobbie curled up in an overstuffed chair with a Jack Skellington plushy toy. A half-eaten grilled cheese sandwich and some cranberry juice remained on the scuffed coffee table beside him. Constance pulled the blanket over him and gently kissed his nephew's forehead. The boy couldn't have looked cuter if actual visions of sugarplums danced in his head. Bobbie having been fed informed Constance that Rayna, although she may be unhappy to see him, wasn't mad enough to ignore her big cousin duties. Constance and Rayna had taken turns raising the child since his parents, the deputy's's sister and her husband, had passed in an untimely winter trip to explore Michigan's Upper Peninsula. Raising a child was something neither had been fully accustomed to, but proved to be quite the bonding exercise between them. Maw Maw Williams had done her share to help out as well, but now that she was an octogenarian and was quickly on her way to needing full-time assistance herself, Constance had his hands full.

He made his way to the adjacent open kitchen area and removed all the items from the canary yellow refrigerator needed to make himself a Dagwood sandwich. He proceeded to call up to his daughter. "Rayna, you hungry?" No answer came back. *Was she still mad at him or had she just not heard him?* He couldn't help but feel guilty for the way he had handled the situation at her school, but first, like any good soldier, he would complete the task at hand. Deep down inside he acknowledged, as a single dad, that sometimes his emotions got the best of him. He was, after all, only human.

★★★★

Vincent rounded the corner at the end of Rayna's street. He had made his temporary escape from the Horseman and now sought solace. Rayna seemed like just the person he could talk to. Despite his outburst at school, he knew she didn't think he was crazy, like even his best of friends did. He needed to talk to her before it was too late. Things were already quickly getting out of hand in his mind, so he needed to bounce everything off her. At the very least, he needed to apologize for his previous actions.

A lot of the houses here looked the same. Every other one a gray or blue with white trim. Either that or boxy and plain white.

Bedford Falls came to mind as Vincent surveyed the area. He knew she lived on this block, but couldn't remember just quite where. He was counting on some dumb luck. *Bingo!* The police cruiser was a dead giveaway as to which was her house. It also meant her father was home, so he'd have to be extremely careful. The rebel inside him was up for the challenge. He headed straight for Rayna's house, where he scampered up a tree and onto the ledge near her window. He paused for a brief moment, then softly rapped on the windowpane.

★★★★

Rayna had moved on to some 80s pop-up videos she had heard about online. She couldn't believe people used to dress like that. *My God the hair!* The synthy pop was contagious, however, and she felt herself lost in the rhythm of the night. She was completely oblivious to any sound from Vincent or otherwise. Right now, her heart belonged to that silver-tongued, red haired demon, the front man for Oingo Boingo. By his own admission, he liked little girls anyway.

★★★★

Constance had just finished making his sandwich when he thought he had heard something. His mind immediately went to "The Raven" by Edgar Allan Poe, as it was indeed the faint sound of Vincent rapping on the window that he had heard. Constance walked toward the door to investigate, the tapping sounds getting louder. He opened the front door and listened alertly. The night was dead silent, like after a fresh coat of snow had fallen to cushion any reverberation. The stillness was sharp and almost painful. He looked around, waiting for the noise to start again. He could have sworn he heard something, or had he only imagined it?

Above him, Rayna closed her bedroom window just before her father looked up. Luckily for the teens he hadn't noticed, but his

155

intuitive policing skills told him something was off. Shrugging it off for now, he headed back indoors, happy to escape the now chilly clime.

★★★★

Rayna had finally taken notice and, after a brief moment of panic at the sight of peering eyes, opened her window just in the nick of time. She saw Vincent, sweaty and panicked, and immediately hugged him after reeling him into her room. She was too sweet and naturally maternal to give in to her former anger at him. After a quick embrace, she made a face. The smoky smell of his clothes was overpowering.

"What are you doing here? If my dad sees you, he will kill you!"

Vincent sucked in air, finally able to catch his breath. The full weight of the events that had unfolded dawned on him all at once, like an oversized wrecking ball. His heart sank and his shoulders slumped. Tears streamed down his cheeks, her clemency acting as the final straw. Then the panic switch flipped back on.

"He's after me. I saw him!"

"I know he's after you. He told me I couldn't see you again. He probably has his police buddies looking for you across all of Westchester County by now. This is the last place you should have come."

Vincent looked down, suddenly too self-conscious to explain.

Rayna followed his gaze and noticed the gash in his knee. "Oh my God, what happened to you? You're bleeding."

Vincent had to tell her, no matter what she thought. It was why he came here, after all. "No, not your father; the Horseman. He's real, Rayna. There was a fire. That old lady is dead. He was chasing me!"

Before she could respond, there was a swift knock at the door. "Rayna, you awake honey?" came her father's voice from the other side of the door. There was a brief scramble in the silence that followed. Constance knocked a second time, but didn't wait for a response before entering his daughter's bedroom.

"Hey, why didn't you answer me?" he softly chided before catching himself.

"I'm sorry, Dad. I was listening to my music. Or more like your music, I should say." She showed him the screen on the device as a distraction, trying to buy precious time.

"Nice. Elfman and Bartek. Classic." He smiled. He liked where this new line of communication was headed. He knelt beside her bed to plead his case. He didn't realize it consciously, but he was using the same logic someone uses when approaching an aggressive animal. Make yourself smaller, get down on their level and extend the olive branch. "You're still mad with me about today, aren't you?"

She wasn't really that mad at him. She had realized long ago he was just doing his fatherly duties, and sometimes, as was the current case with Vincent, his actual police duties overlapped with them. This was one such time and was completely forgivable and understandable. But that by no means meant she couldn't milk a few daughter sympathy points out of dear old dad. She gave him a brief stink eye, but couldn't keep the ruse up much longer. Besides, she needed to get him out of the room. Unbeknownst to him, a panicked Vincent was squeezed under the bed, mere inches from the genuflecting police officer.

Constance cut her off before she could think of a witty enough response to get him to leave. "Someday, you'll realize how hard—" he began.

Rayna cut him back off in return, parrying like an expert swordsman, trying everything in her arsenal to get rid of her doting dad. "No, Dad, I'm fine. But he's really not a bad guy, you know." She couldn't resist jabbing in the plea for her future love interest.

Under the bed, Vincent took long, deep breaths. He became extremely conscious of the rise and fall of his chest, and he could swear his slow swallows of saliva were deafening. Even the slightest move could be capable of alerting the deputy. From where he was lying on his back, the kneeling officer's gun barrel was coincidentally aimed right at him. It didn't help the panic attack that was about to set in. To make matters worse, Vincent now realized that small but noticeable drops of blood from his wound had pooled right where Rayna's father was currently kneeling. He prayed to God above they didn't soil his uniform, or worse, that the deputy wouldn't notice the bodily fluid in real time.

"Look, I really am sorry, but you need to trust me on some things. I just want what's best for you." Constance had an apparent realization and began to sniff around. "What's that smell? Lorraine, have you been smoking in here?" He started to shift his weight to rise up off of one knee.

Rayna quickly put a hand on her father's shoulder, causing him to stay in the same position. "Ewww. Dad, no. Gross."

The officer was skeptical at first, but saw no evidence that betrayed her. Her untarnished record caused him to believe her. Plus, their talk was going too well to ruin it with baseless accusations. Then she leaned in for the kill with soulful puppy dog-eyes as big as saucers.

"Dad, you really need to trust me on some things too."

Touché. Right for the heartstrings. He couldn't argue with that, and was actually quite impressed with her timing. This prompted a smile from him. "Okay, sweety. You hungry?" He rose up to leave.

Rayna shook her head no as he kissed her forehead.

"Okay, honey, have a good night. And try not to stay up too late. That thing's bad for your eyes."

She shot him a supercilious look, by which he knew winning the battle was more important than winning the war at this particular juncture. He smiled again and shut the door behind him.

Rayna jumped up and gave it five seconds in case her father decided to return before she promptly double locked the door. She proceeded to help Vincent to his feet and tried to lighten up the situation.

"We really need to get a bell on that door," she said with a laugh.

The impeccable flashback humor was just what the doctor ordered. Vincent let out a deep sigh and even smirked a little to himself. Once again, she was winning him over with her angelic charm. Having diffused the tension, a look of concern again came over her face.

Vincent took notice and tried to address his previous comments the best way that he could. "Look, I'm really sorry about how I acted at school. There's no excuse for it. But you've got to believe me," he implored.

Her face showed sympathy, and her eyes began to water. "I want to. I really do. But you need to let the cops handle this."

Vince remained silent.

"Look at me, Vince." She pulled his chin toward her so his eyes met her glance. The charismatic aura she gave off was almost unbearable, like staring at a demigod. "I know what it's like to feel alone, but you need to let other people help you." She paused, then sincerely and softly said, :You can trust me.

Vincent finally gave in to his emotions and sobbed. The weight of his stress caused his body to convulse in heavy, weeping contractions. His face contorted into the lachrymose frowns of a deeply wounded boy. Rayna's feminine instincts kicked in and she held him gently, caressing his hair as he cried it out. Vincent could actually feel her heart beating next to his. It was uplifting, spiritual and intimate. After a brief moment of eye contact, they shared a deep kiss. After another pause, came a final reconciliation. She smiled, he reciprocated.

After several moments of reeling from their emotional outburst, Rayna's survival instinct kicked in. They were clearly pressing their luck. "You'd better leave before my dad decides to check in on me again.

Vincent stood to go, knowing she was right. He paused, only for a moment, then asked, "Will you help me get to the bottom of this before someone gets hurt?"

"Of course," she said without hesitation. "You should know by now, I would do just about anything for you." She pondered a moment. "But promise me one thing, first." She was a master negotiator, even if she hadn't realized it yet.

"What?" Vincent said, more curtly than it had sounded in his mind.

"You'll talk to my dad—"

Vincent's head mechanically shook from side to side before she could even get the rest out.

"—or at least to the sheriff," she concluded.

Vincent weighed his options. On one hand, he had just shared the most passionate moment of his life with the one person he knew he could trust. On the other, turning himself into the authorities was surely a death sentence. He wasn't sure how to respond, but he knew his time was running out like a countdown on *Jeopardy!*

"Running just makes you look guilty," Rayna continued, unexpectedly giving him a moment's respite from the line of fire. "Besides, I want my dad to like you."

Oh, that did it. She was good, real good. The implication of having her dad like him was more lethal ammunition than his powerless mind could combat. Once again, she was victorious: two for two tonight.

"Okay, I promise. But right now, I'm pushing my luck. The Horseman is targeting my family. I have to check on my mom. I'll explain it all to you later, and I'll talk to the cops first thing tomorrow, okay?

She nodded, not fully understanding but slowly coming around to believing him. Or at least, believing he believed wholeheartedly in his own revelations. "Tomorrow?" was all she could get out.

"What about tomorrow?"

"Dutch Down-Home Days. It's Halloween. I thought that you and I…"

Vincent's mind raced. *A dance is all she can think of? Wait, the dance. That's perfect. That means skipping school, and the authorities will be distracted*, his inner voice rattled off. This would buy Vincent some extremely needed planning and recuperation time. He wasn't about to look a gift horse, or Horseman, in the mouth.

"Not even the Horseman could keep me away," whispered Vincent, almost seductively. *Damn that was smooth*. Vincent couldn't believe he had said it like that. Valentino himself couldn't have managed a better delivery.

With that proverbial mic drop, he leaned in for one last sweet kiss on her forehead, then effortlessly scaled the windowpane.

Enamored, but a bit confused and worried, Rayna waved goodbye to her peculiar version of an unconventional and most unlikely Romeo.

Chapter 22

Vincent was experiencing an existential crisis of teenaged proportions.

He seemed to glide along aimlessly, as if following a more frantic version of himself that was somehow tethered to him. Sometimes he occupied the lead body, and sometimes the follow body occupied him. It was hard to keep them apart, nor was he sure he had even wanted to.

The follow body was more serene. It was caught up in the feeling he had gotten in the pit of his stomach as he felt Rayna's warm tongue search out the insides of his lips. It thought of the true inner peace he had felt in his very soul as the warmth of her bosom had embraced him so maternally. It thought of a future without consequence, of happiness and the potential to dream. It drifted along about a meter above the ground, plotting how to shear the imaginary bind that kept it shackled to the other Vincent.

The other Vincent was panicked and frantic. It stutter-stepped and tripped over doghouses and yard sprinklers. It stumbled through yards and back alleys and bounced off of trash cans. And it was afraid; very afraid. Paranoid, sweating profusely, eyes bulging, he nervously looked around every corner. An inventory of questions suddenly bombarded the lead body much faster than its racing mind could answer them. The foremost among them, *Was the Horseman real or imagined?* It had certainly seemed real when it attacked him and killed that woman, and that farmhouse certainly hadn't set itself on fire. *And who or what the fuck was she anyway?* She seemed extremely knowledgeable, encyclopedic almost. *But how did she know what he'd ask about, and how the fuck did she know who he was? And what was that nonsense about his father?*

Vincent had never known his father, nor had he cared to. All he could remember of the old man was a brief incident in which young Vincent had accidentally sprayed him with a water hose. He had gotten slapped in the ear so hard by the tyrant, his ear bleed, and he had permanent tinnitus in that ear from that day forward. Everything else, Vincent's mind had selectively forgotten.

Why was the Horseman chasing him of all people? He had been infatuated with the Legend and imagined himself as the Horseman back when other kids had been playing with *Star Wars* figures and Xboxes. If anything, the Hessian should have known Vincent was an ally, not an enemy.

Then he heard it. The whinnying war cry of the Horseman's Hellsteed. Once again, he was off to the races. It was clear whomever, or whatever, this thing was it had no need for a fandom or friends. It was out for blood, and for some reason it wanted Vincent's.

He ran, catching glimpses of the mounted apparition between trees and houses. Its athletic ability was such that it seemed to be toying with the youth, only taking large strides to intimidate. Circling and pinning its prey in, like some demented Australian sheep dog herding cattle. That's exactly what Vince had felt like his entire life—cattle. So why should he expect this escapade to be any different. Well, cattle he might be, but sheep he was not. Besides, last time he checked, some cattle had horns. *All the better to fuck you up with, my pretty*, came an inner voice Vincent hadn't heard before. He liked it. No, he embraced it. *Wanna play, motherfucker?* "Then let's play!"

Finally near his house, he only had another fifty-yard dash to make it to his porch. He was close enough to see that his Jacks's truck was gone. She was probably out fucking that asshole somewhere. *Had this bitch no shame? Home fucking sweet home.* He stooped behind a gnarled tree trunk. The ashen white bark bit into his cheek. A small trickle of blood came down, which reminded him that he hadn't thought about his knee since he left Rayna's. He looked down and noticed it festering. All of sudden, the pain seared back, like a piece of bacon hitting a cast iron skillet. The epinephrine was coming in waves as it subsided the pain temporarily. He just needed to keep the sharp jolts off his mind. He tried to muster the courage to make a run for it, but his balls weren't quite as big as his mouth had been. He might as well have been about to dodge bullets from a clock tower sniper given the amount of adrenaline coursing through his veins.

Finally, he sucked it up and made a mad dash for it.

In the middle of the street, the giant lifted pickup truck of Mack & Saunders turned on its lights and revved the engine like Stephen King's *Christine* on a joy ride. If there was one person, fictional or not, Vincent could completely relate to right now, it was Arnie Cunningham.

For a brief moment, the shock had Vincent stone-cold still in the street like a deer in the headlights. His eyes honed in on the monster Terra tires peeling out. The vibrations they made cutting rubber into asphalt sent shivers down his spine. He could practically smell the pungent singe of melting petroleum in his mind's eye. It burned his nose, even if he was only imagining it.

Billy Bob Greenfield slammed the accelerator forward while the others, in the back of the pickup, hooted and hollered, beer bottles in hand.

Vincent made a run for it as the truck lurched forward. *Game on, bitch!* He could practically read the vehicle's mechanical mind.

He made it to the porch just in the nick of time. The front tires of the vehicle barked over the curb and shredded part of the yard into a muddy goulash. Vincent managed to trip on one of the loose boards of the steps. He landed squarely on the wounded knee, getting a porcupine's quill worth of wood splinters for his troubles.

So this was what was meant by salt in the wound. Thank God the door wasn't locked. As Vincent ducked inside onto the floor, he slammed the door shut behind him. Saunders had chucked a beer bottle with laser-like precision. He might not have gotten either of those Division I pitching scholarships from Binghamton Bearcats or the Fordham Rams like he had hoped, but that shit was right on the mark. The bottle slammed against the front door, shattering into tiny shards like the Death Star. A small, decorative windowpane on the door also shattered in a seawall of stale beer foam. Had it been under different circumstances, it might have been beautiful to see through a high-speed shuttered lens.

Vincent breathed heavily, his face now firmly planted on the floor. Add rug burn to the list and who knows what foul bacteria. He could hear the drunken boys as they peeled away and screamed obscenities at their victim. Vincent was simply glad to be home. He would deal with those assholes later.

He righted himself off the floor. As far as he knew, the Horseman was still after him. Maybe he would chase after those fucks instead, but doubtful. He went to the nearby coat closet and grabbed a Louisville Slugger, which had been propped up inside it next to some winter coats, boots and umbrellas. His mom had always kept it there for the times when strange men followed her home. It worked wonderfully to threaten bill collectors, Jehovah's Witnesses even the occasional cookie-selling girl scout, he had later found out. Now, bat up, elbow out in a stance that would have made Babe Ruth proud, he cautiously moved toward the front door.

Outside, shadows of the Horseman and his Hellsteed circled the house. The predatory silhouette bounced through small openings in the window blinds and doors and made an eerie shadow puppet show on the walls inside. It was like an extremely erratic cucoloris from a low-budget high school theater production.

The sounds and images seem to be coming from different, sometimes opposing, directions. The frightening part was that both seemed to be simultaneously nowhere and everywhere. Vincent felt like someone on a bad acid trip in a funhouse full of mirrors. *Why hadn't it chased Mack and the guys? If this had been some morality play of a horror film, they certainly were the perfect of fodder, no?* His thoughts were racing again. In his mind, he was final girl material all the way.

Vincent stood with bat at the ready, resolved that he may die, but that he would go down fighting.

The unmistakable drum of a horse's hooves approached, pounding just outside the door. The methodic clip–clop was menacing, like the metronome of a Hammer film score. The snort of the horse sent shivers through Vincent's very core, a chill raking over his bones from the inside, then outward.

The door broke wide open and in a flurry of activity. Vincent closed his eyes and swung for the cheap seats with all his might. He lunged his entire body's weight off-balance from his bad leg. He connected with maximum brute force, letting out a primal scream as he did.

Wood cracked bone with a resounding thud. The wet noise that immediately followed was stomach churning. A tall figure tumbled to a heap on the floor.

As Vincent opened his eyes, he saw a paper bag filled with cheap whiskey bottles and junk food smashed on the floor. Brown whiskey from the broken bottles elegantly swirled in mini whirlpools of blood. A fine peppering of bright orange Doritos nacho cheese powdered the shiny, tiny rainbows of alcohol as it formed wispy curls in the blood oozing from the base of Jack's skull. It was quite beautiful. It was morbid, yet colorful. It was final.

★★★★

Holy Shit! That had really happened. Vincent sat in a corner hyperventilating. *Where's Mom? Where the fuck was Mom?! Calm*

166

down, Vincent. Think. Fucking think! He did. He slowly tried to piece things together in his mind. *Okay, I'm definitely home, and that definitely is…. was… Jack.* Vincent rocked back and forth, still cradling the bloodied bat in his hand. Dried blood and matted hair eclipsed the dark letters emblazoned onto the burnt wood, so a bold, black **SLUG** starred back at him. A blueish-gray substance like hamburger meat had started to ooze out of the crack on the top of Jack's skull.

Taco Tuesday! It was Tuesday. Marisa was being taught hearts by a bunch of elderly ladies at a local hospice care home. Visiting them every other week was the one good thing that kept Vincent from knowing she wasn't pure evil. Sometimes, she even spent the night there if a patient was borderline about to die. With any luck, one would die tonight.

Vincent needed to know what time it was. He figured he had at least an hour, maybe more. He skipped awkwardly to his room, almost in a gallop. His knee absorbed the shots of pain as he raced for more medication. Not the kind for the scrape, the good kind. He rallied into the bathroom and emptied half of one bottle and a third of another into his pocket. He was going to need all the help he could get in order to pull this off. He picked up two pills that had fallen onto the rust-stained drain and dry swallowed them. *Thank God.* Now, back to the task at hand—Jack.

Vincent waded through the discarded underwear and alcohol bottles in his mom's bedroom to get to her personal bathroom. Now he knew where he got it from; the room was a sty. It smelled like sex; bad, disgusting sex like in the back alley of the Tenderloin. The giant dildo and half-used box of condoms wasn't helping his mental imagery any. The mop and bucket were in her bathtub, neither of which had been used in quite a long time. The bucket had a thick layer of brown, flakey dust and a multitude of tiny spiderwebs on it. He dumped it out, which formed a dust cloud that looked like Swiss cocoa mix, mini-marshmallows and all. The mop was so hard that it stood on its own in an upward, crispy curl. It made Vincent think first of Wendy Lou Who and then of Ben Stiller's character in *There's Something About Mary*. He couldn't believe his ADHD had gone to comedy films at a time like this. *Goddammit, focus! Jesus Christ, there's a dead man in the living room, Vincent!* That sobered him up quickly. He opened the faucet and murky, rusty water spurted out with tiny blasts of putrid air. He wondered if the inventors of the E-Z-Mop had imagined it being used to clean up syrupy blood, bone chips and brain matter. He was betting at least one of them had. The water sloshed around like swamp water from planet Dagobah.

He reluctantly passed one more time though the bedroom. His mother's ass cheeks had left imprints on the satin sheets. *Gross. They were disgusting humans and Jack deserved to die.* He couldn't believe he had just thought it, but also couldn't deny to himself that it was true. "No. He was a prick, but no one deserves to die. Keep calm and carry on, Vince," he said out loud as he dragged the mop and bucket toward the corpse. He kept trying to rationalize Jack's death in his head. But if he was completely innocent, why was he trying to clean up evidence? He debated back and forth, until he got back to the entranceway and Jack's body served as a stark wake-up call. *This was real. This was murder.*

He could forget about Rayna. Accosting Constance's daughter was one thing, killing a man, even if he was a complete douche who was fucking your mother, was another one completely. *No! It was an accident, right?* Now, more than ever, he had to prove to them the Horseman was real and that he was after Vincent. *Perhaps he was after all of them!*

Vincent propped up Jack against the wall like an extremely large, heavy rag doll. His head swiveled unnaturally backward on his neck like a Pez dispenser and hit the wall with a sickening whack. More ooze got flecked around. Vincent tried to hold back the gag reflexes that were coming in waves, but the smell was too strong and the sight repulsive. Vince vomited over the corpse's head. My god, this was an actual living nightmare. He wondered what kind of karma he and Jack had in a past life to deserve to be in this situation.

After finally composing himself, Vincent wrapped one of Jack's old Ed Hardy T-shirts around the top of the dead man's head to keep the rest of his brain from leaking out. He didn't want the top of his cranium flapping around like that one skeleton guy he remembered hilariously mixing potions in the *Corpse Bride*. He dunked the mop and got to work, sloshing around dust bunnies, dirty water and gray matter into a primordial soup. It was mostly dark, as Vincent was afraid to turn on the lights. Right now, a visit from prying eyes, much less the Horseman himself, could prove to be fatal, both metaphorically and literally. Vincent continued the task robotically, Jack's cadaver smiling up at him with a permanently frozen grin the entire time.

★★★★

In the backyard, he watched his tethered self drag the body by the armpits, then throw it in a small gulch and cover it in a shallow grave. He watched as it poured the viscous mixture of bathwater and brains on top of it, and he watched as it absentmindedly flung the bat far off into the nearby woods. Maybe there was a case to be made that Vincent hadn't done any of these things at all. He certainly didn't feel like the Entity that was doing it. And if he was, how was it he was able to so easily watch himself from afar?

He could still smell the stench of the Van Tassel fire on his clothes and looked down at the frayed edges of the rip in his jeans. *A change of clothes was in order,* one of the Vincent's thought. He couldn't tell which, as the line between them was getting progressively blurred. After being completely immersed in what he had been doing, he had forgotten about everything except the task at hand of hiding the body. It was only temporary anyway, until he could exonerate himself.

He walked back toward the house with the intent of changing clothes before going on the lamb. That was when the weight of his actions settled in on his shoulders. He bent down in a genuflecting position. The full weight of his body on top of his injured knee, coupled with the gravity of the situation, made it difficult for him to stand. Suddenly, he got the feeling he was being watched.

As Vincent slowly rose, he puffed his chest as large as it would expand. Something he had learned in Boy Scouts about facing mountain lions had decided to make its awkward appearance now. His eyes racked focus to just a mere twenty yards away. Near the tree line of Vincent's property sat the Horseman high up in his saddle. His gloved hands grasped the leather of the reins tightly. Vincent didn't quite understand how, but he heard the audible gripping sound it made as the fingers pursed together. Even the Hellsteed looked straight at Vincent. Neither made a sound nor moved a muscle, save the steady breathing and methodical ebb and flow of the animal's massive torso. The fleshy filet of the animal's meaty chest muscles was flicking involuntarily.

Was this some sort of other dimensionally nervous tick, or a warning that it was about to spring into action?

Vincent slowly started to back away, as he had no intention of waiting around to find out. The Horseman made no notion to pursue, but remained steadily, silently and perfectly poised high up in his lofty saddle.

How did it seem as if it could stare daggers at him like that, even without a head? It was unfathomable.

Vincent gathered his senses before he set off in a flash. He ran as fast as his legs could carry him. Even his injury could not keep him from imitating an Olympic gold medalist. If only he had been this athletic in PE class, he might have passed. His mind hadn't even had time to calculate a path or a step, he simply bolted past the tree line and off into the dead of night.

The Horseman remained. The steady breathing of the Hellsteed blew rhythmic puffs of mist into the still of the brisk night. It was as if it was making the only sound for miles. A small gust of wind blew a leaf off of Jack's dormant corpse, exposing a mere glimpse of the white of his one remaining and unmutilated eye. It starred up at the Horseman, but unlike Vincent, it couldn't see a thing. It was the blind seeing the blind.

Chapter 23

The next morning, birds chirped, the sun rose over moss-draped and disfigured driftwood, and yet another day began in the quaint village.

A Northern Oriole landed atop a vibrant jack-o'-lantern. It was unseasonably still in residence, as most had already flown to South America for the winter. Perhaps the male was attracted to the bright orange of the pumpkin's shiny skin, upon which it had alighted. The pumpkin had a shocked look carved onto its face. Stringy pumpkin seed "guts" spewing from its mouth made it look as if it had vomited. The oriole fed on the rotting seeds in the morning sun, crunching its potential mate's innards like some type of cannibalistic love ritual akin to that of the Praying Mantis. It was the perfect metaphor for the evil that had now made itself at home among the town's unsuspecting inhabitants.

Not much bigger than the one in fictional Mayberry, the tiny combination office and holding cells of the sheriff's office was all the small town needed, or so it had thought. A smattering of Halloween decorations adorned the walls and cabinets throughout the confined space. It was all Geraldine, the single secretary and dispatcher, had managed before her maternity leave. Eustice couldn't remember a time when she wasn't knocked up, and told her as much, which promptly lead to her bargaining for an additional two weeks in lieu of a sexual harassment complaint. He had granted it, not knowing if she was joking or not, and hence she had left Eustice and Constance alone for what was traditionally the village's busiest night of the year: All Hollows' Eve.

Sheriff Eustice had his feet propped up on the desk while he read the morning paper. The only local headline noted that the Van Tassel fire would eventually be investigated as arson, but that probably wouldn't happen for at least a week. Eustice just didn't have the resources, and in another stellar policing decision, he had decided he wanted the holiday to pass first before raising any alarm bells. He would send Constance out late that day to cordon off the debris at the former manor site, but figured it was far enough on the outskirts of town not to mandate any immediate surveillance. Besides, if history was correct, any potential vandals would be causing mischief at the Dutch Down-Home Days festivities. He didn't believe it was arson anyway, as that old lady's house was a virtual rat's nest of flammables waiting to go up in the first place. He was simply surprised it hadn't happened sooner and genuinely surprised she had managed to live as long as she did.

Deputy Constance walked in with a box of beautifully decorated Halloween cookies and some coffee. Tiny frosted jack-o'-lanterns, skeletons, and of course, Horsemen, jostled around the confines of their diabetic shock-inducing box. Constance threw it on the desk near the sheriff's feet. "It's the most wonderful time of the year," he sang off key to the tune of the familiar Christmas carol. "Breakfast, boss."

Eustice looked up from the paper and then composed himself, swinging his legs off his desk. "Cookies? Seriously?"

"It's all Von Landshort's had this early in the day, so it was either that or donuts, and I figured despite minding your girlish figure, even you wouldn't want to be associated with that stereotype." Constance sat down, grabbed a cookie and bit the head of an unsuspecting bat, Ozzy Osborne style. He had gotten away with the weight jab, but it hadn't gone unnoticed.

The cops had just started to settle in, and Eustice was about to go over the plan for the busy day ahead of them, when Marisa Douglass barreled through the door. Constance was so surprised, he spilt his coffee onto the khaki pants leg of his uniform and almost went for his gun. A wet brown blotch now stained his crotch like a Rorschach test. Eustice remained undeterred from his seasonal pastry consumption.

"Sheriff, I want to file a missing person report," she said, frantic.

This wasn't atypical for her when she was worked up in a state, so neither Eustice nor his comrade sensed anything immediately unusual right out the gate. Nor was it unusual in a prank-susceptible town on Halloween.

"Please have a seat, Marisa, and calm down. Donut?" asked Eustice.

"Cookie," corrected Constance, which earned him a side-eye from his superior.

"Two actually, maybe two," she said.

As Eustice reached for two cookies, she took the chair offered her but waved off the confections.

"Two missing persons." She said *dumbass* with her eyes rather than lips. "I still haven't heard from Vince. And now Jack, my boyfriend, is missing. And someone broke into my house. There was broken glass and blood, I think."

Now she had his attention. Eustice sat upright, the chair creaking under the weight of his hulking mass. "What in the hell is going on in this town? I got two deaths in as many days. Old lady burnt so bad she was unrecognizable, and now this?"

Marisa had no reply for the sudden outburst.

"Alright, Constance, give her the paperwork."

Constance dutifully started shuffling through a stack of blank forms as the sheriff returned his attention to Marisa. "When's the last time you saw him?"

"Which one?" came her curt reply. Unlike Vincent, it came out sounding exactly as she had intended it.

"Vincent. I don't care about the other guy," said Eustice as he stuffed a cookie in one mouth while fumbling a pen into his free hand, preparing to take notes.

Disbelief registered across her face. Constance knitted his brow, giving Eustice the clue to have more bedside manner.

The sheriff realized his flub. "What I meant to say, Ms. Douglass, is that your son is of particular interest to us." Now he had become the one batting a thousand.

Constance intentionally pivoted his chair to avoid seeing her reaction.

"It's important that I talk to him, 'Ris," Eustice said in a more humane tone.

The sheriff's eyes met hers dead-on and serious. He may not have had the most couth, but it was clear he was trying to help, for once. Marisa looked at his earnest expression, then her eyes darted toward the ceiling as she began to backtrack in her mind. She had been too drunk to remember her son walking in on one of her many acts of fornication, and the police themselves had asked his whereabouts just that day. *Had it been that long since she saw or spoke with him?* She still couldn't think of a clear answer to the sheriff's query.

"Did they ever fight? I mean the two of them. Did they get along?" asked Constance as his mind played out potential scenarios.

"I mean, I wouldn't say they were in love with each other, but they had no more animosity than typical brothers," Marisa said.

The two officers exchanged an incredulous look, both at the thought of zero grudges between the two and also the fact she referred to her son and lover as brothers.

BAM! The door flew open so hard, it nearly cracked at the hinges. Vincent, looking haggard and disheveled from stress and lack of sleep, burst in. His clothes from the previous night were dirty and torn, with a small evidence of blood. He still faintly smelled of the kerosene fire. "You guys are all in danger!" he yelled.

Apparently, Vincent's pills had worn off. Either that or they were having a doubling effect. He obviously had not watched enough episodes of *Cops* to understand that police officers didn't appreciate being taken off guard, especially while in the midst of an interrogation, or worse, morning coffee rituals.

In one fluid movement, Constance put down his coffee and pinned Vincent against the wall. His actions were smooth, calculated, and methodical from muscle memory. His time in the service would allow for no slip ups, nor spilt coffee, while he was in this mode. His police baton had Vincent in a powerful chokehold against the wall. It was a lightning fast reaction that gave Constance the literal upper hand.

The sheriff rose to his feet as Marisa let out an alarmed yelp.

"You touch my daughter again, I'll—"

"Constance!" The sheriff had his oven-mitt sized paw clamped down on the deputy's shoulder. He pushed his thumb into Constance's brachial nerve, exerting just enough pressure to keep a commanding physical control over the altercation. He easily outweighed Constance by a hundred pounds. It was like a mother cat clamping down on its kitten by the scruff of the neck. "Let him go," he barked.

Constance released the boy, who clasped his throat with both hands. Vincent, looking every bit a child for once, struggled to suck in gulps of air. Marisa ran over to him, checking him for abrasions and bruises like only a concerned mother could do. Even the most deadbeat of mothers wouldn't have failed to react to such a spectacle. The two police officers remained in a standoff, neither quite satisfied with the outcome thus far.

Finally, Vincent was able to get some words out. Of all the things he had to say, for some reason the need to explain himself to Rayna's father took precedence. "I never touched her. I.. I like her. A lot."

"You stay away from her. Not one more fucking word out of you." It was unusual for Constance to lose his cool, but these were extenuating circumstances.

Unexpectedly, Eustice was the one who became the voice of reason. "Sit down, Michael." It was extremely rare for him to call Constance by his first name. Next, he turned his intentions to Marisa, using the width of his shoulders to physically get between the parties. Utilizing the girth of his body as a deterrent was a tactic he'd learned in wrestling that had come in handy the few times in his career in volatile situations, like this one. "Marisa, we are going to have to ask you to leave so we can question your son."

The tension in the room seemed tangible, and this comment from Eustice sucked the air out of the room.

Marisa's eyes turned downward, momentarily deflated. Then, like a balloon pop, she ramped up her agitation again, this time full throttle. "Shove it, Van Wart. I'm not going anywhere! Especially after that." There was fire in her eyes now. Even the mountain of a man couldn't ignore it.

"Okay, okay. Fine. Let's all sit down and talk this out." He pulled another chair around the desk. Constance, still visibly steaming, cuffed Vincent to the chair. Vincent looked like a wet cat pulled from a bathtub. Marisa wore her disapproval openly. Like four bleeding alley cats after a knock-down, drag-out fight, none of them were eager to spar again just yet.

"First of all, son," the sheriff began, "I want you to tell us everything you know. Don't leave out any detail, no matter how trivial you might think it is." He leaned in closer, giving the agitated youth his full attention. It would have been nerve-racking even for the hardest of criminals.

"There was fire."

The distrust came immediately. It was as if a gun had gone off in the tiny room.

"What do you know about that fire?" Eustice wasn't wasting time with any more cordialness.

"Look, if you're going to sit there all accusatory, I'm not saying anything," came Vincent's brash and unexpected reply.

Eustice stared daggers at him. Constance's muscles were flexing involuntarily, like a rabid pit bull. Marisa remained quiet. Her mind was racing, trying to put any clues together. She felt completely helpless and actually wanted to know the answer to this line of questioning herself.

"I know because I was there."

Constance stood up. Vincent obviously just majorly implicated himself. "Alright, I've heard about enough. We're taking him into custody." The deputy strong-armed Vincent, manhandling him out of the chair and into a standing position. As Vincent's hands were re-cuffed behind his back, Marisa protested vehemently.

The sheriff was in complete agreement with Constance on this one. "Marisa, til we can sort this out, I'm afraid I'm gonna have to ask you to leave."

"It's the Horseman. He's real," Vincent insisted, nearly frothing at the mouth.

"Enough! Call Paulding for a psych evaluation," the sheriff ordered. "No, better yet, I want a second opinion. Someone new. Call county."

Vince was locked in a cell, where he sobbed from exhaustion and frustration.

Marisa bolted past the officers. Constance tried to restrain her, but she managed to grab the bars of the cell and refused to let go. Vince and his mom were now face-to-face, only the cold steel bars separating them.

"Mom, why don't you ever talk about my father?"

His question shocked her. *Where was this coming from?* "What? What are you... I told you he—"

Constance now had his hands in a bear hug around her waist. The wind was getting knocked out of her, but she hung on for dear life. "Vincent!"

Tears started to flow on both sides of the bars now.

"Constance, let go of her," ordered the sheriff over the chaos.

She reflexively back-kicked the deputy through his spread legs, hitting his ass instead of the intended target, of his testicles. By doing so, she added assault to her long litany of offenses.

Vincent looked her dead in the eyes. "Don't lie to me. I want his real fucking name." Vincent looked her dead in the eyes. He wasn't playing.

Marisa, gobsmacked, was unwilling to divulge the information.

"I swear to God, Mom, tell me my father's real name!"

His accusatory tone hit her like a sack of cement. She doubled over, only managing to keep one of her hands tightly clamped to the caged bars. Constance wrestled one hand across her back and snaked his other arm behind her, trying to break her seemingly supernatural grip.

Eustice now stood behind the two, using his power to separate the woman from her child. "Goddammit, Marisa, I've had about enough of this shit! If you don't leave now, I will arrest you! Don't make me do that."

Constance finally gained control and begin to drag her back.

Marisa could tell by the look in his eyes that if she didn't answer her son truthfully, it would do irreparable damage to their already fragile relationship. "It's... Acker," she managed before Constance bunny-hopped her toward the door in a sideways suplex.

"I knew it! All these years, you lied to me." Hatred spewed from Vincent's mouth.

"I'm sorry, honey. I'm so sorry. I never meant to hurt you. Your real father was horrible. I was trying to protect you."

Constance continued bum-rushing Marisa toward the door.

"I want my lawyer here," screamed Marisa over Constance's shoulder. "Vincent, don't say anything else. Not a word more." She was seething as she said, "And don't you dare touch him," directly into the deputy's face.

Her spittle and hot breath made him question his life choices.

Unable to control himself, Vincent blurted out, "The Horseman killed the librarian and Lady Van Tassel and all of you are next. Don't you understand? You're all in danger." Something in his mind had been jarred loose by his mother's confession, and it was all coming out now. Everything was on Front Street.

"Vincent, shut up," she pleaded as Constance pushed her through the doorway and bolted the door.

Constance could still see her through the glass in the door. It was one of the times he had wished they had blinds on it to shelter them from being a fishbowl to the outside public. She hit the glass so hard, had it been tempered it would have shattered into a million tiny pieces. Instead, a single hairline crack appeared across it, and Marisa's knuckle went unnaturally flat. She used her good hand to dial someone on her cell. Probably her divorce lawyer. He was the only lawyer she knew and, coincidentally, had also slept with. She normally avoided him all costs, except at desperate times like these.

Vincent continued to break down in his cell, devastated and betrayed, while outside, Marisa paced back and forth like the angry cougar she was.

The beige 80s-era phone on the sheriff's desk rang obnoxiously, startling everyone. Eustice quickly picked it up. "Yeah. What? Where?" He just as quickly hung the phone back up. "Constance, let's go."

He threw the box of cookies into the cell, like a bone to a dog, and they scattered everywhere in an explosion of sprinkled lard icing and holiday décor.

The cops grabbed their coats and rushed out the door.

Marisa, climbed in Jack's old jalopy of a truck—license be damned—peeled out, tires ripping across the pavement as she fishtailed in a blur headed to only God knew where.

"Can't we have just one normal Goddamn Halloween like the rest of the country," Eustice wondered out loud as the two officers boarded the Volare and sped off in the opposite direction.

Clearly, nothing about the day would be normal.

Chapter 24

Marisa rattled the loose frame of the F-250 as she sped away with East Tarrytown in the rearview, and left the sequestered glen westbound via Interstate 287. The salt from snow clean up had rusted out its underbelly over the years, and the tie rods on the old truck had gotten worn down to nubs months ago, leaving the truck to sway from side to side like George Washington's skiff across the Delaware. Like General Washington, she too was trying to escape seemingly unstoppable Hessian forces and was crossing an icy, vast expanse of water.

Marisa had a lot of names—Marisa Adelaide Diane Bakker Acker Douglass. Being raised a Catholic, she had her middle name, assigned at birth, as well as a confirmation name she herself had picked. She received this when she was fourteen years old once she had proven she knew, at least by multiple choice memory, the catechism of the Roman Catholic Church. Marisa was her mother's favorite actress's name, but her parents had high hopes for her, assigning her the middle name Adelaide at birth. Adelaide of Italy had been crowned a regent of the Holy Roman Empire by Pope John XII, and Marisa's parents were hoping some of that piousness would rub off on her. They couldn't have been more wrong.

We all know the stories about Catholic school girls getting fucked out of their parochial school uniforms, all while building up a tolerance to a pack or two of cigs a day. In Marisa's case, the stereotypes were true. There was nothing she loved more than rebelling against her holier-than-though parents, who were lovingly referred to by locals as Ma and Pa Bakker. As far as her other names, they were inherited from her former husbands. Had

Jack stuck around, she would have been his third, but definitely would not have proven to be the charm. She had always just lazily added another name at the courthouse or DMV, as it seemed the simplest thing to do. Delores, the County Recorder, always had some offhand remark every time Marisa stopped by. She might as well have just called her a slut; Marisa knew everyone already thought it.

The freeway snaked around. The entrance to the bridge would be coming up soon. Traffic reports jumbled over the radio. Marisa punched it with her still tender knuckle. The radio swiveled over to a local AM station playing sea shanties. As her knuckle swelled, it made it harder for her to grasp the steering wheel. Somewhere far below her, the Manitou River spirits were colluding with Lorelei's siren song in an attempt to get Marisa's undivided attention.

"Well I thought I heard the old man say, leave her, Johnny, leave her. For the voyage is long and the winds don't blow. And it's time for us to leave her."

Marisa had chosen her confirmation name after Diana degli Andalò for several reasons. She had been instructed to choose a saint's name, as was customary. She also knew that her father had Italian ancestry, as well as Dutch, and he preferred his church and the names associated with it as such. But Marisa impetuously chose the name for two disobedient and defiant reasons. First, she loved the thought that her initials would spell out MAD. She knew that would secretly piss her parents off, and she was right. Technically, though, she had followed the rules of her parents and those of the Church to the letter, so there was little they could protest. Secondly, after being forced to read up on saints to find a name, she found that Diana degli Andalò was rumored to have had a scandalous affair with Jordan of Saxony. Him being a holy man of the cloth, and her being a cloistered nun, that was understandably of extreme taboo, particularly in the thirteenth century. There was no proof, of course, but a series of letters had survived her in death, and it was enough to keep the rumors afloat. Just like Catherine The Great getting off with horses rather than getting on them, the whispers wouldn't die easily. Diane sounded more contemporary than Diana, and so MAD Dog Marisa was born. The moniker stuck all through high school, except for a few close friends who called her Little Ma Bakker. She preferred the former, or Dirty Diana, but all monikers labeled her precisely what she was—a willfully rebellious badass.

"Oh the work was hard and the voyage was long, The sea was high and the gales were strong. Leave her, Johnny, leave her!"

A soft mist enveloped the windshield making it harder to see. The tattered windshield wipers just made smudges across the glass, then screeched back into their seated position, permanently scratching it. They were best just left off. Marisa wondered where it had all gone wrong. She had no business ever having kids in the first place, and she knew it. But sex was her favorite hobby, and she never once had thought of consequences. Getting pregnant with Vincent was no exception. Driving in her current state wasn't either. "Where the fuck are you, Jack?" she yelled at the taillights in front of her. The only release she could have currently was unadulterated road rage. She saw signs for the Tappan Zee bridge and knew soon she could clear her head, as the grayish curls of water often gave her solace. She took the exit directing her toward New Jersey.

Marisa had never intended on having Vince, but his father, John Acker, was such a charismatic playboy. Like Marisa, he too liked to fuck, but hated the stifling feel of condoms. It never took much to persuade her to go bareback. The sex was intense, electrifying, mind-blowing and satisfying. It was the only real reason they were together, as they had absolutely zero in common otherwise.

"We'll pump 'er out and we'll leave 'er dry. Just one suck, oh! And then belay. Leave her Johnny, leave her.

Vincent's father had tried to stick it out. Not out of any real sense of duty, more so than the fact that living with Marisa was relatively easy… until the fighting started. She was a great piece of ass and never said no. The least he could do was try to raise the brat. But troubles started early for the couple. With barely a pot to piss in, an impoverished life didn't lend itself to boozing and gambling. John had even suggested that Marisa should start hooking to support his habits, all while having other girlfriends of his own on the side. It was the beginning of the end. She could deal with the infidelities—Hell, even her Bible-toting father had been guilty of those transgressions—but John had been the first man she had actually started to love.

Vincent's disabilities were especially trying. He had been a colicky baby and a rambunctious toddler, crying, breaking things, beating anything or anyone he came into contact with, and had uncontrollable mood swings that were often unbearable. All the drugs and alcohol she did while pregnant most likely exacerbated his condition. She often felt alone in parenting, and was constantly paranoid about Vincent having an episode or how John would react to it. There were many times she herself had wanted to beat the child, but even she couldn't bring herself to do it. John, on the other hand, had no qualms about smacking the kid around, and he made it clear he wasn't patient enough to stick around until Vincent's teenage years. He turned to local watering holes and the solace of "fat-assed hussies" to ease his mind, many of whom were within Marisa's circle of friends. The honeymoon was over, but there would be no love lost between them.

**"It's pump or drown, the old man said, It's pump ye whores or
we'll all be dead.
And it's time for us to leave her."**

The inciting incident had been the only one Vincent could remember vividly; one of his first memories as a child, and the only memory of his birth father. Vincent was a toddler but had remained mute, refusing to speak. It had been the first sign something was wrong with him. John and Marisa had neither the means nor the inclination to seek the professional medical help they probably needed for the infant. Vincent, unattended and barely old enough to move about, had discovered the magic of the water hose while his father had been day drinking on a lawn chair. John had been several bottles of malt liquor in when Vincent hosed down his drunken father at the most imperfect time whilst he was lighting up a "most righteous doobie." The toddler had ruined any possibility of his afternoon high. John was infuriated, and extremely inebriated. The man took the small child's laughter as a personal affront. He hauled off and stiff-armed the child, boxing him right on the ear. Vincent had fallen to the ground bleeding. Marisa witnessed the whole thing. She wanted him out, and that was final. John left of his own volition, happy to finally have an excuse to dump "the retard kid and his washed up whore of a mother." A Haitian maid had found his body nearly decapitated by a self-inflicted shotgun wound in a pay-by-the-week motel just two years later.

Marisa never bothered to talk about him to Vincent again, always skirting the subject or weaving little white lies. With any luck, she hoped, he would forget his father entirely. Her plan had seemed to be work until today. The little faith she had in men died along with John, and she thought, as she always had, that it was much easier to get by on instant gratification. Besides, in the grand karmic spinning wheel and scheme of things, whatever happened to Vincent was already predestined. All she could do was try and steer him in the right direction and hope for the best. At least that's what she kept telling herself to keep from seeking out an actual solution to her bad parenting.

"He could blow you down with a sigh and a curse, and it's time for us to leave her."

Although it wasn't the Sabbath today, just like Rambout van Damme the Reveler amongst the Spouting Devil before here, she had disobeyed Tarrytown's Golden Rule. Mainly, that there is a time and place for everything.

There were sporadic gaggles of congested traffic zooming under the gray steel girders of the Tappan Zee bridge. Occasional K-rails, called jersey barriers in these parts, and traffic cones created an uneven gauntlet for the aging truck to navigate. They were building a new suspension bridge to take its place. The memory of John Acker had made Marisa cry, and her vision blurred with the teeming of tears. Outside, the humid sprinkles of the afternoon sun-shower had mixed with the oily slick residue on the top layer of asphalt. Marisa punched the gas, not knowing where she was going, just that she needed to get away. Her mind raced with each rev of the engine.

Had she been wrong to not remind Vince of his father? Why was it that everyone else could do good things in life, but not her? Why the fuck had God cursed her with such a bothersome child? Why could everyone else fuck whomever they wanted, but she was looked at as a promiscuous skank? Her own mother had often referred to her as a "wanton woman with overly amorous intentions." Marisa knew if there ever had been gossip of improprieties whose side her mother would have ended up on, and it wasn't hers. Not that she had been such a stellar role model herself. *Why the fuck had she ever been born in this one-horse, dead-end, shithole of a town? Life was unfucking fair!*

***"I hate to sail on this rotten tub. Leave her, Johnny, leave her!
And the captain was bad but the mate was worse, Leave her,
Johnny, leave her!"***

Vinnie Douglass was a salesman from out of town whom Marisa met in the local watering hole. His pressed suit and white, collared shirt told her all she needed to know about him. Marisa's mom had vowed to babysit to give her some much respite after the breakup, which meant Marisa had the night off and could finally get laid, unencumbered. When he had said his name was Vincent, it made her wet. It was such an easy in. "That's my son's name," she said as she angled her shoulder forward so the meaty part of her breast would perk up through a strategically placed missing button in her tight top. The rest was history. They fucked every time he came into town, which was a few times a month. His single quirk was a fetish, unusual to Marisa, of having her jerk him off while he wore her silk panties. It hadn't mattered, though. He had always treated Vincent very well. They married after just two months of dating, and Marisa had her son's last name changed. She'd thought she'd be happy then; her and her two Vincents. Then, one day he just never came back. Days turned into weeks, weeks turned into months, months turned into years. Turned out he was already married and had a family clear across the country in Ojai, California. Swing and a miss!

***"No grog allowed and rotten grub. And it's time for us to leave
her. She's poverty-stricken and parish-rigged, And the bloomin'
crowd is fever-stricked. Leave her, Johnny, leave her!"***

It happened quickly. As if to answer the questions swimming around in her head, the great karmic sickle of the Grim Reaper answered her in a stringently decisive manner. An Infiniti Cefiro slammed on its breaks in front of her to avoid a barricade that had been intended to slow down traffic on the South Nyack side of the bridge. The ironic branding of the vehicle was the last thing she would register before catching an infinite breeze of her own. She had a split-second decision to make. Either rear-end the vehicle at breakneck speed but likely survive if possibly paralyzed, or swerve the truck to the right and try to fit through a space that was questionably thin, at best. Only Marisa herself knew why she chose the latter.

> ***"Oh the rats are gone and we the crew,***
> ***It's damned high time we left 'er too. It's time for us to leave her."***

The truck went up on two wheels. As the driver's side wheels took out the roof of the car in front of her, it sandwiched that vehicle's passenger side with fatal force. Physics did the rest. The unstable truck's center of gravity shifted and it began a steep barrel roll to the right. The Jersey barrier, which might otherwise have kept the truck from a plunge, came up to just below the vehicle's window level thanks to its lift-kit. Consequently, it had the opposite effect. The green plastic netting above the barrier was largely ceremonial, and even with a few rebar stanchions for reinforcement, it did nothing to keep the truck from its imminent demise. The F-250 rolled through the construction material at unstoppable speed over 400 feet above the menace of the water's surface below.

> ***"And now it's time for to say goodbye,***
> ***Leave her, Johnny, Leave her. Those pilings they are drawing***
> ***nigh. And it's time for us to leave her!"***

Out the passenger window, Marisa saw alternating stripes of clear blue sky and the gray brackish water of the Hudson River as her centrifugal rotation increased. Rivulets of her blood were floating along in midair and formed tiny, bright-red balls like mercury in a thermometer. Under any other circumstance, it would have been beautiful, captivating.

For a split moment, Marisa had had such great plans for her son. She had even lied to herself for a brief stint while pregnant, wondering if she could ever be mother material. Reality proved she couldn't. Every day since then had been a steady decline of letdowns, culminating in this very moment in time. *And today of all days; Dutch Down-Home night.* Jack was supposed to take her to dinner; they would get drunk and make love on a hayride under the harvest moon.

The quickly approaching concrete-like surface of the water had other plans for the evening. Not one for seatbelts, Marisa finally felt the g-forces slipping away out from underneath her. Her nerves tried to inform her to scream, but her mind fought against it. It wouldn't have mattered anyway. She looked death in the face and embraced it. The final splash killed her on impact.

Rip Van Winkle and The Flying Dutchman were waiting to welcome her with extended arms into Davy Jones' Locker. The gossamer galleon blended into the overcast horizon just off the coast of Hook Mountain as a spectral mist descended down the Hudson and enveloped Irving's sleepy stomping grounds.

It was the first among many fatalities, on what would prove to be a very long evening. Neither Sheriff Eustice, nor the Port Authority, would have to deal with it just yet. Tonight the accident was all Rockland County's problem.

Marisa would no longer be a problem for anyone.

"Leave her Johnny, leave her. Oh, leave her, Johnny, leave. For the voyage is done and the winds don't blow. — And it's time for us to leave her..."

Chapter 25

Eustice and Constance arrived at the covered bridge to a scene as disturbing as it was incredible. The truck pointed in the direction of the wagon trail that served as the unofficial boundary between wilderness and civilization. Like the River Styx before it, something seemed sacred about the traversing span. Perhaps, too, it connected the world of the living with the deceased. Right now, its occupants were certainly the latter.

The pickup dangled precariously off the bridge. The hood was crunched like a discarded soda can, the windshield completely shattered. The 1981 GMC K-2500 Wideside looked nearly identical to the one in the 80s TV show *The Fall Guy*, right down to its two-tone paint scheme. Its front tires, free from impediment, were spinning in seemingly perpetual motion. It was beyond the investigators how it could have gotten up enough speed over such a short distance to ride up the bridge like a pole cat. Its not-so-aerodynamic lines and driveshaft were at a nearly fifty degree angle facing skyward. There also seemed to be more blood than should be possible from just the single occupant in the driver's seat. So much for that peaceful night.

On the ground outside the truck was a multitude of broken beer bottles, windshield glass, and blood. The owner of the one tiny gas station in town, where there had always been parked two or three 50s classic convertibles, was also a beer connoisseur. As such, he always had a rack of seasonal pumpkin beers this time of year. He made sure to go to any length to secure them. Now, some of his most treasured imports were lying crushed into the bloodied and soupy mud. New Holland's Ichabods were among them, as well as several Shipyard Smashed Pumpkin ales. A more appropriate name couldn't have existed in the situation at hand.

Inside the truck, Billy Greenfield's head was cut clear off; a gruesome, bloody mess. The head was currently missing. Flies buzzed around the pulpy flesh, laying maggot larva in the rotting wound. The corpse held the steering wheel with its left hand, the thumb broken outward and facing the wrong direction. The other hand was still tightly clasped around a limited edition Headless Horseman Pumpkin Ale from the Four Horseman Brewing Company. Nary a drop had been spilled.

"I've been meaning to try that one. It's still cold." Indeed, there was still condensation on the bottle. Eustice pried the beverage from the cadaver and took a long swig.

Constance watched the unspeakable act, took one look at the laceration, and moved to the side of the truck to vomit. These small-town cops hadn't seen much like this, and certainly not to this extent. "You serious?" He came up for air wiping the bile off his lips with the back of his sleeve.

"Hmmm. Pumpkin and spice and everything nice." The sheriff drained the bottle and discarded it with a fling. Then he took a ball point pen from his shirt pocket and started to poke around the severed neck of the victim. This made squishy noises that produced an occasional squirt of blood. "Mmmm, that's odd."

Constance held a handkerchief to his mouth to mask the strong smell of iron, as he prepared for another wave of retching. He tried his best to compose himself. The disgusting actions of the sheriff weren't helping. "What?" he couldn't help but ask.

"See this? The flesh is jagged. Not a clean cut." He accidentally poked a hole in the skin near the throat.

Constance needed one more round of vomiting to cleanse the cookies and coffee from his system. The frosting and coffee ejecta took on a brilliant pinkish hue. The sheriff barely noticed.

"You'd think if the windshield caused this it would have been clear through. One fell swoop. This looks almost... hacked," he noted with the assuredness of Barney Fife.

"We should call the feds, or at least the state," Constance suggested. He started to do that thing he did when he got nervous, shifting his weight from foot to foot.

Eustice lowered his mirrored aviators with his forefinger, just enough to give Constance a condescending look. "Look, boy. Don't tell me what to do. Are you that stupid? This is so obvious."

Constance furrowed his brow and gave a Michael Keaton-esque sideways laugh. "What, drunk driving? Then where's the head?"

"Well, animals would've taken care of that. But I was talking about the Douglass kid, genius. We already got him placed at the scenes of two deaths, and he is obviously delusional. And by the looks of it, there was more than just Humpty Dumpty here," reasoned the sheriff.

It sounded good on the surface, but Constance wasn't sure he was buying it. The sheriff kicked broken bottles and beer cans around. Not tampering with evidence obviously had not been part of his training. As Constance picked up a shattered bottle of booze from the wreck, absentmindedly caressing blood from the label with his finger, when he noticed an axe mark cut deep into the wood next to the vehicle. With his eyes, he then followed something vaguely resembling a set of footprints leading off into the woods.

"Those look like footprints to you?" Eustice asked. He had noticed the tracks at the same time.

"I don't know. We should call for a proper—"

"I'm gonna have to stop you right there, Constance. Don't make me say this again. We do nothing, until I say we do something. Understood?" He stared daggers through the deputy.

Constance glanced at his shoes. "Yes, sir," he said meekly. He could see this was going nowhere and knew there was no use arguing with his superior once he started to act like this.

Then, from the direction of the covered bridge, came the war cry of the Horseman's Hellsteed.

Startled, Constance dropped the bottle he was holding and drew his gun, a look of fear in his eyes. "Jesus, what the hell was that?"

The big man chuckled at his colleague's expense "Whoa, calm down there, Lone Ranger. Put that thing away before you hurt yourself."

Constance searched the forest with his eyes, gun at the ready.

Eustice forcefully, but gently, lowered Constance's arm and looked his deputy in the eyes. He was almost amused. At least the earlier standoff between them had been defused. "Don't tell me you're starting to believe that happy-ass Horseman bullshit." He chuckled.

Constance didn't know what to believe anymore.

"Come on, man, you're a law enforcement professional. A grown man," the sheriff jested, nudging Constance with his elbow, the only boney part of his body.

Constance broke a nervous smile. "You're one to talk, Mr. Tampering With Evidence. Besides, every legend is based in some truth."

"Constance, I can't believe I'm actually hearing those words come out of your mouth."

Constance tried to rationalize what he knew deep down was an irrational fear. "It's been part of our history for centuries."

Eustice blinked in disbelief. This was a page right out of Vincent's book. You'd almost think this propaganda had been programmed into the residents from birth.

"Come on, man, you know my history," said Constance. "This night always puts me on edge."

"Now wait one cotton-pickin' minute," Eustice said, the smile suddenly gone from his eyes. "I will not tolerate this. Get yourself together, man. Go question Vincent and check his clothes for blood, wounds, whatever. When you get a confession out of him, then I'll decide who to call."

The war cry rang out again.

Eustice took the gun out of Constance's grip. "Look, I'm sorry about your wife. I truly am. But it's a Goddamned horse." Eustice reversed the weapon, grip side toward Constance, and slammed it to the deputy's chest. The metal of the Glock's slide clinked against his badge. "Go!"

As the dejected deputy went to the squad car, the senior policeman made a call on his cell. "Principal Carter? It's Sheriff Eustice. Look, close school for the rest of the day but don't cause any alarm, alright? Let those kids enjoy their holiday. It's just a precaution. Also, can you grab Price and meet by the old covered bridge? I'll call you back in fifteen with details."

Constance pulled the Volare next to Eustice and rolled down the window as if to ask a question, but the sheriff had already anticipated it. "I'm gonna stay here and search for more clues. I got help coming. You can reach me on this if you have to." He tapped his walkie with three pudgy fingers.

Constance was too defeated to try and reason with him, and too tired to fight. He pressed the accelerator and the steel-belted radials dug into the soft earth, which was still wet from the afternoon's sun-shower. Dark mud splattered on the sheriff's pants cuffs. Eustice couldn't see it, but a smile broke across Constance's lips as he watched the irritated lawman curse him in his rearview. *That'll leave a stain*, he thought as he navigated the muscle car away from the scene of the calamity.

It was time to protect and serve the good people of Sleepy Hollow.

Chapter 26

In Mr. Crane's classroom, Mack, Saunders and Vincent were noticeably missing from their assigned seats, along with a few of their classmates. Crane was speaking about Benedict Arnold. As was tradition, he had come in early to decorate the classroom with posters from some of his favorite Hammer films. He was a movie nerd as well as a history buff, but then again, some would say the two went hand in hand. It was the reason Vincent had related to him more than any other adult. Christopher Lee, Vincent Price, Peter Cushing, and several vampires and goblins stared down from the walls over bright florescent fonts and large-breasted damsels in distress. Even Rayna could barely curb her excitement. It was an exciting time on a special day. The community took their Halloween seriously.

"It was Arnold's defensive maneuvers at the Battle of Valcour that actually allowed patriots right here in Tarrytown, as well as White Plains, to prepare for the impending British Invasion. Little did they know he would soon become one of America's most infamous..."

Rayna was staring at a poster of *The Shadow of The Cat*, in which, Barbara Shelley's breast looked exceptionally feminine and curvaceous. *I wonder if my boobs will ever look like that*, she thought as she subconsciously adjusted her bra.

The brown speaker box that was mounted high atop the chalkboard and stuffed under the American flag begin to squawk to life. It interrupted both Crane's monotonous speech about the patriot turned traitor as well as Rayna's train of thought.

"Attention, students, faculty and staff. The remainder of the school day has been cancelled. All staff meet in the cafeteria. Happy Halloween, kids. See you at Dutch Down-Home Days tonight!" The voice sounded like it had been filtered through a fish tank.

A cheer of joy went up from the collective student body as they started to get up from their desks. The usual chaos of students ending class ensued.

"Traitors! All of you, traitors." Mr. Crane threw up his hands in playful submission. "This will all be on the midterm," he tried to yell over the din of chatter and scuffling, but it was of no use. Most of the kids, including his star pupil, Rayna, had already left the classroom.

★★★★

Vincent lay wide-eyed and awake on a cot inside the holding cell. The cookies were still on the floor, now with the added addition of a tiny trail of ants. Since the cops had left, his stomach had been in knots. He wasn't hungry and had been unable to sleep, or even think, for that matter. A migraine had begun, and he went to his signature move of pounding his fist into his temples. He had no way of knowing in the short time since they had left his mother's limp and bruised body was trapped in her submerged vehicle. Nor that the cops had found Billy Greenfield, without his head, but hadn't found Mack and Saunders at all. He couldn't have. He might as well have been a Shiroiwa 9th grader waiting for Sakamochi's announcements. All he knew was that he was innocent. Except for Jack, of course, but that had been an accident. He made a plan. As soon as the police returned, he would make up an excuse to get out of the cell and then make a run for it. He was sure he could outrun the sheriff, and he was counting on the deputy to show restraint with his firearm. It was a long shot, but it was all he had.

The jail, simple in its design, was rudimentary, but seemed extremely effective.

As he looked around the room for any possibility of escape, Rayna walked in holding a bag full of sandwiches.

"Happy Halloween, Dad! I brought you some—"

Rayna saw Vincent locked in the cell and dropped the bag. Then, composing herself, she picked up the stuff off the floor, put it on the desk and ran over to the cell. He stood up and went to her. They tried an awkward hug through the bars. It was a natural, albeit cumbersome, attempt.

"Oh my God, Vince! What happened?"

"So much for doing the right thing." He blushed, looking every bit like an irresistibly cute Marty McFly.

"What? Wait, my dad locked you in there?" She was pissed, like only a teenager daughter could be at her own father.

"Rayna, please, you got to get me out of here. The Horseman will come to me. I'm our only chance. I can bait him and trap him, or something. I don't know."

"Vince, you're scaring me a little bit. What are you talking about?" She noticed he looked tired and hungry and turned to get the sandwiches she had brought.

Vincent extended his arm as far as he could, grabbing her jacket collar and spinning her toward him. "The curse, Rayna. One of my ancestors is William Acker."

Rayna didn't follow. He saw the confusion and a tinge of fear in her eyes. Vincent let go of her jacket. He hadn't meant to be so aggressive; he never did. He was desperate, and it was simply an impulsive reaction. He began anew. "William Acker helped kill the Horseman, along with the sheriff and half the people in this town's great — however many — grandfathers."

She took a step back. "You're not making any sense."

Vincent got impatient, his dark side briefly surfacing. "Goddammit, it's a curse! Don't you see? I don't have time to explain every little detail."

She looked hurt by his forceful tone and use of profanity.

Alright, third time's the charm, he thought and began once again. "Sorry, okay? Sorry." He drew a deep breath, filling his lungs to capacity. "Look, I never told you this, but ever since the Halloween season has started, I have been obsessed about the Horseman. A lot more than normal. I mean nonstop. I can't sleep 'cause I have nightmares about him constantly. I can't focus on anything but his legend."

Rayna looked concerned.

"I know now he's coming after me 'cause I'm an Acker too. One of my great grandfathers is responsible for killing him." The words were pouring out of him like a geyser. Rayna listened, starting to soften. "Don't you see? If the Horseman gets his head back, he'll be whole again and there will be no one who can stop him from seeking revenge on his killers. He wants his head back, and I think I know where to find it. But if I can destroy it, I can destroy him. You have to let me out of here... Please, Rayna, it's a matter of life and death!"

Rayna was conflicted.

"Damn it, Rayna, please! At the very least, you know I did nothing to justify me being locked up in here like a dog." His eyes watered with desperation.

In reality, Rayna was still a child. But right now, there was an added air of mischief on All Hallows' Eve. Everyone knew it was there, but no one could quite explain it. Call them imps, spirits, instincts, or simply traditions. Either way, there was a reason it was called Mischief Night; Devil's in some circles. Whatever the unseen power had over them, most kids, and even some adults, partook of pranks ranging from toilet papering to vandalism, and sometimes even more sinister or lewd acts. Something was indeed in the air tonight.

Rayna made a judgement call — probably a bad one — but one definitely influenced by the heat of the moment. She went to the desk drawer, where there was a lockbox. Then she pulled down a key that had been taped behind a filing cabinet and used it, along with a code, and opened the lockbox. Inside, there was a circular set of keys, presumably to the holding cell. Small towns had their benefits and their curses. Rayna had grown up here, and was many a time left alone with Geraldine to babysit when her dad would be out on the beat. This happened all the time, usually unplanned—after school, weekends, some late nights. Whenever Rayna was at the station while her dad was out, she would be there with very little supervision, if any at all. Needless to say, she had an intimate knowledge of the inner workings of the tiny operation.

After slight hesitation, Rayna unlocked the cell.

Vincent gave her a hug, rethought it, then kissed her hard on the lips. The kiss was as emphatic as his fiery plea had been. He was truly grateful. In her world, that simple gesture made it all worth while.

Vincent grabbed the bag of sandwiches on the desk and went to leave.

"Wait," she said. "Use the back door. Just in case."

He smiled and headed out the back.

The slam of the door reverberated through the holding cell. Rayna blinked in disbelief. After a few beats, she went to lock the cell. Lost in thought, she sat down on what had been Vincent's cot only moments before. Her foresight to have Vince leave through the back proved to be prescient. As she sat quietly mulling things over, Deputy Constance walked in and caught her red-handed, keyring still hand.

"Lorraine Constance! Please tell me you didn't," her father yelled with every ounce of his being.

Rayna just sat there dumbfounded, not knowing what to say. Then her mind shifted into damage control mode. "Daddy, I'm sorry. I—"

But it was much too late for that. Her father was seething. Constance stomped across the room and slapped her hard across the face. She fell in a heap of tears to the floor. No amount of sad, imploring puppy dog eyes could save her now.

"That kid could be a murderer! Do you realize what you've done?" His hand stung from the blow. "You could be an accessory to murder!"

Rayna cried like a schoolgirl, finally showing the fragility of her age.

Constance's rage started to slowly dissipate as the father inside him gradually returned. "Jesus. I'm starting to sound like Eustice," he mumbled to himself. The good cop inside him knew there wasn't an ounce of evidence so far implicating Vincent in any wrongdoing. He went to his daughter, helped her to her feet and wiped her tears, then he held her close to his chest. A few tears stung his eyes as he cradled her in his arms.

"I'm sorry, baby. I just don't know if I can protect you on this one. For now, just don't tell anyone what happened here, okay?"

She didn't respond.

"Okay?" he said more forcefully. He had been referring to her letting Vincent free, not to him hitting her. She understood the implications and nodded her head yes.

"You have to tell me where he went."

"I don't know."

"Rayna, I've told you before, you can't keep on protecting this kid. You're obstructing justice and there are consequences to his actions." He acknowledged the words hadn't sounded very fatherly as they nose-dived off the tip of his tongue, but he was desperate to get through to her.

"I don't know. I swear dad! He said something about the Horseman and finding his head. He thinks the Horseman is real." Now it was her turn to doubt her own words.

"That boy needs a doctor." Constance became pensively silent.

Rayna took the brief pause in tension to come clean with her father. "Dad, I have to tell you something." She showed the bruise on her wrist. "Vince, didn't do this. Mack, Saunders and Billy did. Vince has always tried to protect me. He's innocent. He would never hurt anyone."

Constance remained silent. Rayna had no way of knowing that at least one of those kids, and possibly all of them, were dead. He knew, however, and his detective's mind started piecing together a timeline that was slightly off. *If Vincent had been pinned down in that cell most of the morning, something just wasn't adding up.*

Rayna drew him back into her confession. There was a lot coming at him at once. "Daddy, those boys were going to... to... They tried to…" Something in her psyche prevented her from saying the word rape. It was just too painful.

Subconsciously perhaps, Constance wasn't ready to hear it either. He again drew her close into the shelter of his protective chest. "I'm sorry, baby. I'm so sorry." Time seemed to have stopped as the two shared the consoling embrace.

He kissed her on the top of her head. It reminded him of all the times he had held her as a baby and comforted her cries. She had long lost that new baby smell, but hers was still a pure one. She had always told him the truth; there was not one precedent for him not to believe her. He started coming around to being convinced about Vince, and truly listened for the first time in a long time.

She picked up where she had left off. "He told me it had to do with a curse, and that Horseman was after anyone responsible for his death. He didn't tell me how he knew this, but he says he can prove it."

Constance continued to process the information.

"He said he had to find its head, and he was going to bait him."

At this revelation, Constance met her gaze, a look of determination in his eyes. "Come on. I think I have an idea where he's headed. Let's go get your boyfriend." He helped her compose herself and gather her things, then the pair made their way out.

As they closed the door behind them, a vintage cutout of an admonishing witch mounted there seemed to stare a glaring warning down their backs. The aura of the Sleepy Hollow legend had taken on a life of its own.

Chapter 27

Rows of Victorian homes were decorated more elaborately than the North Pole at Christmas time. Many homeowners had chosen themes like *The Nightmare Before Christmas* or *Trick 'r Treat*, while still others displayed effigies of Michael Myers or Freddy Kreuger. The older, more conservative contingent, went with more traditional pagan and occultist dressings. The Headless Horseman, being the antiheroic creation of the townsfolk's favorite son, was of course the most prevalent. If he really had been lurking around somewhere, he could have easily hidden in plain sight.

The first crowds of tiny costumed candy seekers made their way through the otherwise barren streets, trick or treating in the shadows. The sun had just started to dip behind the horizon. Orange and pink hues of sunset lit the mostly younger kids and their unsuspecting parents as they trudged along methodically like a group of absentminded zombies; almost as if they had been enchanted with the Dutch sleeping spells of reverie, which their ancestors had endured. The day had already been a long one, but the activities of the evening were just getting started. Every year, some pop culture phenomenon would make one costume more popular than others. This year was no exception. A viral video had appeared on a popular social media app. The video was an EDM mix-up of Marshall Applewhite's Heaven's Gate "Final Exit" video—the cult leader's last video before he and thirty-eight of his followers had committed mass suicide—to which some entrepreneurial youth had added an Avicii-esque beat and even doper bass drop. Black track suits, matching Nikes, and purple shrouds were in extremely high demand as a result.

Neither the kids nor their parents had any suspicion about the challenges facing the authorities that night. The fact many of them were wearing all black, making their visibility extremely low save a reflective Nike swoosh, only added to the chaos soon to come.

★★★★

In a vast, overgrown field of winter wheat not so far from the gruesome crash site, the men assembled there had just started to organize. The last rays of sun splashed across their perplexed faces. Eustice had already explained to them that he had reason to believe there might have been more victims of the untimely accident. He had also kept the search party small and relegated to a close group of personal friends. He didn't want the village's most prized celebration to be spoiled by an unfortunate discovery of idiotic teens. Although he thought Vincent fully capable of what he had accused him of, the sheriff was hoping they would quickly find the other boys simply injured and chalk it up to an unfortunate accident on a night of unadulterated merry-making. Tragic, sure, but nothing that could point to his incompetence as the town's law enforcement authoritarian.

After dividing the men into groups, they began a flashlight search of the area. He led Mr. Price and Principal Carter into the marshy area adjacent to the covered bridge.

"Thanks for coming out. A shotgun?" Eustice looked at Price with a half-cocked smile.

"You never know. How was I supposed to know why you wanted us out here. Your call couldn't have been anymore vague. Besides, bought this down at Moe's Hardware for turkey season. Been wantin' to try it out. Not like either of us had any holiday plans anyway." Price laughed.

"Truth," Carter agreed.

"Well, Charlton Heston, careful with that thing. This is a search party, not a public lynching," Eustice said. He made a half-assed sign of the cross toward them. "Alright, you're now official deputies or some such shit. Just in case this comes back to bite us for some reason."

The guys exchanged an excited glance, as if they were kids with secret decoder rings.

"Cool," Price said. Carter nodded his agreement.

Just as the group was about to disperse, Constance pulled up in the Volare, Rayna in tow. He had purposefully decided to keep the lights off, but the beefy idle of the mechanical Goliath made its presence immediately known. He jumped out, barely managing to put the vehicle in park. It skidded to a stop as the differential gears harshly locked the wheels from spinning. All the others looked up, excitement on their faces.

"The boy's gone," Constance said.

The sheriff shot him a look that could kill. Constance's averted eyes betrayed Rayna's involvement in the getaway. All eyes descended on her like accusatory locusts.

"I'm sorry," came her guilty response.

Eustice was in no mood to debate. He didn't even care how it had gone down, it just complicated matters. "Find him," he shouted.

"To think I stood up for that kid," Price said.

"I've always said he was a weird kid. 'Pumped Up Kicks' kind of nutty." Principal Carter always had to put in his two cents.

"At this point, he's our number one suspect," said Eustice as he began to walk away. It was clear this would easily turn into a witch hunt.

"He's innocent," said Rayna.

"Don't, Rayna. Just don't," her father said curtly. Turning to the sheriff, he said, "My gut tells me he'll turn up close to the Van Tassel fire scene. Keep your walkie on, Eustice. I'm starting to believe there's more to this Horseman thing than you think. The kid mentioned it too. Be careful." He pulled his daughter with him.

Eustice was too miffed to care about some urban legend at this point.

"Something you want to tell us, Sheriff?" Carter was beginning to feel a little uneasy about his newly deputized status.

"Nothing's changed, Carter. Who'd you say was missing at school today?"

"Douglass, Klimchak, Mack, Muskas and Saunders if memory serves. But you know how kids play hooky on Halloween. Hell, it's practically a tradition."

"Like I said, precautionary. I'm gonna search past the tree line. Just holler if you find something. I won't be far." Eustice began to slowly move the large bulk of his frame toward the depths of the forest.

"I'll check the old Dutch cemetery," Price yelled to the sheriff's back as he walked away. "Middle of the night on All Hallows? What could possibly go wrong," he said to himself as he took a bear-sized swig out of a flask and cocked the cumbersome shotgun.

"Great. I'll just be over here I guess, seein' as nothing's changed and all," Carter sarcastically remarked as he headed in a third direction.

The group fanned out as the sky darkened under a reddish harvest moon.

The further Eustice got from the others, the more muffled any other sounds he could hear became, until they disappeared altogether. He was left alone in the dead of Devil's Night. He took notice of the full moon that hung just over the ridge, like a foreboding lighthouse signal. *Land ho! Turn back lest ye be dashed across the rocks,* it seemed to say in the recesses of his mind. He began to feel uneasy.

Alone, he warily headed toward the hallowed Weckquaesgeek burial grounds.

Chapter 28

Aaron and Allister planned to meet up not far from the Old Dutch Church near Sleepy Hollow Cemetery. They hadn't seen Vincent since that night at the video store, but they knew he had been at school because of his outburst in Paulding's office. All the kids in class had been talking about it, but they paid no attention. Vincent was always skipping school and didn't exactly have a satisfactory conduct rating. He eventually would find his way back to them; he always did. Plus, if they knew their pal, tonight of all nights he wouldn't miss the opportunity to meet up with them for some proper misbehavior. Running around like teenaged insurgents in the dark of night, pranking neighbors, and underaged drinking, were long honored traditions that stood the test of time. What better place to set up home base than in the century and a half old resting place of their ancestors. They couldn't think but how fun it would have been to share a flask with Washington Irving, himself, or even William Rockefeller.

Aaron smiled at the thought. Allister had told him to meet up on the sloped side of the cemetery east of the river. Section 95, Row E, plot number 205 to be exact. The boys changed it every year and didn't send it in texts or emails so there would be no record of their correspondence should something go awry. It was a fun little exercise in their own private game of espionage. As the cemetery was usually locked up on this night due to obvious reasons, Allister darted across Highway 9 once the sunlight faded and scaled the Sacchi Pass main gate. Aaron came from the opposite direction after spending most of the morning taking a self-guided tour of the Spratt House ruins, where Barnabas Collins had once visited. He made his way north through Tarrytown Lakes Park, jumped a few fences and crossed through some creeks, then was finally there. This was all part of the adventure, and fun, of Mischief Night.

The cemetery's own publications described it as "A sleepy resting place where little seems to change." Red sandstone grave markers, magnificent statues, mausoleums and even beautiful stained glass depicting Irving's life and his story "The Legend of Sleepy Hollow" created an unparalleled atmosphere full of spooky themes. The Pocantico snaked its way through the back of the cemetery, separating the area where the fresh bodies were interred from the more historical area where the Dutch settlers had been laid to rest. The church still stood in the same spot dating back to 1685, and held within it a bell that had been cast in Holland. The grounds were sacred, ancient, and filled with the spirits and corpses of past and present lineages.

Aaron remembered from one of Crane's history classes that some preacher guy named Coffin was also buried there. The irony was delicious. Someday, most of the town would probably end up being six feet under here, but for now, it was their playground. Tonight, however, when the afterworld could commingle as it pleased, perhaps the boys would have additional otherworldly pranksters on their team.

Allister raced up Dingle Road, passing Andrew Carnegie's grave. It was a meager looking granite post, which seemed to have some sort of Celtic cross carved on it best Allister could tell. It seemed awfully minimal for someone purported to be one of, if not the richest, man in the world at one point in time. It reminded him of something Mr. Crane had told the class upon returning home from a trip to London. The teacher had visited Westminster Abbey in London where many Royals like King Henry V, most of the Tudors, Mary Queen of Scots, and other celebrated people like Sir Isaac Newton were buried, but Roald Dahl was decidedly not.

Although a simple, humble teacher born to an impoverished family from upstate New York, he could walk around and touch their very graves. A common man, a tourist, simply needed to pay the price of admission to walk amongst kings, queens and notable poets. The oil of his fingerprints could leave an indelible smudge-like impression on the very granite face of a royal's tomb. In fact, they probably were all envious of him, as their bodies decomposed in their encased sarcophaguses, he possessed the one thing their money and fame could never buy; life. The moral of the story? We all end up in a box. Death was the great equalizer.

Allister thought much along the same lines as he raced along the aptly named Headless Horseman Bridge, which led into the wooded part of the cemetery where Aaron should be waiting. The planks beneath his feet sounded like horses' hooves to him as he pressed his body forward into a full-on sprint. He wondered if the design had been intentional.

As he reached the meeting point, Allister pressed his tongue toward the roof of his mouth against his two front teeth and whistled a tune similar to a birdcall. Aaron returned the call, which they had rehearsed several times. The boys met up over the grave plot, high-fived each other, then began to empty an arsenal of fiendish goods from the contents of their backpacks.

"I raided my dad's liquor cabinet. What'd you get?" Allister was excited to show his friend his booty and quite happy with his accomplishment.

Aaron pulled a load of junk from his black JanSport. "Whippets, TP and…" He drew out the revelation of the third item like Pat Sajak announcing an all-expense paid luxury getaway to Tahiti. "Cherry bombs!"

Allister squealed in excitement like a kid half his age. Aaron revealed a cluster of tiny, red, fuse-laden balls from his pocket and brandished a ninety-nine cent Bic lighter. The kids laughed underneath their blacked-out masks and high-fived once more.

"Come on, let's head over to the old churchyard and have a drink, then we can come up with a plan of action." Allister held up a nearly full fifth of Johnnie Walker Double Black.

"Oh shit, the good stuff." Aaron motioned for the bottle and began the walk toward the south end of the cemetery.

As they walked and took nips from the bottle, their lungs started to burn with the intense bite of the alcohol. "All right, that's enough for right now. I want to put some of this back in my dad's cabinet. After I water it down, anyway."

Aaron took an obligatory swig, then answered. "Yeah, remember it's a marathon, not a sprint." They both laughed.

They were traipsing down one of the narrow footpaths that took them between mausoleums, statues and a multitude up crumbling grave markers. The crunch of a bed of dead autumnal leaves echoed their footsteps underneath them. Suddenly, a dark shadowy figure appeared on the path just ahead. It was cresting the hill and coming toward them.

Allister stopped Aaron dead in his tracks, and they hid behind the statue of a crying angel. "It's the Horseman," he joked, then ducked down as if he were actually scared. He removed the cap on the whiskey, thinking twice about his resolve to stop. "And he's holding something. Is that an axe?"

Aaron could barely stifle a laugh. "No, asshole. Clearly it's not the Headless Horseman. First off, he has a head. And secondly, he doesn't have a horse. Horseless, not headless. Talk amongst yourselves."

Allister nearly spit out the capful of Johnnie as he laughed. "Oh yeah." The whiskey was beginning to take effect. He sucked in dry air though his chapped lips. "I need some water."

Aaron started rummaging through his backpack for water, when suddenly Allister nudged him, spilling some whiskey on him.

"Shit. What the fuck, dude? Stop wasting it."

"Shhh. Oh shit, it's Price, homie."

They exchanged an incredulous look.

"You gotta be fuckin' kidding me. What the hell is he doing out here?" whispered Aaron.

Mr. Price had made his way through the same wooded landing Aaron had only moments later. It was a miracle they hadn't seen each other, and probably a good thing too, as Price had the shotgun at the ready and alcohol was coursing through the canals of his cerebellum.

"Oh shit, he's got a gun." The boys exchanged impish, nefarious looks with one another. "This is rich," continued Allister.

"Too good," agreed Aaron as they begin to ready some of their cherry bomb munitions. It didn't get any better than having your abhorred boss, alone and drunk, dead in your sights like a sitting duck in the middle of a cemetery on All Hallows' Eve. It simply didn't.

Price sat down on the ground and leaned his back against a mausoleum sporting an angel on top. The look on its stone face seemed to be judging him from high atop its Godlike perch. "What, you want some?" He held the flask up like a sacramental offering before putting it to his lips for a man-sized pull. He had already made the decision to head back to the accident site, as this seemed to be a dead end. "*Ha. Dead end. Cemetery.*" He laughed out loud as the thought came to him. Before he headed back, however, he would enjoy the peace and solitude of his dead predecessors, and the burn of a nice rye malt.

If he had been a knowledgeable historian, like Crane, he could have appreciated the sheer amount of legacy and historical figures that surrounded him. Their combined accomplishments were encyclopedic and unmeasurable in their contributions to modern humanity. But alas, he was just a simple man, enjoying a little nip. Much like the kids, now within his earshot, he was humbly along for the ride on this, the third rock from the sun. He felt every bit as small as a pebble in the Grand Canyon. The fact he was surrounded by personages of such achievement meant nothing. As they slept in their graves, he continued to merely pass the time.

Chapter 29

Sheriff Eustice had finally made it to the now familiar burial grounds. Despite him telling the men otherwise, he had to follow his gut, a large one at that, and had unwittingly been swallowed deeper into the pastoral countryside. He used his flashlight to look through every nook and cranny. A black beetle scurried up a tree and disappeared into a craggy crevice deep inside its bark. He could manage many things, even grotesque ones as the accident had proven, but insects gave him the creepy-crawlies. Even a large, boisterous, and sometimes obscene man like himself had an Achilles' heel.

Something rustled in the trees nearby. Eustice spun his body, surprisingly gracefully, to face the sound. From behind him, he heard the gallop of the Horseman's Hellsteed. It sounded as if the Horseman was headed right toward him, but when the sheriff turned again, there was nothing there.

"Who's out there?" he yelled into the night. "Carter? Price, that you?" Eustice became agitated. "Constance?" He unholstered his service revolver out of reflex. He was shocked at himself for doing so, as he'd had no intention of using it prior to now. It illustrated his heightened sense of unease.

Again he heard the sound of a horse, but this time it sounded like it was approaching from his left. He turned, but still there was nothing. Eustice began to panic, questioning his own ears. The sound of pursuing hooves came again, pounding out like a marching band's drum line.

Eustice startled himself and set off into a run. But all those cupcakes and jelly donuts over the years were finally catching up to him, and he had to stop to gulp down oxygen. As he struggled to get air, he heard the sound of his own heart beating and felt the rush of the blood pounding through the inner canals of his eardrums. Soon, the noise was again drowned out by the cadence of a horse's hooves. The stalwart, bastion of a man was truly frightened.

This time when he spun toward the sound, the Horseman was there, charging at him full speed. Eustice fumbled, but managed to reach his shoulder mic just in time to call into it, "Constance, the Horseman!"

The Horseman raised his arms holding what appeared to be a long black leather Colonial whip and cracked it at the sheriff, ensnaring his ankle. The law enforcer's revolver discharged, sending an errant bullet where the Horseman's head would have been had he had one. The overweight lawman hit the ground hard on his stomach. The force of the impact caused him to regurgitate the contents of his gut. The acidic fire of the vomit burned his throat as the Hellsteed began to drag him across the field by the ankle. The mud was a slick, dark brown and provided the perfect lubrication as the Horseman dragged Eustice down a mild embankment, causing him to roll onto his back. Eustice had managed to hold on to his gun. *Never, ever, fucking fumble the ball!* His mind raced. He couldn't reach the whip around his ankle but had managed to somehow re-holster the sidearm and snap the brass fastener over it. He might need it later, if he managed to get out of this.

The animal picked up speed and the many sharp twigs and jutted rocks could give little resistance to the mass of the overweight man's body. Eustice looked up at the sky and watched as the moon ducked in and out of clouds. Just like Marisa before him, the thought came unprompted: *Beautiful under any other circumstance.*

The beast's speed was too immense for him to be able to lift his head in order that he might get a good look at his assailant. The sheriff's body briefly paused as the small of his back caught the sharp edge of a tree stump. The horse plunged forward, wrenching Eustice across it, sending spikes of pain up his spine. The force of the pull shredded his uniform, along with some flesh, into bloody, stringy scraps. The physics set into action flipped Eustice back onto his stomach. Facedown, he could no longer see anything. The whip wrapped around his ankle had cut through his leather boot and deep into his flesh, burning like the fire of a demonic hand dragging him straight to hell.

Many have told of seeing their life flash before their eyes during a near-death experience. All Eustice could think of was his utter humiliation. He had made a career out of coming across as the unbreakable adjudicator of the indisputable law of the land. Since his early training in wrestling and football, he was taught that a sturdy stance, a menacing scowl, and an unwavering opinion was what a man should always project, even if he actually had much less confidence in himself. Eustice had used this facade all his life. It got him through any and all challenges he faced, and somehow managed to get him elected sheriff, more than once.

But now, here he was being literally dragged off his ass. He had never tried to run for Senate, like he had promised his father before he died. He had never got back to his football fighting shape, like he had promised himself. In fact, he never aspired to achieve anything, other than a false sense of peace he had perpetrated throughout the community. He was an abject failure. A racist, misogynist, homophobic one at that. He had bought into the patriarchal system as a child and had never done one Goddamned thing to break out of it. He hated himself for it, correctly so.

He prayed it actually was the Horsemen executing this last vile act upon him. If he somehow managed to fight his way out of this, or even if he couldn't, it would be much more respectable if it became known he had fought a Demonic Immortal rather than the more likely scenario that it was a revenge seeking, punk-ass kid.

He felt the warm trickle of urine running from between his legs, over his lumpy sack, through his ass crack and up over his back. Once it hit the air, the body temperature was released and his soaked back became wet in the cold of the night. The smell, like him, was vile and pungent. It smelt of fear. Mortified, with no shred of dignity left, the Great Big Al Eustice had pissed himself like the "tiny widdle boy" he had always known deep inside that he actually was.

★★★★

Deputy Constance and Rayna had arrived at the former Van Tassel Manor site. A thick layer of smoke still rose in the cold night and embers crunched beneath their footsteps. Constance had instructed his daughter to remain on the fringe of the area and let him know if she saw anything out of the ordinary. Now just a pile of soot, bricks and wooden planks, Constance searched through debris with a flashlight. He didn't feel great about having Rayna there, but he was hoping she could help him apprehend Vincent and they could clear things up.

Rayna also had a flashlight her dad had given her, but she was too on edge to look for any clues. Every time a bird or night critter rustled in the bushes, she would shine the powerful Maglite into the woods expecting to find a killer, arsonist, or worse yet, a maniacal Vincent. If there was one thing she didn't want, it was a confrontation between the two of the men she loved. Little had she known, that they already had tangoed at the jailhouse.

Constance's walkie crackled to life with the last communication of Eustice before he got pulled out to pasture. The garbled message was difficult to understand.

"I didn't copy," Constance said into his mic. "Say again, over." He turned to Rayna. "Did you hear that? I could have sworn he said Horseman."

Rayna shrugged. "I don't know, Dad, but you're starting to sound an awful lot like Vince."

Touché. He shot her a look, choosing to ignore the jab. "Listen, I want you to go around back. I know he's out here somewhere. If you find him, tell him I'm not gonna hurt him. I just want to talk, okay?" If he was committed to believing her boyfriend, which he was now, he was all in.

"I'm scared," she said.

It reminded him of all the doctor visits and roller coaster rides over the years. The unnecessary, but honestly felt, fright of a young girl.

"There's nothing to be afraid of. I won't lay a hand on him, promise."

A smile split across his face, but in the shadows she couldn't tell if he was being sincere or facetious. She didn't exactly trust him just yet. What's more, she wasn't being completely honest with him, or herself. She was actually a little afraid of Vincent, and even crazier, the thought of the Horseman. Yes, it was irrational and borderline silly, but they had all grown up with the Legend, and sometimes, especially on nights like tonight, it was hard to separate fact from fiction.

Constance saw the look of doubt register across his daughter's face. "Look, so far I have a heart attack, an unrelated burn victim, and what's probably no more than a drunk driving fatality. No crime's been committed as far as I can tell. But the boy has issues." It sounded good coming out of his mouth. It seemed logical, authoritative, and the most likely scenario. Both the deputy and his offspring agreed he was probably right.

Rayna reluctantly headed deeper into the surrounding property. They both begin to call out Vincent's name. The unanswered calls bounced off the invisible walls of dark matter, and burned out of existence, just as the embers of the house had not so long ago.

Constance's walkie keyed up, making muffled and incoherent sounds. He smacked it, but it was still garbled. "Sheriff, that you? Sheriff, copy?" He tried again but received nothing more than static, followed by dead silence.

Chapter 30

Price had nearly made his way to Broadway. He stopped at the cast iron gate of a stone crypt. Tiny American flags surrounded its entrance. He pulled out the flask to take another swig. It was engraved with the words, *I'm not as think as you drunk I am,* which were written upside down. Aaron and Allister had been watching the whole time.

"Aw, fuck it," he said as he upended the flask, fully emptying the contents into his mouth. As the drops spiked his tongue, and his eyes faced skyward, he noticed the words etched into the surface of the edifice's small rocky-faced ledge above him. THOMAS DEAN ERECTED… The alcohol started to blur his vision, so he couldn't tell if said 1850 or 1860. "I feel like I haven't been erected since 1850." He laughed to himself as the intensity of the alcohol overcame him full force, like a cannonball aimed at his head.

BOOM! A cherry bomb went off over his shoulder.

Price swiveled and instinctively fired his gun. The shotgun blast took the head off of an angelic guardian statue. Granite shards and a cloud of plaster exploded into the air. The force of the discharge knocked Price right onto his drunken ass.

Aaron and Allister took cover behind a nearby mausoleum, snickering uncontrollably. Clearly, they felt young and invincible, not realizing how close they had come to being headless themselves.

"Holy shit did you see that?" Aaron squealed as he playfully punched Allister square in the chest. "Give me one."

Allister fumbled through the backpack to quickly grab anther.

"Damn I wish Vince was here to see this. Where the fuck is he?" Aaron seemed genuinely frustrated.

"I don't know. Let's go find him."

Allister dexterously lit another of the potentially lethal fireworks and lobbed in Price's general direction like a Kyrie Irving no-look pass. The youths took off running. They weren't going to wait around to see Price's reaction, or be in the line of fire.

"Off with their heads!" Allister couldn't resist yelling over his shoulder as they fled. It had been long accepted among locals as the thing to say on Halloween night in these parts. They heard the muffled bang of the cherry bomb hitting its mark. They were hoping to reconnoiter later in town once they had found Vincent.

★★★★

The village was small enough that the cemetery was not that far from where the sheriff was experiencing his tortuous ride through the underbrush. That, in turn, was not far from where Rayna and Constance were inspecting the Van Tassel Manor fire detritus. Neither were that far from the main street of the literally one Horseman town, where corn mazes, food courts, band pavilions and decorated gazebos awaited nighttime revelers. Anyone who has been to New Orleans for New Year, Bangkok during the World Cup, or Chennai during Diwali can attest to the fun, chaos, and disorientation such a night brings. Screams, gunfire, fireworks, and music all seem to blend together in one beautiful cacophony of unadulterated pandemonium.

Such was the atmosphere Sheriff Eustice found himself in now. He had briefly passed out from the sheer shock, coupled with the intense pain of his now-broken ankle and other injuries. His eyes started to blink open as his shoulder mic crackled to life.

"Eustice, do you copy?" came the voice. It sounded like it was filtered through a futz device, but it was definitely Constance trying to reach out.

Eustice tried to reach the mic to talk back, but the numbness in his arm prevented him from being able to lift it in that direction. If the Horseman didn't kill him, a heart attack surely would. That and a hefty dose of humiliation would probably do the trick. He was just grateful he wasn't being dragged any more. "Oops. Spoke to soon," came his stifled words immediately after he had the thought.

As his eyes came into focus, he had a clear view up the billiard ball sized nostrils of the black Hellsteed that hovered over his tattered body. It was almost as if the larger-than-life animal winked at him before it reared back and, once again, began its deadly steeplechase. The horse bolted forward with such a jolt that it broke the sheriff's ankle in a second place as it jutted unnaturally in the opposite direction nature had intended. The limp foot now flailed along with the whip still firmly in place. He screamed in pain, but got a mouthful of iron-ore mud for his troubles. The salty grit of the dirt condensed itself onto the palate of his upper mouth, making it even harder for him to breath.

After a few merciless, serpentine slaloms through the damp bed of the woodland fields, the sheriff was dragged right on top of a gutted Saunders and a petite boy named Walter Erickson, who had chosen the wrong night to acquiesce to his former bullies. The body parts still let off visible steam, and a fetid stench. The Horseman released the whip with a swift jerk of his wrist. The sheriff lay slumped in a pile of blood and strewn about entrails. The force of the horse's momentum had shot him forward into the carnage and entangled him in the bloody and revolting mess.

After a few moments of silence, where seconds had seemed like minutes, and minutes like hours, the sheriff tried to right himself to his feet. He was exhausted and had been overcome with emotion, but he was, thankfully, still alive. Every time he stood, he lost his footing, slipping on the blood and intestines of the Horseman's previous victims. It was a clumsy, disgusting nightmare of a situation. Eustice was so busy trying to untangle himself from the gory entrapment, he hadn't noticed the Horseman mounted atop the Hellsteed right in front of him the entire time.

As he finally righted himself and managed to stay upright, he took full stock of his attacker. He kept the weight off the broken ankle, but the pain was severe. Eustice would record this vision to memory, and would never forget as long as he lived. Unfortunately for the sheriff, the Horseman didn't plan on letting that be very much longer.

The Horseman spun his Hellsteed around, pivoting the animal in the opposite direction, and retreated a distance. It seemed like he wanted to get a good running start for his next act. He pivoted the animal once again, hunched down and charged full speed as he brandished the ancient belt axe. Even though the metal of the blade had been tarnished over a couple of centuries, it still glinted in the available light, revealing its predilection for moonlight massacre.

Eustice propped himself down on one knee and reached for his sidearm; it was now or never. With a steely resolve he hadn't entertained since his line of scrimmage days, he pulled his service revolver out and took careful aim at the quickly moving target. The Horseman stooped low like a polo player looking to score as he charged forward with the energy of a freight train.

Eustice got distracted for a brief second, as what was left of little Walter's head stared back up at him with wide, unblinking eyes, as if pleading. His face had been cleaved in two and Eustice could literally see what had been on his mind. Eustice's attention snapped back to the Horseman, but his brief lapse in focus would turn out to be one with dire consequences. The sheriff got a last-second shot off, but it missed. He remained focused—far more than if a state championship had been on the line—and quickly took aim for a second time, perhaps getting one last shot at redemption.

★★★★

Constance's ears perked up. He could hear off in the distance what sounded like a gunshot. His thoughts immediately went to his daughter's safety. He circled back around to their starting point and called to her. "Rayna are you okay?" His voice wavered with uncertainty.

"Yeah, Dad, I'm okay. What was that?" She ran to her father's side. "Did you hear something?"

He shrugged. He had definitely heard something too, but he didn't want to aggravate the situation so he chose not to divulge his concern, or his own nervousness. In the distance, they both heard what sounded like the battle cry of the Horseman. The two looked at each other, not exactly sure what it was they had just heard.

"Van Wart do you read? Eustice, please respond!" Constance pleaded into his shoulder mic.

A few anxious moments of silence passed. Rayna's eyes were huge as they imploringly searched her father's face for reassurance.

"Alright, let's get the hell out of here." He put his arm in the small of her back and forcefully escorted toward the Plymouth Volare.

As they were leaving, the deputy's flashlight hit the white of a single shred of paper amongst the rubble. It stood out like an unblemished diamond in a coal mine. He wondered how he had missed it before, but being that dark, it was most definitely because the light had to hit it just right.

"Get in the car, honey, I'll be right back."

Constance walked over to the pile of soot where he had seen the object's reflection. He picked it up, dusted it off and looked at it. It was the tattered piece Vincent had ripped from the book at the library. Constance unfolded the small fragment. It was creased, frayed and burnt around the edges, but the inside had remained protected and relatively unmarred. He read what he could of the circled names. There was definitely Williams, Van Wart, and what looked like it could have been Paulding.

Rayna disobeyed her father's wishes, likely only a strong-willed daughter could, and walked over to him. "What it is, Dad?" she asked as she trudged through the ash, soiling her white Keds beyond recognition.

"Lorraine! I thought I told —," he softened—"asked you to stay in the car."

She shot him her rebellious teenager look.

"It's a list of some sort. Appears to be names. Probably just an old book or something."

She took the paper out of his hand so she could examine it more closely. "Williams? Like Maw Maw Williams? Is this about her?" she wondered out loud.

Constance hadn't thought of that. The lightbulb still hadn't yet gone off in his head. "Doubt it." He needed more time to think. His policework had always been slow, methodical and calculated. The events of the last couple of days, much less the last couple of hours, weighed heavily on his mind. His eyes darted back and forth between Rayna and the paper. Then, with resolve, he finally made a decision.

"It's probably nothing. Look, why don't you go to the Down-Home Days. Things are going to take serious turn after the weekend and there's really no need for you to be out here anyway. I need to check in with the sheriff, but I'll drop you off at home first so you can get ready for your big night. Okay?"

She looked up at him, tears welling in her eyes. It was the nicest thing he had said in a while and exactly what she had been hoping for. "You sure, Dad?"

He pulled her in close to him and initiated a father-daughter-sized bear hug. He loved her more than anything. After briefly relishing the moment, his mind started racing once again. He truly did need to find Eustice. Maybe this list was somehow connected to Vince, but he couldn't be sure. Either way, there was urgent policework that needed to be done.

"Look, out here is no place for a chi—" He immediately corrected himself, something he was becoming more and more used to doing. "A young woman, anyway. Besides, if there is one thing I know, it's that Vince will come to you, but not if I am always hovering over you like this. Let's go."

They jumped in the car as the deputy pocketed the evidence. The Super Coupe roared off into the night, flexing its American muscle and leaving behind a trail of exhaust like will-o'-the-wisps swirling amongst the spectral wraiths of impending ruination.

★★★★

Back in the marshy field, the sheriff's second shot had somewhat hit its mark. The Horseman had taken a bullet hit in the bicep. Incredibly, he hadn't been the least bit fazed. He threw the battle axe back to his good arm, catching it with laser accuracy. He then raised it in one fluid motion high into the air to maximize the swing of its fulcrum. The hefty weight of the war implement soared downward, in a powerful circular motion of inertia.

Eustice pivoted, but the action caused his weight to shift onto his twice-broken ankle. With a grotesque snap, his body lurched forward. The blade sliced a thin baseball mitt sized chunk out of his stomach with the precision of a delicatessen butcher. The patch of flesh went sailing through the air, a fountain of blood trailing it in a high-arching rooster tail. Eustice used his arm to hold his body upward, like some sort of mutilated tripod. The second snap had been the shin just above the broken ankle. The burden of the man's large body had been too much, and the tibia and fibula had simply buckled out from under him. The stump of the bones had been driven forcefully into the soft ground under the burden of his upper mass, essentially pinning the sheriff to the earth with his own appendage. Being just like Joe Theismann before him, was not the kind of NFL-fantasies Eustice had always dreamt of, but life had a wonderful way of giving its victims the most unwanted irony. He screamed in unparalleled agony.

The awkward position he was now stuck in didn't allow him to turn his body enough to see what the Horseman was doing. Sweat poured down his scalp and into his eyes, burning them and blurring his vision even further. He could tell, however, by the pounding sound of the hooves and the Doppler effect they created that the horse was circling back around so the Horseman could have another go. Eustice waited until he could sense the Horseman virtually on top of him to pull the trigger of his gun in rapid succession. He fired blindly over his shoulder emptying the revolver, hoping some of the hot lead would find a home inside flesh. With any luck, his non-regulation hollow points would leave softball-sized exit wounds.

Eustice took the axe slice to his side full on, effectively being filleted from navel to sternum. His innards released from his body with a gush of fluid that sounded like a water buffalo giving birth. The ground beneath him became soaked in wetness, adding to the corpses that had already been stacked there before him. Eustice fell backward into the pile of human remains, eyes wide open in shock. What remained of his rib cage separated like a rack of lamb upon impact.; The not-so-honorable Sheriff Albert Eustice Van Wart was DEAD.

The last thing he thought of before punching his ticket was the incomparable beauty of Marisa's angelic smile.

Chapter 31

Harvest moons are rare. Most almanacs claim they only show up once a year, around the autumnal equinox in September within the norther hemisphere. Blood Moons were even more rare, and only occurred within total lunar eclipses when the sun's light threw the moon into a red-tinted shadow. The triple threat of one being a supermoon, appearing closest and most visible in the night sky, was undocumented and unheard of, until today.

Scientists had predicted the four full moons of the lunar tetrad that would culminate into tonight's full moon, but they hadn't seen the rest coming because it was, in fact, unnatural. Halloween revelers felt the moons tides awash in their blood streams and saw the bright-red ball dangling from the sky, seemingly close enough to be touched. They had no idea what supernatural events might have been occurring amongst one another, or among the celestial bodies up above.

The "Blood Moon Prophecies" was all Reverend Graham James Todd could talk about for the last two months. Much like Father Lester Lowe in Stephen's King's *Silver Bullet*, the locals dismissed his proselytizing sermons as the ranting and ravings of a zealot. They were more interested in getting back to their Sunday football games and salty stacks of potato pancakes and pumpkin-spiced ales. Of course, like any members of a decent cult posed as a religion, they would nod their head in agreement, all the while ignoring Todd's message of ultimate repentance. No one amongst them could fathom the end of times. Even more inconceivable was the end of his infernal sermons.

The last time the blood moon had fallen on the first night of the Triduum of the Hallows was the night Rayna and Deputy Constance would soon rather forget. A night that would haunt them every year since then, tonight being no exception. The last time all three of the lunar events occurred on All Hallows' Eve was the night the Hessian had lost his head. And the last time prior to that was over eight hundred years ago, well before the Western world had even started taking stock of the heavenly bodies looming over North America.

The Native Americans had known, though, and in their own way they knew what gravity the night beheld. In fact, they would sometimes spend two or three harvest seasons prior to the event purging themselves from sin and making right with even hostile tribes in order that no Indian nation would have to endure the curse of the Triduum of the Hallows. Traditionally, the three days that followed was a time of peace, joy, and reconciliation. A night when the dead and the living coexisted and could atone for their sins against each other. It was a time for generations present to recognize the generations past. The youth would pay homage to their ancestors, while the dead would instill a sense of hope and progression to their children and children's children.

But nights like these, and like the day the Hessian died, were no such measure of celebration. Instead, they were a means of the greater good to cleanse the spiritual palette of the universe. A time when the only way to wash away sin was not through the blood of the lamb, but from the blood let from the transgressors themselves. Nights like these were not notions of reconciliation, forgiveness, or peaceful visitations. On the contrary, these nocturnal traditions were solely intended for karmic retribution. No amount of self-inflicted penance could be seen as proper reparation on nights like tonight.

In the case of the Horseman, it was a night of restitution. He wanted his head back and his honor restored, but what's more, he wanted revenge on those who had taken it from him. It is said that those who die violently and suddenly receive such a shock that they spend the entire afterlife trying to make heads of it. At least that's what the legends and folklore would have you believe. But tonight, it seemed like even bigger things were at play. One could see the Horseman as a harbinger of atonement, but in the grand scheme of things he was nearly a pawn. A great cosmic reckoning was afoot, and it was using him now just as it had so many moons ago.

The Triduum of the Hallows was bigger than any one Hessian. It had long been established by the Greater Entities as a time for the living to pay homage to their predecessors. Occasionally though, like with all good parenting, there needed to be an equal does of punishment to balance out the reward. Unlike in movies and fairy tales, life wasn't always clean and perfect. Resolutions didn't always come quick. Sometimes they took generations. Sometimes they took millennia. Furthermore, the endings weren't always happy. It didn't matter in the larger scheme of Creation if light had triumphed over dark, or good over evil. It was a constant ebb and flow with no beginning or end. Reasoning, logic, statistics, or even science or religion could not predict it. Hell, they could hardly explain it.

But none of that mattered tonight. The great tarot cards in the sky had been dealt and the Grim Reaper put on notice. As fate would have it, tonight was not meant to be a night of ofrendas, candles, or altars clad in marigolds, but rather a night of pain, suffering, bloodletting and loss of life. Tonight would be a mass reunion of the living and deceased all right, but it would also be one of reckoning and disciplinary measures.

There was a certain feeling in the air that the other shoe was about to drop. The telluric warning signs of danger seemed imminent. They couldn't quite place it, but just like New Year's Eve 1999, if the world was going to end, they would do it the best way they knew how—drunk of their asses, partying, and completely flippant toward any impending doom. Just like the warning printed on the side of cigarette packs people ignored even as their uncles were in ICUs on ventilators from lung cancer. *Red Asphalt* may have made you want to throw up your cafeteria macaroni and powdered cheese, but it did little from keeping you from drunk driving on prom night. So, too, did they ignore the admonishments of Reverend Todd, who was written off simply as a paranoid doomsayer. The main reason they went to church, was because they were all expected to.

The townsfolk went about their ways, doing as they had done every Halloween night for so very many years prior. But the Blood Moon in the sky rose to its peak, and very soon the real games would begin. One by one, the kids with plastic goblin masks and jack-o'-lantern candy buckets felt the drowsiness hit their eyelids. So too did the adults wring their hands together in a perverse manner. The hive mind didn't totally understand it yet, but for some reason, a sense of dread trickled down their brainstems like a lethal IV drip full of phenobarbital. It was time for the real Devil's Night to commence, kill or be killed. For some it would be metaphorical, for others quite literal. It was a cosmic roll of the dice as to which befell whom.

★★★★

Vincent stumbled from the woods looking worse for wear. He had been digging around the Indian Burial grounds, sometimes using just his bare hands, and he now appeared more haggard than he ever.

The Volare charged through the woods like a bootlegger on a moonshine run, and its tires barked as they slung off mud, finally gripping the rigid pavement once again.

Vincent ran from outside the tree line, barely getting a glimpse of Rayna in the passenger seat of the police cruiser; He wasn't sure if she had seen him, as the car had flown by at breakneck speed.

The interior lights of the dash that refracted off the windshield, when juxtaposed against the dark of the forest, guaranteed that she hadn't. Inside the car, and inside her head, she was lost in her own little world.

Vincent scrambled to make any kind of contact with her, but it was too late. The car quickly moved on, and Vincent got a whiff of the strong carbon monoxide from the high-powered combustion engine for his troubles. He thought the smell was sweet, and a menacing smile cracked across his face.

Suddenly, Vincent's rational side took over. *Oh shit. Down-Home Days.* The sight of Rayna caused him to recall his commitment to her. He was torn between his quest to stop the Horseman and his teenage hormones. *Hadn't it been clear that the Horseman would kill again? Yes, that was definite. But if anything were to happen on a mass scale, it would definitely be in town, the epicenter of Dutch Down-Home Days. Was it possible he could accomplish both? See Rayna and stop the Horseman?*

He was off in a blaze toward town. "Not even the Horseman could keep me away."

Chapter 32

The high school treated Down-Home Days and Halloween with the same reverence the rest of America gave to Christmas. In this town, no matter what day it fell on, it would always be extended throughout the entire weekend. As tonight was a Wednesday, Dr. Paulding wouldn't have to be back in service until Monday. It would make for a very long weekend indeed. As the feel-good doctor was technically off the clock, he made his way to the back of the house, where he kept the adult versions of prescription medications that he was more than happy to self-medicate with. Paulding's mind drifted to a simpler time.

Before his parents had died, they took in a retired university provost from SUNY Binghamton who was also African American. The Paulding family had vowed to help any fellow Blacks within their community as much as they could, including a place to stay. The man paid little rent, nor was it ever asked of him, and as one might have expected, he became somewhat of a mentor to the college-aged Conrad, who was forty years his junior. The man, Dr. Adheem, had a penchant for collecting vintage items, many owned by former Rockefellers and others transported from the Voigt house in Grand Rapids, Michigan. Each one had a story, and every night Adheem would tell the younger Paulding about some of the item's historical significance.

One such item had been a beautifully carved Black Forest cuckoo clock from Bavaria. It was a dull brown with bright white ivory roman numerals on the face and had shiny, elongated silver pine cone weights, which dangled from its chain gear. The elderly doctor loved the metaphor of the clock. He'd often ask the younger

Paulding what he noticed first. The answer was always the same—the white numbers. Dr. Adheem always jubilantly agreed with the youth.

"Yes, indeed. The whites are definitely more polished and prominent and are put up front so you accept them at face value. But what really makes that clock work?" he would enquire. "All the brown and intricate wood beneath it. The gears are tough and sturdy, hardened and strong. They last for sometimes centuries doing all the work, while the face takes all the credit for time itself."

This was quite a revelation the first time Paulding had heard it. He distinctly remembered admiring the carved wooden birds and flowers, the pendulum, intricate architecture and very infrastructure of the clock that held it together. The strong linden wood and walnut casings were the real heroes of the masterpiece. All beautiful, all brown. Dr. Adheem had said that God himself was a skilled artisan clockmaker and only He could know the objective behind the design. Only God knew how each piece worked together and what they each had contributed. The white pieces weren't any more or less important than their brown counterparts. It was a simple lesson from Paulding's elder to love who he was, despite the face value society had assigned to him.

But as nice and inspiring as that teaching may have been, over time young Paulding became bored of hearing the same metaphor used over and over. He was much more interested in an old apothecary medicine cabinet Dr. Adheem had recreated to look like an exact replica of W.G. Herpolsheimer's, who had been Voigt's business partner back in the Mitten. The display had four shelves worth of items, including a small round mirror, dental implements, vials of elixirs with deteriorating cork stoppers, plungers, and many, many boxes of 1800s-era medications. There was a mortar and pestle, bottles upon bottles of various snake oils, and even an electroshock collar. Name brands like Caulk, Penotape, Beechams, and Carters all graced the eye, but the one

Paulding had somehow sniffed out amongst all of them was a pharmaceutical-grade narcotic for toothaches and headaches. It was simply labeled cocaine, and would change the way Paulding saw his future profession forever. Adheem had never suspected it, but had he checked his brick of the powdery substance, known as coca colloquially, he would have realized it had been replaced with cheap baking soda. The irony wasn't lost on Paulding that the substance was the most brilliant of whites on the color spectrum.

Paulding now picked through some prescription meds, which he used widely for recreational use. He had among them Adheem's vintage display right in plain sight. For nostalgia's sake, he had left the old man's museum much as it had probably appeared in the home of Carl G. A. Voigt back in 1895. If anyone had ever found it, he could simply claim them as antique display items. Besides, as a psychiatrist, he was allowed to have a modicum of prescription drugs on hand. The Xanax, Vicodin and Percocet should be fine, but the OxyContin and Special K, along with hypodermic needles, were pushing his luck.

He eagerly popped his happy pills with a healthy swig of scotch before he made his way back toward the front of the house. He knew if any last stragglers of trick-or-treaters were coming, they would soon be there. It was getting later and the real fun was soon to get kicked off. He sat back in his overstuffed, deep-chocolate brown reclining chair and began to slowly but surely enjoy the oncoming ride.

★★★★

Rayna also had a large display of items splayed out before her in her bedroom, but unlike Paulding's, hers consisted of makeup and arts and crafts accoutrement.

She sat at her makeup table adjusting her ring light and mirror, surrounded by glitter-bedecked nail polishes and trendy fashion palettes. The closest she ever got to a controlled substance was ordering from Jeffree Star. She took the utmost care to do her hair in luscious blonde curls, and her glamour makeup had been set to perfection. On the bed lay a crumpled heap of blue satin, frills, and lace.

Constances sat on the other edge of the bubblegum-pink, laced comforter starring intensely at Rayna's laptop. A man of his stature, fully dressed in a police uniform, looked quite comedic hunched over the hot-pink encasement that had little puffy stickers of various Furbies plastered all over it. It was hilarious contrast that made Rayna giggle every time she snuck a peek at her entranced dad through her mirror's reflection. *How could she have ever been mad at him?*

As he surfed the web, he came across a page that mentioned Acker and his small part in the Revolutionary War. Constance unfolded the page of names from the Van Tassel Manor and compared it to those listed in the article. He shielded it from Rayna's view. "Son-of-a-bitch. A target list?" Constance thought he said it to himself, but his daughter overheard the softly spoken words.

"What?" came her razor-sharp query.

He chose to ignore her. He was good at that.

It was clear to her that he was hiding something, so she determinedly broke the silence, so as to engage him. "Dad, you ever think about Mom?"

He stopped reading and looked up over his reading glasses. Any other night, that would have seemed to come out of nowhere. But the father in him knew exactly where this was coming from, and where it was going.

"Honey, I always think about your mom. Every minute of every hour of every day." No lies were there to be detected.

"I know, but especially now. You know Halloween was her… and how she, you know…" She couldn't bring herself to finish any of the thoughts. Her eyes welled up with tears.

Constance felt a pang in his chest. He placed the laptop down on the bed and edged closer to his daughter, gently embracing her with one comforting arm. "Honey, if your mother were still alive, she would want you to have fun tonight. This was her favorite time of year." Now it was his eyes that were moistening.

"I know, Dad. It's just that we never talk about how she…" Rayna trailed off.

Constance seemed taken aback. He had no intention of revisiting his wife's death. He returned to the laptop and wiped his glistening eyes. He honed in on a graphic of the Horseman on the computer screen, where his internet search down the rabbit hole had led him. "I'd rather not." It was a throwaway line he gave her over his cold shoulder.

Rayna put the makeup down with a pronounced whack and shot him a glance of disbelief; she had honestly thought they were finally connecting. "Dad?" was all she could muster.

"I'm sorry, Lorraine, just not now, and especially not tonight." He tapped the name Williams on the screen. "Where'd you say Maw Maw was taking Bobbie for trick-or-treating tonight?"

"Evergreen Street." She had already started to apply concealer, knowing full well her father was avoiding the conversation. "There's hardly any traffic there, so she figured it'd be safe. Why?"

"Right. Nice homes too. Probably giving out full-sized candy bars over there." Constance stood up and clasped the shell case of the laptop together. "Okay look, I need to go check on the sheriff, and then your grandma. You'll be okay?"

Damn, that was harsh. She stared up, her crystalline eyes unblinking in their disbelief. "Yeah, Dad, I'll catch a ride from someone. Or maybe I'll just walk," she finally said when she realized her father had refused to give up in the impromptu stare down. She looked dejected. She put her had under her chin and wasn't even pretending to be sad this time.

"Rayna, I promise we'll talk about your mother some other time, but now's not the right time."

"Okay, Dad," she acquiesced. At least he had acknowledged the subject this time. It was a start.

"Just promise me one thing." He paused, then leaned in for added fatherly effect "When you see Vince, you call me right away. And don't do anything stupid with him. Please."

"I promise, Dad." As much as Rayna played with him, she didn't like to see her father this distraught.

Constance kissed her gently on the forehead, then they shared a sincere hug before he left.

Rayna went back to primping herself in the mirror and watched in the reflection as her father shut the door behind him. Her eyes were looking, but instead of seeing, they glared off into the distance; a hollow thousand-yard stare.

★★★★

The effect of the medication had started to hit Paulding hard, and the good doctor rode the wave high. This was the good shit, and he let it engulf him.

The doorbell rang, startling him from his dreamscape.

He stumbled up and grabbed a bowl of Halloween candy, knocking over the scotch. "Fuck!"

The doorbell again.

"Hang on, you little shits." Paulding was cursing more at the loss of good whiskey than the impatience of the pint-sized brats.

He chuckled in spite of himself as he opened the door to the cutest trio of trick-or-treaters imaginable, plus one older boy. The kids screeched, "Trick-or-treat!" in perfect unison. The smaller boys had Lock, Shock, and Barrel costumes on, and the older boy had an ill-fitting PeeWee Herman suit. His budding stubble, however, betrayed the getup as it poked through the white face paint. They were obviously big Paul Reubens fans.

Dr. Paulding happily, if not drunkenly, handed out generous portions of candy, patting each kid on the head, even the taller adolescent.

"Pee Wee, right?" asked Paulding.

"I know you are, but what am I?" the tall kid said in a snarky tone.

"Happpy Halloweeeen." Paulding slurred his words as he ushered the kids off the porch. He nearly tumbled down the uneven steps, but caught himself just in the nick of time. "And stay out of the basement of the Alamo," he yelled at the kids. They looked back in profound appreciation.

He quickly closed the door on the lovable tykes, as he was eager to punch his ticket and jump back up on the freewheelin' Peace Train.

"Better check for razor blades…", said the Pee Wee boy.

"…or Propofol!", came Barrel's witty, and unexpected response.

All the kids laughed and disappeared down the darkness of the thinned-out street.

★★★★

Rayna was glossing her lips when she suddenly became curious about what her father had been searching online. She made her way over to the bed. No need to search the history, as the computer opened right to the page.

It was an urban legend page dedicated to the Horseman. There were tons of them, actually. This particular one, entitled "Revenge of the Fallen," was some sort of conspiracy folklore page. It was a very common style of page, which often mixed various religions, folklores and urban myths together to create its own mythology. Boring and typical, like a bastardized version of Dungeons and Dragons. It claimed the Horseman, who was also known as Allocer, would ride his Nuckelavee, apparently a kind of demonized version of a Karabakh horse, and exact revenge on his enemies. It allegedly would happen in due time, and was a curse that would outlast generations.

Rayna had heard most of this stuff before and wasn't at all interested. She checked the browser history and went back a few more pages. All she could find was American Independence historical pages. They were long, filled with facts, and exactly *not* what she was in the mood for. She hadn't, however, forgotten about her discussion with her dad, so she typed her mother's name into the search bar.

An obituary came up, along with several articles about her mother's never-ending humanitarian efforts. She had read them all before, and it wasn't exactly what she had been looking for. Then she pulled up an archived article from New York State's Department of Transportation. It listed several details about her parents' car accident, which had occurred when she had been around six years old. Some descriptions were clinical, others rather morbid, but she found herself drawn into the article. It explained how her father had crashed the car and her mother had died, but reckless driving charges had never been filed against him.

She had very foggy memories of the incident. Most likely, her developing juvenile mind had wisely chosen to block it out for years. Her eyes started to glaze over as she began to get lost in her thoughts and relive snippets she recalled of the incident. They were now forming clearly in her head, like the unwanted crystallization of a long-forgotten nightmare.

Chapter 33

Helen Constance was beautiful. She had the air of a silver screen Hollywood goddess. She had often been compared to Ingrid Bergman, and in fact shared some of the star's Swedish lineage.

The striking blonde woman trudged through the rain, pulling the decade-younger Michael Constance from the bar by the scruff of his neck. Michael wasn't yet a deputy then, but rather a park ranger who worked part-time in the Catskills. The bar was an English Pub called the Grimalk Inn. Its faded neon sign had a dark-gray hissing cat that sported an arched back with raised fur. Half of the bulbs flashed intermittently across the flaking white paint of the words, creating a subdued and spooky atmosphere.

Michael had a sullen expression as he was literally dragged by the collar by his infuriated wife. A six-year-old Rayna sat in the back of a used late 90s Volvo 740 sedan. Its green paint had been peeling for some time, and the fresh coat of rain made some of its veneer appear turquoise while other parts sheened a dull blue. Its front bumper dangled just inches above the ground, and its brakes were rusted down to the drum. It looked like a half-scaled mackerel that had been discarded at a fish market. The rain pounded the vehicle's windows, muffling the raised voices that were coming from outside the car.

"Damn it, Mikey! You promised me." Helen's hands were firmly placed on the hips of her mom-jeans. She didn't even care that she was getting soaked. In his drunken state, Michael had wanted to tell her that she looked sexy when she was mad like that, especially being all wet like she was. It wouldn't have gone over well, at all, if he had.

Young Rayna alighted from the car holding a purple stuffed horse with a rainbow-colored tail and mane. Its large plastic eyes seemed almost mocking, as did its tiny upturned mouth. "Mommy, can we go home? I'm tired," she beckoned. The car door behind her was still open, taking in buckets of rain.

"Lorraine, I said to stay in the Goddamned car," Helen railed at her daughter, misdirecting at her the anger she felt toward her husband. The distraught young girl started to cry as she climbed back into the sedan's roomy backseat.

"Look what you made me do." Helen composed herself. She tried to look her husband in the eye, but he simply stared down at his feet. He had no answers for her. They both were getting drenched. "Michael, what's gotten into you? You never used to be like this before…" She couldn't bring herself to say whatever it was she was going to.

Whatever it was, it triggered her spouse. Michael aggressively snatched the keys from his wife's hand. "Let's go." He started to walk toward the driver's seat.

"I'll drive. You're in no shape—"

But the young lush had already started the car, and on every word that left her mouth, he would rev the engine, more condescendingly each time. He was acting like a petulant toddler, and all Helen was immediately concerned about was getting her now rain-soaked child home safely and into dry clothes. Besides, it was just a couple of miles journey through the wooded connector, and there was no traffic on that road at this time of night. She reluctantly got in.

★★★★

The windows fogged as the car careened down the backroads through the rain. It was pitch-black, save for the car's failing headlights. The years of oxidation had given them a faint yellow glow. Every tree the beam caught seemed like some demonic figure waiting to pounce on the unsuspecting couple from out of the shadows. The Blood Moon was hanging like a dollop of blood high above in the autumn sky.

Helen turned to comfort the pouting Rayna. "Mommy didn't mean to yell at you, honey. We're almost home."

Rayna defiantly crossed her arms tight over her stuffed animal and stuck out her lower lip in endearing, but adamant, dissent. Her mother tried not to laugh at her daughter's overwhelming cuteness.

Once her mom turned back around, Rayna pretended to make her stuffed horse fly about. "Fly, horsey, fly," came the timbre of her childlike innocence.

Michael rubbed his eyes, and the car nearly hit a downed tree branch. It swerved hard left as the inebriated driver over-corrected. Helen was nearly thrown against him with the force of the swerve.

"Watch out!" she shouted. Then, realizing her husband's delicate state, she tried a more maternal approach. She had seen him like this in increasing intervals, and it hardly ever turned out well. The steely focus, glassed-over eyes, and angry stare were all predictable signals. "Are you okay? Please pull over and let me drive," she implored.

"I'm fine, okay? I don't need to be babied." His response was also run-of-the-mill for how this scenario usually played out between them.

"I wasn't babying you, Michael, but you promised to take your daughter trick-or-treating." It had become harder for Helen to hold in the rage that had been boiling up inside her. "It's nearly midnight now. You couldn't even manage a Goddamned phone call? And for what? Beer?" She was ramping herself up into a full-on tirade. He fucking deserved it. "Where are your priorities, Michael Constance?" The full names were coming out now.

Michael shot his eyes forward, every word fueling his anger. He punched the accelerator, throwing caution to the wind. The rain came down in sheets, making it even harder to see. He didn't care. He was rallying the car as it glided along, on pissed-off autopilot now.

Young Rayna pointed out the window at something in the darkness. "Look, Mommy!"

Helen turned around, again facing her daughter. She could feel the hot trickle of tears streaming down her own face. Her anger had pushed her to the brink, and she could barely look at her husband. She was very close at that moment to wishing he was dead. Perhaps she had even though it, albeit briefly.

"What is it, honey?" Her voice lowered several octaves to console the child.

"Horsey, Mommy. Horsey," Rayna chanted. She held the stuffed animal parallel with the road, pretending it was running alongside the vehicle. It reflected off the glass.

"Aw, is purple horsey running with us, baby?" Helen asked, their bond quickly reconciled.

"No, Mommy. The other horsey," the child adorably stated.

Helen strained her eyes, but the night was just too dark when compared with the interior glow of the vehicle. She laughed in spite of herself. Little Rayna could always cheer her up, even if she was in the shittiest of moods.

Out of nowhere, the Horseman and his Hellsteed flashed through the headlights, scaling the hood of the speeding vehicle untouched. It happened so fast, it was almost undetectable.

In the chaos, the car swerved wildly toward the giant oak tree near the Indian burial ground.

"Oh my God, Michael! Look out!" Helen swallowed her words in a gulp of fear.

A loud crash stopped the car, and all its occupants, dead in their tracks. Glass shattered and rained down upon them in an explosion of silvery, razor-sharp shards. The boxy Volvo had rightfully been billed as one of the safest vehicles of its day, but this worn-out jalopy was no match for such an impact, nor such a daunting curse.

★★★★

Small drops of rain beat down rhythmically on Michael's face. He slowly opened his eyes, only to see the limbs of a solid oak leaning toward him like the claw of a gargantuan sylvan Kaiju. His conscious mind slowly came to, now completely sober. It had been about ten minutes since the impact. Suddenly, his thoughts were lucid and his brain began racing with the probable horrific outcomes of the accident. He tried to turn his head, but a searing pain streaked up the very core of his spine. He drew a deep breath and tasted blood in his mouth.

"Helen. Rayna," he sputtered. *My God, Rayna!* The child remained silent.

He felt the warmth of his wife's body stir beside him. The rain trickled to a stop. The night was so still, the quiet hung in the air like an invisible, stifled cloud. It amplified his wife's softly spoken words.

"Rayna, Mommy loves you, baby."

Michael was able to raise his neck a couple of inches in order to look at his wife. He wished he hadn't. It was a vision he would have nightmares about for years to come and would never once forget. A large tree branch had filled the car and impaled a now quickly dying and bloodied Helen. The once beige seats were now stained a deep crimson red. Michael could see shattered glass over the car's crumpled hood, as steam and blood congealed into a syrupy pool upon the vehicle's crinkled bonnet. His eyes shifted to meet his wife's gaze. Her life was rapidly slipping from her.

Michael wrenched his arm backward. He ignored the intense spasms of acute pain that would have paralyzed a lessor man. He felt around behind him, his hand searching for his child, and prayed with any ounce of faith he had that she was alive. He felt the wet and matted mane of her tiny stuffed animal, and his eyes began to water as he imagined it was blood from his daughter, spread throughout her disheveled hair.

Little Rayna, battered and bruised, lay crunched down into a ball on the backseat floorboard. Crayons, half-eaten lollipops, glass shards, and lost fries were stuck all over her body. The entire contents of the back of the car had been flung onto the floor mats along with the child. Rayna clutched her billowy horse companion tightly, silently bawling. Luckily for Michael, the dampness he'd felt had been tears and the remnants of rain, not blood. Her barely audible sobs revealed to her petrified parents that she was still alive. He let out a father-sized sigh of relief.

"I'm so sorry, baby. But didn't you see that thing? That fucking thing outside?" He was mad at the vision. He was mad at the rain. At the reasons he drank, at his wife for yelling at him. He was mad at the shitty, balding tires and the failing brakes. He was mad at everything but himself. He wasn't yet willing to take responsibility for his actions, especially with the consequences being so dire.

Helen turned to him. With a brief moment of clarity, she annunciated her words perfectly and her breath seemed normal. He almost convinced himself that she would live, that everything was fine. "Mike, please. Just stay with me now." She reached her hand over to caress his cheek. It was drenched in her blood and made a vile red smudge across his face. His salty tears muted the blood into tiny vermillion splotches.

For a moment that seemed to last an eternity, the three members of the close-knit family simply cried together. They wept softly amongst the calm of the noiseless and still night air. They wept for what was, and what never would be again.

Finally, Helen sensed her last moments were nigh and turned to her beloved husband, forgiving him. With her dying breath, she proclaimed, "I believe you, Michael." The air escaped her punctured lungs, but the glint in her eye lasted a few seconds longer before her pupils turned an impenetrable black and she was gone.

With a flash and a war cry, the Horseman and his Hellsteed jumped over the crumpled hood of the car. The animal's hooves clambered over the dented metal as it sought out solid footing. The entire car shook in their wake as the entity ran off into the night, falling off into the infinite blackness of the barely visible horizon.

Inside the car, Michael experienced near full-on hyperventilation. His eyes were filled with fear, his tongue dry. He could barely breath, much less speak out to his daughter. He looked over at his wife's gaping eyes and bloodied corpse. The smile she had died with had frozen and was now permanently plastered across her face. Though her dying words were meant to comfort her ungrateful husband, he couldn't help but wonder. *Had she seen the Horseman or had he imagined it, first in his drunkenness, then in his grief and delirium?* It pained him deeply, and served as the turning point in his commitment to fatherhood. He hadn't touched a drop since that night.

A traumatized Rayna gripped her stuffed animal in utter fear as she tried to inch herself under her father's seat. She had attempted to make herself as small as she could, if only in her mind. In her head, she was about the size of pumpernickel loaf. Fear gripped the child, and she cried into her animal, the hair of its mane getting stuck in her throat as she sucked in air between sobs. "Horsey," she cried as she rocked back and forth.

It would be two days before anyone informed the traumatized child that her mother was dead, gone forever.

★★★★

Rayna now closed her laptop. She noticed the same tattered stuffed animal on her bed. It still had a few brown stains on it from that fateful night. Its protective eye had long since gone missing.

With a deep sigh of anxiety, she started to get ready to leave for the fairgrounds. If there was one thing that could take her mind off her mother, it would be enjoying the festivities. It was what her mother would have wanted her to do. Besides, her father was off playing Rambo somewhere, and tonight was Goosey Night. Tonight and May Day were the only two times a year they had an excuse to let their hair down. Turn over some trash cans, move around people's porch furniture, drink, paint some cats with hair dye, whatever. Generally harmless pranks, and hell, the adults practically encouraged it, all in the name of tradition.

Rayna sat and contemplated her life. Her gaze lost in the mirror, she took an intense, long look at herself. She became immersed, down into the deep fathoms, with her hazel eyes. It was a moment of silent admiration. She deserved to let loose tonight! She walked over to the crumpled satin atop her bedspread. This dress, and all its frills, was saved for special occasions exactly like tonight. She picked it up and lost herself in a brief moment of thought before her actions steadily built up into more decisive movements.

She began a flurry of activity, catching a glimpse of herself as she passed her reflection in the mirror. It was almost as if she was looking at someone else. Whoever it was refused to look back at her. If she was going to feel good about herself, she'd have to confront these demons inside her head on. Once again, she sat in front of the mirror staring into the windows of her soul. After the attempted rape, her father's never-ending discipline, and Vincent's unpredictable outbursts, she was confused and adrift. Now, throw into the mix remembering the dramatic death of her mother, whom she never really got a chance to know, and she became overwhelmed.

And yet, tears wouldn't come. Rayna felt as though an invisible hand had reached inside her soul and turned her feelings inside out. The sadness didn't quite become resentment, and it certainly hadn't yet festered into fear. It did, however, turn into an unquenchable desire for independence. For once, she would live life on her own terms, starting this very night. She was going to take charge!

If you had told her at that particular moment she was only experiencing typical teenage rebellion, she would have slapped the words right out of your mouth. It was much more than that. It was beyond even a revelation. It was an epiphany, and it was about Goddamned time!

Chapter 34

Constance pulled the squad car into the field where he had last spoken with the sheriff and the other men. His headlights illuminated the ground, causing eerie, elongated shadows to creep over the uneven terrain.

He exited his car and, after a quick scan of the area, determined no one was around. Constance tried his shoulder mic one more time. "Eustice, you copy?" He waited for a response but none came. A snow-white owl flew over the treetops above him. The beating of its wings had a pronounced cadence. It was unusual to see those birds in these woods, though not entirely unheard of. Could have been someone's stray pet, or a lone Canadian expat.

"Sheriff, do you read me?" he implored again. The crackle of static came back, which made the deputy furrow his brow. That meant either the sheriff was trying to return the call, or at the very least, something was keying up his walkie button.

Just past the shrubbery, Constance could hear the faint sputter of the sheriff's radio. It made a noise similar to what an AM radio makes as it glides between channels—static interspersed between brief moments of dead air. It certainly sounded like someone was trying to respond. Constance keyed it several times to try and pinpoint the location. The sound seemed to be coming from one direction one moment, then a completely different one the next. He had experienced this aural hallucination before in the service, when the beating of helicopter rotors would ricochet off buildings in confined spaces giving the illusion they were coming from often opposite, or even multiple, directions. In this case, it was probably the insulation of all the tree foliage that was causing the sensation.

As he continued pressing his mic, he unwittingly began playing a perverse version of Marco-Polo with the missing sheriff. There was no doubt in his mind that it was in fact the sheriff's radio. After a few moments of basic field triangulation, he narrowed down the sound as coming from just beyond the tree line. Constance slowly unholstered his sidearm and tentatively approached the muffled chirps with a churning sensation in his stomach. He had a very bad feeling about this.

★★★★

Doctor Paulding was just about to sit back down and comfy up with another round of scotch, when there was a pronounced knock at the door. It was getting too late for kids, but whatever, you're only young once.

He sighed and grabbed the candy bowl once again. Definitely too high to care, whatever little sugar goblins were out there, they were in for a treat. He was prepared to dispose of the entire remainder of his stash, bolt the door, turn out the light and drop some more feel-good candy of his own.

He had the bowl already halfway turned up and ready to pour as he deftly opened the door. "Here ya—"

The vintage pumpkin-faced Homer Laughlin bowl fell to the porch and shattered into exactly thirteen jagged pieces. The confections bounced off the hardwood porch, some making it as far as the lawn. The doctor stared up at the towering Horseman with complete terror in his eyes, dropping down to his knees reflexively.

The headless strongman grabbed the largest pottery shard and shoved the burnt-orange implement point first into the doctor's chest. The sheer force of the object caused the air to escape out of Paulding's lung like a punctured tire. Paulding instinctively grabbed the spike and tried to pull it out, but received a slashed wrist in return. The Horseman used his superior strength to impale the

251

ceramic weapon deeper, which hooked just enough to catch onto the doctor's rib cage. The Hessian used it to make Paulding rise to his feet and then pushed him backward back over the threshold and into his house. He was a supernatural puppet master, and the doctor his unwilling marionette.

The Horseman held a flaming pumpkin head perfectly balanced in his other hand. If an Entity such as he had any patience, it was long gone by now. After all, there were so many people to kill on All Hallows' Eve, and oh so very little time. He kicked the doctor square in the chest, lodging the spike so far in it was no longer visible. Paulding was sent flying backward and landed on the ground in a flurry of broken ribs, candy, and pills. He hit his head on the way down and lay unconscious on the floor, mouth agape.

The Horseman gently placed the flaming pumpkin head on the console table just inside the door. The motion was fluid and refined, almost genteel. Several bottles of medication were always within arm's reach throughout Paulding's home. The Horseman picked up an oversized prescription bottle with a large print label, spinning it around inside his hand. He used his thumb to turn it like a carousel music box, almost as if slowly reading it. Of course, one needed eyes to accomplish such feats. If one had to guess, it might have seemed that the Horseman was purposely waiting for Paulding to regain consciousness. He soon got his wish, as groggy moans of pain escaped from the physician's mouth. His breathing was extremely labored, his olive skin had turned a pasty bleachy-blue color, and thick, dark blood trickled from his nose and mouth.

"Why? Why would you…" the doctor couldn't quite manage to fully get the words out between garbled mouthfuls of blood.

The Horseman stood over Paulding and spun the pill bottle cap off like a toy, stripping the thread out of its plastic fasteners with the strength in his powerful fingers. Slowly and methodically, he began emptying the contents of the bottle into Paulding's mouth. One by one the pills hit his face, some going in his mouth, others degradingly bouncing off his forehead and cheeks. He was like an unwillingly participant in an aggressive bukkake gangbang. Degraded and humiliated, the doctor's mouth fought between shutting in order to stave off the pills and gasping for air to stay alive. It was an impossible tug-of-war of survival. Every time he would try to scream, another pill would enter his throat, causing him to gag and choke.

Paulding had lost a lot of blood, and his attempts to spit the pills out was slowly diminishing. One by one, the pills began to mount up. The doctor was falling in and out of consciousness, but the Horseman seemed to have all the patience in the world. As his airway started to get blocked, the doctor again gained consciousness. Finally now fully awake, his eyes bugged as he gasped for air, his entire mouth filled with pills. Every time he sucked in a breath, the pills would wedge deeper in his airway. A frothy pink saliva began to bubble from his mouth and nose as he slowly and painfully suffocated.

The Horseman may as well have been the Empire State Building as the doctor looked up at him. From his point of view on the floor, the mountain of a man, the height of his legend, and the sheer magnitude of the situation seemed insurmountable. In fact, they were.

The Horseman undid the belt axe from his utility belt so that its blunt side was facing forward. He raised it high above—where his head would have been if he'd had one—and brought the flat side of the weighted axe down as hard as he could. The forceful contact of the device, which had been made specifically for barbaric battles, smashed teeth, breaking them at the roots, and cut off Paulding's air supply for good. Pills, teeth and a severed, swollen tongue were now irreparably lodged into the doctor's esophagus. He stared up in shock with bloodshot eyes as he experienced a few final moments of unfettered terror.

Paulding's body reflexively entertained a few small convulsions before it went limp. The Horseman couldn't help but dole out a few more authoritative blunt-force blows to his skull. The doctor's head rocked back, making grotesque squishy sounds as it did, like a rotting pumpkin. It was hard to tell the exact moment during the brutal killing the doctor actually asphyxiated, but it hardly mattered. He lay there, a victim of his own devices. Eyes wide open, mouth and jaw obliterated. DEAD.

Chapter 35

The steady beam of Constance's industrial-strength flashlight danced across the piles of leaves as he searched for the sheriff's walkie. Finally, the chirp of the recall was mere paces away. As Constance pulled back some entangled kudzu, his light caught a glint off of Eustice's gold badge. The horrific visions seemed to all come at once; a visceral tsunami of blood and guts that revealed every limb, entrail, and ghastly detail of the murderous rampage. Constance had finally discovered the disfigured corpses of Sheriff Eustice and the other boys. Eustice's face was still intact, but the others were mangled and disfigured. It was impossible to identify the remains at first glance. Constance was neither prepared nor trained for a scene of such magnitude.

"Jesus!" Constance would have vomited again, but his body had already ejected any semblance of food hours ago. Instead, his abdomen contorted in several dry heaves as the bitter acidic taste filled his mouth.

Constance was breathing hard now. He recognized the noise of his own high-pitched wheezes as being identical to those he had exhaled the night his wife died. His entire body pulsed with adrenaline as unbridled waves of fear rushed over him. It cascaded down his body like unseen tributaries of a diabolical waterfall. He again had one thought on his mind, and it coupled with a sheer commitment as protector. Constance fumbled the flashlight as he went to cover his mouth. He tried his best to quiet the spasms in his stomach, but the entirety of his movements seemed to be on autopilot now. It was as if his body's actions had a good three-to-four second lead before they registered across his mind. He became an unwilling participant in a thrill ride of life and death. There was nothing he could do now but react.

From out of nowhere, the monstrous black mass of the Horseman's Hellsteed barreled through the woods toward him. Constance stumbled backward, managing to get off a few wild shots. He side-rolled in a pivot that would have made a professional running back proud. Had he not pirouetted when he did, he would have undoubtedly been trampled to death. Constance felt a whoosh of hot air pass over him as the animal came within mere inches of his torso. But it was much more than that; the surge was one of dark energy as well. A feeling of dread and helplessness overcame Constance upon realizing he had been in such close proximity to a clearly evil being.

The riderless horse continued on in the darkness, bolting, practically floating in a full gallop. It impossibly blended into the shadows of the night like a Hellish apparition. Constance had no way, or desire, to track it on foot.

Briefly getting his wits about him, the deputy made a beeline for the squad car. He ran so fast, he had to extend a stiff-arm to stop himself from crashing full-speed against the vehicle. The impact was so hard, it dented the door, bruised the officer's hand, and rocked the car with momentum. Constance frantically threw the still–lit flashlight onto the seat and jammed the manual lock on the doors. Not that they would have helped against any supernatural Rider, and most certainly not against a 2500 pound animal from Hell. But Constance was far from thinking rationally at this point. He did manage, however, to engage his inner survival mode. Decades of military training were once again paying off. Once safely inside, he properly tuned the frequency on the police scanner and spoke into the CB mic.

"Hello? Hello, state patrol, do you read? State patrol, this is Deputy Constance, Sleepy Hollow. Officer down! I need back up, over!" His pleas for help went unanswered. He tried again, but there was nothing but static on the radio.

Constance reached for his cell phone, but was deflated when it read NO SIGNAL. Clearly, out here in the woods there were no towers, but the police radio should have worked. He barked a few more distress calls into the mic without any response in return.

He started the car. If this had to be one, he could make it a race between horses. The horsepower rating on the Plymouth made the odds 380 to 1 in his favor. He needed the Volare to show its superiority, now more than ever. Constance gunned the accelerator like a rookie at the quarter mile on drag night. He had forgotten that the wheels of the car weren't on solid ground. As the drive train torqued with full American muscle, the steel-belted radials carved out a deep trench into the dampened earth. The wheels spun, coating the white, raised letters in a thick chocolate soup of raw earth. The might of the Detroit-made car bogged itself a good half a foot down, deep into the muck.

"Fuck!" Constance slammed the car into park and bolted outside.

★★★★

Back at Paulding's, the Horseman had kicked through the screen door, knocking it off its hinges. He breached the door as if on a mission. The cantaloupe sized Jack-o-lantern, which he had set on the table inside the door, had a brainless grin plastered across its skin. Jolly in appearance, the flame inside its hollowed-head danced in the ridiculing delight of vengeful revelry. But like the Horseman, this was simply a veneer of the malicious spirits embodied within it. A much more sinister intent floated through the air. In the deep background, Paulding's body laid lifeless on the floor.

The same snow-white owl from the forest now perched itself on top of the Evergreen Street sign. The white of its plumage was in stark contrast to the bright-orange placard and black lettering of the sign. On the nearly deserted street, Maw Maw Williams held little Bobbie's hand. Being geriatric, it had taken her quite a long time to make the rounds. Her steps were tiny and sporadic, but she had refused to be babied or pampered. This was extremely ironic for someone nearly in their 90s, but Maw Maw had always been unwilling to give up her independence. Tonight was no exception. She had promised Bobbie that she would escort him down every street in the area, and Paulding's was the last house on the list.

Bobbie, dressed in a vintage Eddie Munster costume, marveled at the sight of the hulking Horseman who appeared before him. Maw Maw had lived through several generations of the Horseman's legend, and had heard and seen things that today's generations could not have even imagined. She had long believed that her daughter, Helen's, untimely demise was an act of revenge for the sins of her fathers. Though Maw Maw had been expecting this day all her life, she still cowered in fear, knowing something was terribly wrong with this situation. She felt it deep down in her brittle old bones, even more than when her rheumatoid arthritis signaled before rainstorms. For the first time in her life, she displayed the true fragility of her age.

The young boy craned his neck upward in admiration. If that was makeup, it had to have been done by a Hollywood-caliber SFX artisan.

"I think we should go, Bobbie. It's getting late," said Maw Maw in direct opposition to her previous vigor and insistence. Now it was the defiant child's turn to resist, as he spun himself in the opposite direction. Even at his age, the youngest Constance was stronger than the octogenarian.

Conrad Paulding's blood was still dripping off the belt axe in the Horseman's hand. Little Bobbie focused his eyes on the blade, then they quickly darted back up to the cauterized amputation of the Horseman's meaty neck.

"Coooool costume!," said the unsuspecting boy, with an ear to ear grin.

The Horseman paused, slowly spinning his body to face the youth, his shoulders taught as he stiffly pivoted. If he had a head, it would've been mad-dogging the kid right now.

Even though she felt cold to the touch, Maw Maw, now sweating, clutched Bobbie hard, sending a pain up his tiny hand where the bones of her skeletal digits pressed against his fingers. She stumbled back as the Horseman raised the belt axe high above him.

"Shit!" was the only word that escaped the old woman's dry lips. For being such a proper woman her entire life, it was a hell of an unorthodox last word to go out on.

The Horseman swung the axe down in one skillful swoop.

Bobbie noticed the sound of the sharp blade splitting tender flesh was just like it was in the movies. The child had seen so many horror movies, he had a hard time distinguishing fantasy from reality. If this was some kind of trick, it sure was an impressive one. He couldn't wait to tell his buddies.

Maw Maw's head landed directly inside Bobbie's jack-o'-lantern bucket. It still had the same look of concern frozen in place, but now was a sickly pale blue. As blood came spouting out of her torso like a low-pressure fountain, it finally dawned on the boy that all this was real. He felt the warm release of his bladder run down his leg. Bobbie dropped the bucket in disgust, screamed in bloody terror, and churned his little legs as fast as they would go in the opposite direction. He fell hard on the pavement, skinning his knee and tearing his costume, but got right up and kept on running. He didn't have the presence of mind to remove his mask, which made navigating through the torrent of tears and tiny plastic eye slots near impossible. Under any other circumstance, it would have been hilarious watching a mini Eddie Munster dodging trash cans and smacking headfirst into a parked car. The little kid was laid out cold, his body splayed in the street.

The Horseman had no desire to follow the boy. He had accomplished what he had come there to do and there were much bigger fish to fry. The boy could wait for some other Triduum of the Hallows. At least then, maybe the adolescent could put up a decent fight. It always proved more entertaining that way.

Chapter 36

The town's Dutch Down-Home Days Ball had been a long-standing tradition in the village since its early settlement days. New Netherlands, as the area had been previously known, was a safe haven for Dutch fur traders. They originally had no intentions of staying there. It served as a nice resting place, a tarry town if you will, on their way to Fort Orange. They often made it a point to respite there on their way to trade goods with Native Americans in Albany. Soon, the Dutch West India Company implemented the patroon system, rewarding tracts of land along the Hudson to extremely wealthy Dutch colonists who didn't mind settling there. It was here that these tiny little towns, including what would eventually have the moniker of Sleepy Hollow, would be settled. Hunting and shipping would be an integral part of their society, and the settlers needed an escape from the complexities of rural life.

There were minimal perks compared to what they were used to back in Hollander civilization. Their society, accordingly, became increasingly more Puritanical, leading many to need a release from the strict day-to-day constraints of their religion. Although predominantly wealthy, and scarcely treated like the African slaves, they were in a foreign land after all. This led many to become quite nostalgic and homesick. So much so, they would do anything they could in order to make life feel more like the Motherland. The local governors, patroon investors, and Native Americans proved to be a three-pronged threat to a gentile society, at least in their eyes. So once their religion became reformed and recognized, they used events like the Dutch Down-Home Days to further their foothold in the area. This served a twofold service, as it also helped implement their own newfound sense of tradition, belonging, and identity.

The English eventually sought superiority through their own means of tyranny up and down the Hudson, and in 1664 took the area for themselves by force. By then, however, it was too late to uproot the culture of the Dutch, and to this very day, events like Dutch Down-Home Days have prevailed, along with countless additional practices and culturally significant contributions.

As Washington Irving, himself, mentioned in his magnum opus, the whole "family of cakes" was represented at the celebration. In fact, every fruit, pastry, delectable meat, scrod, baked good, and seasonal offering was in abundance. With the inclusion of the Polish immigrants, who had settled mostly west of there in Pennsylvania, and the Italians who came up from the city, the influx of delicacies heeded no bounds. In recent years, every imaginable incarnation of pumpkin and pumpkin spice flavored items had been represented across the full spectrum of gourd-related cuisine delights. The confluence of the Tappan Zee and Hudson River was also that of many peoples and cultures. It was the literal amalgamation of every culinary delicacy, which spanned a minimum of a two hundred mile radius, and at least an equal number of years.

The townsfolk were extremely proud of their history, and the Dutch Down-Home Days celebration was a way to show that off. It was one thing that seemed to unite the community in an esprit de corps despite their differences throughout the previous year. It was bonds over traditions like these, as well as that of the Horseman, which rendered the community's fellowship ultimately unbreakable. The festivities usually took place on the old fairgrounds near the center of town. There was plenty of space there on the old calvary parade grounds to set up the multitude of booths, rides, haunted houses, dances, contests, exhibits, and the perennial favorite Headless Horseman's Corn Maze.

The attraction had been born out of a particularly witty pun on the word maize one Halloween at a dad's-jokes face-off. The very next year, they created the sprawling, nearly ten-acre attraction where everyone was welcomed to try their very best to escape the maze without getting lost, and before the dreaded Horseman could "get" them. The maze would also have the occasional scare actor, who would pop out of a hidey-hole to give patrons quite the jump scare. Some adults partook of the installation, but it was mostly geared at the high schoolers and young adults. It was a safe space where they could quite literally hide from authority, and no one was checking IDs or coolers for snuck-in alcohol or other contraband. All in all, it was good fun and the star attraction. Everyone from school knew that sooner or later that evening, they would eventually end up there.

Everywhere one looked, people were in a festive mood. Kids wore costumes and townsfolk were having fun. Whatever particular brand of evil was surfing the comic waves of Sleepy Hollow that night hadn't yet permeated the celebration in the heart of town. Nor was anyone remotely aware there was a killer on the loose, or that Heaven and Hell were conspiring for their collective assassination.

Banners, Halloween decorations, and county fair-type booths were everywhere. Face painting, bobbing for apples, pumpkin carving contests, and more were in full swing. It was as if a thousand Spirit stores had regurgitated their wares across the land as far as the eye could see. The smell of fresh baked pumpkin pies and apple cider drifted across the air, so thick you could almost see it. The crowds of youths were celebrating life against a backdrop of death, and the adults were all pretending it was the only time of year they chose to indulge in their vices of avarice, lust, and gluttony.

Near a gazebo in the center of the grounds, a small quartet played traditional Dutch Stockade-type 1700s dance music. They would alternate that with Mozart, or Vivaldi's *Four Seasons*. Lots of up-tempo violin and fiddle gave the commemorations a light and festive air. Teens in every Halloween costume known to mankind pranced about saying hello to friends and meeting strangers who had come from miles around. Many, like Rayna, chose to wear traditional Dutch Settler costumes, some extraordinarily designed and quite valuable. The village's parties were just as legendary as their famed equestrian. Couples begin to pair off, as romance wafted through the air atop the sensual aroma of a bed of cinnamon and nutmeg flavored baked goods.

Rayna was impeccably dressed in a robin-egg blue satin Dutch Colonial wedding dress. The bodice, lace, and frills would have been enough to impress the Queen Mother herself. She was radiant. Tonight would be her one night to make a solid commitment to Vincent. If she waited any longer, it might have taken a traditional Dutch Charivari to trick the couple into quickening the timeline of their courtship. Tradition had it, if one officially kick-started a relationship at the Dutch Down-Home Days Ball, it would last well through football season, Homecoming, and most likely the remainder of the school year. It was a big commitment for Rayna, a junior, to make, and she was fully ready for the long-honored mating ritual to begin.

Her eyes scanned the premises, apprehension and restlessness clearly visible across her countenance. She looked for Vincent, to no avail, then headed to a nearby punch bowl. As she approached, she noticed a sweaty Allister and Aaron standing just off to the side.

Just back from the cemetery, the long walk had sobered them up and cleansed their system of a good amount of alcoholic content. The boys had needed a liquid refresher, and spiked the punch with the remaining liquor they'd pilfered from their fathers' liquor cabinets. They had just finished some of the tainted concoction and were laughing uncontrollably as Rayna approached. Both simultaneously saw Rayna and ditched the empty bottles under the table. She was not quite a close enough friend to know if she would tattle or not. Underage drinking was, after all, illegal, and her dad was a cop. Besides, she was known not to be a drinker.

"Hey, guys," she called over to them. She was actually glad to see them, because that probably meant Vincent wasn't too far behind.

The boys giggled like girls half their age.

"You guys seen Vincent?" she asked. Her nose cinched at the stinging smell of alcohol as she approached the two.

Allister mimicked her inflection exactly. "Nope. You try the punch, couz? It's killer."

She saw it as kind of dickish, but once the corners of his mouth curled into a smile, they all shared a hearty laugh. No harm, no foul.

"Have you guys been drinking?" She knew the answer before she had asked it. It was fine. They were harmless, and Rayna was fully ready to indulge them. Throwing caution to the wind, she filled a party cup and took a large swig. The look on her face registered the pungent taste of the alcohol. She hadn't been expecting that much of a spike. Her taste buds rebelled, and a stream of liquid sprayed out from between her teeth. The pink mist dissipated in the air as she put the empty cup back down.

"See, the good shit! Am I right?" The boys laughed. They were proud of themselves, their work here done.

Rayna wiped her mouth. "Uh, sure. I guess." The rose hue of her embarrassment nicely complemented the celestial tones of her dress. Despite her outfit, the last thing she wanted to come across as tonight was an inexperienced prude, especially to Vincent's closest friends.

Chapter 37

Vincent made his way back to the Hallowed fields of the Indian burial grounds. Halfway to Rayna, his paranoia had kicked in once again. He didn't want to admit it to himself, but part of the reason he had left was that he was actually afraid to confront the Horseman. His entire life had been filled with confrontation. Years of medication, therapy, and the never-ending parade of his mom's lovers had trained him to be quite proficient in it. He considered this an invaluable skill set, but something was different about the Horseman. Vincent couldn't understand why it was that he always seemed drawn to the Legend. He was having a hard time digesting that it was somehow tied to his own family history.

He had never studied Theravada Buddhism, Carl Sagan, or reincarnation, but if he had, he would have found many attempts at explaining some of the feelings he innately carried inside. They gnawed at his insides like a rat in a burlap bag. There was definitely some sort of cosmic connection there that at times became overwhelming. It was like the feeling you get knowing you stand in the place where some historical event happened. Tangentially inexplicable, but somehow tied to your own destiny by a higher power, which was perhaps beyond your comprehension. Vincent felt like the microcosm of the man that he was in this exact moment was at odds with the very Universe he had always been a part of. There was no denying a sense of lingering doom had overcome him.

Frantic, Vincent now fell to his knees as he once more paused at the exact place he had when being chased by the Horseman previously. He had managed to nip a shovel from one of the shacks in a backyard in the few minutes he had been near town. *What was a little petty theft during a time of crisis?* Several erratic holes where he had dug just prior littered the field. It looked like a drunken fox's den. Vincent began to hone in on an area in the field near the towering oak tree. Something drew him toward it, an unseen invocation beckoning to this very spot. As if in a trance, Vincent began to dig in the moonlight. Visualizing, adrift on the hyper focus of concentration and thoughts, he forgot about everything but the desired task. Neither Rayna, the celebrations at hand, nor even time itself were present within his thoughts. Undistracted, he robotically continued on, answering the call in his soul with prodigious efficiency.

After what could have been hours, or only moments, a thunderous crackle could be heard across the entire town. Far away, banshees and fae shrieked on the chilling winds in unbridled anticipation. Thousands of glowing fingers of lightning stretched in unison across the night sky. There wasn't a drop or precipitation to be seen, only the kind of static when cold and hot climates try to intersperse together in vain. So, too, were the living and dead now trying to co-exist. There was push and pull. A palpable friction skirted the air. An invisible tug-of-war would soon engulf the village and all its inhabitants.

Vincent's shovel hit something hard. He dropped the shovel and emphatically dug with his hands like a Rottweiler after a T-bone. After a few moments, his fingertips brushed against something relatively silky. He reflexively pulled back his hand, not because of being surprised he had actually found something, but more because of the power he had felt that the object possessed.

Whatever it might be, it was soft and shiny. It certainly didn't appear like something that had been buried for a century or two. He wrapped the black strands of braid around his wrist and gave it a bear-sized tug. The item unearthed itself like a root from freshly disturbed soil. The momentum caused Vincent to fall backward off his haunches and onto the ground. The other end of the item had been wrapped in tattered fabric much like the canvas of an old shipping sail. It was dotted with rust-colored blotches and swaths of earthen stains.

Vincent's eyes went wide as he slowly unwrapped it. The thrill of discovery spiked the base of his brain. The black braid was not cloth or rope at all, like he had initially thought, but a jet-black ponytail attached to a weathered and demonic-looking human skull. Two hollowed-out eye sockets stared back at him. The few remaining teeth it had were jagged, some even appearing as if they had been purposefully filed down. The jawbone being totally pulverized gave it an unsightly sadistic grin that could almost be misconstrued as a crooked smile. Two bony nodules protruded from its forehead, and the cheekbones remained razor sharp. Strangely, a solitary peach pit appeared to have taken root inside the cranium.

Vincent rotated the artifact in his hand, looking at it askance. His pulse throbbed so fast, it felt as though it would rip out the veins from inside of him. His body surged with adrenaline and unwonted energy. Vincent looked like he'd found the Ark of the Covenant. As he righted himself to his feet, he muttered, "I got you, you son of a bitch," then raised the object high above his head in the pinnacle of triumph.

As he held the skull to the sky in a victory stance, the electricity in the air once again surged. Thunder intensely crackled as lighting illuminated the ghoulish skull. The expression on the dead man's bones was unmatched, save the sinister appearance of Vincent's own deranged visage. If it was not previously clear he had slowly been going mad, it seemed quite probable now.

The change in Vincent was noticeable, though it was unclear if his devilish reactions were due to lack of medication or because of it. His appearance became noticeably deformed, but not physically. It was something much more sinister than that, more of an inner transformation, the magnitude of which could not be clearly defined.

He screamed at the top of his lungs to the heavens, or perhaps to hell.

"Is this what you're looking for? Is it?" A long strand of saliva released itself from the confines of his mouth and dangled from its pronounced corners. It was hardly noticeable, but the implications were of great magnitude. "Well, come and get it, asshole!"

Vincent continued to shout into the dead of night. Leaves, wind, electricity and malevolent spirits all danced a whirling dervish over his head. Thunder and lightning angrily crackled in the distance. The mythical kent-kow dance of the Thunder Beings had been set into motion. Dead natives began to initiate an En-na-shee—thank you ritual, as the stage for an epic showdown had been set.

★★★★

Mr. Crane was dressed in full period Dutch regalia for tonight's festivities. He looked every bit the part of his literal namesake. He wore a black long-tailed duster with an upturned collar and brass buttons over beige breeches. The white ruffled shirt underneath was immaculate, and his pointed shoes had large, gold brass buckles the size of a fist. His hair was braided back in perfect symmetry, a pink satin bow tied in a knot at its furthermost tip. The cherry on top was a black tricorne hat made from the same felt that his coat was. The young buck had spared no expense to impress the visiting Emily Jiompkowksi tonight. The mischievous Peter Crane had made no bones about wanting her to try any flavor of sausage, tonight, other than Polish, including his own. He loaded the last bit of baked goods into his car, a white 1991 Mustang GT. A cool car for the single man, but one he could still afford on his modest salary as an educator. More importantly for him, if needed, the seats could fully recline into a supine position. Or prone, depending on the desired effect of the subject.

Crane's ample ears perked up, as he thought he heard the snort of a yet unseen horse. He slowly stretched his neck to reveal what appeared to be the real-life Horseman seated atop his horse just a few yards away. As Crane's line of sight crested the ragtop of the convertible, the Horseman appeared to be in a stance atop the horse that was practically identical to the position he held on the Sleepy Hollow High School's marquee next to him. Reality mimicking folklore, or folklore mimicking reality? It was impossible for Crane to tell.

There was a brief standoff between the two. They studied each other intently, Crane surveying to see if this could be a prank, some ludicrous underclassmen dressed up. If so, the getup was extremely convincing. The Horseman stared as if meeting a kindred spirit, perhaps someone he had known from a past life. Although the close proximity with which they stood absorbing each other's aura was frightening in its own right, there seemed to be an unspoken feeling of contrition between the two. There appeared no imminent danger to Crane, simply a feeling of disbelief deep within him.

The Horseman reared abruptly, causing Crane to fall the pavement. The front hooves of the animal had come so close to his face that he felt a gust of air and could smell the fresh sod on its shoes. Crane hardly felt the ground below him, but rather sat there in contemplation.

The Horseman rode off into the night, having spared Crane's life for reasons known only to the Great Cosmos.

Chapter 38

In an alcove on the fairgrounds that had been inadvertently fashioned when crowd barricades were placed adjacent to the corn maze, a few older teens drank and generally ribbed at each other. An enterprising and creative intern had hustled up enough ingenuity to one-up her male counterpart and had decorated the area into a makeshift pumpkin patch.

There were a few teens making out, and there was some heavy petting going on. Particularly disturbing was a young girl, who wasn't even yet a freshman, making out with an older dropout of approximately nineteen. She had ridden with her older sister to the Ball, as they had promised to their parents, who also wanted some of their own alone time. The older sister, of course, immediately split up with the younger in order to engage in her own brand of premarital bliss. In essence, each of the family members had put their own selfish desires of lust above the rest of the clan, with the end result of the youngest now being compromised. If only Daddy could have seen! Instead, the self-centered drive of gratification blinded them all into becoming victims of their own set of vices, baby girl included.

One of the boys, lovingly known as Jimmy Poon, yelled over to the teen macking on the underage girl. His name was Charlie, which hadn't helped his case any when he had actually been a student attending school there. "Chuck the Fuck" and "Molester Chester" being his most common monikers. The boy's father had never been around, and his mother was a functioning alcoholic. As a result, he was raised with no real moral compass and often needed to fend for himself; a latchkey to the max he be. The harder truth to swallow was that he believed the world was his for the picking, and he simply had no inner monologue to dissuade his increasingly evil actions. Blame the parents, the boy, or society, or take the nihilistic approach of "The Lord's will be done," but either way, the kid had every intention of committing statutory rape.

"Get a room, Chester," jocundly blasted Poon.

He took it as encouragement rather than insult, again illustrating his lack of virtue or any sense of self-awareness. "Up yours, assclown," came Chester's profound and witty reply. He was already at second base with the girl and quickly rounding third.

"Hey, where's Mack & Saunders?" barked Jimmy Poon in a sudden moment of clarity. His date got sprayed with peppermint Schnapps flavored spittle as he yelled. Not that she had cared. It could have been worse. At least he didn't have the ashtray-breath of the older, smoking boys she often played tonsil-hockey with.

"How the fuck should I know? You know those guys. I'm sure they're planning a huge prank or some shit." Chuck was tired of horsing around. If he was going to fuck this girl, and he was, it had to happen while she could still consent. At least that would lessen the charges as a first-time offender. *First. Ha, if only they knew!* The thought made him laugh into the girl's cherublike face. She looked up at him with an age-appropriate innocence that she was on the verge of losing, forever.

"Yeah. You're probably right," said Jimmy. His full-on erection informed him that this topic needed no further debate. The kids went back to nursing their hormones, beers, and underage victims.

★★★★

Vincent stood in the center of some invisible ceremonial circle as he held the raised skull like some barbaric war trophy, screaming and taunting the Horseman. His voice cracked as a sensation of fire pillaged the valleys of his vocal folds.

He could sense something circling him. He couldn't see it, but he knew it was there. Alone in the middle of the field, it seemed as if nature had gone silent to witness his acts. He might have believed he was in complete solitude before, but now his mind denied him of that sensation. Whatever wire had tripped in his brain was not going to let this go. He remained defiant and relentless, now the undeniable center of attention of the Universe.

"Come on, you son of a bitch! Come get your head!"

Complete silence.

As Vincent began to lower his arms, the wind started to howl through the upright sentinels of birch before drafting up the solid trunk of the massive oak, which acted as their fearless commanding officer.   Vincent hadn't realized it, but he had been holding his arms out in beckoning gesticulation for quite a lengthy amount of time. It was almost as the Kohnstamm phenomenon had demanded him too. In those maniacal moments, he couldn't have put them at his side if had wanted to. The muscles started to cramp up as his blood pressure finally dipped from exhaustion.

Vincent slowly turned. The confrontational spite with which he previously seethed was now replaced with an overcoming fear. He instinctively bent over and grabbed the discarded shovel with his free hand. His fight or flight responses rebuked each other. Thunder continued its meaningful chant, serving as an atmospheric undertone to Vincent's feelings. The constant ebb and flow of emotion and adrenaline caused Vincent to lose it. He began to laugh and spit out his words. It was patently obvious, even to himself, that he had gone off the deep end.

But wasn't all the world an illusion anyway? Hadn't the Mayans called it that? Or was it Shakespeare? All the world's a stage, right? So why the fuck not, Billy Shakespeare!

Vincent's mind had taken a turn for the worse, and he was having an inordinate amount of trouble reeling it back in this time. "Here horsey, horsey, horsey! You want to come to Pa—"

The Hellsteed and its Rider now stood before him in defiance. It appeared even larger than Vincent had remembered from the manor fire. It was silent and defiant, as if a statue fashioned from heated black zirconium.

"—pa?" Vincent tossed the last syllable out like flavorless gum, finally completing the thought.

The smart-ass side of Vincent's brain wanted to make a wisecrack. It wanted to throw out a witty quip or a memorable one-liner that would properly clap back at the Entity that had caused him so much pain. He wanted to show that he had the upper hand, that he could never be defeated in a battle of wits or endurance. He wanted to say "Fuck you!" to the Man and "Damn the patriarchy!" He wanted to do all those things that he was so wired to emote through acts of defiance and rebellion. Who the hell was this Horseman to tell him how to react anyway. He was channeling it all through his soul at this very moment—his mother, Jack, the cops, Rayna, fucking Paulding. All of them. Years of institutionalization, quack doctors, bullshit psychologists. It was all coming to a head, motherfucking pun intended!

"Well, come and get it," was all that escaped his lips instead. But he delivered it with such snideness, contempt and slick-backed class that the point struck sharp.

As if in slow motion, in one fluid action Vince threw the skull high into the air and drew back the shovel. As it came back down, just as the skull seemed suspended eye to eye, Vincent swung the shovel in a perfect sideways parabolic arc. The force of the collision between rusty metal and ancient bone rocked the skull, exploding it into a dust cloud of bone and dirt, sending fragments and clumps of hair into the treetops.

The Horseman's saddle leather cracked as his torso leaned back, as if watching it hurl through the sky like the Hale-Bopp comet.

Straightaway, the world seemed to speed back up to real time. Vincent's demeanor changed in a split-second from one of profound victory to utter, unbridled fear. The boy became so astonished at his sudden change of reality, a pronounced "bark" actually escaped his throat. As the Hellsteed raised itself in a full-tilt rear, thunder once again cracked overhead. Both horse and Rider let out a diabolical war cry.

Vincent didn't even wait for the mighty horse's hooves to hit the ground before he took off running into the dead of night.

Chapter 39

Constance jockeyed the car back and forth a few times before bowing his head in defeat. He wasn't giving up just yet, but he needed to gather his thoughts before continuing on.

The Volare would certainly be the fastest option. Nearly 400 cubic inches of unparalleled power purred beneath the deputy's feet. The warmth of the transmission crept through the floor boards; The car exuded a plethora of kinetic energy with its raw power, like a third-generation thoroughbred stallion vying for the Triple Crown. His foot barely tapped the accelerator and the car rocked back and forth in the sludge, practically on its own accord. Even at idle, the RPMs ached to punch the tach near red, like the beating pulse of a restrained warrior itching to return to the bloodlust of the battlefront.

"Come on, you son of a bitch." Constance was talking to himself, not the vehicle. He'd never insult it like that. He got frustrated at times like this, when his mind couldn't think itself out of a proverbial hole. Whether that be a complex logistical solution in his mind or a literal quagmire of muck, like he was in, he always seemed to find quick and efficient workarounds by problem solving on his feet. Normally, his brain could ferret out a solution even when faced with moving goal posts. He could remember a few times when he hadn't though. One was when his college sweetheart left him, another in an IED ambush during combat, and still a third the night his wife had died. Each of these times had been momentous occasions, and at each of those moments he had lost something very dear to him. He didn't want that to happen again tonight. His mind immediately returned as his thoughts snapped back to Rayna.

Growing up, he had watched enough winged-sprint car racing on muddy Saturday nights to know there was surely a way out of this. He would have to trick the car at its own game. The vehicle was born and bred to lunge forward full-throttle at high speeds, just like certain dog breeds with malicious owners were taught to be aggressive, or others to chase a mechanical rabbit in circles—one track minds.

Constance aggressively pulled the steering wheel with several turns to his left. The Plymouth sign, embossed on the leather of the horn pad, looked like it was in a tumble dryer. He slammed the gear in reverse and punched it. The car lurched backward, cresting the thick rivet it had dug itself into. Before the full weight of the nearly two-ton vehicle could settle back into the comforting embrace of the wet bog, Constance jacked the wheel to the right, threw it in drive, and once again punched it. The gearshift on the steering column fought back, and felt as though it would break in two. The veins in Constance's forearms bulged like a heroine addict's on score night, pulsating with each fuel-injected dragon chase. The fat treads of the tires chewed the sludge and finally decided to take hold. The steel belts dug in and the vehicle, incredulously, rocked forward. As it fishtailed hard, it was finally freed from gravity's embrace, once again emboldened to charge into the dark of the night. The front lights had been caked in mud, dimming the deputy's view of the open road before him.

Constance pounded the wheel. "Yes! Yes!" he screamed, losing all inhibition and throwing caution, quite literally, to the wind as the Super Coupe rocketed into the dark abyss of the night. Rather than maps and coordinates, it navigated the beckoning darkness with primal urges and the need to survive.

★★★★

As Vincent crested another tree line out into an open field, he saw the taillights of the deputy's car off in the distance. The thick red streaks of light quickly faded into the darkness.

The gallop of the Horseman and the whinnies of his Hellsteed were not too far behind him; they were faint, but still distinctly audible. There was no time to stop. He would have to rely on the lactic acid breaking down in his bloodstream now. Hopefully it hadn't been too tainted. There'd be no time to suck in air now, if even for a moment. Racing away came as second nature to him, as he had been running from things most of his life.

Vincent lunged forward off his back foot, springing up as if in a canter. Up ahead, the moonlight caught a reflection of something shiny on the ground. At his speed, he was able to just barely dodge it, but when he did, his foot hit a wet patch. He stumbled face-first across the splayed out remains of the sheriff. The two boys' bodies were illuminated only by the luminescence of the moonlight. They reeked of death and were postured unnaturally. The glassy eyes of the sheriff stared up at him. He wore no shaded aviators to refract the gruesome gaze. The carnage before him of eviscerated bodies turned completely inside out didn't shock him as much as he thought it once might have. Years of video games, terrorist videos and horror films had already desensitized him to that. *Guess there's no need to worry about the damage to the cruiser door anymore. Maybe he could use the money for the Horseman figurine.* His mind betrayed him. Maybe it was some sick, apathetic version of a coping mechanism. Or maybe he really was deranged.

Vincent had no choice but to grab one of the exposed rib cages to get leverage in order to stand up. As he did, the corpse's head tilted forward like a lifeless rag doll. It was clear in the bright-red light of the blood moon that it was Saunders. The recognition of someone whom he had interacted with so closely on a daily basis jarred Vincent back to reality. He grabbed his mouth in horror, and in a barely audible tone, whispered, "Oh my God." He couldn't actually say that he was sad the boy was dead, but it registered a real fear inside him—this was no first-person shooter video game or movie special effect.

The rhythmic pounding of the Horseman's gait was upon him once again, and it was deafening. There was no more time for shock to set in. He had no choice but to suck it up and keep running. The adrenaline had caused Vincent's muscles to shift into hyperdrive, but the amount of physical torment he was inflicting on his lungs and legs had become apparent. A relentless fire burned inside his chest, spurring him onward in order to try and stay alive.

★★★★

The height of the corn maze was particularly daunting. It was clear that whomever had designed it had been a fan of *The Shining*. It was easily eight feet tall, but on a night like tonight, felt more like ten. It seemed awfully quiet for a party night. Rayna wasn't sure if she actually was there by herself, or if someone was tactically lying in wait in order to scare the "popular girl" from school. Either way, it was extremely unnerving. As it was not possible to see over the tops of the corn stalks, nor to delineate the various offshoots and corridors, the moonlight high up above was her only solace.

In fact, the moon and the constellation Orion had often helped her deal with her mother's death. They were always permanent fixtures of the night sky, and helped her believe that wherever her mother was, it was conceivable these heavenly bodies could be used as a mutual point of reference to find her. Orion the Hunter was always there, armed with bow or club, watching and protecting. The thoughts may have been considered childish or superstitious by others, but they gave her fortitude and the comfort to go on. The alcohol was also helping bolster her false sense of courage. Its effect was now settling in throughout Rayna's bloodstream. Her senses started to dive into a topsy-turvy spin. She was at the moment of intoxication where one either embraces it intrepidly, or where one fears every uncertain nuance is a threat and goes on a very bad trip.

She caught a glimpse of a dark, fleeting figure. She comforted herself by acknowledging that the attraction was meant to be a bit scary. She should respect the design and the season and go with the flow. She trudged on, following the specter through the never-ending assortment of cornstalks and hay bales. She was sure this was meant to amuse her. It hadn't. Scarecrows, witches and creepy jack-o'-lanterns adorned the maze turned haunted cornfield. The addition of pitchforks, torches and other implements, although adding nicely to the ambiance, did little to assure anyone that proper safety protocols had been in place. The obstacles scattered throughout the area would probably have been hazardous even if it were well lit.

The alcohol now kicked even harder. Like a dose of ecstasy at an underground rave, the pulses of oblivion came in droves. She was trying to keep her "Aliceness" from stumbling off the ledge down into an infinite rabbit hole. Rayna tripped on the train of her costume and the fabric tore beneath her, a victim of collateral damage. The momentum of her body thrust her forward into the waiting arms of a scarecrow. It spun around, revealing a terrifying skull with razor-sharp teeth. Lightning struck and illuminated the *Jeepers Creepers*-esque monstrosity, every pore breathing and very much alive. Then, much worse, its ragged checks became full as apples as its thin lips stretched into a wicked smile, followed by a startling guffaw. Rayna, aghast, fell over straight into an oversized prop guillotine. The blade dropped directly onto her arm, prompting a high-pitched scream from deep within her diaphragm. Alas, it was only plastic, and the scarecrow just a scare actor.

Rayna composed herself and laughed it off, as did the Oscar-calibre performer. However, it was clear to the scarecrow, and her, that she was genuinely not in the joking mood. Her heart raced like a frightened rabbit's, pulsating a torrent of alcohol into her already laced bloodstream. But as no harm had been done, other than being startled, she tried to return to the jovial spirit of the evening. It was too late; she had already fallen through the abysmal depths of the looking glass.

Chapter 40

Vincent was in a full sprint through the darkness of the woods. Only occasional reflections off of shiny slate rocks or stagnant water told him areas to avoid. Thoughts of Saunders's and the sheriff's mutilated corpses began to ambush his perception of reality. Images suddenly flashed in front of him that he had no control over, as if someone was deliberately projecting them from the deep recesses of his mind. They were repulsively gory and brutal, and made it hard for him to focus on delineating the patches of gray that carved out specific shapes before him. His depth perception was skewed, and his faculties dulled.

An elongated, thin black stripe stretched out before him. His mind wasn't fast enough to calculate that the divot ahead was actually a vast ravine deep enough to escape the light from the moon overhead. Heinously miscalculating, he misstepped and took a somersaulting tumble down a steep gulch into some thorny underbrush. Rocks and branches cut into his flesh on the way down. He was simply a passenger along for the ride. White bursts of sparks flashed across his closed eyes every time an object struck a blow near the soft tissue surrounding their lenses. He couldn't tell up from down as his body plunged earthbound before coming to rest in an abrupt stop.

He lay in the ditch, which was the perfect size for a human body on its side. His head hurt more than the rest of his limbs, even though they had received the most damage in the fall. If this was the end for him that was destined to be, there was exactly nothing he could do about it. He lay sideways in the gully, eyes tightly shut. The depth of it, at its very bottom, not nearly as shallow as his breathing had become. His body having taken the brutal pummeling of the drop without hesitation or the smallest resistance had actually increased his chances of survival.

Overhead, although Vincent could not see it, he felt the presence of the Horseman and his Hellsteed as they leapt over him. They thundered along, seemingly oblivious to his presence below them. Although Vincent was facedown, semiconscious and badly bleeding, he felt the same rush of an energy one might have felt if blindfolded next to railroad track as a locomotive passed by at full speed. It was simultaneously hair-raising and skin crawling. A sensation of an incredible force passing mere inches within doing one irreparable personal harm washed over his senses. He moaned in the damp underbrush. At least he would have a moment to catch his breath, albeit under the least ideal of circumstances.

His mind drifted to Rayna, to Allister and Aaron, and yes, even his mother. What they said about your life flashing before your eyes like a projected home movie was not true for Vincent. Parts of his body were broken, but his mind functioned like a rebooting computer as it calculated the possible sequences of events to follow. If the Horseman made it to town before he could, he would have no time to warn any of them. He had given up saving himself eons ago, but would never forgive himself if he at least didn't try to be Rayna's savior.

★★★★

Deputy Constance had feed the Volare a steady diet of high octane as he gunned the squad car toward town. He knew from his days of maneuvering ATVs over all kinds of uneven terrain that the faster you went, the less likely it was the wheels would catch on an obstruction. This also meant reaction times were extremely minimized, but created the sensation the vehicle was actually floating at breakneck speed unabated. Racers colloquially called the perceived state of being of rider and agent morphing into one "the flow." All Constance knew was that he was in the zone. He was hoping and praying to get to his daughter before the unknown culprit did.

He had already gone through several scenarios in his mind, including Vincent, as well as connecting the manor fire and deadly crash to a single potential murderer. There was no way to be certain of anything, but after what he had seen in the field, he was taking no chances. His mind fabricated several plotlines faster than he could process them, let alone flesh them out. He even imagined having to confront a much stronger killer, or even the fantastical idea of the Horseman himself, however remote that scenario might be. Constance was frazzled, and deeply distracted, as he looked down quick enough to key up Baby Girl in his cell phone's contact list. The phone was showing faint bars again.

At that exact moment, the Horseman and the enormous Hellsteed cut off the vehicle, leapt across it, and cleared it to the other side of the road. As the deputy momentarily looked up from the phone, he caught a glimpse of the massive Beast as it crested his hood. His impulsive reaction caused him to swerve to avoid it. The car bottomed out, then shot up on what was left of its bruised suspension. It lost contact with the ground's already tenable surface and hit a tree.

This was the same maneuver the Horseman had pulled on him so many years before, the night Helen had died. Only this time, the deputy was completely sober and knew exactly what he had seen. The car absorbed the impact of the thick and meaty tree trunk much better than expected. Nothing was quite comparable to the bulky undercarriages of 70s American muscle cars. The cell phone had gone flying as the windshield cracked in the ironic shape of a peace sign. The downside being there were no airbags or thick impact foam to cushion and absorb the transferred energy of the hit.

Steam poured from the bent hood, and Constance felt as though he had been sacked by a 350-pound Georgia nose tackle. As he slowly came to his senses, it felt to him as if waking up from a nightmare, only to find out it wasn't an altered state or imagined, but rather a real-life experience. Constance was confused and trying valiantly to stave off the fog of his confused stupor. His senses had been dulled by the impact and were slow to reignite at first. Upon seeing the sleek lines of the classic machine wrinkled like an accordion, Constance wondered what his superior would think, before he remembered Eustice was dead. Languidly, but surely, anger began to boil up inside him.

Once his minimal strength had returned, the thwarted deputy exited the car and kicked the tires in utter frustration. "Damn it! Not this time, you son of a bitch!" Although he couldn't comprehend why, Constance sobbed in powerful heaves as he screamed into the night. He wouldn't even dare to imagine losing his daughter. His voice box strained in desperation; he felt as though he had swallowed broken glass.

The salt of his tears and the iron of the blood from a gash in his forehead only spurred him into more of a determined rage. The harsh jolt to reality had triggered him into action. Nothing in this dimension, or the Horseman's, could match the resolve of a protective father. He tightened his belt, pulled up his pants, and got ready for the long sprint ahead of him. With waning energy from his barebones breakfast of mostly ejected coffee and cookies, he began the journey toward the center of town. Provisions of hatred, discontent, and resentment would be all the nourishment needed to spur him on.

Like a pawn, he had precisely played into the negative power the Universe was using to rebalance itself. As he fed on it, so did It feed on him, accepting no remorse or contrition for sins of the past generations. They were like host and parasite in a symbiotic feeding frenzy, only they were mutually detrimental to each other rather than beneficial. Like it or not, there was a blood–debt owed, and a reckoning yet to come.

A faint crackle spiked the radio inside the still running police cruiser, but Constance was no longer there to hear it.

★★★★

Rayna, as if sensing her father's concern, composed herself with renewed strength. Her confidence amongst the towering corn stalks quickly faded, however, as she once again saw the figure in the distance moving effortlessly toward her. Whomever it was, was athletic and agile judging by their ability to duck into the shadows and hide just out of her view.

"Hello? Someone there? Vincent, is that you?" Rayna's voice faltered as she tried to drum up enough courage to confront the daunting character. She felt by projecting her voice she could somehow avoid another embarrassing confrontation, like the one she'd had with the scarecrow.

A half-rotted pumpkin landed at Rayna's feet, exploding into a million stringy pieces from the M-80 inside of it. The ripe smell from the flesh of the rotting gourd was as powerful as the explosive. Rayna was showered head-to-toe in a deluge of sinewy orange innards and brittle pumpkin seeds. The slime splashed the satin of her dress, leaving unapologetic snail tracks in its wake. Rayna shrieked in horror and fell to the ground. Even her ample backside wasn't full enough to properly absorb the impact. She sat in a heap of dull aches and mortification.

Aaron and Allister, drunk off their minds, stood over her and laughed. Alcohol now superseding their best judgement, all propriety had been lost.

"Come on, guys, are you fucking serious right now? What are you, like eight?" She was humiliated and her ass was more than a little sore, neither of which she had bargained for tonight. Her tailbone pulsed to the beat of a painful rhythm.

The boys remained in silence for a good beat. It was the first they had ever heard such a vulgar profanity uttered from such a sweet mouth. Once over their initial surprise, both cracked up at her fright. The boys were dressed in black capes and had been taking turns luring Rayna deeper into the maze. They would shift into her line of sight from opposing directions, causing her to become even more confused and disoriented. Knowing she had gotten drunk from the potent punch concoction had made their diabolic plan all the easier to execute. Aaron slapped Allister, causing the last of the whiskey to spill from the bottle he held. The boys fumbled for it, but it had already been drained. They took off deeper into the maze, giving themselves "Atta boys" and proudly quipping, "Bro, did you see her face?" and other immature banter.

Rayna tried to shake it off. *This is Down-Home Days. It's part of the deal.* She balanced herself upright as she tried to get a better bead on the awkward confines of her costume. Like the Dutch settler who might have worn this exact dress before her, she imagined generations of female degradation at the hands of their male counterparts. It was salt on top of her injury. Her momentary flash of anger only added to the wave of negative energy that was becoming increasingly more prevalent as the evening passed.

Again she saw movement in the far distance. If that's how the night was going to go, at least she was prepared with the right mindset now. She wasn't going to let those drunken idiots get the drop on her again. "Assholes!" she defiantly yelled at the top of her lungs into the chilly night air.

The cornstalks peered down at her in apparent derision. Somewhere in the distance, immature laughter cracked the still of Devil's Night. At that moment, any playfully innocent sentiments of mischief had transitioned into more embittered and evil ones. A sinister pervasiveness permeated the night air, evoking the cataclysmic retribution of an entire generation.

Chapter 41

Gilbert Price was happily inebriated as he sat on the steps of the John Dustin Archbold Mausoleum in Sleepy Hollow Cemetery. He stumbled to his feet and drunkenly started to snoop around with his awkwardly aimed shotgun and flashlight. He was positive he would find absolutely no clues as to the location of the missing boys, but had convinced himself the night might still be salvageable. The last of his hooch was long gone, but luckily, he'd had the foresight to pack two 75mg dosed edibles for whatever the night may bring. He had consumed one after the shock of the last firecracker had worn off. Price never saw who threw it, but it didn't matter much to him anyway. He wasn't even angry. The kids were merely partaking in long-honored traditions, and in this town "boys will be boys" had no negative connotation, but rather was a well-adhered-to credo.

Just when Price assumed the last edible had been canceled out by the alcohol, it started to kick in, hard. The ramp-up had been so subtle it was scary. He hadn't noticed the exact moment he recognized the kaleidoscopic patterns forming in front of his eyes, but they were obvious now. Everywhere he looked, shattered prisms of color and light interlaced and distorted what would have normally been ordinary everyday images. Now, they were taking on a life of their own. Of particular note was how the porous granite of the columns appeared to be crawling, like waves of tiny insects. It was fascinating, if not slightly disconcerting.

Out of nowhere, the Horseman bolted by him at full speed. The coarse hairs of the Hellsteed's tail whisked across the bridge of Price's thick nose, giving him a scratchy slap across the face and a thick dose of Charger musk. Although the sensation roused the nerves across his puffed face, he wondered if the Horseman had been a part of his involuntary hallucinations. In fact, he was sure if it. He pulled the empty box from his pocket. Had he misread the label—ICKY-BUD CRANE 100mg. It had been a larger dosage than he thought. "How strong are these fuckers?" he mumbled as he pondered the potent effect of the cannabis now coursing through his system.

The whole time he had been distracted reading the label, the Horseman had slowly and stealthily made his way closer. He was now perched atop the mighty Hellsteed, seemingly calculating Price's every move. This time, Price knew he was very much real. The timed beats of the horse's breathing were full and ominous. Its lungs expelled air in powerful bursts, almost mechanically. Price knew this was no costume, and certainly no well-intentioned prank. Blood dripped down from the belt axe, and pieces of sinewy flesh still clung to it. The overwhelming smell of death, unheard of to this degree even in a cemetery, pervaded the air.

The Horseman walked the Hellsteed back, before horseshoeing it around to face Price from about forty yards away. He brandished the axe high into the air, and the Beast whinnied its war cry so loud that it nearly pierced Price's eardrums. He shielded his ear from the sonic onslaught the best he could with his one free hand.

The Horseman began his gallop toward Price with the very clear intention of causing maximum damage.

Price took aim with the shotgun. The blast stole through the air, relieving the dead of their peaceful slumber. His drunken state and frayed nerves guaranteed he would miss. Without so much as a flinch, the Horseman rushed past the bewildered man once again before finally stopping. The demonic duo stood there in defiance, obviously mocking Price as he clumsily managed to chamber his last and final round. A futile exercise they were willing to entertain.

"Die, bastard, die!" Price had no time to think any of this through, and his reactions were as cliched as the movies he collected. If the Horseman had been a person — especially a kid in costume — there would have been consequences that would have caused irreparable damages. All the mayhem would have stemmed from his inexcusable actions. There was no way of knowing that, however, so he followed his instincts, which for once in his life, were dead on.

The Horseman spun once more and bore down heavily upon his victim. Price leveled the weapon best he could at the quickly approaching equestrian, but knew he had but one shot left. Adrenaline had a sobering effect. He fought his nerves in order to steady his hand, rewarded only with fleeting moments of respite from intoxication. When the whip was just within reach, the Horseman adroitly flicked his wrist and wrapped up Price's ankle with the braided tail of the hided bullwhip. The expertly calculated maneuver had landed with masterful precision.

The Horseman tugged hard with the full of his supernatural might, sending Price ass over tea kettle. The video man, and chronic sex offender, landed hard. As his skull was curb-checked at the base of a concrete tombstone, the shotgun simultaneously went off, sending a cloud of buckshot into the night. The spurt of blood released by the man's weight hitting the granite careened up the side of the building. The unsightly red streak made it all the way to the engraved cross above the weathered-green brass doors, a good eight feet above the grounds hard surface. The complimenting colors of blood red atop mossy green were more akin to Christmas revelry than those traditionally associated with Halloween. It looked like an avant-garde art masterpiece. *Ars Gratis Artis*; Quite beautiful under any other circumstance.

There was nothing but a soupy, bloody pulp left above Price's shoulders. His body didn't even have the decency to twitch a few more times in its last struggle for life. Like the man it once belonged to, it also took the shortcut and had perished upon impact, giving Price an instantaneous one-way ticket to Hades. No goodbyes would be given, no time of reflection or remorse allotted, no prayers spoken. He would be flung, literally headfirst, into whatever penances waited him on the other side for his numerable transgressions.

Chapter 42

Chester and Jimmy Poon had unsuccessfully tried to convince the underaged girl and her friend to go down on each other. They had just recently conquered their fears of the dreaded same-sex French kiss. The drinking teens, now completely sloshed, had paired off and were having a go at their own awkward attempts at fornication.

The Horseman and Hellsteed languidly sauntered up, dragging something behind.

"Holy shit!" Charlie dropped his bottle. He was naked from the waist up, and his inadequate boner had been aching to be released. The young girl lay naked beneath him on a hay bale, prepared to be deflowered. The bastard hadn't even bothered to put anything down to keep her back from getting scratched up. The girl had been itching uncontrollably, and the little alcohol she had consumed was just enough to impair her beyond recognition.

"That costume is lit, yo," slurred Charlie, not at all embarrassed or shy about being caught literally with dick in hand. His indifference to the fact he was about to commit a sexual act in public that was illegal in nearly every state of the Union only proved the height of his privilege.

Jimmy Poon cocked his head as if he were a Labradoodle hearing the mechanical gibberish of an animatronic Furby. His brain was just a little too daft to make an absolute conclusion, but it was trying. "Dude, I don't think that's a costume" The kid was a Goddamned rocket scientist.

"You drunk pussy. That's totally Mack & Saunders. You're such a dumbass." Charlie was entertained now and walked away from the girl. His semi-aroused penis was a badge of honor in his Cro-Magnon mind. He hadn't even heard the girl as she released an audible sigh of relief at his departure.

Charlie, unbelievably, walked right up to the Horseman. "Damn, dude. You totally scared the shit out of me, but I'm gonna kick your ass when you come down off that thing." The teen went to pet the horse, which snorted in defiance, edging its head away. Even a Beast so symbolically diabolical abhorred the thought of his vulgar touch.

The previously horny adolescent got an eerie feeling. The animal's eyes began to glow unnaturally red, and Charlie's hand started to burn before it even touched the animal's pelage. He slowly looked up in disbelief. "Whose horse is this?"

The boy's face went ashen as the gruesome remains were slowly revealed to him just as the horse edged forward. Poon started off in a stilted run in the opposite direction, but his synapses weren't quite getting the impulses to run that this brain were sending. In his mind, as if in a dream state, his legs were moving, but he wasn't gaining much ground. Neither girl had yet realized what was happening and remained blissfully unaware.

Charlie glanced down at the body being towed. "See, I told you. There's Mack right there." He realized how ignorant the words were the moment they escaped his mouth; this was no joke. He was right about one thing, though. It was Mack's lifeless corpse that stared, unblinking, back up at him. The Horseman raised his axe.

As Rayna rounded the corner of the maze adjacent to the pumpkin patch, she could hear the sounds of the brutal slaughter taking place. The Horseman's back was to her, but she was close enough to see the looks on the kids' faces as the blade striated them with surgical precision. In the fight or flight moment, her instincts choose flight, and she doubled back into the unknown of the expansive cornfield maze.

Charlie's headless body slumped down to its knees in a lifeless heap, its penis once again erect. The young girls began to scream, but anytime they tried to make a move, the Horseman would use the girth of the Hellsteed's chest to corral them like wayward sheep. There was no escaping. Jimmy Poon had a few feet head start, but his steps were ill-timed. The Horseman rib-kicked the animal into a trot forward and cracked the whip around Jimmy's shins. One of his knees bent sharply, knocking into the other, and the youth violently fell like an AT-AT at the Battle of Hoth. He hit the ground so hard, three of his teeth loosed beyond repair when his face abruptly came into contact with the hardened earth.

The Horseman was in no mood to waste time with artistic endeavors, so he simply flayed Jimmy from behind, ass crack to nape. The hot steam from his body dispersed into the air, along with the fresh smell of alcohol-tainted blood. The sharp tinge of iron was palpable. The air became noticeably thicker.

Under other circumstances, the young female victims might have been spared. But that was not the way of the Horseman, and certainly not that of the Triduum of the Hallows' Curse. Just as aiding and abetting was often seen as equally guilty as the crime committed, so too was the placement of the young women. They were simply in the wrong place at the wrong time. It was not the Horseman's place to be judge and jury; he was merely Executioner. The Horseman had exacted an unrelenting, unapologetic, and unsurpassed death sentence on all present. The fragile young lovers, if you could even loosely call them that, were snuffed out in an instant. Perhaps the death sentence was a much more favorable fate, than the sexual assault and years of guilt they would have soon endured. The murders here had occurred with the same zest as those in Amityville, only difference being those were less brutal and allegedly undeserved. The Horseman was a mere vessel, acting out the judgment of the Higher Powers of the Universe. The bodies were displayed in a gruesome arrangement amongst the faces of jack-o'-lanterns that were scattered throughout the patch. There was no doubt this time that the carvings across each candle-lit visage were unarguably derisive.

Rayna had made a perhaps fatal mistake, as she now fled the scene through the infinite labyrinth of the maze. That was no scare actor, and those had been real bodies. Any inkling of innocence Rayna may have had until now was gone forever. She was running for her life with no escape in sight.

The Horseman followed and tracked her every move with supernatural precision. The day of reckoning was upon her, and even as the strong-willed and independent woman she had become, she was decidedly powerless to fight it.

Chapter 43

As she fled for her life, Rayna realized the total scale of her insignificance. It was as if she felt the full weight of the vast rock known as Earth beneath her feet and understood how little her presence on it meant. What's more, she felt its position in the Universe, spiraling around the unfathomable galactic drain of the Sun's gravitational pull, spinning endlessly in circles with no real sense of direction or orientation. She felt, in a word, minuscule. A trivial, trifling, inconsequential spec in the Grande Design. It was amusing to her that only moments prior, events like her mother's death, followers and likes on social media, her all-important appearance, kissing a boy, or drinking alcohol had seemed relevant and important. What a fool she had been! She only realized now, after what she had just witnessed, and after being pursued by the Horseman, that none of it mattered, or was even pertinent to her continued existence.

Rayna felt as though she was an astral projection gliding alongside the now-foreign body of the girl known as Lorraine as she continued to run through the maze, the Horseman in hot pursuit. Lighting and thunder kicked up. A storm was brewing, ever evolving, and certainly here for the duration. It may have been meteorological or supernatural in origin, but either way, it was leaving an intensified damper on what was left of the evening.

Rayna finally came to a dead end in the maze. There was a moment so intense that she could no longer hear or feel the sound of her own breathing. Time seemed to stand still. The sound of the Hellsteed's whinnying seemed to be coming at   her from every angle. Rayna's reality imploded in on itself, creating a vacuum of any semblance of tactile substance. She heard a death-defying reversed sucking noise, which ended with the absence of all sound and senses. Then…WHAM! The Hellsteed barreled straight through some cornstalks, missing Rayna by mere inches before disappearing yet again.

Rayna looked around, her mind playing unpredictable tricks on her. Her state of being was fragile and precariously hinged on the edge of insanity. The shadows seemed to be playing with light and darkness right before her very eyes. Rayna began to run through the maze once again, each corner seemingly a dead end. Finally, she whipped around the corner to reveal Allister holding a mostly empty liquor bottle. He was visibly plastered and appeared to have been having a great go at celebrating.

"What up, couz? Damn you look really—" He was going to say hot, but unlike most boys his age, he had a good grasp on his inner monologue. "Spooked." He settled for the word as it fell flat. "Wish I had a little more to offer you." He held up the near empty bottle in front of him. The whiskey had given him the false courage to tell the prettiest girl he knew what he had actually been thinking. He didn't care if Vincent knew; that guy was hardly ever around anyway.

"Allister, look out!" she screamed as the Horseman appeared behind him.

SCHLOP! Off went his head. The Horseman again disappeared. A demented game of cat-and-mouse now at play. He would let Rayna stew on that for a while.

The head rolled toward Rayna's feet. She was able to stop it by firmly placing the tip of her satin heel across the bridge of its nose. The boy probably had barely registered his demise, and it was debatable if he could have still inhaled the scent of her perfumed stockings. His blood infused itself in the fabric of her dress, saturating the sweat and pumpkin stains already present. Her dress was now splattered with an offensive amount of vital fluids.

The breathless young woman backed away, nearly hyperventilating. She was too panicked to scream, but the sharp breaths she drew in released high-pitched wheezes as they were expelled from the confines of her imprisoning rib cage. Her mind swirled blindly. She fled in the opposite direction, through which she thought the Horseman had ridden, but the rapidly firing impulses of her brain made it impossible for her to map out the maze. It would have been difficult under normal circumstances, but with her senses now heightened in panic, it proved unthinkable. She simply ran, the grays and browns of the stalks blending with the angry sky.

The clouds barked in ominous unison and seemed portentous of an ill-fated outcome. Unseasonably warm rain spewed forth from the sky. She wanted to curl in a ball and cry. She wanted her father to protect her, or her mother to console her. Even Vincent's presence would have been better than being here all alone. The gravity of seeing kids she knew murdered in cold blood finally started to weigh heavily on her mind. She was at a breaking point. Her legs keep churning beneath her, like a massive waterwheel fighting upstream currents, and she became soaked by the acidic rainwater as she ran. The full moon ducked behind a bank of inky, earth-toned clouds, making it impossible to differentiate between the rain, mud and human blood she was now thoroughly soaked in.

Up ahead, the maze opened up. It seemed to be the center of the arrangement, with eight passages all leading in different directions. A broken windmill methodically churned in the center of the field like a discarded sentinel. Ripped canvas was draped over its twisted arms, and it had been intentionally weathered by a theater scenic artist. It was a subtle nod to the historical significance of the Dutch Colonists from the area. Then clearly, unmistakably, she saw the silhouette of the Horseman. In its hand, the glint of the belt axe it was holding flashed. Only a short distance separated them.

Rayna screamed, and the noise of her own voice jolted her back into the reality of the situation. Her scream was so loud, a pounding pain shot from her vocal cords all the way up through her eardrums. If there was anyone in a mile radius, they should have heard it, but perhaps they were already all dead. She tried not to allow her mind to consider this unfathomable, but very probable, possibility. She fled in the opposite direction, not sure where she was going, simply trying to escape her imminent demise.

The Horseman dismounted. Now on foot, he moved forward menacingly, calculating each step with euphoric exuberance. His movements and swagger seemed larger than life.

Unfortunately, Rayna once again ran into a dead end and had to double back. She came within feet of him, but rather than attack, he sidestepped and let her pass, toying with the panicked young girl. When Rayna's escape was foiled by yet another dead end, she returned to the center of the maze, and the Horseman. This time, he purposefully jockeyed in front of her to cut her off and corral her around the next bend.

She turned and ran down a longer outlet of the seemingly infinite maze. The bass of the thunder sent intervals of truncated low pitches throughout the atmosphere up above. Patches of lightning illuminated the clouds from the inside. The rain had become steady. Rayna was actually glad to have some of the human remains residue wash off of her. She looked up and, for a brief moment, noticed the constellation Orion in his fixed position in the sky. If she was going to die here tonight, she was finally willing to accept it. The celestial Hunter would protect her if he so chose, but if not, perhaps her fate was already predetermined. She gave in to his will. An all-encompassing peace of acceptance washed over her.

Then, one last burst of survival mode coursed through her veins. Adrenaline reared another head where a precious one had been cut off. She turned to run again. If her calculations were correct, she was running out of options to escape from the confines of the corn stalks. The walls almost seemed to be closing in on her, like in an inescapable nightmare. She turned to bolt, and ran smack-dab into…Vincent!

Rayna collapsed in his arms, sobbing like a lost child. The full weight of her body fell out from under her as he held her up from under her armpits. Her tears were completely lost in the deluge of rain.

"Rayna, it's gonna be okay." He kissed the top of her head, tasting the salt of perspiration in her hair. The smell of fear radiated from her skull. It was intoxicating. He was covered in filth from digging in the fields. She barely recognized him, but the kindness in his eyes was enough to register her salvation. She let herself go and melted into him.

The sound of a horse's hooves echoed about them like a drum cadence in a sonic house of mirrors. Vincent's ears perked up as he heard the coming onslaught. His eyes went dark and his pupils dilated into an unfathomable bottomless brown. A devilish smile cracked the purple of his lips. "Trust me. This will all be over soon."

Out of nowhere, the Hellsteed charged, sans Horseman.

Vincent threw Rayna to the ground. The force of the fall caused her to sprain her arm, and in her current mental state, the action injured her fragile ego. It almost felt as though he had discarded her, though she knew deep down that he had only been pushing her out of harm's way. Rayna stood up and slowly turned around. Vincent was nowhere to be seen. Scared, alone, and jumping out of her skin, seconds seemed like an eternity. After an eerie silent beat, she again heard the methodical sound of a winded horse's breathing. She turned around and her mouth fell agape.

As powerful lightning flashed, the blade of the raised axe was revealed. It came down with a fury unequaled to even the brutal assaults of Genghis Khan. The contour of the blood-slicked blade cut through the silky sleeve of Rayna's dress, giving her arm a deep, bloody gash. The singe of the burn seared her arm like a red hot curling iron. She screamed in pain, immediately grasping at the wound. Her blood-alcohol meant the sanguine life-force flowed more freely as it sought out the path of least resistance. Instead of congealing, the wound flowed freely. Her lifeblood's viscous stream left unabated, lubricated by the atmospherically charged downpour. Her pain pulsated with each beat of her ebbing heart.

The Horseman edged forward. On the ground, Rayna attempted to crab-walk backward in the face of His domineering and overbearing advances.

He spoke with a deep, almost non-human resonance. "Behold! I taketh revenge unto the last living heir of the curse of the Unhallowed Horseman of Hallowed Grounds." The Horseman raised the belt axe up for the final death blow.

Rayna buried her face in one of her hands, the other outstretched out of the instinct to defend herself from the deadly blow. But the blow didn't come. Bleeding and sobbing, she tried to focus through the blur of tears and rain mixed in her eyes. Perhaps one last attempt at reasoning could stop him. Rather than seeing the Horseman, Vincent's rain-soaked face slowly came into view.

"Wait! Vincent, no!"

Chapter 44

"Look at yourself, Vincent. This is not you. I know you never meant to hurt anyone," she pleaded, knowing her very life depended upon it.

"The Horseman didn't do this, Vince... you did! Look at yourself, please!"

In his mind's eye, Vincent had pictured himself as the Horseman in full costume, sans head. But as reality slowly began to pierce the fog of his mind, it was as if his vision circled around his own self. What it revealed to him was what had been apparent to Rayna once she had finally mustered the courage to look up again at the exact moment she'd thought she would die. It was actually Vincent, wearing the tattered cloak from the burial ground and holding the dripping belt axe in his forcibly shaking hands, who was the threat.

Vincent's eyes widened like a madman. His stare pierced right through Rayna, seeing past her, into the very depths of Hell. The splitting headache came to him harder than ever. Still holding the axe, Vincent pounded his temples as the agonizing pain delivered its unrelinquishing blows. He screamed out in pure agony. Rayna's mind blocked out the terrifying guttural sounds he made. Vincent's jaw appeared to become practically unhinged, and the bulging veins across his forehead looked as though they would burst.

A series of visions flashed before Vincent's mind's eye, separated by blinding thermal-white pulses.

★★★★

"You know, horses make very good therapy animals, Marisa," said the petite farmhand.

"I know, Ms. Masson, but we simply can't afford this," said a much younger Marisa.

"Oh no, honey, don't you worry. The Bellino Foundation pays for everything."

Nine-year-old Vincent shuffled his feet; his signature move, even way back then. "Mom, can we go now?"

The two woman exchanged glances.

Young Vincent's eyes went to a much larger horse walking with a limp in a circular round pen a few yards over. "What's that one's name?"

"That big fella's name is Solomon, but you'd need a lot of practice before you could ever ride him. Let's go say hello."

Masson walked the distracted boy toward the animal. Marisa admired the fit of the trainer's breeches over her curvaceous backside, like only an envious fellow woman could. She silently wished her ass could look only half as good as she focused on the sensuous cut of the tight-fitted jodhpurs, quickly forgetting her wayward son.

★★★★

Vincent stood seething with the belt axe in hand over the cowering librarian, who begged for his life in raspy, apologetic tones. Lightning struck outside the library, serving in Vincent's altered state of mind as a blinding transition into his next vision.

★★★★

At the Van Tassel Manor, Vincent held a conversation with the elderly woman near the barn.

"You mind if I take a look around?" he asked.

"Not all, Vince. I really missed you coming around. I hoped you would stop by again before the season got too cold. I've baked your favorite, gingersnaps. I'll just go check that wood-burning stove. Best not to leave that unattended too long."

A much healthier looking Lady Van Tassel slowly headed back inside as Vincent made his way out to the decrepit old barn. One by one, he picked up sharp implements and other tools, as if studying their build and calculating their usefulness.

The Horseman sized up a riding whip and handed the belt axe to Vincent, who checked the sharpness of the blade, getting a nasty cut to the fingertip in return.

In the wide shot of Vincent's mind, he sees himself acting out both roles, the Horseman and himself, handing the axe from one hand to the other, eyes glazed over in a stupor of self-medication.

★★★★

Vincent relentlessly hacked at the base of Billy Greenfield's neck with a rusty hacksaw. As Mack, Saunders and the other boy came to, they looked on in horror. Vincent threw the axe at them, just barely missing, and it boomeranged itself back in his direction. The drunk, wounded boys fled into the woods.

★★★★

Vincent dragged the lifeless, bloodied body of the bludgeoned Jack to a suitable hiding spot in his backyard. He looked up at the night sky, but this time, there was no Horseman there.

★★★★

He stared into the stained bathroom mirror at the dark circles under his eyes and traced them with his hand. He had just read the article about the special edition Horseman figurine. Vincent opened the medicine cabinet, and his hands aimlessly glided over the menagerie of pill bottles inside.

When he closed the mirrored door, he no longer saw his own reflection, but rather the bulking mass of the Unhallowed Horseman.

★★★★

A sharp pain drove itself like an ice pick into Vincent's temple, bringing him back to the painful reality of the corn maze. He couldn't believe his fantasy world and reality had finally collided into unimaginable tragedy too grotesque for even him to comprehend. He had gone completely off the deep end, his mind a turgid current of unrestrained psychosis. Something in his mind that previously had the pliancy of a green willow reed, suddenly snapped like a rotted twig.

Rayna's eyes widened as she saw Vincent but heard him speak in the deep, unnatural voice of the Horseman.

"Hell hath no fury more powerful than blood vengeance. Victory shall be mine," he growled as he raised the belt axe. Now completely enthralled by the hypnotic incantation, Vincent lunged forward in a full swing, taking aim for Rayna's head.

"Vincent!" Rayna screamed as her body became paralyzed with fear.

BLAM! The sound of the close-range gunshot was deafening. The bullet slammed into Vincent's shoulder. The meaty part of his upper shoulder was torn off and ejected like discarded pulp, causing the axe to be violently and involuntarily thrown to the ground, barely missing her feet. Rayna could only hear a sharp ringing in her ears. Any outside noise, including the shouts of the men who now surrounded her, was silent to her sense of perception.

Trooper Parent, a seasoned veteran of the New York State Police, and his partner had received Constance's distress call just after the deputy had abandoned the Volare. The faithful steel steed had come through after all. They were able to pinpoint the vehicle's location and serendipitously met up with Constance on his way back into town.

The two state police officers advanced on Vincent. Grabbing him, they bent his wounded arm unnaturally backward, slammed his face down into the mulch, and applied pressure above his neck while aggressively pinning him to the ground. They flex-cuffed him so violently, it drew blood across his already multi-colored wrists.

Deputy Constance lowered his still smoking service revolver and scooped up his daughter in his arms. Listless, she stared into space, catatonic, as full-on shock set in.

Vincent was in tears as the officer kneed his back and pinned his head firmly to the ground. In obvious pain, he sobbed heavily in between seething grits of his clenched teeth. "Rayna! I'm sorry. I love you. I love you!" he screamed with a hoarse, stripped throat.

Constance kicked out toward the maniacal boy with the heel of his boot, as if defending his daughter from a rabid feral dog. "Shut the fuck up," he screamed. He no longer gave a fuck about police protocol, prisoners' rights, or perceived improprieties. At that moment, he was just a father protecting his daughter from a sadistic killer.

The other trooper kept his firearm leveled at Vincent, trained on the youth for a kill shot between his eyes. If he wasn't careful, Vincent would have become headless in a heartbeat, just like he had always wanted to.

Vincent continued to scream, his voice echoing up into the last resounding storm clouds. The last thing Rayna heard before she blacked out were the final words that he would ever say to her: "I love you!"

Somewhere that night, the ubiquitous presence of wickedness had gained the upper hand. The Triduum of the Hallows moved on to the next set of victims it intended to cull. The Unhallowed Horseman born once again.

Chapter 45

Somewhere, a lone Fazioli yielded a solemn death dirge. No one knew the source of the music, but no one really cared either. The following days had brought the full extent of death and destruction to light.

The murders attributed to Vincent were vast, more numerous than previously suspected. Anyone missing, specifically students, was presumed dead. News of the first half dozen bodies came as a shock, but eventually, as the count continued to climb, the novelty wore off. Everyone just assumed there had been a serial killer amongst them, and something in him had finally snapped. The town elders knew better.

Vincent maintained his innocence.

It took a week before any lawyer would even defend him. In that time, Vincent learned of the death of his own mother. Seen as a monster by the authorities, he wasn't even allowed to go to her pauper's funeral. Being that Vincent was her only known living relative, they quickly, and perhaps spitefully, cremated her body before Vincent even got a chance to say goodbye. He was finally assigned a New York City attorney by the State. This didn't bode well, as the metropolitan legal eagle had been raised with a disdain for upstate country folk.

The collective mind of Sleepy Hollow became downright ashamed of their association with the Unhallowed Horseman after the great Down-Home Days Massacre. Concerned and dejected citizens almost ashamedly removed the Halloween decorations from in front of their Victorian homes. They wanted nothing to do with the holiday, or the Horseman, that had inspired the murders.

Like the confederate flag before it, any sign of the former icon symbolized a period of ignorance and blind allegiance.

Constance had the Super Coupe Volare towed to the back lot of the police station. The Volare was washed, waxed, and a had new windshield refitted. The iconic steel steed would prove much harder to be put down. It was back to near showroom-quality. Constance had put a lot of hours into it as a much need distraction. Anything that would take his mind of his ailing daughter. At the moment, Constance had his leg against the police cruiser as he struggled to remove the decal of the Horseman from the door. He began to pull it off, shifting his full weight into his back, and the adhesive slowly gave way. As it did, the force of suction caused the dent left by Vincent's bicycle to pop out. *Perhaps order would be restored*, he mused. He took it as a sign things would be starting anew, but little did he know, that wasn't necessarily a good thing.

Everywhere across the village, people removed the imagery of the Horseman.

Near the covered bridge where the decapitated Billy Greenfield had been found, there was a small bouquet of daisies fastened to the wall of the enclosed crossover; a makeshift memorial. The planks of the wall with the axe marks had been replaced with new pine, giving the patchwork an awkward zebra-stripe facade. A maintenance man swung a newly installed gate shut, designed to prevent automobile and foot traffic from crossing the bridge toward the old Van Tassel Manor. It essentially cordoned off the village from whatever lay on the outskirts of town; A clear delineation between civilization and wilderness. A meaty chain was pulled taught and locked with an enormously thick padlock. A "NO TRESPASSING" sign swayed on the chain as if moved by an invisible force. It would only be a matter of time before the town passed legislation meant to discourage outsiders from going to the scene of the gruesome murders.

At the cemetery, several distraught families were gathered. Many were dressed in black and several had spent the better part of the last few days there burying the dead. Some had even attended multiple funerals or interments on the same day because of the overlap of victims amongst their inner circles.

A two-toned silver and black hearse was parked atop the hill. It was a custom-made Prinzing hearse designed to mimic the Victorian-era horse-drawn hearses of the 1800s. The ghost-looking, elongated chassis had been driven all the way from the Andrew Strish Funeral Home next to the Potato Pancake Shack in Larksville, PA. The luxurious and elegant motorcar seemed out of place amongst the excruciating circumstances of mass killings. It belonged in a museum, not at the site of such a catastrophic calamity. Nevertheless, the car had arrived as the last request of the now deceased Emily Jiompkowski. Although Mr. Crane had barely dodged sure massacre himself, his newfound love interest had not.

Townsfolk had laid flowers at the foot of the many newly unearthed grave plots. The brown dirt and upturned sod dotted the hillside like a morose checker board. It was doubtful the cemetery had seen this much action since America's War of Independence. Even the old ACKER gravesite had a large wreath of black and blood-red roses placed upon it, next to a tattered swatch of Ol' Glory. The compounded cries of the communal mourning lifted up to the Heavens, but fell on the deaf ears of the mourners' God. It was all part of the Natural Law, and what had occurred could never be undone. Nor should it.

Near the back of the cemetery, Preacher Todd presided over one of many burials. It was hard to see who, as it could have been any of the numerous victims. Whoever the person had been must have been popular judging by the amount of mourners attending the service. Todd's eyes were dark, as he had clearly lacked sleep, but his spirit remained undaunted, and his faith was not only upheld, but if anything, bolstered. The Bible had warned him of things like this, and he had no doubt in his mind that there would be more reparations to come.

On the high school marquee, the symbol of the Horseman now had black paper taped over it, obscuring its view from the general public. It had been heavily vandalized following the revelation of the slaughter, and crime scene tape now cordoned off several areas in the immediate vicinity around and behind it.

Mr. Crane was not dressed in his usual flashy attire. His heart just hadn't been in it since Emily had been killed. It wasn't even that he had known her all that well that hurt the most, but rather the fact that her life was so promising but had been snuffed out so suddenly and violently. He also selfishly mourned for himself. It had been years since he'd had any amorous intentions toward anyone, and even longer since anyone had any toward him. He correctly feared it would be years more before it would happen again. He knew deep down in his jaded heart it was not the person he was mourning, but rather the loss of their presence in his own life; it was a very real problem of the living. Maybe he had a tinge of survivor's guilt, but like most things, it would eventually wear off over time.

He continued putting up letters on the marquee.

— In God We Trust —

Although, no one was quite sure if that would be the case anytime soon.

Chapter 46

A custodian took Paulding's nameplate off the door outside the former psychiatrist's office. He replaced it with one that read *Dr. T. Tamimi, Grief Counselor & Psychiatrist*, then gave it a smooth stroke with his dust rag.

Inside the office, Rayna sat in a newly unwrapped high-backed leather chair. The office had been redecorated with intentionally muted oranges and pinks and an uplifting cheerful undertone of yellow trim. The school had no issue directing some of its budget toward the students' psychological welfare. It was the least they could do, given the circumstances. Rayna's eyes remained permanently red from crying, mourning, and trying to cope. She barely blinked or responded, as her mind was in a constant state of daze.

An attractive middle-aged Middle Eastern woman leaned across her desk with a glass of water and two giant horse-pills, similar to the ones Paulding had given Vincent. They weren't Neuropreen, as those had been quickly taken off the market in light of recent events and the newly discovered side effects. If Marisa had lived, she surely would have had grounds for a lawsuit. The new pills were all the rage, and were being peddled aggressively by the drug reps. If the thought of getting better wasn't lure enough, the charm and curves of the specifically chosen doctor seemed to have a beguiling effect on patients and parents alike.

"Lorraine. Here ya go, hon. Just take these. They'll make you feel better." The appealing psychiatrist subtly nodded her head yes in an encouraging gesture. The use of her birth name seemed as fake and foreign as the doctor's concern, but Rayna robotically obeyed.

Rayna's arm that had been slashed was in a bandage and sling. Like a zombie in a trance, she reached across the desk with her good arm and took the pills in silent compliance. She popped them in her mouth and grabbed the waiting cool glass of water from the table in front of her. Without turning her head or breaking eye contact with the doctor's intense brown eyes, she downed the pills in a single swallow. Remaining unresponsive, she sat wide-eyed, lost in her grief; truly a broken soul.

"Now, let me just write these up and you'll be all better." Tamimi refused to engage the dilated pupils of her patient. She had seen it all before, and in her experience, it was much better to treat the situation clinically, with only a thin veil of familiarity. It was truly the best thing to do.

Rayna knew exactly what was happening, but unlike Vincent before her, she had no control of her own now sullied destiny. She picked up the glass, now half empty, and stared at her reflection. Her gaze traveled past the deep blue seas of her irises, into the dark recesses of her fully dilated pupils. There once had been an innocent beautiful soul in there, but all she could see now was a deep, dark void.

In a pitch-black void, Vincent sat within the padded walls of a filthy asylum for the criminally insane. He had been confined on the sixth floor, for offenders in need of the staunchest of security, of one of the State's most forsaken and notorious mental health facilities. It had long been left to its own devices, far from the public's prying eyes.

The walls were covered in every human bodily fluid imaginable. The orderlies only bothered with the severely incapacitated patients, like Vincent, once a week, and even then, it was with a high-powered hose. It was clear that here inmates were left to die a slow, inhumane, and lonely death. They had no family who visited, so there was no need for appearances. The prisoner-patients were seen as human animals, available for entertainment, sadistic experimentation, or sexual gratification, but definitely not reform of any kind.

Vincent rocked back and forth in a filthy straitjacket, sweating profusely. The stench of urine, feces, and sadness permeated the room. Several scratches, some deep, made indelible marks across his blanched face. His eyes were bloodshot and permanently dilated. Fresh blood marks stained the jacket's shoulder from where the gunshot wound had never fully healed. Instead, it remained only partially cured and forever festering. He was as broken on the outside as he was down deep within. The sad reality was, even wayward cockroaches and rats steered clear of him. Unattended in solitaire and listless, Vincent remained left alone by society, left for dead.

He squinted through a small, barred window as he thought he heard something outside. *Maybe it was a bird, that would be nice*, he thought. He could only form complete sentences in his mind, no longer with his spoken word. The small bars were his only gateway to the world outside and beyond. They were open to the elements, which wreaked havoc in the extremes of winter and summer along the Hudson. If he managed to get close enough, something he rarely did, he could look out down onto the field far below. He preferred not, though, as it was only a reminder of all the things he would no longer ever have.

The sun had just begun setting as the evening lazily lulled the overgrown field below to sleep. An orange hue wrapped the sky in a cloudy blanket, neither liberating or suffocating, but somewhere in between. The weather had been still and temperate, making it all together manageable this day. It had been nearly a full year since Vincent's detainment, and the dying leaves of autumn signaled the return of the Triduum of the Hallows once again.

Vincent heard the noise again; a familiar one. A feeble, listless fluttering of escaped air punched its way out of his lungs. He scooted himself over, dragging his haunches across the floor like a dog with an itchy ass. It was the only way he could be mobile, as due to the heinous nature of his crimes, he remained permanently restrained. His continued psychotic outbursts hadn't aided his case any, either.

Vincent slowly looked out the thin slit of the window, almost afraid of what he might see. Nothing was there. He sighed and leaned his weight back onto the curve of his brittle spine. Then, he heard the sound once again, only this time much louder. He realized he had only been searching the far end of the field with his eyes, where he'd thought the noise came from. But if he knew anything, it was that the Demons that haunted him were malevolent tricksters. He now traced a path with his eyes to right below him, just barley within his sight line at the base of the building.

There sat the Horseman, headless and plainly visible, high atop his Hellsteed.

The Horseman pulled the reins, rearing back the Hellsteed to the pinnacle of its height. It let out a demonic whinny that shot waves of omens through Vincent's very bones. His ribcage rattled with fear as the deep onslaught of emotions of reliving the massacre of his friends hit him like a mighty deluge of terror. The Horseman arched its headless body toward Vincent's cell as a hellish laugh resonated through the charged air. No longer telepathic, the noise was distinct and clear, and soon followed by the war cry Vincent knew all too well. The Harbinger made a final gesture with the belt axe before spurring the diabolical Hellsteed forward.

The Horseman's chortling reverberated in Vincent's head as Horseman and Hellsteed galloped off into the now dark of the night. The patter of rain began to hit the windowsill. Droplets of sulfuric water slapped him across the face like the vengeful vitriol of the final Judgement Day itself.

Vincent sucked in a deep breath through his teeth, his eyes wide. For a moment, he percolated in complete silence, before the realization hit him as hard as a bullwhip directly across the face.

The Headless Horseman of Unhallowed Grounds rode on!

Author's Note

I have been a fan of the Headless Horseman for as long as I can remember. I think it probably first started on lazy, rainy afternoons in Cloud Springs Elementary School around October, when the teachers would sometimes wheel in the old AV cart to class. This was a sure-fire signal you were in for a treat. Disney's 1949 classic *The Adventures of Ichabod and Mr. Toad*, which includes *The Legend of Sleepy Hollow*, was a kid-friendly, animated version that fit well into the school's curriculum as being on the fringe of its literary counterpart. For us, and probably the teachers as well, it was just an excuse to take the afternoon off and get lost in the spooky world of Ichabod leading up to the Halloween season.

As a child, I couldn't quite place what was so gripping, intriguing, and yes, scary, about the *Legend's* antihero being the Headless Horseman, even if in animated form. Maybe it was the fact he loomed larger than life. Perhaps it was that he came from out of nowhere and chased you down, the finale of which would either end in decapitation or the greatest fright of your young life. Even still, it could have been the fact that for me on late-night bike rides around the far side of the neighborhood on Edgewood Circle, where streetlights were burnt out, or houses had their own sinister stories, you always felt someone or something could be lurking in the shadows, ready to give chase at any moment. It was, in fact, the love of getting scared in a relatively safe environment. These were same reasons people decide to go on late-night romps into secluded crypts, abandoned buildings, and antiquated cemeteries.

As childhood changed from a time of blind admiration and allegiance to the characters, an enlightenment and appreciation for the classic literature beginnings of such tales sprung up in their place. It was in my high school years in the vaulted ceilings of dark and mysterious libraries and corridors of two-hundred(plus)-year-old seminaries that I began my quest for all things frightening. The Harry Potter-esque surroundings of those cathedrals of learning were more than enough to titillate and spark the dark side of my imagination. From there, all through college I fed my voracious appetite for literature a steady diet of Edgar Allan Poe, Roald Dahl and eventually Stephen King and H.P. Lovecraft.

As I got older, and my tastes developed into a deeper appreciation for the dark and macabre, I began to develop an appreciation for all things cinema. Having a brother who is ten years older than me meant that as a youth I often got my fair share of age-inappropriate entertainment. This included everything from "Satanic" rock-and-roll to Hammer films and Harryhausen stop motion, and of course, horror films with a touch of the sexual trappings of bare-breasted and half-dressed damsels in distress.

Once I started down a path of actually having a career in feature films—first as an actor, then producer, and eventually writer and director—I realized my personal aesthetic was akin to, and had been heavily influenced by, Tim Burton. That is to say, my particular brand of horror tended to lean more to the fantastical, rather than solely the gore-fest of slasher films. In 1999, when Burton did his take on the tale with the much celebrated *Sleepy Hollow*, I knew the cycle had come full circle, eating its own tail and solidifying the perpetual motion of creativity like a ravenous ouroboros. All my influences—literary, cinematic, pop culture, music, and otherwise—were coming together in one great identity as an admirer of the genre.

From there, I somehow managed to write and direct a film called *The Incantation* with my partner at Blue Falcon Productions, Dan Campbell. I was able to use all these influences, including those of the seminary, and piece them together in one story that had played out in the dark recesses of my mind. After scoring a castle in France and a favor from former Superman Dean Cain, everything fell in place. Something I often jokingly attribute to "the film gods." It was a good start to leaving my own, individual mark on the world, albeit a minute one.

But something always kept drawing me back to Washington Irving's classic tale of terror, "The Legend of Sleepy Hollow." It remained haunting, yet still user friendly, like a nightmare world in which you are afraid but really don't want to leave. I still, to this very day, feel a connection with that story and its characters closer than any other piece of literature or pop culture. I somehow wanted to indelibly merge whatever legacy I would leave behind with that of Irving's.

Around Halloween of 2009, I was on one of my many sojourns for film work back to Los Angeles. (I split my time between there and Thailand, where I live with my wife and kids.) At that particular time, I was feeling extremely inspired, and although my career had been going great, it was by no means stellar. My good friend Peter Liu allowed me to stay in one of his homes in the quaint neighborhood just to the southeast of downtown Los Angeles known as Monterey Park. The community is a quiet and peaceful one of predominantly Chinese immigrants and their families. Just the kind of place one could get the peace of mind to reflect on life and let the creative juices flow. I obtained a library card at the city library just across the street, and selfishly checked out every Poe and Irving book they carried. I reread their classics from cover to cover all day, and all night by candlelight. As the timing was around Halloween, my love of the Horseman— pardon the pun — reared its head once again. So, I again read the Irving classic and decided to create my own version of the everlasting tale.

Being that I was, and still am, a filmmaker at heart, it only seemed proper the piece would take the form of a feature film screenplay. This was before everyone and their mother were getting series projects greenlit by streaming giants like Netflix et al., so I set out to write the story, not knowing where it would take me. I only knew the basic components of story, taught by greats like Joseph Campbell, and of course every filmmaker since Charlie Chaplin, talkies, and the days of German Expressionism. The result was a script that eventually would carry the same name *The Unhallowed Horseman*. As of this writing, it still hasn't been made, but has been "greenlit" and considered by many insiders in the industry; an achievement in and of itself.

Writing a novel has always been one of the things I personally wanted to achieve. My grandfather was a self-educated and self-published writer. He was never properly schooled, but he nevertheless taught himself to read and write. As a result, growing up, I would see him spending hours reading literally stacks of books from his local library under a cloud of cherry pipe tobacco. He ended up writing at least four books and several short stories. My admiration of the man has no bounds. So if he, an "uneducated" man, could do such a feat, why was I so intimidated by the thought of writing a novel? So I did it, and you're holding the result.

In the beginning, it seemed like a gargantuan task. Every word, page, and chapter a minuscule chip off of a daunting iceberg. But as I continued to write, the story often took on a life of its own. Sometimes it felt as if I was merely channeling the thoughts of some Higher Power. Perhaps Irving himself was adding his take on his beloved character as seen through my eyes. Eventually, it started to take shape, and achieving this goal seemed like a reality that could actually happen. Many, many hours and months later, I managed to get it into a somewhat presentable shape. It is up to literary agents and publishers to decide if it will eventually be on their roster or if I will continue to self-publish. Either way, the story is out there now. It has been exorcised from my system and expelled from my imagination. From all the influences in literature, art, film, and pop culture of nearly five decades of my life—Washington Irving the least of which having inspired me—as well as any intelligence or style I might have accrued along the way, the result is here in a real and tangible form.

After I wrote the original script over a decade ago, I had a chance to visit the real Sleepy Hollow, New York, formerly known as Tarrytown but renamed to honor the famed author posthumously. I was thrilled to discover it was every bit the way I had imagined it in my head, sight unseen, and I can only hope that I have honored its citizens and heritage. I may not make a splash like our forefather Irving did, but in some small way, I hope I can add to his and the Horseman's legacy.

Someday, we will all be dead and buried, of that we can be sure. But with or without us…

The Horseman rides on!

About The Author

Jude S. Walko is a film producer (Producers Guild of America), director, screenwriter, and actor (Screen Actors Guild). Among notable works is his 2018 award-winning film *The Incantation*, which stars former Superman Dean Cain. Walko won the 2018 Eclipse award for Best Direction, among several other awards, for the film.

Jude has been a lifelong fan of classic literature and has a special love of all things Washington Irving. He even owns a grave plot at Sleepy Hollow Cemetery in New York. Jude is passionate about Halloween, Tim Burton, stop motion animation and all things dark and mysterious.

He spends his time between Los Angeles and Thailand, where his family now resides, and has multiple film and writing projects in development.

RELEVANT LINKS

THE UNHALLOWED HORSEMAN

https://www.goodreads.com/book/show/59316303-the-unhallowed-horseman
Twitter – https://twitter.com/HorsemanRides
Facebook
https://www.facebook.com/TheUnhallowedHorseman
Website – http://www.theunhallowedhorseman.com/

JUDE S. WALKO

IMDb – https://www.imdb.com/name/nm0908351/
Twitter – https://twitter.com/judeswalko
Facebook – https://www.facebook.com/JudeStephenWalko/
Instagram – https://www.instagram.com/judeswalko/
YouTube – https://www.youtube.com/c/HollywoodhoBRO
LinkedIn – https://www.linkedin.com/in/judeswalko/

9 780057 830356 7